ALSO BY SCOTT SPENCER

Last Night at the Brain Thieves' Ball

Preservation Hall

Endless Love

ENDLESS LOVE

by Scott Spencer

ALFRED A. KNOPF   NEW YORK   1979

THIS IS A BORZOI BOOK
PUBLISHED BY ALFRED A. KNOPF, INC.

Library of Congress Cataloging in Publication Data
Spencer, Scott.
Endless love.   I. Title.
PZ4.S7465En [PS3569.P455] 813'.5'4 79-2089
ISBN 0-394-50605-7

Manufactured in the United States of America

Published September 19, 1979
Second Printing Before Publication

For Coco Dupuy

I no more wrote than read that book which is
The self I am, half-hidden as it is
From one and all who see within a kiss
The lounging formless blackness of an abyss

How could I think the brief years were enough
To prove the reality of endless love?

—DELMORE SCHWARTZ

Part One

I

When I was seventeen and in full obedience to my heart's most urgent commands, I stepped far from the pathway of normal life and in a moment's time ruined everything I loved—I loved so deeply, and when the love was interrupted, when the incorporeal body of love shrank back in terror and my own body was locked away, it was hard for others to believe that a life so new could suffer so irrevocably. But now, years have passed and the night of August 12, 1967, still divides my life.

It was a hot, dense Chicago night. There were no clouds, no stars, no moon. The lawns looked black and the trees looked blacker; the headlights of the cars made me think of those brave lights the miners wear, up and down the choking shaft. And on that thick and ordinary August night, I set fire to a house inside of which were the people I adored more than anyone else in the world, and whose home I valued more than the home of my parents.

Before I set fire to their house I was hidden on their big wooden semicircular porch, peering into their window. I was in a state of grief. It was the agitated, snarling grief of a boy whose long rapturous story has not been understood. My feelings were raw and tender, and I watched the Butterfields through the weave of their curtains with tears of true and helpless longing in my eyes. I could see (and love) that perfect family while they went on and on with their evening without seeing me.

It was a Saturday night and they were together. Ann and her husband, Hugh, sat in front of the empty fireplace, on the bare pumpkin pine floor. (How I admired them for leaving their good wooden floors uncovered.) Ann and Hugh, sitting close, paged through an art book, turning the pages with extraordinary slowness and care. They seemed enraptured with each other that night. At times, their relationship seemed one of perennial courtship; hesitant, impassioned, never at rest. They seldom took each other for granted and I had never seen married people whose moments of closeness had such an aura of triumph and relief.

Keith Butterfield, my age, the oldest son, and whose passing curiosity in me had been my original admittance into the Butterfield household, also sat on the floor, not far from his parents, where he fussed with the innards of a stereo receiver he was building. Keith, too, seemed to be moving slower than normal, and I wondered if I was seeing them all through the gummy agony of a dream. Keith looked to be exactly what he was: the smartest boy in Hyde Park High School. Keith couldn't help learning things. He could go to a Russian movie and even as he concentrated on the subtitles he'd be picking up twenty or thirty Russian words. He couldn't touch a wristwatch without wanting to take it apart; he couldn't glance at a menu without memorizing it. Pale, with round eyeglasses and unruly hair, in blue jeans, black undershirt, and beatnik-y sandals, Keith laid his hands on the spread-out parts of the stereo, as if he wanted not to build it but to cure it. Then he picked up a small screwdriver and looked at the overhead light through the mango-colored plastic handle. He pursed his lips—sometimes Keith looked older than his parents—and then he got up and went upstairs.

Sammy, the younger son, twelve years old, was sprawled out on the couch, naked except for a pair of khaki shorts. Blond, bronze, and blue-eyed, his prettiness was almost comically conventional—he looked like the kind of picture little girls tuck into the corner of their mirror. Sammy was somewhat outside the Butterfield mold. In a family that cultivated its sense of idiosyncrasy and its sense of personal uniqueness, Sammy's genius already seemed to be taking the form of profound regularity. Athlete, dancer, paperboy, bloodbrother, and heart throb, Sammy was the least retiring, the least internal Butterfield; we all really did believe, even when he was twelve, that one day Sammy would be President.

And then there was Jade. Curled into an armchair, wearing a loose, old-fashioned blouse and a pair of unflattering shorts that reached almost to the knee. She looked chaste, sleepy, and had the disenfranchised air of a sixteen-year-old girl at home with her family on a Saturday night. I scarcely dared look at her; I thought I might simply hurtle myself through the window and reclaim her as my own. It had been seventeen days since I'd been banished from their home and I tried not to wonder what changes had taken place in my absence. Jade looked at the wall; her face seemed waxy, blank; the nervous knee jiggle was gone —cured by my banishment?—and she sat unnervingly still. She had a clipboard wedged between her narrow hip and the side of the chair, and she held in her hand one of those fat ballpoint pens that have three separate cartridges, a black, a blue, and a red.

I still believe the statement that gives the truest sense of my state of mind that night is that I started the fire so the Butterfields would have to leave their house and confront me. The trouble with excuses, however, is that they become inevitably difficult to believe after they've been used a couple of times. It's like that word game children discover: you repeat a word often enough and it loses all meaning. Foot. Foot. A hundred times foot, until finally what is foot? But even though the truth of my motive has worn a little thin (and through its diaphanous middle I can detect other possible motives), I can still say that indeed the clearest thought I had when I lit the match was that starting a fire on the porch was somehow a better way of rousing the

Butterfields from their exclusive evening than a shout from the sidewalk or a stone against the window—or any other desperate, potentially degrading signal I might make. I could picture them: sniffing the smoke sent off by the pile of old newspapers, trading glances, and then filing out to see what the trouble was.

This was my strategy: as soon as the papers catch fire, I hop off the porch and run down the block. When I'm at a safe distance, I stop to catch my breath and begin strolling back toward the Butterfields, hoping to time my arrival with their emergence from the house. I'm not sure what I planned to do then. Either jump right in and help put out the little fire, or stand transfixed, as if surprised to see them, and hope that Jade or Ann would see me, wave, invite me in. The point was not to allow them to go another day without seeing me.

I don't recall debating this plan of action. Nerved-out and lovesick, I simply proposed it and then a short time later was lighting a match. I waited for a moment (my legs shaking from their desire to vault off the porch and run like hell) to make certain the fire had really taken hold. The flame lifted the corners of that stack of papers page by page, increasing the depth of its penetration but not the breadth. I could have put it out by stepping on it a couple of times and I came close to doing so, not out of foresight but panic. I remember thinking: This will never work.

The flame, after burrowing through a few layers, at last made its move to the heart of the pile—it seemed to have found the perfect dry bridge to race across. It was still not an impressive fire, by any means. It would not have done for cooking a trout and, at the point I fled and left it to its own nitrous fate, you would have been hard-pressed to toast a marshmallow over such a feeble flame. But the fire had established itself; it was not likely to shrink to nothing at the slightest breeze, nor did it seem destined to extinguish itself. It was real, alive, and I leapt off the porch and onto the tall unkempt grass that distinguished the Butterfields' patch of lawn. I turned back for a moment to look at the house, gothically eccentric, a New England frame house in the middle of Chicago, then at the softly lighted living room window, still empty of curious faces, and then at the stack of newspapers, gauzy now behind the first sheet of smoke and capped by a rooster comb of flame. And then I ran.

The Butterfield house was on Blackstone in the Hyde Park section of Chicago. I ran north, knees locked, toward 57th Street. As far as I remember, I passed no one. And no passer-by walked near the Butterfields to notice those smoldering papers. Hyde Park had not yet turned into an indoor society because of crime-fear. You still had accidental meetings in the street, and though the University of Chicago already had its own private police force and a separate busline to transport students around the neighborhood, Hyde Park was an open, busy place, even at night. (Jade and I, before her parents accepted our love affair and all of its inflexible demands, often walked those streets at two, three, even four in the morning, leaning on parked cars to kiss, embracing and even lying on top of each other on darkened porch stoops, and we never felt unsafe—our only fear was interruption.) But that night, when one watchful pedestrian could have changed everything, I had that long block to myself.

When I reached 57th Street, I went into the second stage of my plan. I paced slowly on the corner for perhaps a minute—though knowing my tendency to rush when I'm uncertain, it was probably less time than that. Then, while trying to invent a quick, plausible excuse for being on that block in case Jade or any other Butterfield asked me, I walked south, retracing my tin-soldier steps back to their house. My heart was clapping with lonely, lunatic intensity but I can't say that by then I was wishing I'd never struck that match. I hadn't seen or spoken to Jade in seventeen days (though when Hugh Butterfield had told me, as he banished me from the house, that he and Jade had decided I would have to stay away for thirty days, I had unfounded but powerful suspicions they had engineered a separation that might never end). This banishment, this sudden expulsion from the center of my life, was the core of all thought and feeling. And while misgivings and second thoughts buzzed around my determination, they were as ineffectual as houseflies. I was scared that I'd done such a strange thing as burn the newspapers that had collected on the Butterfield porch, but there is no sense calling this nervousness, this surprise-with-myself, *regret.* My major concern was that the ploy would work.

I stood in front of their house. The sidewalk was fifteen yards from the porch and I could see perfectly well that the flame had not gone out. But neither had it grown. A steady haze of smoke wafted off the newspapers, yet still no Butterfields had been aroused by it. I had an impulse to sneak back onto the porch and blow on the flame or perhaps loosen up the papers so they could catch fire more easily. But I didn't want to nudge chance with too firm a hand. Since my whole faked-up meeting was to be based on the pretense of coincidence, I wanted to leave a little room for the quirky meanderings of fate: if I engineered things too carefully, I might not be able to imitate astonishment when the time came. I walked past the house, southward this time to the corner of 59th.

On 59th Street I did see people walking around, but no one I knew. I saw a rather glamorous older woman (meaning, then, a woman in her twenties) walking a large, nervous red dog. She wore sunglasses, a floppy straw hat, and smoked a cigarette out of a long black and silver holder. I think I may have stared at her, just to occupy my thoughts. She cocked her head and smiled at me and said hello. Her voice startled me and I experienced that quick intestinal collapse you sometimes get in bed when you think you are falling. I made a brisk British military nod (that month's mask, picked up in the psychological warehouse that stored other people's discarded personalities) and I thought: I'm getting the timing screwed up. My life would have had to be a movie for the plan to really work the way I wanted— I wanted to time my passing the Butterfields' house just as they were coming out. But I felt there was some split-second urgency involved and so I quickly started out toward the house, first at a trot and then at a dead run.

Was I running for the sake of my masterplan or did I somehow know that the fire I'd set had leapt out of control? Did I smell smoke or did the part of me that had understood from the beginning the consequence of my actions finally fight its way through the thicket of wilfulness and heartsickness to scream its alarm? I ran and now my heart was not beating with a lover's mournful nervousness but it seemed to bound against my chest like a furious dog against a fence.

I don't understand how fire works; I haven't learned the scientific explanations for its cunning and greed. A lick of flame can scurry like a cat while it hunts for the choicest morsel of fuel. An infant flame is subject to the government of the elements. But by adolescence, fire is as brave and artful as a revolutionary band, snatching easy victories here, extending the limits of its power there, consolidating, attacking, brightening with triumph. At its full force, its victory over the stable world complete and everything from Doric columns to magazine racks within its mercy, fire is messianic—it rules over its domain with a blistering, totalitarian authority and seems to believe that all of creation ought be in flames. By the time I reached Jade's house, the fire I'd set was not in its uncontrollable maturity but it had advanced to its daredevil adolescence. The central flame, headquartered in the stack of newspapers, had sent attack parties of smaller flames to menace the house itself. Points of flame scattered along the side of the house and fluttered like small orange pennants. A circle of fire had been dispatched to the floor of the porch and seemed to race around the newspapers for a short time, and then, thrilled with the very fact of its existence and drunk with the berserkness of its cause, spread out in a dozen different directions.

I backed away. I already felt the heat on my face, burning through the passive warmth of the August air. I backed off until I slipped off the curb and rammed myself against Hugh's car, a ten-year-old Bentley that he nursed and loved to excess and beyond. I rubbed my back—a moron checking for a bruise on his spine while everyone he loves sits in a burning house. The flames that darted this way and that on the house itself were all on the feeble side, but there were so many of them and they had enough confidence in their power to continually divide themselves. And then, almost as if the fire was controlled by a dial like the flame on a gas stove, in an instant the flames—all of them—tripled in size and power. I let out a cry and rushed toward the house.

The porch was already half covered with flame—there were shoots of fire everywhere, an intermediate garden of fire. I flung the screen door open and tried to open the big wooden door, which was usually unlocked (not as a gesture of trust but an accommodation to the constant human traffic). Tonight, however, the door was locked. I pounded on it with my fists and shouted—no, not "Fire!" but "Let me in! Let me in, goddamnit! Let me in!"

Sammy opened the door. He was, in fact, on his way out because now, finally, they all smelled smoke. "David," he said, and put up his small hands as if to stop me.

I pulled him out onto the porch and then ran into the house. The small, cluttered foyer already smelled of smoke and when I made the familiar right turn into the living room, Hugh was backing away from the window with his hand over his eyes.

"We're on fire," I said. (Hugh was later to testify that I'd said this in a "casual" tone of voice. It seems incredible; but I don't remember.)

The living room was hotter than any summer's day. It didn't so much seem that smoke was rushing in as that the air itself was turning into smoke. The fire, with its tactical instinct, had surrounded the frame of the largest window on the outside, maneuvering toward the easiest entry into the house. It raced around the pulpy, half-rotten wood, multiplying its intensity, dancing, dancing like warriors working themselves up before a battle, until the heat was powerful enough to explode the window and a long orange arm reached in and turned the curtains to flame.

It is here, at this point, when the window blew out and the curtains caught fire, that the sequence of events become irretrievable. We were, I would suppose, like any other group of people in a burning house, fighting back our terror with the worthless fantasy that really nothing so terribly serious was happening. Only Hugh, who had fought in a war and had spent time in a prison camp, only Hugh knew firsthand how sometimes ordinary life is completely overturned. The rest of us, even as we breathed in the heat and the smoke, even as our lungs burned and our eyes teared and we heard the crackle of the wood, held onto the possibility that disaster would suddenly stop in its tracks, turn around, and disappear.

I forced myself to be calm as I went to Jade's side, and I put my arm around her in the manner of someone taking charge during an emergency—but really, all I wanted to do was touch her.

"How are you?" I said, putting my lips near her ear. Her hair smelled from the curling gel she had set it with; her neck looked naked and vulnerable.

"I'm OK," Jade said, in her low, porous voice. She did not look at me. "Except I'm . . . high. I'm very, very high." She covered her eyes against the smoke and coughed. "And scared," she said.

Perhaps there had been something more than Jade had said, but I knew immediately that the family had not been smoking grass: for the past couple months, Ann had been in correspondence with her cousin in California, trying to seduce him into sending her some of the laboratory LSD he had access to, and tonight, with all ceremony and seriousness, they had swallowed it, ingesting the spirit of the new consciousness in a square of chemically treated blotter paper, just as they from time to time ingested the spirit of Christ in the form of an Episcopalian wafer.

Now, suddenly, horribly, I understood the pages of that art book being turned in slow motion and Jade's waxed features as she had sat immobile in the chair. . . .

Across the room, Ann was at Hugh's side. He was trying to pull the curtains down and she held onto his shirt and said, "Not a good idea, Hugh." Sammy was back in the house. He stumbled and fell to his knees; he began to right himself but it was too much effort. (Or did he know that close to the floor was the safest place to be during a fire? It was the sort of thing Sammy would know.) Looking up at his parents from his hands and knees, Sammy said, "You should see it. The whole house is burning." Ann finally pulled Hugh away from the curtains—they barely existed anyhow: they were just a sheet of flame sending out more flame. There was fire on the walls now and, a moment later, fire on the ceiling.

When the ceiling started to burn, Ann said, "I'm calling." She said it in a fed-up voice, a put-upon citizen forced to call in the officials. But she made no move toward the telephone in the kitchen, even though the kitchen was still free of fire. We all stayed together in the most perilous part of the house, knit together and nailed to our places by astonishment, and I was one of them.

It seemed that that house longed to burn, just as a heart can long to be overcome with love. One moment I was saying to Jade, "Are you OK?" and the next one whole wall was covered in flame. Freely, wantonly the house yielded to the fire, donating its substance to eternity with the reckless passion of someone who'd been waiting for years for the proper suitor. If any of us were to that point still debating whether we were faced with a household mishap or an emergency, it was now certain that all previous bets were off and it was time to do what we could to save our lives.

Sammy was on his feet. "We can't go out the front. The porch is burning like crazy."

Ann was shaking her head. Annoyance had given way to

grief—and a certain weariness that made me wonder if she wanted to save herself. She felt the lure of the fire, as someone on a high balcony will suddenly have a curious desire to jump off.

Hugh was kneading the sides of his skull as if pacifying its contents. "Everyone stay together," he said. "Hold hands." (He repeated this two or three times.) "We go out the back door. And we stay together."

I took Jade's hand. It felt like melting ice. She wouldn't quite look at me but she gripped my hand with all her strength.

"On the floor," I said. "We'll crawl out." To my surprise, they listened to me. And then I knew: as out of control as I felt, I was the sanest person in the room.

"I feel scared, I really feel scared," Jade said.

"We just have to keep our heads," I said.

"Oh my God," said Hugh. "I knew we shouldn't have. I can't get it straight." He dug his knuckles into his eyes.

Sammy was on the floor, talking away to someone he imagined was next to him; he sounded perfectly in control of himself as he conversed with the apparition.

"OK, I'm all right," Hugh said. "I can feel myself getting all right."

Jade took my hand and pressed it against her breast. "Is my heart still going?" she asked in a whisper.

"It's incredible," Ann said. "All we have to do is get out of here and we can't. . . ." She made a short laugh.

"Where's Keith?" I cried.

"He's upstairs!" Jade said.

We were on the floor; the room was more than half smoke, much more. I could barely see the staircase, and as I ran toward it my only hope was that by the second floor I'd find more clear space. A thousand other things must have been racing through my mind but the only one I remember was the hope that someone—Jade—would grab my leg and stop me from going up for Keith.

I took the stairs two at a time and the smoke filled the air with deeper and more absolute authority. I felt the intensity of the heat but saw no flames—they were inside the walls and burning in toward us. Inasmuch as I could open my mouth, I called Keith's name. On my hands and knees, I felt the heat coming up through the floor, so tangible that I thought it might actually lift me. Coughing, nauseated, I spit onto the floor. I was on the second story of the house now. Down at one end of the hall was the room where Jade and I had been sleeping for the past six months. At the other end was Ann and Hugh's room, vast, cluttered, and open to all. In the center of the corridor, on the left, was the bathroom, and on the other side was Sammy's small room. The door to Sammy's room was closed and as I looked at it, it burst into flame.

The stairway to the top floor was just past Sammy's room, and through the layers of smoke, which were dyed by the color of the flames like fog tinted by headlights, I saw what looked like a moving figure. I called Keith's name. I didn't know if my voice could be heard; I could not hear it over the pounding of my blood and the sound of the fire. I crawled down the hall and tried not to think about dying—my thoughts were not brave but neither did I turn and run. The figure I'd seen had disappeared. I didn't know if it had been obscured by new dark layers of smoke or if Keith had turned back. I wondered if he even knew that his house was on fire, knew that this danger was not illusion. I knew he must be high and no Butterfield was less likely to handle the shattering of his personality than Keith: Keith the sleepwalker, Keith the mystic, Keith the hyper. If some people's intelligence is evidence of their mind's strength and hunger, Keith's genius was the product of his mind's extreme vulnerability: everything touched him and left an impression. Any other time I would have thought that the Butterfields' taking LSD together was simply further proof of their extraordinary openness, their willingness to become a part of their times and share in the risks of the current year. But as I thought of them stumbling aimlessly below me and looked for Keith through the sheets of darkening smoke, I judged them for that moment as harshly as I ever would. I was not remembering altogether that it was me who had started the fire.

I forced myself toward the stairway to the third floor and Keith emerged again. His shirt was pulled over his face and he was coughing and weeping. I called out to him and he staggered toward me as if he'd been pushed from behind. My face was so hot I slapped at it, thinking in a panicky instant that my skin had caught fire.

"Please," moaned Keith. "I can't see and I don't know what to do."

I scuttled over to him. Keith had one arm over his eyes now and his long, thin legs bent at the knee. His other arm still reached out toward me—though I don't know if he realized who I was. I grabbed his hand and tried to pull him down to the floor; he stiffened as if I'd shot him through with electricity.

I shouted his name as loudly as I could and pulled again. He yanked loose of me and stepped back, like a spirit preparing to disappear into the ether.

I struggled to my feet and reached out for him. He looked at me with a momentary flash of recognition.

"Take my hand goddamnit," I shouted. "Take it!"

Keith stared at me and took another step back. I was terrified that at any instant he would burst into flames as Sammy's door had, a human nova. I lunged for him and as I grabbed his shoulders I felt the strength leave his body. His legs buckled and he swooned into my arms. It was dead weight and I was not really equal to it. I staggered back but Keith kept coming; his forehead banged into me, his bony chest slumped against mine, and in a moment we were both on the smoking floor, he on top of me, and now my heart was wild, beating at an incredible rate as if to compensate for the eternity in which it would remain still.

And then I heard someone pounding up the stairs. I turned my head to see Hugh rushing toward us. He was roaring Keith's name. His ferocity was nearly as awesome as the fire; even through the smoke, his eyes shone with paranormal intensity. And though I knew that Hugh had come back to rescue Keith, as he came charging up the stairs I could not help but fear that he was coming after me—not to rescue me, of course, but to take my head between his strong capable hands and crush it. Like a madman, Hugh raised his arms above his head, breathed deeply through his clenched teeth, and brought his hands down on Keith's back to lift him up as easily as if Keith were a sack of feathers.

It was the last thing I saw. Limply, with no more than instinct's shadow, Keith tried to hold on to me as his father lifted him up, and with that faint plucking at my shirt I lost all consciousness. The world began to ooze away from me. The last thing I saw was Hugh looking down at me and then I felt his hand on my wrist. It wasn't until he testified against me that I learned that Hugh had carried me down slung over his shoulder (with his arm around Keith, who sobbed and stumbled at Hugh's side) and brought me outside, where the firemen were finally arriving, their sirens whooping and the red lights skittering through the trees. To his everlasting regret, Hugh had saved my life.

I confessed it was me who'd started the fire while I was in the Jackson Park Hospital. (The Butterfields were being treated in the same hospital but I shared my room with strangers.) I told the first people I saw the next morning, which means that in the ambulance, the emergency room, and all through the night, while I drifted in and out of consciousness, I concealed that central fact. But when I woke the next morning to find my parents sitting in folding chairs—Rose with her legs crossed and her fingers drumming on her patent leather purse, and Arthur with his large head bowed and needlepoint drops of perspiration in the bands of scalp that divided his thinning hair—I cleared my throat and said, "I started the fire."

They both sat up and looked at each other, and then Rose leaned forward, pursing her small full lips and shaking her head. "Shut up," she whispered, and she glanced with conspiratorial panic at my two sleeping roommates. But I wasn't about to leave myself open to the horrors of detection and from that moment began a process of confession, defense, and punishment that was to dominate my life for years.

My father is what people call a "left-wing lawyer." By 1967, both he and Rose had been separated from the Communist Party for fifteen years, but he was still a left-wing lawyer—meaning that he would never defend a rich man against a poor man and he didn't charge his clients fancy fees. Arthur aged faster than he should have from the long hours he put in at work. He often stayed in his office until midnight and once—this was a story Rose liked to tell about him—the lightbulb in his desk lamp popped and went black and Arthur continued to sit there in his feeble, whinnying swivel chair writing down on his long yellow legal pad an inspired line of inquiry he wanted to pursue in an accident case. He was afraid that if he got up to switch on the overhead light, he might lose the rhythm. The next day, checking over his notes—now if this were a joke, they'd have been non-sense or illegible, but the three pages of blindly transcribed ideas were perfectly readable and absolutely essential to the case. It wasn't something as bloodless as addiction to work that made Arthur put his whole heart into every case: Arthur truly longed to defend the weak against the strong. He wanted this more than money, more than glory, more than comfort. Sometimes his passion to save his clients destroyed him in court. He often grew angry and his voice would crack like an adolescent's if he sensed a case slipping away from him.

Arthur wanted to handle my case, just as a surgeon would need to perform a vital operation on a loved one. But this was clearly out of the question: with the charge of arson and reck-less endangerment wrapped around me like a hideous ceremonial robe, I certainly needed someone more plausible to plead my defense than my own father. Arthur had done his share of favors, and when it became clear that the full complexity of wrongdoing was to be mine to untangle, two of his friends stepped forward and offered to take my case for free—Ted Bowen, whom I'd known all my life, and Martin Samuelson, who was treated by my parents as a transcendent hero of intelligence and nerve, a dialectician *extraordinaire*, a man who could quote Engels with the same lyrical brilliance as he could cite Hugo Black and whom my parents, in a holdover from their Party days, considered more important than they themselves, so that his interest in my case was greeted with stunned gratitude.

Briefly, the sequence of events was this. I was arrested in the hospital and placed, without hearing, in a juvenile detention center on the West Side. There was a great deal of haggling between the police, the district attorney's office, and my lawyers over what my legal status was: the question was if I would stand trial as an adult or be treated as a juvenile offender. I was seventeen and Martin Samuelson—this was his major effort; he soon wearied of the case and he especially grew tired of me—was successful in defining me as a juvenile so my fate would be decided not before a jury but in judge's chambers. By now, I was out of the juvenile detention center and undergoing a marathon sequence of psychological examinations—they seemed to be a mixture of Scholastic Aptitude Tests and the kind of baffling, embarrassing questions a cornball pervert might ask a child in a schoolyard. I gave my impressions of inkblots, added columns of three-digit numbers, identified pictures of Washington, Lincoln, and Kennedy, and answered True or False to questions like: "I feel I go to the bathroom more than other people." I went through this process of psychological testing twice, the first time at the hands of a court-appointed psychologist. Then Ted Bowen arranged that I'd be retested by a private psychologist. This was Dr. White, a gentle old man with conjunctivitis. (Dr. White was the first doctor I'd ever been to who wasn't a personal and political friend of my parents: the Party created its share of internists and dentists but few psychiatrists.)

All the while, I was in my parents' custody. It was the autumn I was to begin college. A few months before, I'd been accepted by the University of California, but since Jade was still in high school and bound to stay in Chicago, I had switched my choice to Roosevelt University, which was hardly a place to study astronomy but *was* in downtown Chicago. It didn't matter any longer; I wasn't going anywhere. I was told by the police, the psychologists, the lawyers, and my parents that I wasn't under any circumstances to even try to make contact with Jade or any of the other Butterfields. At the outset, this wasn't a difficult rule to follow. I was incapable of even imagining what it would have been to see them after what had happened. I had no illusions of their sudden compassion or their willingness to see through the act I'd committed to the innocent, lovesick spirit that had triggered it. I could not stop hoping that Jade would contact me, but she didn't, even though it would not have been that complicated to do so.

One day I forced myself to walk past the house in which I'd lived so deliriously and which I'd set on fire nearly causing the death of five people. The police had tied a cord from one iron porch banister to the other and from the center of the rope hung a printed sign warning people to keep away. Astonishingly, the house still stood and aside from the broken windows seemed unchanged—except it was no longer brown and white but a deep fuzzy black. The porch was gone, the wizard-cap peak of the attic was half collapsed, but other than that the Butterfields' was structurally intact. At first, it was a relief to see this, as if it might help me begin to fill the immense emptiness that I'd created within myself that August night. But that relief was more wished for than felt, just as the wish to see a departed lover will trick you into seeing her on the street. In fact, it was a thousand times more painful that the house still stood—for it stood not as a reprieve from absolute loss but as an accusation. I was, I knew then, a member of a vast network of condemned men and women: romance had taken a wrong turn within me and led me into mayhem. I was no better than dialers of anonymous phone calls, hounders, berserk pests, ear severers, committers of flamboyant, accusatory suicides, hirers of private detectives, or a medieval king ready to deploy an army of ten thousand souls in order to gain the favor of a distant maiden—and when the fields are scorched and the bodies lie in heaps beneath the sun, the king will clutch his breast and say: I did it all for love. The relief was gone and I stared at the house and wept—though I hardly knew I was weeping because I'd done little else but weep since the day after the fire, as I suppose anybody in their right mind would.

Of course, the question of whether or not I *was* in my right mind was central to my fate. Though my lawyers, like my parents, viewed psychiatry as a kind of high-priced astrology, their dedication to my cause led them to discuss my circumstances as if I was totally victimized by the irrational navigation of my unconscious.

My mother, however, whether out of guilt or rancor, wanted my defense based on the fact that the Butterfields were strange people and as such deserved to have terrible things happen to them. As Rose's theory went, the Butterfields could no sooner hold me responsible for what had happened that night than a host who makes a guest falling-down drunk can hold that person responsible for a piece of broken china. The Butterfieldian *milieu* had been my downfall, according to Rose. This included Jade's prescription for Enovid, and the fact that when I began spending nights in that house it was decided that Jade wasn't getting her sleep and (in an appallingly democratic family meeting) this was solved by getting us a double bed, a used bed from the Salvation Army which we sprayed for bugs and drenched in Chanel No. 5, a bed with rollers on its legs and that moved from the east wall to the west when we made love. Rose would have given anything to prove that the Butterfields were "on dope" the night of the fire, but I never said a word about it.

My mother was prepared to subpoena half of Hyde Park to testify against the Butterfields. I tried to mock her out of this idea but I think I knew even then that there were hundreds of people who found Hugh and Ann unsavory. Ann herself told me this. Once, taking a casual stab at ordering her unraveling life through religion, Ann attended services at a nearby Unitarian church. Though the adults in the congregation were strangers to her, she said she could feel their eyes on her when she entered and heard them whispering about her. "Distinctly," said Ann, "I heard them distinctly. I'm not the sort who imagines things like that. There's no profit in my believing such a thing. But I heard it quite clearly." I told her she must have been stoned or having a reaction to Unitarianism and the foolishness of religion (I was the household's official radical, so I could say such things). But Ann was probably right; even though she didn't know those Unitarians, they knew her and they *were* judging her. They were the parents of kids who'd used the Butterfield house as a hangout, who'd run away from home and slept on the Butterfields' couch or in the back yard, or who had learned how to smoke and say *coitus interruptus* at the Butterfields'. Or perhaps they were the neighbors who had seen the lights blazing in that lovely house, burning through the summer nights and mellowing into the dawn—to this day I cannot see electric light easing into the fresh day without feeling I am standing in front of the Butterfields', gliding home after making love. And when Mrs. Who-Ha came collecting for the March of Dimes and saw Ann flat on her back listening to Tibetan ritual music, with a big square candle burning in the middle of the day—oh boy, did that get around. Everything did. The fact that Hugh and Ann had gone to Ivy League schools and had come from what we call "good families," carried, as it turned out, a lot more weight with me, the son of lifelong Communists, than it did with anyone else. I thought that Hugh and Ann's inherent respectability, their lean bodies and strong bones, their straight teeth, straight hair, and the incurably upper-class *ping* of their voices would protect them from a lot more unwholesome gossip than it did. In fact, though they had very little money, their "breeding" may have left the Butterfields open to an unkinder scrutiny than they might ordinarily have had to endure.

It's a measure, I think, of "my side's" moral disarray that Rose's suggestions were taken seriously. I don't know why, but my parents and the lawyers still seemed to hold the hope that I'd be judged innocent. Not only did I refuse to testify that the Butterfields were the immoral, freebooting scum my mother described them as ("Immature, subjective jackasses—even the children are immature") but I didn't have any desire to be judged innocent. I don't mean to make myself sound more calculating and self-possessed than I was (it had been a month of sweating and weeping; there were teethmarks at the top of my bedsheet and a drawerful of unsendable letters), but I *wanted* to be punished. I knew the fire was accidental but it was not as accidental as it should have been, and I wanted some agency outside of all of us to intervene and take over the job of making me suffer for what had happened. I thought my fate in the hands of the police and the courts would drain some of the vividness from the hatred the Butterfields held toward me. With someone else to punish me, someone else to say I was bad and unfit to live with decent people, then Jade and the rest could allow themselves to drift toward the other side, my side, to stop punishing me in their hearts.

So I would not say that the Butterfields were on acid that night and I would not volunteer anecdotes about the far-flung Butterfieldian lifestyle. Ted Bowen, a lawyer very much like my father, with his sturdy amber teeth, peppermint breath, and the one long uninterrupted eyebrow growing from temple to temple, arranged for a private meeting with me. He took me to a working-class cafeteria on 53rd Street and, in a long speech that was both tender and formal, informed me of the consequences of a guilty verdict. He described juvenile detention and the humiliations I might suffer. "These are guys from the bottom of the heap, David. Simple socialist theory will tell you what that does to a person. They have nothing, they believe in nothing, and they'll kill you for a half of a cigarette." Then he leaned forward and gave me one of those I-wouldn't-be-telling-you-this-if-I-didn't-think-you-could-take-it looks. "I don't know if you've heard about homosexuality. . . ." And with that his voice trailed off and his eyes looked so sad and so astoundingly serious that out of sheer nervousness I smiled.

When I thought of how I'd set fire to those newspapers on the Butterfields' porch, it seemed fair (that is, not cowardly, not evasive) to say that I wasn't in my right mind. And the root of this temporary insanity? Clearly, it was my love for Jade—a love blocked and turned frantic by my banishment from the Butterfields' house. Love, that is to say love thwarted, severed me from my senses. The fire was not mischief, not hatred, not some crazy act of revenge.

From the time I learned to love Jade and was drawn into the life of the Butterfield house, straight through to the wait for my case to come before the judge, there was nothing in my life that wasn't alive with meaning, that wasn't capable of suggesting weird and hidden significances, that didn't carry with it the undertaste of what for lack of anything better to call it I'll call The Infinite. If being in love is to be suddenly united with the most unruly, the most outrageously alive part of yourself, this state of piercing consciousness did not subside in me, as I've learned it does in others, after a time. If my mind could have made a sound, it would have burst a row of wineglasses. I saw coincidences everywhere; meanings darted and danced like over-heated molecules. Everything was terrifyingly complex; every-thing was terrifyingly simple. Nothing went unnoticed and everything carried with it a kind of drama. This agony, this delight did not recede when Hugh told me it would be best if I kept away from Jade for a month, nor did it quiet down after the fire and the weeks I spent in limbo—not knowing what was going to be done with me and, above all, not being able to see her. But the actual decision by Judge Rogers slipped by the perpetual watchfulness of my overstimulated consciousness. I had no idea that a ruling was near, and the whole affair was suddenly ("I guess we were lucky," said Rose) decided behind my back—a deal between Ted Bowen, the district attorney, and Rogers.

No prison. No juvenile home. And, if my parents were willing to pay for something private, no state institution. I was judged psychologically irresponsible and assigned to a psychiatric hospital for one year, until my eighteenth birthday, after which my case could be reviewed. It was not even a real conviction; the time in the nuthouse was parole.

My parents' aversion to psychiatry was so deeply ingrained and so reflexive that they could have just as easily related to my being sent to a seminary. ("Let's consider ourselves very, very lucky," my mother said through her tears, but I knew that she would soon be thinking—if she wasn't already—that as deadly as prison might have been, it would have been something I could hold in common with Stalin, with Eugene Dennis, with the Spanish Freedom Fighters, and thousands of other revolutionary heroes, whereas time in a mental institution would put me in league with some chain-smoking wisecracker, Oscar Levant, say, some pampered little fool in love with his own feelings.) I was, however, relieved at the judge's decision and felt, by and large, that I'd been treated fairly. I could have imagined a complete excusal—and often I fantasized it, the judge saying, "David didn't mean to do it," and leaving it at that—but the prospect frightened me. I thought a measure of punishment would be best, all around, and I was grateful that this punishment would be in a private hospital, with rolling green lawns and adolescent flip-outs from privileged, tolerant homes. The judge had indicated that my assignment to psychiatric care could be reviewed after a year, but I felt that with any luck and one or two sympathetic ears to hear the truth of my feelings, to sense the enormity and stability of my feelings, I would be out in a few months, ready to pick up the thread of my life at the point at which I'd snapped it.

The judge devised his sentence after a parole officer interviewed anyone who might give the court a sense of my character. ("It's like a cockamamie FBI check-up," said Arthur. "The FBI," said Rose, nodding and looking at me with sorrowful intensity—trying to remind me of who I *really* was.) The parole officer spoke to the psychologists who'd tested me. And he spoke to me. (He was a young man, Japanese, longing to pass for friendly. "Why do *you* think you set their house on fire, Dave?" he said, in a cagey voice, as if it were the first time anyone had put the question so directly. I stammered out the beginnings of a reply and then lowered my face into my hands and wept—out of habit, partly, because I cried constantly during those weeks, out of helplessness, and, in a peculiar yet undeniable way, out of boredom, because that fire, for all of its horror and devastation, was just a *part* of my life, a *part* of my heart's passionate destiny, and it seemed atrociously unfair that now it was *all* that was important.)

The parole officer spoke to my teachers at Hyde Park High School, who told him I was a good student. He spoke to my few friends and he spoke to my friends' parents. I don't know what he learned—that I liked astronomy, jazz, baseball, that I read books, baked cakes, and liked to turn the volume off the TV and supply absurd, dirty dialogue in a variety of voices. He asked me to give him the names of past girlfriends and he spoke to them and their parents. I doubt very much that Linda Goldman told of relieving me of my virginity in her family's paneled basement—one of the only paneled basements in Hyde Park. The Goldmans were business people and devoted their basement to pleasure: a wet bar, two couches, a Ping-Pong table, and an octagonal poker table covered in tropical green felt with circular recesses for stacking chips. No, I don't think Linda breathed a word of our afternoon's struggle; I don't even know that she remembered it. All that could have distinguished my turn from all of the other afternoons she's spent with such tender self-destructiveness was the sound of her father's voice rolling through the heat ducts, saying, "I could have sworn there was a chicken leg in the refrigerator. I could have *sworn* it." As to other friends, including girlfriends, they were a part of the world originating with my parents. Though my father in particular didn't want me to be a typical "red-diaper baby," that is to say, a child of Communists who associates exclusively with other children of Communists, the pressure of the times and my parents' own nervousness left me, by default, with a vast majority of friends whose parents were friends of my parents. And, of course, none of them said anything to the parole officer that put me in a bad light. The parents, Rose and Arthur's friends for decades, were probably expert in their testimony, and the children, having learned by osmosis the careful language of political harassment, were probably smooth and earnest and absolutely faultless in answering their questions.

Judge Rogers gave us a week to conclude my adolescence in Chicago and get me ready for Rockville Hospital, which was about one hundred miles downstate in the town of Wyon, Illinois. I was still, of course, forbidden to contact any of the Butterfields—or even to make enquiries after them. It was made clear to me that the Butterfields, Hugh in particular, had been the outraged party in my case. Hugh had petitioned the court a number of times; the only evidence that had tempted Rogers to be less lenient with me had come from Hugh. This wounded me without surprising me and I felt that terrible sickness you get when you must acknowledge the righteousness of your attacker. I understood and, in my woozy, isolated, heart-mad way, even *endorsed* Hugh's complaints against me, his right to want me punished with crushing severity—but I also had to believe that Hugh was alone in this, that Ann, and certainly Jade, did not align with him. But as to making a desperate attempt to reach them—I didn't even know where to begin. I didn't know where they lived. Were they in a hotel? Had they divided up and stayed now in two or three separate houses? Had they gone to stay with Hugh's parents in New Orleans, or with Ann's mother in Massachusetts?

I wrote a hundred letters I didn't dare send. I wrote to Keith, to Sammy, to Hugh. I wrote more than a dozen letters to Ann and more than seventy-five to Jade. I wrote apologies. I wrote explanations, rationales, and attacks on myself that might have exceeded their most bitter impulses. I wrote love letters— one of which was signed in the smeary blood of a sliced fingertip. I begged and remembered and I pledged myself with an exile's choking ardor. I wrote at dawn, I wrote in the bathroom, I woke in the desolate middle of the night and wrote and wrote. I wrote poems, some copied, some composed. I made it clear to the world that what Jade and I had found in each other was more real than any other world, more real than time, more real than death, more real, even, than she and I.

Then, on a Friday, the day before my parents were to drive me down to Wyon, a letter arrived for me. It was cleverly concealed in a Student Peace Union envelope, of which I was a member and with which my parents associated the better things of my former life. It was casually, impersonally addressed D. Axelrod, and it arrived with an issue of the *Saturday Review*, which I'd been given a subscription to by friends of my parents on my seventeenth birthday. My mother handed me both the magazine and the Student Peace Union envelope—a little meanly, I thought, for what could it have contained? An announcement for a meeting I would not be free to attend? I tore open the letter in full view of my parents and there, in a script so per-

fectly devoid of idiosyncrasy that it was hard to believe it was
written by a human hand, much less a young, trembling hand,
was a letter from Jade:
"David, oh David, I want you to be all right."
I wasn't to hear another word from her for as long as I was
in custody.

2

The man who built Rockville Hospital was named James
Marshall Nelson. He built it along sleek modernist lines (modern
in the 1920-ish, Bauhaus sense, that is), shooting for and achieving
a plush functionalism: curving staircases that were nearly impossible to fling yourself down; wooden floors with the somber
walnut tone of inherited wealth and the high gloss of immaculate
efficiency. It is said that Nelson built the hospital for himself
because he suspected he was going mad and he wanted a hospital
he could call home. Nelson, an heir to a rural banking fortune,
had served in World War I and after that so-called Great War
ended he stayed in Europe, where he apparently was introduced
to Sigmund Freud. Freud did not analyze Nelson, but when the
young heir returned home he nevertheless called himself one of
Freud's disciples and he devoted his wealth and soul to something called the Wyon Mental Hygiene Foundation.

When Rockville was built, Nelson used his considerable
wealth to recruit a number of psychiatrists. I've often wondered what sort of doctor would have consented to set up
his practice in Wyon, Illinois. The farmers and businessmen who
were within range of the hospital's services would rather have
hung themselves from the rafter of a barn than set foot in the
place. It was used occasionally by local drunks who wanted a
place to sober up, rather than be teased at home or in jail. And

it quickly gained a certain folkloric notoriety: mothers threatened to send misbehaving children there, husbands suggested to reluctant wives that they spend some time at Rockville, and, naturally, there were persistent stories of the place being haunted, of orgies, of hidden German generals, of rapes and transformations.

When the banks failed in 1929, Nelson's banks failed with the best and the worst of them. The Foundation was quickly penniless, and the last of the staff departed leaving a fifty-bed hospital with forty-nine empty beds—the only patient was James Marshall Nelson himself. He lived alone in Rockville, transferring himself from his room to the chief physician's stern little suite. He treated himself and took voluminous notes on the progress of his self-analysis—these notes, edited by his cousin Marie Nelson Abish, were published in the 1950s under the title of *The Interior Pilgrim*. The jottings seem to be the product of a mediocre, compulsively theoretical, and thoroughly impersonal mind—though Abish may have deleted her cousin's warmth and agony out of some panicky sense of propriety.

Yet Nelson was vindicated. Though Rockville remained empty for years, not long after the appearance of *The Interior Pilgrim*, it was purchased by a group of psychiatrists whose discomfort with the mental health establishment (coupled, I suppose, with a sound business sense) led them to set up their own hospital. Though the surrounding farmlands and the newly burgeoning suburbs still offered no indigenous constituency, Rockville was soon known throughout the Midwest as one of the most humane, progressive institutions—a place where parents might send a baffling, tumultuous child and feel not only guiltless but hopeful. It was a place to be healed; the staff, including nurses and orderlies, were sympathetic to the range of human variety, and it was an unwritten motto that what one day is considered deviation *might* be recognized the next as sheer genius. Of course, those whose treatment was founded on such gentle grounds were bound to be privileged. The hospital tried

to provide funds for an occasional under-class patient—a con-
science-taxing process because the Rockville staff truly believed
that nowhere else could a distressed young person find comparable care and it wasn't easy to choose between the hundreds of
petitioning, penniless patients. And what of those who were
turned away? It was like condemning them to mistreatment,
even abuse; it was like closing the doors to the Ark.

Had it not been for my grandfather's money, I don't see how
I could have gone to Rockville. Even with their savings and the
money put aside to help me with college, Rose and Arthur
couldn't have paid the $25,000 a year it cost to stay there. (Or
so I assume. I never knew for certain what their financial situation was. Of all the vulgar, undignified things I was trained not
to discuss, money was the most forbidden. I wasn't answered
when I asked how much my toys, my shoes, or even the meat on
my plate cost. And if I'd asked them for a look at their Hyde
Park Bank for Savings passbook, I would have been treated—
to put it vulgarly but accurately—as if I'd requested they not
flush the toilet so I might examine their feces.) But Arthur's
father, Jack Axelrod, had money, and though Arthur broke with
his father by joining the Communist Party in the middle of law
school, Jack remained, in a sporadic, long-distance way, my
grandfather—expressing his thwarted tenderness as a kind of
bogus Jewish tribalism: "You're my only grandson. The others
had girls." Jack, retired from business and living a lonely life of
leisure in one of those Florida retirement villages, had framed
photos on his wall of my Uncle Harris, Uncle Seymour, and
Aunt Hannah, and, where the picture of Arthur should logically
have hung, a picture of me.

Resentful and maybe even a bit respectful of the alien values
by which I was being raised, he never knew what to send me on
birthdays or at Hanukkah and so twice a year he'd sent me $25—
in cash, as if people like us might not know how to use a bank.
I kept this money in a special savings account and one day, in
the middle of my dolorous thirteenth summer, impulsively with-

drew it to buy a plane ticket to Florida, leaving in the middle
of the day with my bathing suit under my jeans and without a
word to my parents. Jack kept me and my secret for two days,
introducing me to his card-playing partners and winking at me
to let me know these were not people who he *really* liked,
watching me swim in his pool, and letting me have a half glass
of imported beer with my supper. I told him I wanted to live
with him, though I could not say why. I didn't trust him to
understand. And if he would understand, then I would have
betrayed my parents to an enemy. I suppressed no tales of abuse
or neglect. The truth was—or felt like—that I wanted to live
with him because I was bored with my parents, bored with their
gentle reminders, their sighs, their careful, closed faces. I was
bored with how easily fooled they were, how effortlessly paci-
fied and lied to, and I was bored with how they never told the
truth of their lives to me. They were people whose central lie
has it that nothing is wrong, nothing is strange, nothing is un-
explainable or uncommon. I could have told my parents that
every night I dreamed of traveling in a flying saucer and I woke
every morning to find a small red stone in my closed hand, and
they would have said, "Don't worry, that's very common at
your age." It seemed a much brighter prospect to live with my
grandfather, with his memories of Europe and his rapacious
commercial past of turning one dollar into two and two into
twenty, and his frightening, exhilarating stories of firing a cutter
who looked at him "funny" and firing another who grabbed a
woman's breasts, to live with that soft-bellied, granite-fingered
man beneath the untiring sun, with the fragrant fuzz of imported
beer on my lips and the lazy murmurs of the not-too-distant
Atlantic in my ears.

I wrote often to Jack while I was in Rockville, inconsequential, newsy letters, beginning Dear Zadie and ending Your loving
Grandson. These letters were composed with a false, utterly
trumped-up sense of strategy—it added spine to the dull pudgy
days to make myself believe that it was up to me to keep Jack

on my side in order to ensure his continued financial support. This was completely absurd, of course, but I needed to believe that my life required clever maneuvers on my part, that it would somehow benefit me to keep track of nuances. Like a lonely paranoid with a hundred rituals and a hundred intrigues, I built a bathosphere of strategy in which I might live with some fearful, keen-eyed purpose beneath the overwhelming murky sea of my true circumstances. Not only did this include the needless buttering up of Jack Axelrod, but it meant sniffing food, refusing aspirin tablets or vitamins, though there was no reason whatsoever to think the doctors or staff would slip some tranquilizer into me—drugs, isolation, shock therapy, and all other forms of medical punishment were virtually unheard of at Rockville, and even if such things happened I was hardly a candidate for such treatment, being one of the more docile members of that "therapeutic community." The vigilance added tone and made me feel like a soldier, a prisoner of war, and the we-aim-to-please letters to my grandfather were a part of my grand diplomacy—a diplomacy that sought a truce not between me and the rest of the world but between the part of myself that was learning to conform to life in an institution and the part of myself that was stiff with shame.

I wondered if my letters to Jack Axelrod were opened and read by the Rockville staff and I wondered if the brief, meticulously typed notes he occasionally sent in reply were also scrutinized. If I'd wanted to send him a message of passionate sedition I suppose I could have slipped it to my parents on one of their biweekly visits and had them mail it in the wild, thundering freedom of the Outside World. I don't know what I could have said to my grandfather that would have raised any suspicions (I knew that my sincerity as a patient was in doubt), though I did feel our living situations had something in common: he in his balmy planned community with strangers in the communal garden, me learning to play the guitar and singing "Michael Row the Boat Ashore" with peers such as I would

not have known or looked twice at under any other circumstances. But Rose and Arthur were not likely co-conspirators if
I wanted wide, risky contact with Jack; they were uneasy with
my relationship with him and the one weekend he flew north
to visit me, they stayed home.

Of course the letters I truly longed to send I didn't even dare
seal into envelopes: the letters to Jade. Even if I'd known where
to send them, I wouldn't have risked detection—those pages and
pages and pages of frantic scrawlings were the core of my secret
life in Rockville and I never knowingly hinted at it, not even
to Dr. Clark, the psychiatrist in charge of my case, who I actually
liked and spoke to five hours a week. I prayed that Jade would
know that I was writing those unreceivable letters. I believed,
because I had to, in all sorts of mental miracles, like detailed
telepathy or the power of my rich electrical thoughts to send to
her a vivid, unmistakable sign—a heart-shaped constellation, a
speaking wind, or a caterpillar that would find her alone in a
field of tall grass, crawl up her arm and stop at the elbow, turn
its hard black goggles toward her and implant in her consciousness not only the fact of my ceaseless, obsessional thoughts but
their content as well. Perhaps if someone had told me that my
stay in Rockville was going to be two years, or five, or even ten,
I would have found the cunning and courage to get word to
Jade. But from the moment I was installed in my room and began
unpacking my rolled-up socks and folded tee shirts (it was a pine
dresser with a sweet Butterfieldian aroma), I began anticipating
my release, my return to Jade. I did not dream of this release as
something that was months away—I felt it could happen any
day, any day at all.

I didn't want to do anything to draw suspicion. Like Rose, I
believed I belonged in a prison more than a nuthouse, and was
damn grateful to be stuck in the latter. My psychiatrist mentioned
that the fear of anal rape is the most vivid terror people experience when they contemplate prison—more horrible than separation from loved ones, loss of time, collapse of career, etc. I don't

know quite what Clark was leading toward, whether he considered this a holdover from our pasts as baboons or if he meant to suggest that the phobia was the Halloween mask of a latent desire. But the fact is I did cringe at the thought of being served up to a cellblock of crazed prisoners. There is something so unbelievably cruel about fucking someone in the ass. Of course the opening is there and, I suppose, handy. But it takes advantage of the body. It's like making faces at a blind man. I know that one is suspect no matter what one says about things like this. If you say you like anal fucking, it's a bit strange, and if you bother to say that the idea is horrible then that is somehow even stranger. But I had to think about it when my case was pending and it wasn't certain if I'd get by on my plea of insanity or if I'd be sent to Joliet. I have never been on either end of a brutal sexual transaction—even the old high-school stunt of getting a girl drunk and grabbing her cunt struck me as crazy and wrong. (Though I realize that a lot of the drunk girls wanted nothing more.)

Once when Jade and I were making love in her bedroom, around the time when we first got the double bed, and we'd been making love for so long that she was as wet as a river inside and could hardly feel me anymore and I could hardly feel her but we needed, for reasons that really weren't physical, to keep on making love, she turned over on her belly and raised herself on her knees. I thought she was asking me to come in from behind, where the tilt of the vagina gives the illusion of newness and tightness, as we had done so many times. Her back was soaked with sweat and the sheets were like slush. I was panting and sweating myself and sore all over but I didn't want to stop, neither of us did. The friction, our need of it, wasn't really connected to pleasure at that point. It was more of an attempt to *erase* our bodies and explode out of them into pure matter. It was afternoon, there was soft light in her little room, and when she spread her legs and offered her rump to me I looked at the back half of her vagina, with the dark brown hair sopping wet and poking out in curly spikes. I'll never understand exactly what the sight of her body did to me, I mean why it worked the way it did, but its effect was so powerful, so unfailingly powerful that I believed then and will always believe that I was born to see it, to look at her face, throat, breasts, genitals, and feel a heat and spaciousness that no word in my vocabulary can even begin to express. I think that after all of that wet, wet fucking I was only three-quarters hard but the sight of her backside restored me to my unanimous erection and at once I began to move myself into her. But she stopped me and said something a little bewildering, like Put it in the other one, something uncharacteristically peek-a-booish like that, but which I completely understood. I didn't want to say no but I was immediately nervous. We'd never done that before, and I didn't want to leave her alone in her willingness to go somewhere new. And so I made a clumsy jab at her asshole with my cock groping in its lilac blindness. Like the first time we made love, Jade had to guide me in, only now she was pointing me toward a path my mind and heart refused to follow. I drew back. I can't do that, I said, It'll hurt, it's got to hurt. Do you think so? she said. People do it all the time, not only homos. She'd been reading a book about the Mochican Indians of—where was it, Peru? They were notorious ass fuckers and not only the Spanish conquistadors but the Incas used to punish them to the point of death in order to make them fuck more productively but the Mochicans held fast to their preference. (I don't remember if this lesson in anthropology came right there in bed or if it was later.) Jade pulled me back toward her and pressed my cock to her asshole. She grabbed the pillow with her free hand and breathed out with a kind of yogic completeness as if to open herself further to me, but it was useless because her anus was as cryptic as a belly button. I could feel its stunned rejection of my approach. You see? I said. But Jade was caught in the logic of her proposal and she stuck a finger into her vagina and pulled it out wet and moved it in a circle around her asshole. Try it now, she said. Or why not put yourself inside me the regular way so you'll be wet too? What resourcefulness! I felt the beginnings of sexual terror. Why was she being so determined? What was the cause of this sudden stubborn hunger for a new sensation? Was she nostalgic for the stretch of an untraveled passage? Or was there buried somewhere in the core of our lovemaking a hopelessness and shame she wanted to exorcise? I don't want to do this, I said, even as the head of my cock pressed against her ass's wrinkled middle, lilac to mauve. It was opening to me, slightly. I must have been pressing myself in without altogether knowing I was. Her asshole was shuddering like a puppy, like a small frightened heart, and I could see, in a glimpse, her inner walls, a flash of translucent red as spectacular as slag. Why not? she asked. Her voice was muffled. She was supporting all her weight with her forehead. Don't know, not in the mood, something like that. I was wary enough to be cautious. Suddenly she rolled over onto her back. A gray scraggly feather from the pillow stuck to the sweat between her small breasts and she plucked it by its stem and twirled it between her fingers. I thought you'd like it, she said. No, I don't think I would, I said. My stomach was pounding like a second heart. I stretched out beside her, with my leg resting on her thighs and my arms around her. I'm not ready for it, I said. I think it would be wrong. It would hurt. It wouldn't be right. It would be right, Jade said. Because it's you and me and we love each other. I wanted to do it because neither of us have ever done it before. It would be ours. We were silent for a while. We could hear the casual commotion of her house. Sammy and his crew were below playing poker, screaming at each other over every card. (I hate to think what they'd have done to each other if they'd actually played for money.) Keith was on the third floor listening to Joan Baez with the volume turned up so high she sounded like a middle-aged drunk. "Don't sing love songs / You'll wake my mother." The lyrics of that song curled around our slightly embarrassed silence and first I laughed and then Jade laughed. Though it was only in the future, after my release from Rockville, that I learned the real joke to those words, when Ann confessed the full extent of her obsession with Jade and me, and how she had used the heat we generated to ignite her own elusive passions.

Dr. Clark counseled against it, but I kept a calendar on my wall and put an X through each day that passed—at a minute past midnight, if I was awake. I moved through time with constant terror. It moved too swiftly, separating me from my life; it barely moved at all, keeping me distant from the day of my release. In that way, each day was a victory and a humiliation. Yet a part of me refused to live inside of time at all; something of myself remained distant from those nervous skirmishes with the passing days. I thought of this part as my best and most secret self and I would not submit it to my losing war with time, just as no sane nation sends its finest tacticians and most lyrical poets to the front lines of a raging battle. Throughout my stay in Rockville, half of me remained sheltered in the lead-lined bunker of eternity.

As it turned out, my preserving half my heart in eternity contributed to my undoing in Rockville. It meant that I'd make virtually no friends and that I was more isolated than I ought to have been, more sequestered than I wanted—the loneliness was crushing, for the most part. In a community almost exclusively inhabited by perceptive people, my decision to reserve a part of myself from the reality of our shared circumstances was noticed constantly—causing me to be shunned, attacked, razzed, ignored, or, worse, much worse, wooed, drawn out, seduced, challenged, conned. My own doctor folded his arms and shook his head when he listened to me, and more often than I care to remember said "ho-hum, David" when I offered my careful, tidy descriptions of my feelings. "What's your favorite color?" he once asked me. "Blue," I answered, thinking of Jade, her Oxford cloth shirt, the shade of the ink in her last letter to me. Dr. Clark leaned forward and moved his small face closer to mine—a vein the width of a child's finger beat in his high ivory forehead, as if his heart and brain were joined like Siamese twins. "Blue?" he said, and I avoided his eyes and nodded. "I don't believe you," he said. He slapped his knees and stood up. His hands were on my shoulders now and I squirmed away from him. "I don't believe your favorite color is blue. You can't even tell the truth about that. Do you know how to tell the truth, David?"

Of course I knew how to tell the truth. But the truth of the matter was I couldn't. I wasn't there in the same way as the others. I wasn't an acid casualty or a compulsive eater or someone who believed that the lawn wept at night because I had walked over it. For all the encouragement I was given to whirl freely through my feelings, to become whole again by expressing everything that was inside of me, I hadn't in fact been placed in Rockville to discover my true unbroken self. I was there on court order and I was there to change. And I was willing to change. But I knew there were things I could not say—not if I wanted Clark to report that I was ready to go home. I could not say that I wrote secret letters to Jade. I could not say that all that "getting well" really meant to me was the chance to find Jade, to find Ann, Hugh, Sammy, Keith—but most of all Jade, to find Jade, to hold her again and make her understand, as I did, that *nothing* had changed. I was willing to talk about anything else, but not once did I confess that the part of me I'd been sentenced to transform was as alive and unreasonable as ever.

My belief in the truth of my love for Jade as a higher and untouchable truth kept me from the despair that clawed at the hearts of many of the patients, but it also meant that after a full year in Rockville I was still very much there and had no immediate prospects of release. Ted Bowen (working without pay, refusing the money my parents tried to press on him, and neglecting to deposit the checks they mailed to his office on Oak Street) made a number of appeals to Judge Rogers, trying to get my so-called parole commuted, but it was clear (though Rose

and Arthur tried to conceal this) that my leaving Rockville
wasn't being seriously considered.

A few days after the first anniversary of my institutionaliza-
tion, Rose and Arthur appeared for their Saturday visit. It was
mid-September. The first touches of slate were in the sky and
though Rockville's soft golf-coursey lawn was green, its best life
was gone. I still lived with a student's attentiveness to seasons—
the first cool day always made me think of the crisp promise of
blank notebooks, good intentions, new teachers, reunions with
friends—and the panic and despair I felt at not being set free cut
deeper because it was September. The world was changing and
I was not.

Rose and Arthur always seemed ill at ease and a little pathetic
when they came to Rockville. They did not, of course, believe
in psychiatric cures. It would have been more to their way of
thinking to send neurotic teenagers into a state forest to do a
little conservation work, or perhaps a year on an assembly line to
ground short-circuited emotions. And the high-priced Rockville
with its necessarily privileged clientele might have been invented
to stimulate my parents' scorn. They also felt the ego tenderness
of most parents whose child sees a psychiatrist: they were sure
I said awful things about them. They feared that I talked about
their long time in the Communist Party (which I did) and that
I portrayed them as cruel and uncaring (which I did not). They
walked the halls of Rockville with unnaturally soft footsteps, as
thief-like as my own when I used to return home at six in the
morning from Jade's. They wore dark clothing and spoke barely
above a whisper if anyone else was remotely near. Dr. Clark
avoided them, which frightened them in one way, but was also
a relief. They'd read Clark's book, *Adolescence and Agonia*, and
it disturbed them. It was a chatty, aphoristic book, which enjoyed
a mild success. There were no copies of it in Rockville but I
subsequently read it and could scarcely recognize in it the stern,
skeptical man who treated me—it was faintly anarchist in tone
and put forward such suggestions as parents giving their children

complete control over them one day a week. ("He writes books?" I said, one visit. "Well, it can't be for the dough. He makes a fortune right here." This was just the kind of cheap remark my parents needed to hear and Rose gave me a little squeeze on the arm and said, "That's the spirit.")

This time, however, Rose and Arthur were more uneasy than usual. I thought at first that they shared my desperation over a full year's passing, but something in their muffled voices, stiff gestures, and coolish, guilty eyes made me suspect that their unhappiness was rooted in something more specific than despair. They looked absolutely miserable. And then I knew in an icy, uncaring instant that their unhappiness had nothing to do with me, that it was between the two of them, and that it was connected to the death of feelings between them. Once, when Rose showed up alone for a visit, she hinted briefly that the story of my father being in bed with the flu wasn't entirely true, and the one time Arthur appeared without Rose he said quite explicitly that without her he and I might be able to speak more freely, more meaningfully. (We didn't; he took me to the town, fed me, and then took me to a deserted back road he'd "discovered" and let me drive the car—I tried to scare him by speeding into the sunset but he just leaned back and smiled: it was so odd.) Love gives us a heightened consciousness through which to apprehend the world, but anger gives us a precise, detached perception of its own. I sat in the nautical-style desk chair in my little room and looked at Rose and Arthur seated on the edge of my single bed. Arthur plucked at the nubby spread and Rose poked about her purse for Sen-Sen, and I saw that my absence had robbed them of their last excuse to remain together.

"I've got an idea," Arthur was saying. "Why don't we go to that old farmhouse we pass on our way out here?" He was looking at Rose, but now he turned to me. "It's been preserved, nothing changed since eighteen twenty-something. All the original furniture, everything. It might be interesting."

"Sounds like it could be fun," Rose said. She said it with a frown, as if to put us on notice: even if she enjoyed the antique farmhouse, her spirits would remain low.

"Why do we have to go anywhere?" I asked. "It's always a drag. You two spend half the day driving down here and then as soon as you arrive we get in the car and drive some more."

"We don't have to go anywhere," Arthur said. "It's a beautiful day. We can walk around here."

"I'd think you'd *want* to get out and see the world for a couple hours," Rose said.

"It doesn't make any difference to me. A guy who's here has a pretty fair telescope back home and his parents are bringing it next week. There's pretty good visibility here at night and as we all know I have a lot of time, especially at night. The nights are nice and long and we have supper at five thirty so that gives us even more time at night. You have no idea how much of it we have, time."

"I hate when you get like this," said Rose.

"Like what?"

She shook her head.

"Like what?" I repeated.

"You're not the only one in the world who's upset about this whole situation."

"Drop it, you two," said Arthur. Suddenly, his psychological politics seemed more clumsy and transparent than ever: how he loved to place himself between Rose and me, as if only he kept us from killing each other. It was true, he had stopped my mother and me from fighting countless times, yet he had never brought us closer and the distance he allowed us to maintain was as important as the truces. "I think we should get some fresh air. Before long, winter." He pressed his lips together and swallowed; he hadn't meant to suggest that another season lay in wait for me.

"Of course we couldn't simply sit around," I said. "We couldn't talk. That's what was so amazing to me about the . . ."

I paused, letting my parents become anxious about the taboo that was about to be broken ". . . the Butterfields. To be with a family that actually talked to one another."

"That's a new one," said Rose.

"It's not a new one. You remember what you remember and I remember what really happened," I said. "After all, I've had more of an occasion to talk about the past and remember it. Professional help, you know. The Butterfields were interested in each other and there was *nothing* you couldn't say. You weren't asked not to mention things and if you said something that maybe wasn't so nice you weren't told, 'That's not a nice thing to say.' We always lost track of the time because I'd be talking or Ann would or one of the boys . . . or anyone else. Everyone talked and everyone listened and you had ideas and thoughts and feelings you never had anywhere else because there was nowhere else where anyone would care or would listen."

"Oh, they cared so much about you," said Rose.

"There's no need to argue about this," said Arthur.

"A bunch of fools in love with their feelings, is what they were," said Rose, reddening, leaning forward. "And they didn't give two cents about you."

"When they let me stay with them I felt my life had been saved," I said.

"Well maybe you did, but you were wrong." Rose paused. "As you can see."

"OK," said Arthur. "That's it." He put up his hands.

"I'd rather be here than turn out to be what I would have if . . ."

Rose nodded. "If what?"

"If I hadn't known them. If I'd been what *you* wanted me to be."

"We're putting on a wonderful show for the whole school," said Arthur.

I slammed my open palms on the desk violently. I got up and knocked the chair over. I picked it up and thought I might throw it—at my parents, through the window, against the wall. My parents were silent. They looked at me with that mixture of embarrassment, disgust, and envy we feel when someone gives vent to their ugliest, most unreasonable feelings. I let the chair drop and walked toward my parents. I certainly wasn't going to do them any great harm, though I did have a fleeting vision of taking them by the shoulders and shaking them.

"David," said my father, with pointed neutrality.

Rose planted her small feet squarely on the floor and leaned back, like a drunk trying to sit erect and miscalculating the angle.

"I never asked you for anything," I said.

"David," said Arthur, letting his voice drift toward its natural warmth.

"I've been here more than a year and you haven't done anything to help me."

Quickly I turned away from them and walked back toward my desk and righted the chair.

"I think we should leave while the day's still nice," said Rose.

"Good. Go home. I want you to go home," I said.

"Don't pull this," Rose said.

"We don't want to go home," said Arthur.

"Then visit with someone else. That way you won't waste the long drive."

Rose and Arthur exchanged glances and for an instant I thought they might discuss me in my presence. It had never been their way, of course. I'd almost never seen them disagree or reveal confusion. Running our tiny family on the principles of centralism, they shielded me from their uncertainties—captains of an imperiled ship staving off the panic of the passengers with buttered rolls and routine announcements.

"Well," said Rose, with what was meant to be a sigh of finality, "are you through trying to make us miserable? As I've said, you're not the only one in the world who's upset."

"I really don't care," I said. "With all my heart, I don't care."

"Your mother means that this whole mess is as tough on us

as you," said Arthur. He shook his head and lowered his eyes: it wasn't what he'd meant to say, exactly.

"Do something for me," I said.

"Our life is very sad these days," said Rose.

"Do something for *me*," I said.

"There's no reason to discuss our personal lives at this time," said Rose. "And I refuse to listen if you're going to pretend you're the only person in the world with troubles."

"He knows that," Arthur said.

"Do something for me," I said once again. I thought of getting on the floor and chanting it, the way one of the orderlies had taught me to chant Coca-Cola Coca-Cola until my thoughts disappeared and my mind existed only as a pitchless hum. "Do something for me."

"We want to," said Arthur. "Surely you know that."

"I want a new lawyer," I said. "Who's looking after my case? Who's in charge of getting me out?"

"It's in the hands of the court," said Arthur. "There's not much that can be done."

"Who's handling it?"

"Ted is," said Rose. "You know that."

"Bowen?" I said. "Bowen is a total fucking jerkoff asshole idiot. He's been losing cases all his life—this is the kind of lawyer you get me? A Communist lawyer with as much influence as a stray dog?"

"You have no right to talk that way about Ted," Rose said. "This is a man who's been loyal to you. It's time you learned who your real friends are."

"I know," I said. "Ted Bowen watched me grow up. Well, I don't care. I don't want him to have anything to do with me anymore. Don't I have the right to fire him? I'm eighteen. If you're too fucking loyal to tell him he's through, then I'll tell him."

"You're making a mistake," said Arthur. "Ted's a very capable attorney."

"You *have* to say that," I said.

"I don't have to say that—or anything else."

"Yes, you do. You have to say he's good because he's the same kind of lawyer you are."

I glared at them both and waited for a reply. But they were silent. They didn't sigh, or shrug, or even move their fingers. Their eyes fixed on a space three or four feet to the left of my face, like people you are shouting at in a dream.

Finally, Rose said, "Obnoxious."

"Is it the money?" I said.

"You know it's not," said Arthur.

"Because if it is, I'll get the money. Grandpa will give it to me. It'll cost him less to pay a good lawyer than to keep me here. I want the best. I want someone smart and tough, someone with a little influence for God's sake, someone who won't get walked over and laughed at. I need string pulling and pressure and deals. Ted's not the one."

"He has an excellent record, David," said Arthur.

"But he's not doing anything for me."

"You think you're going to find some outsider and get the kind of dedication we get from Ted?" said Rose. "A man who was struggling for the rights of people before you were even born?"

"I don't want to hear anything about it," I said. I slapped at my shirt in that open-handed gesture of innocence and exasperation; a little coin of perspiration had formed in the hollow of my chest, trapped in its crater by the pounding of my heart and the hardness of my belly. "I want a new lawyer. I'd find one myself, but how can I? If you don't do this for me . . . You have to do this for me. Tell Bowen he's out. He has nothing to do with this anymore. The next time someone talks about my case it has to be a different kind of lawyer—not some little nobody with soup on his tie. I want the best. I want to get out of here. This is completely unfair. You better find me a new lawyer even if it's someone you hate."

3

They eventually got a new lawyer, and it *was* the kind of lawyer they truly disliked, with an office in the Wrigley Building and a picture of Mayor Daley on his wall, but even so it was practically another two years before the court gave me permission to return home.

4

They took me home in the middle of August on a day turned absurd by melodramatic weather. I sat in the back seat of their car with my tan valise on my knees, like a soldier on a crowded train. I'd been advised by my only friend in Rockville, a boy named Warren Hawkes, who had been in and out of three such places, that the best way to make the journey was to remain as lifeless as possible, and I held my mind tightly, as if in two cranial hands. Arthur drove and each time he glanced at me through the rear-view mirror he took his foot off the accelerator and the Ford slowed down. Rose said two things I remember: "This is the last time we'll make this trip," and, "I wonder if you've heard there's been an upsurge in anti-Semitism lately." We traveled a narrow back route, a short-cut to Chicago they'd discovered just recently; nearly ripened fields of corn thronged the sides of the road, pressing forward like spectators awaiting a parade. Above us, the thunder groaned away and first to the west and then to the north leapt platinum branches of lightning —in momentary silence and then with a great electrical crunch.

The cornfields flashed, the air grew heavy, oppressive, almost purple, and before we were thirty minutes away from Rockville it was raining so hard the windshield looked as if it were being splashed with silver paint.

The weather somehow intensified my silence and made Rose and Arthur miserable on a day they'd counted on. I could feel myself failing them and in truth I didn't want to. But I didn't dare make a civil gesture. I was sure that if I let myself come forward at all, I would do something to disgrace myself and terrify my parents. I might holler, or cry, I might curl up in the back seat and whisper "I'm scared." It was better, safer, to remain as inanimate as my raging senses would allow, and before long Arthur and Rose drifted into the haze of silence I'd manufactured. On and on we drove, slowed by the rain and startled now and again when the lightning broke so nearby that it sounded as if it were your own bones being snapped in two. Through the small towns, past the churches, the shopping malls, the hasty clusters of ranch-style houses, the storm and its crazy drama followed us every inch of the way. I dozed off at one point and woke with a start that was doubled by a long roll of thunder. My valise fell from my knees and balanced on the steering-column hump that went through the center of the car. I stared at my lap; the suitcase had left a perfect parallelogram of sweat. "You're awake," said Arthur, looking through the rear-view mirror. The car slowed down. There was a high hum beneath us and I saw we were going over a metal bridge. We were in Chicago, crossing over the Chicago River, dead now but curiously beautiful, moving beneath us like melted candle wax.

My parents took me home to their shadowy apartment on Ellis Avenue, a street which many no longer considered safe. From time to time, Rose and Arthur had talked of moving but it seemed reactionary to quit the backsliding neighborhood. My parents had lived in the same apartment all their married life. It was in a massive stone building and its white was the color of an old tombstone. About a block away was a physics research lab where some of the work on the first atomic bomb had been done and across the street was one of the University of Chicago's libraries. But we were at the western edge of the University's territory and all around us were empty lots where buildings once stood and the woeful evidence of families living with not nearly enough money. The professors and their families were gone from our building as well, and when we pulled in front of it (after a roundabout route that took us as far as possible from the Butterfields' old block) I noticed that whoever had moved into the ground-floor apartment had pasted yellow paper over their windows and that the heavy oval glass in the building's street door was badly cracked, as if it had been struck by a rock or a bullet.

I followed my parents up the stairs, holding my valise. Someone was cooking curry on the first floor and as we approached the second landing I heard "When a Man Loves a Woman" by Percy Sledge. Arthur led the way, gripping the dark wooden banister with one hand and bouncing his keys in the other. Rose seemed to walk with new cautiousness; she lifted her feet higher than necessary at each step and as I lagged back and tried to calm myself I noticed a tiny wet leaf plastered to the sole of her high-heeled shoe. The halls were painted a pale butterscotch color and our shadows bent and swelled as we climbed to the third floor. I tried to feel cheerful by saying to myself, "I'm home, I'm home," but my inner voice sounded skeptical and timid and I was only making things worse.

If my parents themselves gave off accidental evidence of having changed, of having lost patience with their long and puzzling relationship, the apartment itself reflected none of this. As soon as we were inside, my pulse slowed to half its rate. The sensory overload of the long trek was behind me and I was immediately incurious. I knew in an instant that nothing had altered in those rooms. The smells were the same—paste wax, old books, coffee, and Rose's Evening in Paris talcum powder— and the air conditioners wheezed at the same pitch they always had. The same pictures were on the walls: a Utrillo reproduction, a *Guernica*, and five portraits of working hands done by a local lithographer named Irving Segal—hands on rakes, hands on lathes, hands holding knotted ropes. Even the knickknacks were solidly in place: the chunk of quartz on the bookcase next to *Scottsboro Boy* and the little limestone toad from Mexico squatting next to the *Letters of Lincoln Steffens*. The cherry-wood coffee table was still two feet in front of the brown sofa and on top of the table was, as always, the blue pottery vase stuffed with cattails.

I dropped my suitcase onto the pale green rug and sat on the sofa. "Well," I said, "I see you've got the same old cat." It was the punchline to an old family joke—the little boy who runs away from home and returns before anyone notices he'd left.

"Would you like to see your room?" Rose asked. While I was in Rockville she had appointed herself the guardian of my room. Sometimes, as a way of saying goodbye, she'd said, "Your room is waiting for you, David." When they gave the apartment a paint job Rose made certain that the pale blue matched the original color without the slightest variation. When the painters left, Rose took color snapshots of the whole apartment and three of my room and delivered them to me at Rockville. Though I never mentioned the pictures to her—her gesture struck me as somehow out of character, too explicit—those color pictures had survived the steady attrition of my belongings and were now at my feet in the tan suitcase.

"May as well," I said.

It's the same. It was the backdrop of a recurring dream. It was as if the same air I had left behind still filled the little square chamber, waiting for me to please breathe it again. This was beyond preservation—the room had been embalmed. The bed was still covered by a copper corduroy spread. There were still only two pictures on the wall, both ripped from books. One of Ty Cobb, demonstrating his open grip, taken from *The Encyclopedia of Baseball*, and another of Monk Eastman, the notorious Jewish gangster, razored from a book called *The Gangs of New York.* The wooden floors were painted and waxed and, that night, when I turned on the lights, they would dully reflect the electric glare. There was the red and green braided rug and the white dresser, the bowl-shaped glass cover over the ceiling light, the three-legged blond wood desk, the plum-colored coffee mug filled with pens and pencils. My bookcase was still intact, holding boyhood books about prehistoric animals and astronomy, the novels of John R. Tunis as well as the worthy books my parents had given me on holidays and which were unread—though I'd opened each page by page so they wouldn't look unappreciated.

"My God," I said, in not much more than a whisper, but we were so quiet and so uncomfortably conscious of one another that I might as well have shouted it.

"Recognize it?" said Rose, with a brief nervous laugh. "We wanted it to be just like you remembered."

"It is," I said, and impulsively took her hand and squeezed it. It was the first time we'd touched since leaving Rockville and I could tell she didn't want me to let go.

Arthur opened the narrow closet and ran his hand over the empty wire hangers, an innkeeper's gesture.

"Plenty of room," he said.

Obligingly, I looked at the closet and nodded. Toward the side were some of my old clothes.

Rose was gazing around the room and it looked as if she'd suddenly regretted keeping it so frozen in time. Yet how to change it? What would that have meant? What would it have made them?

"Do you like it like this?" she asked, softly.

"Yes. It's just like it was. I really feel like I'm home."

"You *are* home," said Arthur, huskily.

And then, when we least needed it, an enormous silence descended. I sat on the edge of my bed and waited for what I hoped was a polite interval before saying, "I guess I'd like to lie down for a while."

My parents exchanged quick glances, but not nimbly enough to escape detection, like old illusionists helplessly exposing the rigged banality of their tricks. They were regretful not to have planned something definite for my homecoming. But who could they have asked? There was no family to speak of.

"You're not hungry?" said Arthur.

"I couldn't even look at food."

"Maybe a drink." Arthur checked his watch. Two o'clock. An indecent time for alcohol. But it was Saturday and certainly an occasion.

"No. I get drunk too easy."

"We stock other things besides booze," said Rose, smiling and folding her arms.

"I'm just going to rest."

"Well," she said. "OK." Her voice trailed off but her smile remained perfectly firm.

"Well," said Arthur, throwing his hands before him and then clapping them together, like someone making a good choice, "you rest up."

As they left, Rose said, "Should we wake you for dinner?"

"No problem," I said, "I'm sure I won't sleep."

"Open or closed?" said Arthur, touching the door.

I pretended to think about it. "Closed."

The door closed with a soft click; finally I was on my own. I listened to their footsteps go away and then I was up and across the room. I opened my old desk drawer. It was filled with letters. I grabbed them all and leafed through them, first quickly and then, with mounting disappointment, very slowly. All of the letters were addressed to me but none were the ones I wanted— they were birthday greetings from years before, Christmas cards, letters from a South Korean pen pal I had kept up with until my parents asked me to stop, letters from my grandfather.

I'd asked my parents, long ago, if they'd kept the letters from Jade. These letters had been submitted to the court during my hearing and had actually been officially marked as evidence.

They'd helped keep me out of jail, helped to prove the extraordinary emotional pressures I was under. But what had happened to them afterwards?

Once more I flipped through the letters, with a wrist-and-thumb dexterity developed trading baseball cards. It would have been too easy, too kind to find them straight off. They must be somewhere else. I opened my dresser. Top drawer: three new pairs of Esquire socks and a couple unopened packets of Fruit of the Loom underpants. Second drawer: an old white shirt back from the laundry, folded and bound by a strip of heavy turquoise paper. Third drawer: empty. *The important thing is to guard against jumping to conclusions. Not to think ahead of myself.* Quietly, though my hands would not quite behave, I closed the drawers and went to the window.

I sat on the sill, moved the brown curtain to the side, and like a thief, a spy, I looked down at the street. The rain had stopped. A black teenager was walking by with a steel, four-pronged comb stuck in the back of his helmet-like hairdo. In a strange way, I had forgotten about black people. All the staff at Rockville were white and the only black patient who had been there during my stay was a girl named Sonia Frazier, whose father taught logic at Northwestern. Sonia had twig-like scars starting at her wrist and going more than halfway up her arm from countless suicide attempts. Failed suicides suffered a generally low status among the other patients—they were not considered serious people—but Sonia overcame this by not speaking to anyone about anything. She sometimes played the guitar and one day, quite unexpectedly, she sang English folk songs for an hour. By the time she was finished nearly all of Rockville had gathered into the Common Ground to hear her soft, penetrating voice. I admired her remove and guessed that she too wanted her solitude so she might savor secret memories and irrevocable decisions, and whenever we met I nodded at her, as if we were allies in a secret spiritual war. Sometimes she returned my sign. A couple of months into her stay, her parents withdrew her from Rockville. I happened to be crossing the main entrance-way as the three of them left, each carrying two large plaid suitcases, each looking determined and scared. I went to her side, touched her on the shoulder, and said, "I think you're a great person."

I sat at my window now in a state of terror and the terror would not recede. I stared down at Ellis Avenue until it was blurry. I simply could not imagine setting foot on the street below. Two professorial-looking men walked by, one swinging an unopened black umbrella, the other with a raincoat hooked onto a finger and slung over his shoulder, like a TV star. People and their lives. People and their pictures of themselves. It was astounding and it gave me motion sickness to think of it. How could I ever find a place among them and how could I learn to want to? I had nothing to say to anyone; everything I cared about was exclusive. I thought of suddenly braving it, of just going outside and asking the first person I saw—what? Anything. Directions. To the Museum of Science and Industry. Yet what a poor choice, even in fantasy. It was in that very museum that Jade and I had spent our first afternoon alone, in that palace of progress with its towering lobby and the genuine World War I fighter planes hanging from the ceiling on steel cables. Holding hands—it was really more like touching fingers—we had ridden the jolting trolley through the replica coal mine and then, later, spoke to each other in whispers, each facing a scientifically molded sheet of Plexiglas separated by some two hundred yards. Our murmurs had carried with miraculous intimacy and fidelity: it sounded as if we whispered to each other in bed, though we did not know that yet. Finally, we strolled through a gigantic model of the human heart, in the company of twenty tee-shirted children from Camp Wigwam. We walked slowly through the ventricles, listening to the omnipresent thumping that came through a hidden speaker, touching the modeled veins. Jade, in whose house medical gossip was detailed and incessant, presented one of her father's far-flung theories about the

Healthy Heart while I, my mouth so parched that I dared not speak, marveled at our journey through affection's symbolic locus and felt an overwhelming jolt of pure consciousness—I knew from the start that I loved her and knew, as well, that I would never fall back from that love, never try, never want to.

I sat with my forehead pressed onto the window and my full weight was supported by one sheet of glass. With a sudden recoil I sat up straight—I'd imagined myself tumbling out. I looked out at the street again and then pulled down the shade.

The room was mostly dark now and I stood in that darkness. Soon, I knew, I would be ransacking the apartment looking for those few letters, but the search would have to wait. I'd have to be alone. And time passed so slowly—there was no reason to hurry. For the moment it was all I could do to stand where I was, in my stuffy, stupid room, and feel the tears—when had they started?—rolling down my face. I hoped my parents wouldn't barge in and find me like this. But there was no question of stopping myself. I hadn't the strength, nor the cunning disregard for the self's deepest wound. I sat on the bed and blindly groped for the pillow. I wrenched it free from the covers and pressed it to my face. Then I opened my throat to its full aching aperture and sobbed into that soft mound and its millions of feathers.

Rose worked as a librarian in a high school on the Southwest Side, and because it was summer and the time of her vacation, it fell to her to remain home with me during those first humid days of my return. Eventually, I would have no choice but to put my life in order. My release from Rockville was only a new kind of parole. I was required to see a psychiatrist twice weekly, remain in contact with a parole officer, and either enroll in college or get a full-time job. I was not to leave Chicago without the court's permission and I was not to make any attempt to contact any of the Butterfields. But in the meanwhile, I lurked about the apartment, sleeping late, watching TV, and eating with the blind cosmic appetite of an enormous parasite. How Rose suffered my languor. She believed in will power as deeply as Galileo believed in gravity, and the overgrown boy in cocoa brown pajamas staring at reruns of "The Lucy Show" was the apple that falls from the tree only to hover in mid-air.

The weather was repulsive. The temperature was in the nineties and the sky was the color of soiled bandages. Our air conditioners were on perpetually and they dripped cool gray water into the pans we'd placed beneath them. Everything felt damp and slightly soft; the ink from the newspapers came off on your hands.

I could not bring myself to leave the house. I slept as late as I could. When I woke I'd force myself back to sleep, pushing my consciousness back down with the hunger of a man licking the last crumbs off of his plate. Then, when I couldn't take my bed or my room any longer, I'd stagger into the living room, turn on the TV, and lie on the couch, picking at a bunch of oblong green grapes or devouring a box of Ritz crackers. Rose tried to get me to go out. She suggested lunch at a nearby restaurant; she looked at the movie listings with me and asked me what I wanted to see. She claimed to have made appointments for me—with her friend Millicent Bell, who worked at Roosevelt University, or with Harold Stern, who had offered to get me a job with the Amalgamated Clothing Workers union. But I wasn't ready to leave the house and I told her. I never noticed her making a call to cancel one of these so-called appointments; I suppose she was trying to appeal to my sense of order or trying to make me feel there were real live people out there, waiting to see me and make my life real. She offered to take me shopping and when I refused that, she went to my room and took all of my old clothes out. She brought them into the living room and dropped them on the floor and forced me to go through each piece and decide with her that practically none of them fit me any longer—I'd gotten taller in Rockville and I wasn't quite thin any longer. This was on my third day home, and after I admitted that my clothes didn't fit me—and assured her that quite soon I would allow her to buy me new ones—Rose gathered them in her arms to dispose of them in the cellar.

"You could give them away, you know," I called after her as she lugged them toward the door.

"Charity is for the ruling class," she answered.

"Sharing's not!" I shouted, suddenly electric with frustration and shame.

I listened to her heels clatter down the stairs. For the first time since arriving home, I was truly alone in the apartment. I had searched my room and hadn't found any of the old letters to and from Jade, and now at last I could look elsewhere. I ran to the bookcases and opened the sliding cabinet doors at their base: folded tablecloths; aqua and burgundy burlap napkins from Mexico; a few old copies of *The National Guardian;* a chessboard and a White Owl cigar box for the chess pieces; dozens of little boxes of delicate pink birthday candles; boxes of checks; boxes of unsharpened pencils; a portable sewing kit, housed in heavy, shiny paper and decorated by a drawing of an elephant waving its trunk; envelopes; empty spiral notebooks. Just the kind of innocent, chaotic accumulation that at another time might have made me grin with pleasure—my parents' hidden clutter was utterly beyond reproach. It was like prying open a locked diary only to read recipes and descriptions of nature, or hearing someone murmur in his sleep, "I must remember Ezra's birthday."

I closed the cabinets, turned on the TV, and flung myself onto the sofa, trembling in the wake of the missed opportunity. Rose stalked back into the apartment. I could tell that her temper had subsided and she no longer had the impulse to remove my old clothing, but she still had another armload to go and it would have been too complicated not to follow through. She avoided my eyes and gathered the last of them and was gone.

I raced into my parents' bedroom. Even on bright days it was a dark room but today it looked submarine. I switched on the overhead light, which was covered with a convex square of cloudy cut glass. There had never been any sign of activity in that room. They dressed and undressed in the bathroom down the hall. There was no desk, no telephone, and the only chair was an old wooden one pressed against the wall, which had never, as far as I knew, supported human weight. The floors were carpeted and the bed stood in the middle of the room, between a closet on one side and a dresser on the other. There were two Irv Segal lithographs of toiling hands on the wall but no mirror. The bed itself was made so tightly that it looked as if you'd need a penknife to roll back the covers at night. Racing both against time and my own admonishment, I searched through their yellow lacquered dresser. What unvarying innocence! First drawer: socks, shorts, tee shirts, handkerchiefs, and a bottle of Arrid deodorant that Arthur evidently felt was too personal to store in the common medicine cabinet. Second drawer: Arthur's shirts. Third drawer: nylon stockings, one pair still attached to a garter belt, brassieres, panties, a lady's shaving kit. Fourth drawer: an empty wristwatch case, an empty photograph frame with its glass cracked, and stacks of manila envelopes. For a few pounding moments I was certain I'd found my letters. But the envelopes held canceled checks, old income-tax statements, snapshots of me as an infant and a child, old leases, automobile registrations, insurance forms, a loan agreement from the Hyde Park Bank, an envelope marked "Arthur's Will" . . .

"What now?" said Rose.

I was seated on the floor and the envelopes were in my lap. I was silent for a moment, wondering without terribly much fear if inspiration might present me with a brilliant alibi. I had never had any deep attachment to the truth, especially when my personal welfare was at stake. Yet since having confessed to starting the fire on the Butterfields' porch, my sense of personal protection had become sporadic: I rarely felt that more damage could be done to my life than had already been done. "I'm looking for my letters," I said. "My old letters to Jade." I looked up at my mother, prepared for her fury—the only part of my parole she approved of was the stipulation I keep the Butterfields out of my life. I was ready to be screamed at, slapped, even threatened with being sent back to Rockville; I was ready for tears, for panic and grief and even compassion. It really didn't matter to me.

But Rose didn't seem to hear my confession, or else she did not absorb it. Perhaps she had forgotten the letters, or perhaps as far as she knew they'd been disposed of long ago. She swayed in the doorway to her bedroom. Her eyes blinked slowly behind her glasses and her arms were folded over her chest in that schoolteacherish way that was second nature to her now.

"I suppose this was your father's idea," she said.

"Dad's idea?" I said, pouncing on the notion as if it might prove my innocence.

"Dad's idea?" she said, tilting her head, making a face, and trying to mimic my voice. It was, as far as I'd let myself know her, completely unlike my mother to do a thing like that.

I stood up, still holding the envelopes. "I honestly don't know what . . ."

"Checking his will?" she said. She smiled and pointed her chin at the documents in my arms. "I thought you'd be curious to find out if you were still in it. How about the insurance? Did you check that too? You could have asked me, you know. I would have told you. But your father made you promise not to talk to me about it. And like a good little boy you kept your trap shut. Well? Did you have a nice look?" She stepped carefully across the room and pulled the envelopes away from me—for some reason I resisted for a moment. She yanked them away with a surprising jolt of strength.

"Here we are," she said, choosing the envelope that said "Arthur's Will" and letting the others drop and fan out onto the floor. "You won't find any mention of his new family. Or in the insurance. That comes later."

"His new family?"

"Please don't lie. Your father told me he's had a nice little discussion about it with you. And you're so happy for him. Your father has finally found his true love. Now you're a team. 'I'm happy for you, Dad.' That's what you told him. He's got everything he always wanted. A silly woman who waits on him hand and foot and two little brats who wouldn't mind calling him Daddy."

"*His* children?"

"You know they're not his. Why do you join with him against me? I know you love him and not me, but don't you understand that when he leaves here to join them he won't have any time for you? He won't have time. He'll forget you just like he forgot me. You don't have any idea what the world is like, do you? Here," she said, handing the will to me, "you're not going to find any answers in this. Or in any of these packs of lies," she added, kicking at the envelopes on the rug.

That day and the next and through the days that followed, Rose made no further mention of Arthur's other family. I waited for her to approach me again—to apologize, to clarify, to pull me a notch or two deeper into her sorrow. But her small, watchful face showed no trace of those raging moments in her bedroom and I came to see her as one of those patrons of a nightclub who are coaxed on stage, hypnotized, made to cluck like a hen and bay like a hound, and are then sent back to their table without a glimmer of remembrance. It astounded and offended me that she could turn her revelations into a needle in a haystack, but I must admit I was grateful, too. What would Rose be, freed of the bonds of her natural restraints? I feared her. Now, finding me sprawled in front of the TV, all she could do was comment on the stupidity of the shows. But wouldn't it be just as likely that she'd wrap her small hard fingers around my arm and say, "You never respected the things I believed in. You blabbed family secrets to strangers. You've taken dope. You gave your heart to another family."

Yet there must have been more than fear that caused me to join Rose in that conspiracy of silence, because I felt no temptation to speak to my father about his "other family." On a certain level, I didn't believe that any such hidden household existed and I was protecting Rose by keeping her ravings private. But if Arthur had a lover and was waiting for the best time to dismantle his life, it was his part to bring that news to me. I was not anxious to share the secrets of his starving heart. Though he had of course never told me his capacity for love had not been tapped, that it had remained curled within him, that it had been reabsorbed by his body and turned into belly, that the unused love had collapsed his arches and grayed his hair, that it had thickened his voice and swollen his knuckles, turned him into a quipster, a sigher, a snuffler at the movies, a tag-along and a drag-behind, I had always felt this to be true, and from the moment I had my first intimation of romance I mourned Arthur's loss. I was eight or nine years old and the radio was playing Johnnie Ray singing: "If your sweetheart / Sends a letter / Of Goodbye / It's no secret / You'll feel better / If you cry." Arthur put his paper down to listen for a moment and then he smiled at me. And I knew that even though the song was cheap and "made for a profit," it meant something to my father, was taking him by surprise and laying its clammy hands on him. More than once, more than a thousand times, I had longed for my father to honor the unreasonable impulses of his love-soaked heart and break out into some high-flung adventure—to chase after the waitress whose walk he studied with such instinctual longing, to write a letter to Ava Gardner whose films he'd see three, four, sometimes five times over, to live the life of popular romance with picnics near the waterfall and long, spinning embraces. Once, in what turned out to be the middle of my time with Jade, I was in my bedroom, dreamily and pointlessly filling out applications to college, when Arthur drifted in. I looked up from my desk and saw his reflection in the night-backed window. "Hello," I said. "Happy?" he asked. The question didn't sound like it hid a trap and so I nodded. Arthur shook his head—my father, that is, my father shook his head—and he said, "I envy you." I thought then as I was to think later: It was too late in his life for me to help and if I couldn't help, then where was the profit in caring?

Saturday, seven days after my return, there was a little reception in my honor. Clearly, it had been Rose's idea. She had been urging me all week to make contact with the people who had watched me grow up, who had written me birthday notes in Rockville and sent me presents, and who now wanted to enjoy the relief of my return. Rose, a loyal, principled friend, felt she owed her friends a glimpse of me, and I think she was domestically strategic enough to realize that a day with family and lifelong friends might have a sentimentally sobering effect on her husband, might fill Arthur's winged heart with the baffling weight of the shared past. When I emerged from my bedroom that day—feeling as if this might be the day I would go out on my own, take a walk, buy a book, feeling, that is, more confident but holding that elusive confidence in my palm like the contents of a broken egg—Rose was already at the Co-Op buying food and Arthur, dressed in tan trousers and a sleeveless tee shirt, was pulling our old torpedo-shaped vacuum cleaner around the living room and scowling at the carpet. "We're having the old bunch over," he said above the roar of the vacuum. "Some fun, huh?" And he raised his eyebrows comically, inviting me to share an irony he refused to explain.

And oh my parents' melancholy friends! Olga and Leo Greenbladt, Millicent Bell, Tom and Natalie Foster, Harold Stern, James Brunswick and whoever it was he happened to be married to, Connie Faust, Irene and Alberto Nicolosi. They were the people I'd known all my life, better, or at least with more constancy, than I knew my schoolmates or my scattered, distant relatives. If I had been married it would have been these people, my parents' friends from the Communist Party, who would have sat grinning in the folding chairs at the nonreligious ceremony, and if I'd been struck dead it would have been their tired, slightly haunted eyes watching my ashes scatter in the wind. In the old days—old days for me, that is, but for them it was The End— I listened to their incomprehensible discussions at monthly meetings and played the role of servant, passing through the smoke-dense room in my aqua pee-jays, carrying a tray of salami and cheese. Then I'd be sent to my room with a bottle of Canada Dry and a little turquoise dish filled with miniature pretzels. These were the faces who beamed at me over the shine of birthday candles; these were the scuffed shoes and massive knees lined beneath our dining room table where I crawled in a mild social panic hoping to retrieve a dropped Brussels sprout. These were the voices and the aromatic pipe tobacco in the back seat of the old car during rides to the country; these were the hands that grabbed for the check at the pizzeria; these were the names on the bottom of astoundingly corny graduation cards. Here were my parents' friends resting their feet and drinking Italian coffee after a nervous Saturday helping the Negroes picket Woolworth's. And here they were again, visiting me before I shipped off to Rockville, squeezing my hand, memorizing my face, bringing fictitious regards from their children who I'd never bothered to know. (My father's way of leaning away from the truth of his life was to discourage my making friends with his friends' children: "Make friends with real people. Forget these red-diaper babies." But I needed little discouragement. Those boys and girls were not my type, nor was I theirs: they were serious, respectful, unused to wasting time, uncomfortable with the mean jokes I amused myself with.)

To protest the vicious social wound I felt this impromptu party was inflicting on me, I withdrew from the household after eating a long, sticky breakfast. I closed myself in my room—a ten by fourteen chamber that was beginning to tell more of the unpleasant truth about my physical self than a shoe or an old shirt would tell—where I dozed, read, and wondered what to wear. The reception was set for three o'clock (a time no one could expect to be given a real meal) and as the hour approached I began to think seriously of dressing for it. Rose had thrown away most of my old clothes but a blue suit bought for my high-school graduation had survived her raid. I put on a white shirt, a narrow black tie, and my old suit. There was no mirror in my room—the only mirror in the house was on the medicine chest; you'd have to leap into the air to see how your pants fit—but I checked my ghost-like reflection in the window glass. The suit was clearly too small for me and the sight of its snug fit—its tightness at the thigh, its narrowness at the shoulder and chest, the cuffs' clumsy suspension above the tops of my shoes—filled me with a strangely powerful sense of unease. That tight blue suit ambushed me with the reality of my time away.

I lay in bed, fully dressed now, staring at the ceiling and stroking my narrow tie. The tie was altogether unfashionable but I doubted that my parents or any of their friends would notice. That set had a conscious disregard for fashion and products. (It had only been recently, for example, that Arthur learned a TV dinner wasn't just anything you happened to be eating while watching the set.) I dozed off. While I slept, a few of the guests arrived; I might have slept through the day if my mother hadn't awakened me.

"David?" she whispered through the door.

"I'm up," I said. "Are they here?"

"May I come in?" Without waiting for an answer, Rose entered, contrary to established Axelrodian etiquette. She wore a

U-necked pale green dress and green and white shoes. She held a glass of whiskey and water, clutching at it through the thickness of three cocktail napkins. "You're wearing a suit," she said, closing the door behind her.

"Observant," I said.

"It's much too hot, David. And that's a wool blend suit. Look how you're perspiring. Why not take that old thing off and freshen up with a nice cool damp washcloth?"

"No, I want to wear this," I said, with all the maturity and sense of fair play that had made me such a hit at home.

The door buzzer went off. I could hear familiar voices from the living room. Laughter. A high, rapid hoot, like a mezzo-soprano owl. Then a man's voice—Harold Stern's—saying, "No. Don't laugh yet. This isn't the funny part." This was followed by more laughter, over which a woman's voice emerged to say, "Who the hell cares if it's the funny part. We're laughing now, aren't we?"

"OK," Rose said to me, after a panicky glance at the closed door, "you look fine. Why not just pop into the washroom and throw a little water in your face?"

As for the party itself, it went so smoothly and without incident that it could just as well not have happened. No one had an unexpected thought or said an unpracticed word; no one got drunk or ate too much; no cigarette ash was accidentally flicked onto the rug. I was allowed to drink my fill but I could not become drunk. I was led over to the sofa and placed next to Millicent Bell, who was later to help me enroll in Roosevelt University. I was also led into a conversation with Harold Stern, who would get me a job with the Amalgamated Clothing Workers of America. Yet I did nothing to secure these favors that day. They were mine because I was Rose and Arthur's only child and because I'd been so silent and adorable passing out smoked meats during Party meetings in the past, during the best days of all of their lives.

Daylight lingered in the windows and the reception in my honor seemed never to end. What one could or could not ask about my long absence was a mystery to my parents' deferential friends. The deepest into the personal area anyone dared wade was a hearty Welcome Home, that would have been just as suitable if I'd returned from a two-year study of socialist genetics at the University of Leningrad. Even those who had written me and sent me presents during my stay in Rockville avoided touching the truth of my absence. Did they fear what might accidentally appear in their own eyes if they mentioned my incarceration— the tears, or perhaps the scorn? Or were they respecting my mother's ardent desire that everything, everything in all the world, be absolutely as normal as possible? History owed Rose a normal afternoon and even the children of my parents' friends were determined to keep anything reminiscent of pain at bay. Meredith Tarnovsky, sixteen and finally beautiful, with the pure, animal attractiveness of someone whose sexual drive is not yet social but purely hormonal, was just returned from a few weeks in Cuba, where she'd cut sugar cane and attended lectures. She was often at my elbow, talking to me about Castro, who I actually happened to like, though not with Meredith's whole-hearted passion. Her dark eyes glistened, the perfume of her bath lifted off her soft skin, the Havana sun had turned all the soft hairs on her arm bright platinum. I drank gin after gin, wondering if the purpose of this party was to encourage me to violate my long celibacy and drag Meredith into my room. "You were in Cuba," I said to her, "and I was in a fancy little nuthouse. Talk about your separate paths, huh?" She lowered her eyes and shook her head. Meaning what? That it was ironic? Sad? Or that we weren't supposed to talk about it? The other representative of my "peer group" was Joe Greenbladt, an ex-runt who once was called Little Joey Greenbladt and who now, at twenty-two, towered over me. He wore a red shirt, powder blue corduroys, and cowboy boots. I'd never had enough to do with him to join the ranks of his childhood tormentors, yet today he avoided me and glanced at me with a certain dark irony as if his presence in my parents' apartment was somehow settling an old score. He was apparently a great favorite in my parents' set. Meredith may have gone to Cuba but Joe (Josef on his birth certificate) had read all of *Kapital* and referred to the civil rights movement as "the Negro question" and to his own friends as "today's youth." Joe's parents, Leo and Olga, remembered my birthday while I was in Rockville and now and then had sent me a book or a magazine. The year before, they'd gone to the Soviet Union and brought back a small reel tape recorder, which they gave my parents to give to me. Along with the tape recorder was a taped message. "Helloooo, David, this is Olga speaking to you." "And this is Leo." "David," Olga had continued, "we've just returned from the Soviet Union. We had the most marvelous experiences, too numerous to mention. It was very cold but our hotel was perfectly warm. And the people, David, the *people* . . ." "Very happy," Leo said. "Joyous and dignified." I had listened with tears in my eyes, overwhelmed by the stupidity and tenderness of their message. Without realizing, I'd lain my hand on the machine and it got in the way of the reel. Olga and Leo's voices got slower, lower, and they sounded now like stroke victims—that preview of their mortality had gone through me like heat lightning.

Around seven, the rains began. The sky turned a vivid electric green and the rain pounded against the windows and battered against the air conditioner. Like a pack living in the wild, the guests moved in unison, making plans to leave, to share rides, to drop each other off. It seemed the rain panicked them, though I suppose they were seizing a good excuse to leave. Tom and Natalie Foster were the last to go and even they were gone fifteen minutes after the rain began—they'd lingered only to gossip about the Tarnovskys, Meredith's diminutive, gaudily dressed parents. The Tarnovskys owned a movie theater on the North

Side and had taken to booking in an occasional sex film to pay expenses. "We told them it would come to this," Tom Foster said, feigning sadness and concern.

When they finally left, Arthur closed the door and leaned on it. "The first to arrive and the last to leave," he said.

Rose laughed loudly. "What a pair of characters." Then she said, "Hmmmmn," as if she'd overheard herself and found it puzzling.

I sat on the sofa eating a piece of ham that I'd placed on an apricot sweet roll and drinking a gin and tonic. I felt blurry but not tired enough to sleep.

"Well, how did you like it?" said Rose as she began her rounds, collecting glasses and emptying ashtrays.

Arthur stood at the window and gazed out at the rain. I wondered if he wanted to look quite that dramatic. "It wasn't much of a party for you, was it?" he said.

"It was fine," I said.

"Everyone was so glad to see you," Rose said.

Arthur paddled across the room and lowered himself into what we still called Arthur's Chair. He heaved a glutinous sigh and placed his smallish feet on the battered oxblood ottoman. "It could have been a lot worse," he said.

"No, it was good," I said, injecting some conviction into my voice.

"You know," said Rose, in her "family secret" voice, "your dad and I have been shopping around for a welcome home present for you." She sat really quite close to me on the sofa. "Would you like to know what it is?"

"You don't have to buy me anything," I said. "You've already spent a goddamned fortune on me."

"On this party?" asked Arthur.

"No. On the new lawyer. On Rockville."

"Well, money has to be spent on *something*, doesn't it, Arthur?" Rose said.

"Not necessarily, but I know what you mean," Arthur said.

"Are you interested in what we're getting for you?" Rose asked me.

"Sure."

"A little car."

"A little car?" I said, holding up my thumb and forefinger.

"Not quite that small," Arthur said, smiling—I was never more his son than when I made a simple joke, especially if it was at my mother's expense.

"If you're not interested . . ." said Rose.

"I'm interested. It would be great. But I don't even have a license. Mine expired."

"What does that matter?" said Rose. "You'll bone up and take the test. You were a wonderful driver."

"Yes," I said, "like driving you crazy."

"Or driving me to drink," said Arthur.

"Are you happy about the car?" asked Rose.

"Yes. But I don't want you to get it. I don't need presents."

"It's Millicent Bell's car, you know," my mother said. "A green Plymouth sedan. As soon as her new car's delivered, we get to pick up yours."

"So it's a slight case of hurry-up-and-wait," said Arthur.

"That's not the worst thing that ever happened in this world," said Rose, with a brave, incongruous smile. "But how about this? In the meanwhile we'll get you something else, another welcome home present. What would you say to that?"

"Fieldmouse," I said.

"What?" Rose said.

"Nothing, no, that would be great."

"What would you like?" Arthur asked.

"I don't know. I don't need anything."

"Some clothes?" said Rose. "For when you start school, or whatever."

"That would be nice," I said.

"Clothes aren't a present," said Arthur. "He'd get clothes no matter. How about something special, David? Something a little off the beaten path?"

I wondered if he were tempting me deliberately. "Like what?" I said.

"Name it," said Arthur.

"Well," I said, leaning back and preparing my insides for the worst, "there *is* one thing."

"What?" said Rose.

"And it wouldn't cost a penny," I said. "It's something of mine. I've been looking around for it and I can't find it."

My parents exchanged glances; it seemed they knew what was next.

"Anyhow," I said, "I'd like you to give it to me. It means more to me than any old Plymouth, I can tell you that."

"What are you talking about?" said Rose.

"A bunch of letters. The letters from Jade. The ones you showed to the judge." My voice was suddenly unstable, feathery, and overheated—not a voice that could command attention. "And I think there were some letters I sent to her. I'd like to have them, all of them." I took a deep, notched breath and added, "They're mine," because they were, they were completely and irrevocably mine, and it tore at my tenderest parts to have to ask for them.

Rose and Arthur explained as simply and calmly as they could that the letters were gone and I, to prevent making a fool of myself, tried to look as if I believed them and, at the same time, to prevent myself from losing all hope, told myself they were clearly lying.

Later that evening we sat in the kitchen over a light supper. Rose and Arthur yawned frequently from exhaustion and tension. No one was hungry and with the topic of the letters having been instantly elevated to a taboo, there was nothing anyone cared to talk about.

Rose was the first to leave the table. Then I went into the living room and turned on the TV. Arthur followed and sat at a respectful distance from me on the sofa.

"Did you talk to What's His Face about a job?" Arthur asked.

I nodded. A White Sox game was on, tied 6 to 6 in the fifteenth inning.

"You know there's no rush," said Arthur. "You don't have to get a job. I hope you know that."

"I've got to get a job. That's what they told me. It has to look like I'm getting adjusted."

"You'll adjust. It doesn't have to happen right away. I told you what it was like for me when I came home from the Army."

I nodded, but Arthur went on.

"I was of course glad to be back. The war was over and I was alive. I had people I wanted to see and places to go. The whole country was celebrating. But I couldn't do it. Everyone thought your mother and I were having a little second honeymoon but the truth was I couldn't leave the house. It was the damndest thing. I was just stuck here as if I was paralyzed."

"I know, I know," I said. And then, looking away from the TV but not quite at my father, I said, "But there's a big difference between coming home from World War II and coming home from a fucking insane asylum where you've been sent because you burned your girlfriend's house down. No one wants to see me."

Arthur shook his head. "Stop it. With an attitude like that you can't expect very much."

"That's fine. I don't expect anything."

"Don't you understand? Everyone is willing to grant that what's behind you is behind you. Look at all the people here today. I know you don't care very much about them but that's not the point. They were all happy to see you again. It was almost like you've never been gone."

"Right. I noticed."

"Now it's your turn, David. It's time for you to realize to yourself that what's in the past is in the past."

"I don't think I know what the past is. I don't think there's any such thing."

"You want to know what the past is?" said Arthur. "It's what's already happened. It's what can't be brought back."

"The future can't be brought back, either. Neither can the present."

"I'll show you what the past is," said Arthur. He clapped his hands together once, waited a moment, and then clapped them again—the sound was hollow, forlorn. "The first clap was the past," he said with a subdued yet triumphant smile. If we had shared the sort of life that Arthur had wanted for us it would have contained hundreds of conversations just like this one.

"Then what was the second clap?" I said. "That's the past too, isn't it? And right now, while I'm saying this, isn't this the past too, now?"

Rose came in holding that week's *National Guardian*. She wore a light blue robe and her summer slippers; she was smoking her nightly Newport. "I'm going to bed now," she announced. It was something she used to say to hurt Arthur, to make him feel he was being avoided and to emphasize the point that they wouldn't be making love. There had been a time when Rose had felt she could protect her position in the marriage, and protect her privacy, by simply (and it *was* simple) withholding her love. But now that her love was no longer sought there was no advantage to be gained in rationing it. It was clear that the power she once had was not real power—it had been bestowed upon her, assigned. It had all depended on Arthur's wanting her, depended on his vulnerability to every nuance of rejection. He had, she realized now, chosen her weapon for her. He had given her a sword that only he could sharpen.

Arthur checked his watch. "OK," he said. "Good night." Then, to me, "I think we'd better turn down the TV so we won't keep your mother up."

I sat forward quickly and turned off the set. "I'm going to wash the dishes."

"There's a million dishes," said Arthur. "Save them for the morning."

"I don't see anything wrong in doing them now," said Rose. "It's about time people started pitching in around here."

"I agree."

"It doesn't have to be done now," said Arthur.

"What do you care?" said Rose. "You don't lift a finger around here. You're like a rabbi sitting around for people to wait on you."

Arthur forced a burst of air through his lips, to signify a superior laugh that supposedly just happened to escape, and then shook his head to signify patience wearing thin.

I went into the kitchen. At the party, plastic forks and paper plates had been used, but still nearly every dish in the house was soiled. Ordinarily, they would have put them into the dishwasher, but even after the rain the night was too hot and they couldn't run the air conditioner and the dishwasher at the same time. I felt relieved to be alone and felt somehow clever for not having retreated to my room.

I turned on the water, hot and loud, and stared at the window over the sink. (The window looked out on an airshaft, which my mother found depressing, so she had pasted on the window a picture of Leningrad, clipped from *Life* magazine.) I squirted some emerald soap onto a big tawny sponge, then picked up a flowered cake dish, washed it clean, and ran it beneath the hot water. As the water touched my hands I felt my eyes go molten and then I bowed my head and cried. Before, when I had wept, I thought of Jade, and wondered where she was and if I would ever see her again, or I thought about all the time that had been lost, or I thought about how absurd and awkward I felt, how out of place and helpless, or I just remembered past happiness—happiness that had been mine and no longer was. But now, standing before the sink in a cloud of steam, I thought only of those letters, picturing the ink upon the page, recalling the endearments. Those letters were all that I had that wasn't invisible. They were the only tangible proof that once my heart had wings. I had known another world. It is impossible to give it a name. There are words like enchantment, words like bliss, but they didn't say it, they were stupid words. No words really said it. There was nothing to say about it except that I had known it, it had been mine, and it still was. It was the one real thing, more real than the world. I was crying steadily now, aware that I wasn't really alone, trying not to make too much noise. I felt myself sinking, literally falling to pieces. I tried to direct my thoughts toward anger with Arthur and Rose for separating me from those letters, for destroying them in a panic, or hiding them, or for whatever they had done, but the anger, even the hatred seemed thin, insignificant. I tried to turn my thoughts toward my own helplessness, my inability to get on with life, to begin again. But the truth was that I had no will and no intention to begin life again. All I wanted was what I'd already had. That exultation, that love. It was my one real home; I was a visitor everywhere else. It had happened too soon, that was for certain. It would have been better, or at least easier, if Jade and I had discovered each other and learned what our being together meant when we were older, if it happened after years of tries and disappointments, rather than that vast, bewildering leap from childhood to enlightenment. It was difficult to accept, and it was frightening too, that the most important thing that was ever going to happen to me, the thing that *was* my life, happened when I was not quite seventeen years old. I wondered where she was. I thought about those letters, in a trashcan, in a dump, or in a fire. My hands were paralyzed beneath the hot-water tap and they were turning red.

"Do you need some help with those?"

It was Arthur. I didn't dare face him; I tried to stop crying and I shook with the effort.

"I'll grab a towel. You wash and I'll dry," Arthur said. He

was standing next to me now. His shirt was open and the long dark hairs on his chest glistened with sweat. He glanced at me briefly—then dried the one dish in the drainer.

Desperately, I tried to compose a sentence in my mind: I guess I haven't made much progress with these dishes, is what I came up with. But I couldn't say it. My tears had become familiar to me yet I couldn't control them. They had a life of their own. I washed another dish and handed it to my father and he dried it.

"David," he said. I shook my head and he fell silent. We were silent for a few dishes, for all of the dishes, and then I began on the glasses. I was getting myself under control; my breathing was regular again. I glanced over at my father. His eyes were cloudy and his lips were pressed until they looked ivory and transparent. Oh God, I thought, with a flash of annoyance, he's worried about me, he wants me to take him off the hook.

"I'm exhausted," I said. It wasn't much of an excuse but at least it was true.

He nodded, keeping his eyes on the hot glass in his hand. He turned the dishtowel around and around inside of it, until it cracked a little. "Talk to me, David," he said, in a voice full of holes.

I knew how to avoid the curiosity—or even the concern—of others and could do it as easily as a cheat can deal off the bottom of the deck: it was basic, rudimentary, and sometimes I did it even when I didn't altogether want to. I watched myself doing it. "What do you want to talk about?" I said.

"Anything. Whatever's on your mind."

I shrugged. I was going to start bawling again and I didn't know how to stop myself—I didn't know how to want to. I placed the sponge and a soapy glass on the side of the sink and pressed my hands over my face. I felt the tears running through my fingers, warm and oily.

"I wish I could help you."

"I'm just very tired," I said, though I don't know if it was understandable. I was sobbing heavily now and speech was washed away.

"Is it the party?" Arthur asked. "Did you feel strange with all the people here?"

I shook my head.

"Tell me, David. Talk about it with me. Let me in." He leaned forward and turned off the water.

"I'm in love," I said, through my hands and tears.

He touched my shoulder. "I know, David," he said. "I know." Then—and I don't know how to explain this—I heard something that he didn't say, I heard, "I am, too."

"What can I do for you, David?" my father asked. "Please. What can I do?"

I heard my mother come into the kitchen. I waited for her to say something but she felt excluded and shy. I turned to face her, with my red ugly eyes. She stepped back and touched her face, looking at me open-mouthed, both embarrassed and ashamed. I turned back toward the window. I felt the misery radiating inside of me, going deeper, getting fiercer and more immense, and I was suddenly very afraid that I wouldn't be able to stand it. I rubbed my forehead; I clenched my teeth; and then, suddenly, horribly, without even a moment's warning—or perhaps just *one* moment, a freezing, sweating instant—my insides contracted and sent spewing up the day's gin. My vomit splattered onto the sides of the sink and sunk into the soap bubbles.

"Oh God," said Rose, only half in disgust.

My father grabbed my elbow to support me if I were to swoon. "Press your tongue behind your bottom front teeth," he said, urgently. I heard a scraping sound behind me. My mother was pulling a chair away from the kitchen table.

"Sit," she said, in that stern, bossy voice some people adopt when they want to sound reassuring and which has never reassured me.

"I'm all right," I said, hoarsely.

"You're not all right," said Rose.

"If he says he's all right then he's all right," said Arthur, squeezing harder on my elbow.

I turned on the faucet and drank from it, shamelessly squishing the water around in my mouth and then spitting it into the sink. Then I ran some water on my wrists, filled my cupped hands with water, and threw it inaccurately onto my face.

"Are you sick, David?" Rose asked.

I leaned against the sink. Staring into the dark, stinking water, I said, "Why did you throw my letters away?" I waited for an answer but there was silence. Their silence somehow encouraged me—I didn't want an easy answer and now they seemed to be struggling with my question, my accusation. "Why did you do it?" I said, my voice getting steadier. "I mean, why? That's all. Why?"

I stood up straight. The sickness was gone. Arthur was looking at Rose, he seemed to be demanding that the answer come from her. I followed his eyes to her guarded face and now both of us were staring at her.

"We did what we thought was best," she said, calmly, but with an unstable, evasive quality right at the center of her voice.

"Best for who?"

"We didn't want them around," she said.

"Then best for you?" I said. "You threw them away because getting rid of them—my letters—was best for you?"

"Why do you want them?" she said, gripping the back of the chair she'd pulled out for me. I thought: I am that chair. And I watched her fingers go white from squeezing it. "Why do you want to repeat every mistake you made, to, to . . . *wallow* in something that just about ruined your life?"

"Wallow?" I said, my voice rising in volume and pitch.

"I don't want to argue over words," she said. "You know what I mean."

"I don't care what you mean," I said. "I want *you* to know what *I* mean. Those letters were mine. They were all I had. I just want you to know that I'll always want them, I'll always know that you did this. Nothing will make this memory go away. What's happening right now, in this room, happens forever." I stared hard at her; my eyes colored the air between us. It seemed for a moment that she might cry but she clamped her mouth shut and tried to think of how to answer me.

"Don't you speak to me in that way," is what she finally said.

"We try to do what we think is best," Arthur said.

"Oh stop it, stop it, for God's sake, you are both such liars." I heard my voice as an alien thing, the words clumsily attached to my emotions. My truest, most solid impulse was to push them down, to kick at them, to cause them some physical agony—I knew there was no inner pain I could inflict that would match mine. And I knew, as well, that I was not going to hurt them, I was not even going to touch them.

"You're not allowed to see her anyhow," said Rose. "If you even try to, they can revoke your parole."

"They're not going to revoke my parole for reading old letters."

"We're afraid for you," Arthur said. "That's why the letters aren't here."

There was nothing to say. I didn't want to argue with them. It might have been good for me to enunciate my fury but I wasn't interested in that sort of psychological housekeeping. I was angry but I was peculiarly bored with my anger. It was connected to a part of my world that I didn't care very much about —it didn't connect me to the letters. If I couldn't live in the center of the life I had known, once, the only life I believed in, then I would rather live in dreams. And so I may have said more. The argument may have sputtered on for another few minutes, but I no longer cared and I don't remember anything about it. I was gone, elsewhere. I was listening to my heart beat—it was pounding, really. It was going faster than it should but I followed its beat and it took me in, took me away. My eyes remained on Arthur and Rose but what I saw was Jade walking through that enormous model heart in the Museum of Science and Industry, touching the veins with her small hands, gazing this way and that, her mouth a little open, stumbling but not seeming to notice that she had. Then we walked home, back to her house on Dorchester. I took her hand, and she stroked mine with her thumb, knowing that if I wasn't reassured I would lose courage and let it go. When we reached her house she said she hoped her whole family was home. I asked her why and she said she wanted them all to see me. I was so startled that I asked her why and she did me the kindness of pretending she didn't hear. Then we walked up to the big wooden porch that circled halfway around the house, like a broken Saturn ring. There were bicycles parked on the porch. A wicker couch, yellow with white cushions. A footstool, a flyswatter, an open book. On a little oak table was a glass of iced coffee, milky, with ice cubes stacked in it like bricks. There were tiny flies swimming around the top of the glass, their wings the size of commas, trying to stay alive. Jade saw this—we both looked in the glass at the same instant, but that kind of thing would always happen to us, until it would no longer surprise us but just make us laugh—and she said something like Oh those poor things, or Poor little beasts—the whole family liked that word: beasts—and she threw the coffee over the railing, emptying it out onto their overgrown lawn. Just then Ann came out. It had been her coffee. She had only gone in for a cigarette . . .

In the middle of the night I woke up, completely. I had been dreaming about Jade. I knew when I dreamed about her. It felt as if a wheel was turning inside of me. I tried to catch the images before they sank back into unknowing but it was like trying to pluck moonlight off of the water. It wasn't the dream that woke me, though. It was something that my father had said earlier in the kitchen. "That's why the letters aren't here," he'd said. I could hear him saying it and I could see his face, now, the look of pleading, as if he'd been asking me to see through him, to interpret him, to just be patient and give him a chance to be my hero. I kicked the sheet off of me and got out of bed. I didn't know what I was going to do but I couldn't stay down with my new knowledge. It rushed through me. "That's why the letters aren't here."

But where? There seemed only one logical place: Arthur's office.

I was frightened—of letting myself down, of betraying myself. I dressed and wondered how I could get from the apartment to my father's office. I had no money. I wasn't certain how the buses ran or even if they were still going. The elevated train ran twenty-four hours but I was afraid to ride it. I stood at my window. The glass felt cooler; the rain must have broken the heat. It was two in the morning and no sign of anyone on the street. An almost full moon was out, touching the broken clouds with chromium glow.

I crept out of my room and into the darkened hall. I could hear my father's deep buzzing snores. Rose must have been sleeping too: if she'd been awake, she'd have poked her husband in the ribs to silence him. Touching the walls for balance, I made my way down the hall, past their bedroom, and toward the entrance foyer. Arthur had taken to leaving his briefcase and keys next to the door. This presumed forgetfulness was new, and I didn't know if it came from the erosion of age or the delirium of his new romance. But when I reached the door and groped in the dark for the little table upon which he kept his things, all I felt was the smooth, slightly oily surface of the wood. It was Sunday; there was no need to lay out his things.

I stood in the hall. A layer, and then another, of darkness receded and I could see shapes now. The plastered-over beams in the ceiling, the picture frames on the wall, the soft obsidian gap that was the entrance to the kitchen. I slipped off my shoes. My heart was like a barrel end-over-ending down a flight of stairs. With a murderer's stealth I crept down the hall toward my parents' bedroom.

Before Rose and Arthur lost control over me and could no longer stop me from spending my nights at the Butterfields', I had sneaked into and through the apartment a hundred times. I knew just where to step. I knew which spots on the floor twittered beneath my weight and I knew how fast to open a door to stop the hinges from creaking. My way was not the soundless, shadowy glide it had once been—the door to their room, even though ajar, groaned slightly when I pushed it open and the doorknob touched the wall with a hollow click—but in less than a minute I was standing in the faint moonlight of my parents' bedroom, my feet planted at the edge of their bed's long shadow, and I had done nothing to ruffle their slumber.

My father wore no night shirt and the cover on his side of the bed had slipped down, revealing his soft, hairy chest and the dark birthmark (the "chocolate patch" of my childhood) on the top of his ribcage. His large head sunk into the center of his pillow and his chin was slightly raised. His snores were steady and sounded every bit as loud as those given out by those big dopey, innocent animals in old cartoons. It was the sound of the fake snore I used to give when I meant to say I was bored. Next to him, Rose slept in her nightgown. She slept on her side with her half-closed fists touching Arthur's shoulders. Her breathing was regular, deep, and absolutely soundless; oxygen filled her lungs and fed her blood with botanical silence. The light of the moon, divided into twelve bars by the Venetian blinds, quivered slightly on the wall. I stood before my parents' unconscious forms, my heart beating with a terror more befitting a patricide.

My parents were the very models of tidiness and "good habits." Newspapers, if not to be saved permanently, were thrown out immediately after reading. A glass that was used for a midday drink of juice was always rinsed out and placed in the blue plastic drainer. Lights were not left to burn in empty rooms and no unoccupied shoe would ever dare show more than its very tip, peeking out from beneath a fringed bedspread. And so as I surveyed their room, looking for a wallet that might pay my way downtown and a set of keys that would allow me to enter my father's office, I saw nothing but clear surfaces—no piles of change, no rings of keys, no dropped (or even carefully folded) clothing.

Slowly, slowly, slowly I crept across their bedroom, casting my shadow first over the square of broken moonlight on the wall and then laying it like a sword over my parents' sleeping faces. Finally, I opened their closet. The scent of mothballs, the lumpy darkness. I reached forward, rustling the hanging clothes, chiming the metal hangers. Blind, I felt a suit or a dress wrapped in the dry cleaner's crackling plastic, a silkish shirt, cool and melancholy to the touch, my mother's nylon robe. Then came my father's suit, colorless, made of mystery-fabric, but unmistakably his. I stuffed my hand into its pockets—empty.

There was a break in my father's snoring. I turned toward the bed. Rose rolled away from Arthur and raised one half-closed hand above her head, grazing the bedboard with her knuckles before dropping her unformed fist onto the pillow. Arthur's body seemed to veer toward hers, as if to follow its tiny nocturnal migration, but his journey toward her steady, familiar warmth was only hinted at. He remained flat on his back and the snores returned, deeper now, as if coming from a more resigned part of him.

O mother, O father. To be standing in your room. Conscious of you as you were conscious of me during my slumbers, to watch your progress in the womb of sleep, to have the power to plant invisible kisses on your nearly blank faces, or to kneel at your sides and practice the grief of your deaths. I stretched out my hand, as if to touch you, to steady your hold on sleep. My hand completely erased you from my sight, and I marveled at this as I had as a child when I could prove my thumbnail was larger than the moon. I felt myself filling with emotion, as a room might fill with light.

With my back to my parents again, I searched through the unvarying blackness of their closet, and though I must not have stood there very long (because Arthur's sport jacket was the eighth piece of clothing I inspected and in it I found his wallet and his keys) I would not have been surprised to face the room again and find it lightening with the first spray of dawn. With Arthur's heavy, tarnished ring of keys on my thumb and a mint-fresh twenty-dollar bill, I slipped out of the room, moving so silently that I was only intermittently conscious of myself.

I closed their door with a soft, final click and went to the end of the foyer. I turned on a light and opened the Yellow Pages to find the number of a taxi fleet. I chose the one with the largest ad and after I spoke to the dispatcher I sneaked into the kitchen and drank what was left of the Gordon's gin straight from the bottle.

A few minutes later I was sitting on the steps in front of our apartment building, breathing the free night air. It was my first time out on my own but the momentousness of the occasion barely grazed me as it passed. It was three in the morning and whoever was having a late Saturday night was having it else-where. The street was empty. The first headlights I saw coming down Ellis Avenue belonged to the cab I'd called, a battered yellow hulk with a checkered fringe painted around its roof.

"Hello," I said, opening the back door. I wasn't so stupid as to think that you greeted cab drivers like that, but I did it any-how. I had put myself in a trance to make it through the time separating my calling the cab and its arrival and I needed to make contact with someone outside of me. The driver was a youngish man. He wore a plaid shirt with the sleeves rolled and had a pony tail. A huge portable radio next to him competed with the two-way radio from which his company's dispatcher honked and squeaked like an electronic goose. The driver nodded at my hello and placed his hand on the meter's lever so he could pull it the moment my backside touched his upholstery. "I've got to get downtown," I said, still not getting into the cab. I was afraid to. My first time out of the house alone should have been a walk around the neighborhood in the sunlight, not a cab ride downtown in the hot darkness, with stolen money and stolen keys in my pocket.

I got in the back seat, gave the driver the address, and began to tremble. I tried to put myself in an adventurous frame of mind, to imagine a trenchcoat on my shoulders and a cigarette plugged into the corner of my mouth—a man with a mission, a man alone. But those second-hand images could only flicker, they could not sustain me. I couldn't even bear to look out the window, and each time the cab made a turn I felt my insides lurch. My legs were crossed tightly and I hugged myself, with my elbows digging into my ribs and my hands clutching my biceps. I heard a weak, low moan and it took me a moment to realize that it was coming from me.

Too soon, we were in front of my father's office. It was on Wabash underneath the elevated tracks. I looked out of the cab's rear window at the deserted street. The streetlights shined down on emptiness. The stores had steel gates over the windows.

"Four-fifty," said the driver, not turning around.

"All I've got is a twenty," I said, digging it out of my pants.

The driver muttered something and opened a cigar box next to his portable radio and thumbed through a stack of bills. Next to the cigar box was a billy club with nails driven halfway in. He began counting out my change.

"Say, I wonder if you could wait," I said. "I won't be very long."

"The meter's off," he said.

I stopped to consider what this meant; it made no sense to me.

"I'll be about ten minutes. Then I'm going right back to Hyde Park. It'll be hard for me to get a cab. Could you please wait? Here. Take the twenty, OK? That way you'll know I'm coming back." I handed him the twenty and put my hand on the back door handle but didn't open it. I wanted him to reassure me that he would wait. "OK?" I said.

He put the twenty on the dashboard and turned off his motor, the lights.

I'd been to my father's building dozens of times. As a young boy I'd pretended to be his partner, lunging for the phone whenever it rang, stuffing my shirt pockets with his pens, riding on the sliding library ladder. It was a small, whitish building, filled with the offices of marginal enterprises: importers of knickknacks, jewelry repair, the editorial offices of a Serbo-Croatian newspaper, a chiropractor, a Hong Kong tailor. I tried the street door on the off-chance it was unlocked, but it wasn't. There were seven keys on my father's ring and the first one I tried unlocked the door. (A measure of my state of mind was the intense, practically religious exultation I felt at this.) Inside, I found myself beneath a flickering fluorescent light. I listened for footsteps—perhaps they kept a maintenance man on twenty-four-hour duty. I stood there, transfixed, much longer than necessary. Something in me wanted to stay right there, to not walk up the one flight of stairs to my father's office. It was the first time in three years that someone in control didn't know exactly where I was; now, at last, my aloneness was complete and it terrified me. The only cord connecting me to the known world was that cab outside—or had it already left? I didn't dare look and finally the thought of the driver making off with my money and abandoning me was more palpably frightening than anything else and I ran to the steep, dingy stairway and raced up it three steps at a time.

It was dark on the second floor, a solid, unvarying darkness. I staggered forward and kicked a wash bucket that had been left in the corridor. It went crashing down the hall and I covered my ears and said, "Shhh." I waited for the darkness to recede. I stared ahead, blinking slowly, trying to tame the blackness with the intensity of my need to see. Slowly, I began to make out shapes. I could see the glass on the doors along the wall. My father's office was the third one down and I made my way toward it. This time, though, I wasn't so lucky with the choice of keys. I went through the seven keys three times around before I got the door to open.

I turned on the overhead light and regarded my father's small office. I knew that I must move quickly, but that was all I knew. I didn't know which way to turn. I closed the door behind me. I went to his desk and forced myself to sit in his swivel chair: my body was so stiff with fright that it was hard to seat it. Then I went through his desk drawers. I rifled through reams of blank paper, stacks of yellow legal pads, blank contracts, forms, packets, pads, boxes of pencils, balls of twine, envelopes, folders. Somewhere in the middle of going through his desk I took the phone off the hook—I'd imagined it ringing and what that would do to me. I didn't look very carefully. I was too scared to search well, but I satisfied myself that the letters weren't in Arthur's desk. I went across his small office to the file cabinets. They were locked but the key, a small slender one, was on the ring. The files were packed. I looked under Axelrod, under Butterfield, under David, and under Jade. Finding nothing, I even looked under Letters. Everything seemed innocent and impersonal and suddenly I was filled with a boiling sadness for my father and his files, for the work he had done, for the tender, perishable details of his life.

His file cabinet was three gray metal drawers and two of them were sufficient for the alphabet. I opened the third. There were old staplers, phone books, a flashlight, a scarf . . . But in the back of it was a locked metal box, the size of a bread loaf. I picked it up and I knew that if my letters existed, they were in that box. The keyhole told me that it took a key the size of the one that had opened the file cabinets, but there was only one key like that on the ring. I tried it but it didn't fit. I don't really remember what I did next. I was no longer able to move in any deliberate way. I went to the bookcase and randomly removed some volumes, thinking the key might be hidden behind one of them. I picked up ashtrays, fell to my knees and peered beneath the office's two green chairs. I paced wildly around and around, slapping crazily at my thighs and talking to myself, like a prisoner in the violent ward. Somewhere along the way I must have organized my senses enough to sit at his desk again and go through the drawers because soon I was inspecting the top middle drawer where, on a little interior shelf, which it shared with two sharpened pencils and a roll of mints, I found the key. I closed my fist around it, closed the drawer, and then collapsed onto the desk and burst into tears.

But there was no time for that. Still weeping, I made my way across the room again and, no longer with any energy left to hope, I opened the box.

Jade, our letters were there, all of them, folded and packed into a long brown envelope. Your handwriting was next to mine and I held them both and the words that we wrote.

When I finally left the office and went down to the street, the taxi was still waiting. The driver sat sleeping at the wheel, his chin touching his chest. I watched him for a moment and imagined he dreamed of someone he loved. The night had turned cool and the wind touched me as if for the first time. The sky was slatey, with a few bluish stars poking out of it. The moon, practically full, hovered on top of a nearby office building, like a bright cold dome. I looked at that moon as I had so many nights before, for prisoners love the moon, but now I was not looking at it as a prisoner, and not just as a dreamer, but as a free man, a pilgrim, a navigator charting his course.

5

Left to my own devices, I don't know what I would have done with my life. But so much was required of me: I had to enroll in school, I had to see a psychiatrist twice a week, I had to stay in contact with my parole officer, and I needed a part-time job.

Everything was too mandatory, pressing, and I resented it with a deep, helpless passion.

With the help of my mother's friend Millicent Bell, I got into Roosevelt University and was even allowed to apply some of my work at Rockville toward college credits. Roosevelt is a big downtown college, with a student body made up of part-time workers, married people, and a lot of people over forty. There was no campus and because there was no obvious place to meet and talk, it was difficult to make friends with the people you shared classes with—or, in my case, easy not to. I studied astronomy, though Roosevelt was not much of a school for that. I took math, physics, and I did well in my courses, but none of my instructors seemed to recognize me from one class to the next. Even the guards at the planetarium where I showed up two or three times a week to stare at the dome full of lucious points of fire and light never remembered me, never returned my nods.

My psychiatrist's name was Dr. Ecrest, and I liked him as much as you can like a psychiatrist you don't want to be seeing. The parole officer assigned to look after my progress was a nominal Japanese named Eddie Watanabe. Eddie had shoulder-length hair, wore blue jeans, and had one of those peace symbols around his neck, the kind they sell on streetcorners, large as a grapefruit and dangling from a piece of rawhide. It was his strange contention that his being a parole officer represented a victory for "our side." I would have loved to tell him exactly what I thought of his Beatle song lyrics, his freshly shampooed hair that looked as soft as a night cloud, his fake-o belief in "bein' straight with each other," and the enthusiastic, utterly humiliating bicep-squeezes he forced me to endure whenever I told him something he could categorize as "super news." But Eddie, like so many before him, had a great deal of power over me—exactly how much, I hoped never to test.

My parents' friend Harold Stern got me a job with his union, the Amalgamated Clothing Workers of America. Harold, who liked to taunt my parents' crowd with the assertion that only he had contact with the working class (and, thus, with reality), had always seemed shifty and arrogant, but he really came through for me and got me a job only a couple of blocks from Roosevelt University. I was hired to carry a picket sign in front of a clothing store on Wabash Avenue called Sidney Nagle. Sidney Nagle sold a line of cheap men's trousers called Redman Pants, and the purpose of the picket was to inform customers that Redman workers were on strike and to ask them not to buy Redman products. It would have been more gratifying to my romantic sense of trade unionism if the store had a rich clientele, but the customers (most of whom ignored me and my sign) appeared far more humble than my parents or any of their friends, and Mr. and Mrs. Nagle, who ran the store with just one employee, seemed like a thoroughly desperate, unprosperous old couple. They stared at me with outrage and grief whenever the opportunity arose and I had a dreadful suspicion that if I were to see their bare forearms, I would find fading blue numbers.

I started working for the union not more than a week after sneaking into my father's office. The fact that I was out in the world and behaving like a normal person reduced a bit of the tension at home, though my parents were not quite self-conscious enough to hide their own unhappiness. In order to be at work on time, I had to set my alarm clock in advance of the official time, and Rose and Arthur, willing to help me make my adjustments, set all of the other clocks in the apartment ahead as well, including the one in their bedroom and Arthur's wristwatch. If once my parents lived with the belief that they were an epoch in advance of the general population and if that certainty had dissolved along with their political faith, they now lived, quite demonstrably, at least ten minutes ahead of history.

I often thought I could not have found a more difficult job. Every day I saw thousands of faces. Sometimes, the crowds shimmered before me like heat off a highway and at other times each face was momentous and distinct, like those faces in a crowd in an old steel engraving, each rendered in perfect, be-

wildering detail. It was the sort of job ideally made for obsessively thinking how pitiful my life was, of remembering Jade
and longing for her, and accusing even the most distant stars for
keeping us apart. I tried to entertain myself: one day I counted
black people; the next day I counted people under twenty; and
the next I tallied the people with noticeable deformities. I predicted how many women in the space of an hour would pass
holding white pocketbooks, how many couples holding hands,
how many stoned people. I searched my mind for things to recite.
I asked my friends, and the Romans, and the countrymen to loan
me their ears and I claimed to have seen the best minds of my
generation destroyed by madness. Sunlight passed through the
elevated tracks over Wabash, dividing itself into soft bars of
light, falling onto the street like rungs in a gauze ladder. I tried
to find this extremely beautiful. But it seemed far too inconsequential, too unintentional, and finally it awaited some missing
ingredient to make it lovely, something pre-existent in the eye
of the beholder. It waited to be beautiful for someone else.

Everyone I ever knew was elsewhere. Now and then I'd feel
a start within me and it seemed certain that that face coming into
view was someone I'd gone to school with, or an intern from
Rockville, or someone who used to live on Ellis Avenue, or even
a shopkeeper I'd once bought a Stevie Wonder record from. But
it never turned out to be the case. Even when I stopped hiding
my face and remained recognizable by anyone who might place
me, no one broke stride in passing. The only curious eyes
focused on my picket sign.

I had prepared myself to be startled regularly by apparitions
of Jade. I don't know where this knowledge came from—probably from a song or a movie—but it was my understanding that
the hungry heart manufactured mirages. If you see someone in
a gray skirt and blue shirt . . . or someone five foot four with
small breasts . . . with turquoise studs in her earlobes . . .
walking with her eyes down and cast to the right . . . with
biscuit-colored hair, but curly like Little Lulu's. I saw all of

these likenesses, and more. I heard voices that could conceivably have been confused with hers, and one girl could practically have been on her way to a masquerade dressed up as Jade. She wore Jade's khaki trousers with the wide elastic waistband and Jade's green and red tee shirt; she walked with her eyes fixed to the right of her feet; she carried a cigarette, which might very well have been a Chesterfield. Her hair was much shorter than Jade's but the very discrepancy in length revealed a more telling similarity: a brown mole on the back of the neck, just above the shoulder, that was pure, pure Jade. But I wasn't tempted; not for one instant did I confuse these impostors with the real thing and now I couldn't understand those who claimed to see their lovers everywhere. People took these mistakes as passion's proof, yet now it seemed that to mistake a stranger for your lover was really an absurd kind of narcissism. How could one not know? How could there be any mistake? Pigeons in a flock picked their mates without confusion, penguins and titmice were not prone to optical illusions, or any other illusions, for that matter. They knew, and so would I.

The Chicago Public Library was only a couple of blocks from the Sidney Nagle store and I passed most of my lunch hours there. Since I had no idea what to do with the money I made, I was seized with frugality and liked the idea of spending less than fifty cents on lunch and reading for free to pass the time.

One day I discovered that the library had telephone directories from what seemed like every city in the United States. As casually as possible, I looked at the New Orleans directory to see if Hugh or any other Butterfields were listed—New Orleans was the city of his birth and perhaps Hugh had reconstituted the family in some moss-choked ancestral mansion. There were Butterfields in New Orleans, though no Hughs. There was a Carlton Butterfield, an E. Roy Butterfield, a Horace, a Trussie, and a Zachariah. I wondered if any of these were related to Hugh. Was his father still alive? Still running the coffee warehouses, still drinking from morning to night, still listening to Mozart with tears in his cloudy blue eyes? I stared at that cluster of Butterfields in the New Orleans directory and my heart beat hard but slowly, as if resisting the best it could the infusion of adrenalin seeing those names created: even a handful of bogus Butterfields put me closer to my friends than I'd felt in more than three years. I thought of Carlton, E. Roy, and the rest, reading the *Times Picayune* beneath the moving shadows of a ceiling fan, drinking thick black coffee out of clear glass cups, wearing white suits and smelling of bourbon. I stared at the names and tried to remember if Hugh had ever told me his father's name.

Well, where would the family go after leaving Chicago? If not New Orleans . . . There had been talk of San Francisco. Idle, I thought, but who knew? Ann had a cousin who ran a psychiatric clinic in Berkeley: he was the source of the LSD the Butterfields had taken the night of the fire. I took down the San Francisco directory and looked for Butterfields. Again, the name was represented, but no Hugh, no Ann, no Keith, Sam, or Jade. I stopped to remember Ann's cousin's name: I'd paid attention to the correspondence because at least one hit of the LSD would have gone to me if it had arrived before my banishment. Ramsey (Ann's family name). Gordon Ramsey. There was a G. Ramsey DVM on Polk Street. Could it be? Had Gordon given up psychopharmacology for distemper shots?

I went slowly, haphazardly, and did my best not to admit how central it was becoming to my life, but every weekday, without fail, I spent time in the library looking for Butterfields in the phonebooks. I found Butterfields in Los Angeles, Butterfields in Seattle, Portland, Denver, and Dallas. I bought a pocket-sized spiral notebook and wrote the address and phone number of any name that seemed likely. H. Butterfield in Denver, an actual Keith Butterfield in Boston and another one in Milwaukee, and Ann F. Butterfield in St. Louis (the F. made no sense but I recorded the number anyhow), a strange yet heart-kicking

Jane Butterfield in Washington, D.C., and so on, back and forth across the nation.

As long as I was living with my parents, I didn't dare make long-distance phonecalls, nor was I in a position to receive private mail. Sporadically, I called numbers from phonebooths in the Roosevelt University lobby, and one day I turned a twenty-dollar bill into quarters and spent an hour at least calling far-flung strangers. Hugh? I'd say, knowing at once from the enfeebled hello that Denver's H. Butterfield was no one I knew. I called that Jane Butterfield in Washington and said, "Excuse me, I'm calling Jade—not Jane." "Who's that?" said a small child's voice.

At the end of September, I moved out of my parents' apartment and into a furnished two-room apartment on 55th and Kimbark. It was a dismal place, but I could afford it. I was glad to be on my own, though I was lonelier than I'd ever imagined. I hadn't yet made any friends at school—I didn't have any nodding acquaintances, really—and the retired suit maker who picketed in front of Sidney Nagle with me didn't like or approve of me. I'd gotten my job through connections and it was generally something the union gave to retired members, to supplement pensions and social security. My only co-worker's name was Ivan Medoff and he looked the way Jimmy Cagney would have looked if Cagney had been Jewish and worked in a factory for thirty-nine years. The only social gesture Medoff made in my direction was to say one day, "I told my wife I was here working with a youngster and she says I should maybe ask you to have dinner sometime." He didn't take it further and I didn't press it, though I waited for him to name the day because I would have accepted.

My loneliness was at once vague and total. I never missed a class and soon forced myself to ask questions of the instructors, just to hear myself talk to another person. I looked forward to my appointments with Dr. Ecrest, and when he asked me if I'd be interested in joining a therapy group he was forming on Wednesday evenings I almost said yes, on the chance I might make friends in the group. My parents made a ritual appearance at my apartment for dinner, which I cooked for them on my two-burner stove and served in the cracked turquoise and white plates supplied by my landlord. I found more occasions than I would have guessed to make the walk to their house—picking up a sweater, borrowing spoons, spontaneously accepting an old dictionary they'd offered to give me before I'd moved out—and more often than not my arrival coincided with dinner. They both seemed involved with their jobs and though I knew they were in a sad, difficult time, they looked no more unhappy than two old dolls in an attic. I was an absolute pig in how I refused to recognize their misery, but it was what they wanted of me.

Near the end of October, I had a phone installed. Soon, I thought, I'd be in the Chicago directory. It would be widespread proof that I was out of the hospital and living on Kimbark. It would be public record and Jade could know.

As is well known, the telephone is a gloomy hunk of plastic and copper if it doesn't ever ring. My parents had my number and they'd call often, but no one else called me. Oh yes, once my parole officer Eddie Watanabe called and put our appointment off for a week, but other than that the phone was as quiet as the old, stern sofa and chairs the landlord had left for me.

What the phone did provide was a constant temptation to call names from my list of Butterfields. I made these calls with an altogether frantic sense of guilt, as if I were compulsively dabbling with an addictive drug or losing myself in pornography. Each time I dialed I told myself it was the last and then I'd tell myself just one more. I don't know how long I would have kept at it if I'd come up empty each time, but ten days after getting my phone I found Ann in New York.

There were only a few Butterfields in the Manhattan directory. One of them was a K. Butterfield, which could have been

Keith, but I'd tried it from a phonebooth two or three weeks before. I also looked for Ramseys, however, and I had quite a few of those. Ann was listed as A. Ramsey, 100 E. 22nd Street. I remember that when I first wrote it down I thought it was one of the more promising entries, but for some reason it took me a long while to call it, as if I required the lengthy frustration of not finding anyone before deserving success.

Or perhaps it was sheer terror. I called her in the evening. She answered on the second ring and I knew from her hello that I'd found Ann. As soon as I heard her voice I pressed the button down on my phone, like a sneak pinching out a candle's flame. I sat gawking at the phone, as if it would ring, as if it would be Ann. Then I paced my rooms and tried to understand what had happened, how by dialing New York City's area code and seven small numbers I had completely changed my life. I grabbed a jacket and ran outside. Walking aimlessly, I passed a bar on 53rd Street and thought to go in for a drink—I'd forgotten for a moment that at twenty I was too young to be served. I drifted south. Soon I was on Dorchester, near to where the Butterfields once lived. But as I got closer to where their house had stood I lost all courage and, sweating crazily, I trotted back home.

I called her as soon as I was in, still wearing my jacket, panting from the run. This time, she didn't say hello.

"Who is this?" she said.

"Hello, Ann." My voice was tiny and inconsequential.

She was silent for a moment. "Who *is* this?"

I cleared my throat. I wasn't near a chair so I squatted down on my haunches. "This is David Axelrod."

She was silent. You never knew with Ann if those long pauses were proof of amazement or if her speechlessness was a device, a way of turning what you'd just said into an internal echo. I remembered this about her and a ripple of emotion went through me: *I knew her.*

"Hello, David," she said. She sounded as if her eyebrows were raised and her head was tilted to the side.

"Am I bothering you?" I asked.

"Where are you?"

"I'm home. I'm in Chicago. On Kimbark."

"So they let you out."

"Yes. Since August." I waited for her to say something and then I asked, "How do you feel about that?"

"About you being out?"

"Yes."

"I don't know."

"It's only parole," I said.

"Oh? I thought being sent to that hospital was parole."

We were silent again; I listened to the soft electronic rustle of the long-distance lines.

"Well, tell me," I blurted out. "How've you been?"

"David, this is too strange." And with that, Ann hung up.

I was stunned for a moment but I redialed her number. She picked up without saying hello.

"I'm sorry," I said, and then I burst into tears. I thought I was only apologizing for the phonecall but as my tears came I realized I wanted to apologize and be forgiven for everything.

"David," Ann said, "*I* can't hate you."

I tried to stop crying to consider what she'd said, but the tears, once begun, refused to be controlled. I took a deep breath that was broken in two by a sob and then I simply covered my eyes and cried. I turned away from the phone and when I placed it to my ear again Ann had already broken the connection.

Ten days later, a letter from Ann. It was so thick that the mailman couldn't fit it into my box. He left me a yellow slip and after school I picked it up at the post office. Some of it was typed and some was written—in four different pens. I was up past dawn rereading it. The pages were fastened by a huge shiny paperclip and on top, written on a torn scrap of paper, was this note: "Finally decided if I didn't send this I'd be writing it for the rest of the year. Don't know what to make of it—impetuous, improvident, but now it's yours. A."

David, I'm amazed you've found me! Living here on East 22nd, in this cramped, expensive apartment, under what language so daintily designates as my "maiden name," I felt—until I heard your voice and threw the phone into its cradle, in terror—I felt rather safe from any spontaneous visitations from my Butterfield past. Not just safe from you—you haven't been an issue, really, locked away as you've been—but simply and unspecifically *safe*.

I am alone, for the time. All of the Butterfields have scattered—that's as specific as I'll be, though if you've found me then I suppose you've scared up a couple more of us. In fact, I'd put *me* as the trickiest to find, since Hugh, Keith, and Sammy are still Butterfields. I had no particular need for more independence (and now could use a bit *less*), nor did I feel burdened by dragging the Butterfield name behind me, but I *did* want to do something rash, something that would distinguish this particular, this final separation from all the other fits and separations that preceded it. I wanted Hugh to know that I had depleted my forgivenance, just as humankind is depleting the earth's resources. All of my indulgence was gone and I was down to the bottom of me, the driest and most tender part, the most breakable and, I suppose, the meanest. I wanted him to know that and I'm not regretful for having given him the heave. Even though it was only after Hugh had made it abundantly clear that I could in no way interfere with his incessant poking around for his true and elemental self—which in Hugh's case meant running around with his heart on a string like a little boy trying to launch a kite. Sometimes I suspect my pressing for the divorce and forsaking his name was my way of giving some dignity and finality to his awful carryings-on and in a funny way giving him one last chance to come to his senses. But Hugh by then had precious few senses to come back to. He didn't respond at all to my announcement that I was reverting to Ramsey; it annoyed me so that I tried to convince the kids to drop his name, too. What a joke that was. Sammy's was the perfect response: And what? Change my driver's license?

I shouldn't have been so short with you on the telephone. I felt compromised just hearing your voice. The others would never have forgiven me if I'd been friendly— but who am I fooling? They'd forgive this letter even less. I've always had a particular, a special sense of myself when I spoke to you: you hear things the others like to ignore, or misunderstand, and so I like to say them to you.

And you! Back in Chicago. I don't think I could ever go back there. Chicago is a house full of kids and a lawn no one would mow. Hugh's been back, though. Now that he travels around, like a peddler, though with nothing to sell, of course. Nothing at all. He's quit his practice and he works when he and his current girl run out of money. He washes dishes, loads trucks. Anything. But Hugh went to Chicago with a purpose and that was you. He'd heard your case was coming up. I suppose you know that when the trouble all came, Hugh got to know the prosecutor fairly well and they've remained friends? Hugh learned there was a good chance you'd be getting out of the hospital and he did his best to revive the case against you. He mentioned this to me in his last call, and since we're on the subject, I may as well add he was bitterly upset because he knew he'd lost and that you were on your way out. Didn't I tell you you were making a dangerous foe in Hugh? How could you have been so arrogant as to mistake his slowness for laxness? You think that astrology is a joke but Hugh *is* a classic Taurus. And not a bad clairvoyant. The only reason I didn't fall into a faint when you called is that *months* ago Hugh predicted you'd find me and get in touch and in a weird way I've been waiting to hear from you ever since.

Though I'm quite poor, I'm alone and so I can afford a few of my pet indulgences. (Really, I should have been Catholic; no one has a more quantitative sense of pleasure.) It has taken me this long to fully realize that I am never likely to be un-poor—unless, of course, that proverbial rich old man with a twenty-four-carat hole in his heart comes kneeling into my life. Hugh and I started off together with virtually no money but it never seemed altogether serious. We both assumed we were rich, and as educated Protestants we also assumed that the whole society—if not the cosmos—had a stake in keeping us buoyant. We consoled ourselves with that classic semantic sleight-of-hand: we weren't poor, we were broke. Which in our case made as much sense as a shipwrecked family describing themselves as "on a camping trip."

I learned to walk away from many luxuries—and each child caused me to evacuate another set of expensive yearnings. Yet the one that would never die (I protected it like an endangered species) was my love for expensive chocolate. It survived my love of well-made books, magazine subscriptions, alligator purses, and English cigarettes; chocolate survived turquoise and gold, as well as the simpler pleasures of a first-run movie or sending the shirts out to the Chinese laundry. But not only did my adoration of good chocolate survive my other pleasures—it surpassed them. No whiff of a fresh book or feel of Irish linen touched me quite so deeply as the melting, the slow darkening dissolve, of a good piece of Swiss chocolate beneath my tongue.

Since everyone in your family professed to believe in sharing (what ardent egalitarians you people were!), you were more than a little shocked to learn that I hid my chocolate from my own family. I used to savor my hidden sweets and, in truth, as much melted or went stale as got eaten. I felt a definite jolt when I passed a spot where some was hidden. Sometimes, talking to Hugh or one of the kids, with my hand resting on the maple sewing box that held, stuffed beneath the felt snips and empty spools, five dollars' worth of Austrian semi-sweet, I felt a blush spreading like a stain across my face and my heart would literally pound. I would think: My God, I'm giving it away. I'm found, ruined! It was like passing one's lover on the street and he is with his wife and you are with your children—that frightening and that pleasurable. Secrets offer the solace of privacy and possibility. They are the x in your equation, the compassionate unknown. Those caches of hidden candy, those untapped resources stood in for all of the others I pretended were available to me.

Even before you made our house your own, the search for my chocolates was a family sport. Sometimes I'd sleep late, come down, and find the house in shambles. The search for my store of chocolate was a ritual, and like other tribal games, no one in that big drafty falling-down house ever quite outgrew it. Even Hugh got in on the act. But no one had a knack for finding my stashes like you had. Of all the people who traipsed through—family, the kids' friends, the cleaning woman we hired for a month when I had what Hugh liked to call a nervous collapse and what I called simply coming to my senses, and the odd-lots of runaways and dropouts who seemed to land with us because our openness and curiosity was inevitably taken as laxness—of all the dozens with and without names, with and without scruples or conscience, you were the only one who could regularly unearth what I'd hidden. You hadn't been courting Jade for more than a week before you began producing evidence of my stealth. I mean,

David, you discovered chocolate that *I'd* forgotten. You found the bar at the bottom of the Kleenex box, then the semi-sweet buds in the bookcase, stuffed behind the antique *Britannica* that no one used because the language was too high-falutin' for the kids to copy their school papers out of. You found the chocolate in the basement wedged behind a rusty snow shovel and wrapped in rags to protect it from the mice, and you guessed with no apparent effort which brick was loose in the fireplace. Once the others got you into the spirit of the search, the only place safe from you was my bedroom, where I occasionally tucked something into my underwear drawer and where you were—well, what were you, David?—too delicate, too tactful, or too tactical? to look. I must admit it was better to be raided by you. At least you made certain that most of it found its way back to me. You liked to present me with what I'd hidden. You were like a dog with a stick: throw it! hide it! I know you!

I've had a lot of time to think about this and I've decided that because you were starting out fresh, with no resentments or hurt feelings, you could muster an understanding of me that in some ways surpassed my family's—the rest were too anxious to discover I was somehow warmer, more capable, that I had a secret store of womanliness, motherliness, and selflessness, and they saw everything through a mist of expectations. I always thought you had some special instinctual understanding of me—though what we call understanding is as often as not appreciation decked out in robes. With you I could talk with the confidence that everything I said wasn't going to be automatically husked for the kernel of true meaning. I could joke with you and talk around what I meant. I could *hint* —what a relief that was. All of the rest of them were so bloody explicit.

And you were the only one who was genuinely thrilled

that I'd been a writer. When you found that I'd once sold two stories to *The New Yorker*, you went that very day to the University of Chicago library to read what I'd published and came back to the house that night with damp, chilly white-on-black photocopies of those old stories. Who *weren't* you courting, is what I want to know. Those stories were more than eighteen years old but they trembled in your hands and looked new and alive as if they'd just rolled off the press. You gazed at them and at me as if I were still the person who had composed them. You wanted to talk about everything; you interviewed me as if I were Rebecca West, asking me what had inspired me and asking me why I'd chosen one word and not another.

I was the first person you'd ever met who had published anything, and I knew your enthusiasm was naïve but I cherished it and drew it out of you. I made us a pot of coffee and we drank Tia Maria out of those orange juice glasses that Sammy had swiped from a cafeteria. Who were you? I mean then, that night. My daughter's high-school sweetheart. Another newcomer to our household. But you seemed to promise so much. Your big intense eyes and the absolutely masterful trick of slowing your flattery down with little stammers. Before long the family, including Hugh and then Jade, went upstairs to bed, and you and I were alone beneath the kitchen light in an otherwise darkened house. It was nearly eleven but we were far from exhausting our conversation. It felt so damned wonderful to be talking about those stories, and you, I see now, were very cleverly staking a claim, marking off for yourself not only spatial territory but temporal territory as well. In a night you established a crucial precedent—that is, it was no longer expected that you would leave at a normal, decent hour. I remember hoping that Hugh would be asleep by the time I came to bed because I'd sensed earlier that evening that he wanted to, as he actually liked to say, "have me," and I was not in the mood at all. At all. And I remember wondering if Jade lay in her bed, cursing me for monopolizing her new beau. But it just felt too damn *right* to be drinking and talking with you for me to worry about the others. I told myself that if old Hugh wanted me so badly he could come down for me, and if Jade suffered teen-age jealousy then she could confront me with it, and if you, beneath the opacity of your charm, sensed you should be somewhere else—home or with Jade—then you could simply pick yourself up and go there. I was so happy.

I know you feel we somehow lured you into accepting the ways of our family, lured you into becoming one of us. And others, I suppose, feel the same way, that we got what we deserved from you because we tempted you into waters that finally were over your head. The fire you set was, to some, I suppose, the flames of the hell we so richly deserved. I know that your innocence was not proved (or provable) but even your sentence—treatment rather than punishment—seems to hold within it a certain condemnation of *us*, as if you were driven mad by the circumstances of your life in our household. I see it otherwise.

There was something about you that exacerbated every muted struggle, all of the divisions, misunderstandings, and hurt feelings that until then had hung in a precarious balance among us. I still don't wholly understand how you did it. Our house was always open for all manner of roughneck and maladjusted teens, for grubby little geniuses, for the science fair winners and the folk singers, and every kid who passed through us had an effect—to be sure—but no one played Prometheus to our huddled masses, no one really changed the way we felt about each other, and no one ever caused us to renegotiate the complex of treaties that held us together—as *all* families are held together, if there is no single, dictatorial power.

I think it was how you were changing us, more than any other factor, that finally caused Jade to confront Hugh and say, "Why don't you *do* something? Why don't you be a father and say no? Get me out of this." I know you like to believe that the decision to quarantine you from our house for a month was basically Hugh's, with perhaps Keith's jealousy and my perverse nostalgia for the old rules thrown in. But it was really Jade who wanted it, Jade who felt everything was slipping away: Hugh and I were actually too stoned and too obsessed with what we so proudly hailed as "Our New Sexual Freedom" to make any decisions. Our lives were hanging so abruptly, so convulsively, that just hanging on was like a rodeo stunt; we felt brave, certainly, and completely in advance of our contemporaries—we didn't have a good friend our own age, by then. But we also felt utterly shaky and so new to our new ways of living that we didn't feel adult enough to devise codes of behavior for Jade, or for you, or for anyone else. At that point, the best we could do was Judge Not Lest We Be Judged. And it took Jade staggering into our room with a fistful of my newly acquired Thorazines (perfect for short-circuiting bum trips) to prod us into action. "What should I do?" Hugh asked her, with that helplessness he liked to think represented open-mindedness. I occupied myself with prying the Thorazines out of Jade's hand—God, they could seep through the skin of her wet palms and put her into shock. And by the end of the evening, Hugh would have stepped in and been a Daddy such as Jade longed for and he would prove the efficacy of his Daddyhood by keeping you away from our house for a full thirty days and, as well, keep Jade away from *you* for the duration.

But of course it was already too late. Jade was trying to do more than make a last-ditch retreat into daughterdom, and she had more on her mind than somehow recovering her balance—connected to her need to be cared for by us, to live more normally, was her suspicion that a girl her age oughtn't to have a lover and certainly oughtn't to have that lover in her own home. With you in her bed, Jade had no place to be a young girl; with the traces of your lovemaking on her every night she could never sleep the innocent pink sleep she often felt she needed. Yet it was only partly her own self she wished to save by banishing you for the month: it was for all of us, especially Hugh and me.

Everyone who ever came traipsing through our lives brought a message and a challenge, taught us something. Maybe it was because Hugh and I met when we were in college, but we were born students, taking notes on the life we glimpsed through others. It was the privilege of having an open house; even the desperadoes came bearing gifts. Hugh and I, and to a lesser extent our kids, let this rich antic life stream around us; we acknowledged the runaways, the curious, the overnight visitors, as if they were so many minstrels wandering through a vast medieval fair. We were susceptible, we were, in fact, suckers— totally willing to believe that teenagers and even the kids Sammy's age were planting the seedlings of a new con- sciousness and that we, Hugh and I, were lucky to be learning from them. But no one of them had the effect on us that you did. It took us by surprise, or rather *you* did, because compared to such characters as Alex Ahern and Crazy Hector and that Billy Sandburg who beat on his belly like a bongo drum and rolled his eyes back so far that only cloudy white showed in his sockets, compared to some of the real daredevils and casualties we saw, you were relatively a straight arrow. It took me weeks to become interested in you, now that I think of it.

You knew you were up against a lot of competition and it wasn't enough for you to court Jade. You had to make yourself interesting—indispensable!—to the rest of us. Of course you could go a long way toward seducing each of us and you could outdistance the other passers-through in terms of sheer charm—no one else could have possibly *tried* so hard, no one else had your determination or cared about making an impression nearly so much. So it was botany and folk music with Keith— while he could still stand you—and karate workouts with Sammy, and Jewish novelists with me, and a kind of fawning obsequiousness for Hugh, which, unfortunately for you and your strategy, could never quite wriggle free of the superiority complex that spawned it. And for all of us Latvian folk tales you made up to get us laughing and Marxist dogma to impress us with your erudition and to inform us that while you seemed to be living for no principle loftier than your own pleasure you were, in fact, guided by huge historical considerations. Beneath it all, you were a revolutionary something-or-other, and you knew we would be enchanted by your ideals, by their certainty and their hidden promise of a transcendent life. Scorning the liberals was, at least for us, a version of strolling around Hyde Park blasted out of our minds: a way of being in the world and above it at the same time, immune to comparison or judgment.

But forget Latvia and the Russian Revolution, forget *Gimpel the Fool* and your periodic thank yous to Hugh for his hand in winning World War II. The thing that made you vivid to us, in the end, was the one thing you did effortlessly. And that was loving Jade. And it was Hugh, you should know, who recognized it first—not the love, which I saw as inevitable when all you two were doing was *wanting* each other, but the weird, unique force the two of you generated, which Hugh saw *months* before we finally banished you from the house.

It was one thing to allow our daughter the freedom to express love (especially when she had such a hard time expressing it within the family), but quite another matter to see this liberty catapult her into a relationship every bit as intense as what Hugh and I called "mature love." We were OK on letting her be sexual, OK on letting her find her individuality outside of the family structure, but I must say Hugh and I were assuming Jade would begin her sexual life with some sort of puppy love, something more quintessentially adolescent, which was to say something filled with doubts, lapses in concentration, some connection that more distinctly expressed the peculiar mixture of child and woman she was at that time. We felt as if we'd given a child permission to experiment with a little chemistry set only to find she was an undiscovered genius— solving ancient alchemical riddles, bonding once incompatible molecules, filling the cellar with luminous smoke. We simply had no idea of what we were in for; we totally underestimated the incredible emotional reach she was capable of. We were too accustomed to seeing Jade in one way. Yawning, slightly withdrawn, orderly, conservative, evasive, with not much of a relationship with her own body, save worrying abstractly over her weight and lamenting the smallness of her breasts.

It drove Hugh mad; it tore him in half. It absolutely *galled* him to think of his precious daughter naked in bed with a boy. Left alone, I'm sure that Hugh's incestuous fantasies would have atrophied. But having Jade embrace the sexual life just when she was at the juncture between childhood and womanhood triggered a deep, conflicted, painful yearning in Hugh, and he wanted *you* to go away because he wanted *it* to go away. He'd been raised to believe it was OK to be protective and even possessive about your daughter, but poor Hugh was too closely attuned to the truth and ambiguity of his own feelings: more purely passionate than anyone in his family, he could not ignore the measure of sheer jealousy in his feelings about you and Jade.

But, on the other hand, you two had the same effect on poor Hugh that you had on nearly everyone else. That is, you made him recall the most inarticulate, unreasonable romantic hopes he had ever had. All that was betrayed and lost, all that was refined and diminished, all of that raging wilderness of feeling came rushing back to Hugh. I was different; seeing you two in love only made me mourn for the person I never was, for the risks I'd never taken, for my life more or less on the sidelines. But Hugh actually recognized himself in you two. Actual faces, actual moments, the precise emotional content of broken promises came back to him. With me it was mere jealousy; but Hugh experienced all the ecstasy and sorrow of *memory*.

Hugh was wide open for the sucker punch of your example. I saw him reeling and I took advantage. I encouraged him to believe that our lives might safely hop track, that instead of growing older we might grow younger, and instead of becoming more encumbered we might catapult into a vast, vast freedom. The house, our precariously balanced budget, the carefully tended and mended clothes hanging in our closets, the boiled eggs, the tarnished spoons, the Klee prints in their homemade frames—none of it, I argued, need define the real limits of our life. *We could do anything.*

And the rest, as they say, is history. I took one lover and he took a dozen. I smoked a joint and he smoked a pound. I hinted at the contradictions in my character and he poured forth torrents of confession. I shed a tear and he wept copiously. And then when I began to wonder if perhaps we were being a tad indulgent and letting our paternal responsibilities go a little too much, Hugh went into a shuddering panic, reaching out for the familiar controls that now eluded him, or wouldn't respond to his touch. What happened to the family meetings? Who was ironing his shirts? He said he felt like the pilot of a fighter whose tail's been hit—loss of altitude, sudden shifts of direction, the high whistle of impending doom.

Who knows what form that impending doom would have taken if it hadn't been for you? A nervous breakdown? A bad trip? (Ah-ha! I can see you starting to wriggle, imagining that you're being let off the hook. Only it's not your sense of guilt that ought to be relieved, but your megalomania. How dare you even imagine that you and only you were enough to unravel our family.) Yet, in the end, you were the perfect messenger for our special domestic ruin. If it was at least in part on your inspiration that we began to step over the old limits of married life, there was a berserk symmetry in that it was you who finally dragged us further from our old ways than we'd ever intended to travel. It was us who wanted to prove that our lives weren't circumscribed by the walls of our house, by the clothes in our closets, by the Klee prints in the homemade frames. And it was you with a flick of the wrist who turned it all to ash.

A.

6

Ann's letter did everything an important letter is supposed to: it changed my luck, my confidence, it changed my place in the world. In school, my teachers finally recognized me when we met in the halls and suddenly people in my classes were talking to me—asking to see my notes for Tuesday's lecture, asking me to coffee, to lunch, and inviting me with some slight shyness to get together with four or five other students and review the material for an upcoming test, as if it would be *me* who'd be doing *them* the favor. Even when I was picketing, some of the people who passed looked at me as if I really existed, and a few stopped to tell me that they wouldn't ever buy a pair of nonunion trousers. One old man coming out of Sidney Nagle's with a plain gray box in a red and white bag put his thin hand on my arm and said, "I'm sorry. I just bought a pair of Redman pants. My son-in-law gave me a list. It's not for me. For me, I would never. But the son-in-law doesn't know union from Joe Blow. I'm sorry." And he stood there gazing at me until I realized what he wanted and I touched his hand and smiled. I was forgiving other people!

As to the people who kept an eye on my life, I had no intention of telling any of them that I'd made contact with Ann, just as I told no one of the night I'd recovered Jade's and my letters. My parents were not the probing sort and they knew there was nothing to gain by venturing unexpectedly beneath the surface of my life. Eddie Watanabe actually told me that viewing my progress was just the kind of thing that made being a parole officer worthwhile; he liked to rattle off my recent accomplishments, punctuating the list with little sharp squeezes of my bicep. You've got a job. Squeeze. You've got a job with a union. Squeeze. You're in college. Squeeze. You're interested in astronomy. Squeeze. You've got your own pad. Squeeze. You're making friends. Squeeze. All right, tell me. Got a girl yet? Silence. A grin and the hardest squeeze of the series. As for my new friends, my fear of slipping back into isolation often tempted me toward a burst of intimacy, in the way we can throw our self-revelations like a net over others. But they knew nothing of Ann, nothing of Jade, nothing of the fire and my three years in Rockville. I'd begun my new relations in a mood of extreme

secrecy and even as I got bored with the lies in my flimsy auto-
biography, I told myself that my new friendships were too
fragile to withstand sudden changes in my story. As far as they
were concerned, I'd been out of school for three years with no
particular purpose, which was fine and absolutely right for the
times, though they may have wondered why someone who'd
just spent years getting high and hitchhiking (or whatever they
imagined I'd done) wasn't looser than I was, had no stupendous
tales to tell.

The most likely to detect the new light in my innermost
heart was Dr. Ecrest, and for a while I could feel his intelligence
tracking me. I must say, Dr. Clark did his best for me when he
referred me to Dr. Ecrest, especially because their methods were
so divergent. Clark favored dreams, free association, and took
notes without looking at you with the blinds drawn and the
curtains three-quarters closed. Ecrest was tall, his forehead was
creased; he looked like an ex-baseball player, or the kind of
waiter who warns you that today's fish isn't altogether fresh.
His thin, wiry black hair was dryer than a doll's; he risked
setting it on fire whenever he lit a Kent. Although he was large,
his voice sounded unnaturally sonorous, just as some teen-age
boys sound as if their voice is too deep for their body. He
worked in a fully lit office and there was no couch for me to lie
on and pretend I was speaking to myself. We sat in cheap-
looking armchairs, facing each other dead on. I often thought
that Dr. Ecrest would have been equally at home reading Tarot
cards or the lines on my palm. Take the dusty blinds from his
windows and put up dark flowered curtains, take down the
diplomas and the certificates and put up a pale orange gypsy
dress, spread out to show all the embroidery. He was a clairvoyant, in the way that people who end up peering into crystal
balls or massaging the lumps on your skull are clairvoyants: he
had the animal understanding of silence and that powerful, yet
oddly emotionless, sympathy that allowed him to enter into other
people's thoughts. He could have spent his life in carnival tents

or drumming his long fingers on a felt-covered table in a recon-
verted store front, except that he'd had the energy and money to
go to medical school.

It was never clear if Ecrest thought of himself as possessing
"powers," and if he acknowledged his uncanny perceptions I
don't know how comfortable he was with them. Walking me to
the door at the end of a session, he once touched me lightly on
the shoulder and said, "Try not to eat crap. Eat good food, OK?"
And when I looked back at him he seemed to blush and he
glanced quickly at the floor. Once when I saw him I'd missed
both school and work that day and he said, "So what did you *do*
all day?" I asked, "Why?" And he shook his head. "I don't
know," he said, very softly. The day after I sneaked into my
father's office to read the letters from Jade, Dr. Ecrest asked me
if I'd been to my father's office yet. I looked at him with guilt
and shock and Dr. Ecrest said that he was only thinking I might
find work with Arthur until something else came along.

When I began compiling my list of Butterfields and Ramseys,
I lived in horror that Ecrest might guess—so sure was I that he
would fathom my small private life that I came a dozen times
close to blabbing it. It was only when I contacted Ann and then
received her letter that the stakes of my secret were raised im-
measurably and I built an obdurate mental barrier between Ecrest
and that part of myself that lived only for reunion. I felt like a
youth in a medieval saga engaged in a battle of wits with a
wizard: we talked about Rose, we talked about Arthur, we talked
about that time of my childhood when I claimed to have gone
deaf, and all the while our unconsciouses played falcon and fieldmouse. I never really knew if my suppressions were successful.

The day after Ann's letter arrived, Ecrest suddenly and for
the first time picked up Dr. Clark's obsession with my sexual ab-
stinence. "I'm speaking to you man to man," he said, "not doctor
to patient. How much longer can you continue denying yourself? You can't live without warmth." "Warmth?" I said, sending him a *shut up* message. "Yes. Sexual expression. David, you

don't even masturbate." We were silent for at least a minute. My intrigues huddled within me like guerilla warriors, hiding behind other thoughts. Finally, I thought of something to say: "If we're going to talk man to man and not doctor to patient, then I don't think you should charge me for this hour."

My father's office was near my school and once or twice a week we'd meet for lunch. It made me uneasy to see Arthur so much more than I was seeing Rose, especially since she'd always felt excluded from the friendship between my father and me. But the fact (if not the truth) was that Rose didn't want to see much of me. She'd always had a horror of over-mothered children, and now that that was no longer an issue she told herself the best thing for me was to find my own way, or "role," as she would put it.

Whenever I could, I arranged to meet Arthur at his office. I never tired of remembering the night I stole in and found my letters, and as often as not, Arthur would make a quick trip to the bathroom before we left for lunch and I could test fate and my reflexes by reading one or two of the letters in his absence. (I didn't have the courage to steal them, though finally I did take them for a day and Xerox the lot of them.) I waited with confused patience for Arthur to tell me how desperate his life at home had become, but he only expressed his sorrow in asides—in shrugs, in sighs, by calling his wife "your mother," as if she were nothing more. I'd been warned by Dr. Ecrest not to involve myself in my parents' woeful marriage, and of all the psychiatric advice that had come my way none was easier and more natural to follow. I was content to return my father's kisses of greeting and farewell, to feed greedily upon the sentimental anguish of his love for me: it was a pure father's love, effortless and insane. He asked only that I be his son; he scarcely knew how I adored him. Whenever we met for lunch we spoke only of me, and then one day near the end of November I walked into my father's office and he told me he had decided to leave Rose. He sat behind his desk with his hands folded in front of him, like the President giving a little TV chat from the Oval Office. His hair was carefully combed and he wore a new brown sports jacket with wide lapels; he looked like one of those older men who decide to change their "image." Only this was Arthur, and no gesture of his could be entirely free of whimsy: he looked like a good-natured blind man who'd been dressed by someone who didn't know him very well. "Last night," he said, in a voice that seemed a mixture of news commentator and graveside eulogizer, "after twenty-seven years of marriage—many of them, most of them, David, nearly all of them good years—your mother and I decided it would be best for everyone if we were to separate."

I nodded, but couldn't think of anything I wanted to say. My father's eyes were on me; I wanted to brush my face, as if to clear away a swarm of mayflies. The tall dusty window behind him was all lemon glare. His phone began to ring but he didn't answer it.

"Let's get out of here," he said. He glanced down at the phone and it stopped ringing.

We went to a bar and grill beneath the street level on Wabash Avenue. In an area mostly inhabited by clerks, professionals, and businessmen, this was the most proletarian restaurant around. The entrance looked like an abandoned subway stop. You walked down a flight of studded iron steps and then pushed through a peeling green door. Inside, it was cavernous, an underground universe of hardworking men. Drinks cost a quarter or thirty-five cents and the bar alone could seat two hundred people. The smell of beer mixed with the smell of sausages; the smoke from hundreds of cigarettes mixed with the haze from the steamplates. Nearly everyone was dressed in work clothes: flannel shirts rolled to the elbow and ribbed long-sleeved undershirts; zipper jackets with a first name stitched over the right breast; ankle-high, steel-tipped shoes with the laces wrapped around the tops.

My father was the only man in business clothes and I was by far the youngest.

We got our food from the cafeteria serving line. Boiled potatoes, a thick delicious sausage called a thüringer, peas, and rice pudding. I found a small empty table and Arthur went to the bar and bought a pitcher of beer. I took our food off the brown plastic tray and noticed my hands were shaking.

"You know," Arthur said, as we began our meal, "I've never been able to figure out what this place is called, and I've been eating here most all my life. After Prohibition they called it the Step Down Bar and Grill, and after that it was sold and it was called something else, I don't even remember. You notice there's no sign? And some of these guys working here were working here before I even heard of this place—and *they* don't know what the hell it's called.

"You want to know something?" my father said. "I'm just remembering this is where I took Rose the first day I met her."

I speared a few peas but didn't bring them to my mouth. My father remembering that didn't agree with my memory of my parents' meeting, but I couldn't exactly recall what I'd been told. A May Day parade? A picnic?

"It's something we never told you," my father said, "but your mother was married when she was a very young girl. It was to a rich fellow named Carl Courtney, a real William Powell type and as stuck up as a rooster. They got married in Philadelphia. Rose was working fifty hours a week and doing her best to support her crazy mother; Courtney was working maybe two hours a week and getting dough from his mother, old Virginia Courtney who owned a radio station and was quite a reactionary character. It was a very short marriage and it didn't add up to anything. But I guess she loved him in a way because he was a bastard heel and she went along with it. About a year into their marriage Courtney got a job—through his mother—with the *Tribune* right here in Chicago and Rose came out with him. She was already a Communist and Courtney was really nothing more than an isolationist playboy, but she stuck with him, telling herself that maybe she could change him, until he started running around." Arthur looked at his plate and remembered he was supposed to be having lunch. He cut the end off of his thüringer but then put his fork down and took a long swallow of beer.

"Running around with other women?" I said.

"You name it. Secretaries and showgirls, crazy women without a care in the world. Sometimes he only came home to change his clothes."

"God," I said. I felt a very specific grief for Rose, as if it had always existed within me but I was only now discovering it. Had I always known? Was it something I'd heard them talk about when they thought I was asleep? I had a sudden recollection of myself stretched out in the back seat of one of our old cars as we drove at night on one of those long restless vacations we used to take and my parents were talking in edgy murmurs and my mother was . . . crying? and my father was making emphatic gestures that I saw reflected in the dark windshield and . . . But then the memory was gone, replaced by the effort of trying to remember.

"Did any of my psychiatrists know that Mom was married before?" I asked. My question puzzled me. What difference would it have made? When Jade told me that she had talked with Hugh and they'd decided it would be best if I stayed away for a month, the first thing I asked her was *when* they'd had the conversation.

"No. We didn't say."

"Why was it a secret?"

"Rose didn't want anyone to know. It made her ashamed."

"Then why are you telling me now?"

Arthur shrugged. "Are you sorry I'm telling you?"

"No."

"It's being here."

"We've been here so many times."

"It's being here today. I'm sorry if I told you something you'd rather do without. But today my marriage is over, so I'm talking about things that maybe I shouldn't."

We were silent for a while. I finished the beer in my glass and poured another. Arthur's glass was practically full but I topped it off. I touched the food on my plate and it was cold.

"I was her lawyer for the divorce," Arthur said. "That's why we came here. To talk about it. I didn't even know her, but a gal she was close to in Philadelphia had a brother in the Party here, and Rose went to him and said she needed a lawyer and he sent her to me. That was Meyer Goldman, by the way, who sent Rose to me."

"I love Meyer Goldman," I said.

"You never met him."

"But you told me about him. He was the one who smoked pot, right? He played saxophone. He knew Mezz Mezzrow. He wore black and white shoes and he pulled the waist of his pants up so high he looked like he was nothing but legs."

"Curly red hair and a mouthful of rotten teeth. Poor Meyer. Even after the Party expelled him he was always in trouble and he always came to me. Write a letter to his landlord. Call up the musicians' union and scream anti-Semitism. This and this and that and that, I thought it would never stop. I wasn't even supposed to talk to him, you understand. When someone was expelled you weren't supposed to talk to him. I didn't give a damn about that, but the things he'd come to me for. And each time he made sure to remind me, 'If it wasn't for me you wouldn't have Rose.'" Suddenly, my father put his hand to his forehead, as if he'd been struck by a stone. He closed his eyes and shook his head. "I was so much in love then."

I had an impulse to reach across and touch him, just as he wanted to hold me whenever I showed my sorrow. But I held myself back. I didn't want to interrupt his remorse. It reminded me too much of my own and once it did that, I wasn't as close to him as I should have been.

"So you helped her get divorced?" I said.

"I did everything and I knew as much about it as you do. It wasn't my kind of law. I got her moved out of Courtney's house. I found her a place with a very good woman, a sculptor, a very generous, warm person."

"Libby Schuster," I said.

"I told you about Libby Schuster?"

"Something. I remember her."

Arthur's hand moved as if it had been touched by something invisible. His eyes moistened. "You never met her. She died just a little after you were born. Meyer too, Meyer died in 1960, in California, Meyer Goldman. Libby was old but Meyer was young, maybe fifty, fifty-two. It wasn't necessary. A waste."

We were silent while the dead who lived in my father's thoughts passed through him: with leaflets, with saxophones.

Finally, I asked, "When are you leaving. . . ?" Leaving where? Home seemed childish and Rose an accusation.

"Tonight," said Arthur.

"Mom knows?"

"She knows."

"I mean she knows it's tonight?"

"Yes. And she's known the whole thing for a long while. We waited."

"Because of me?"

"We wanted you to get settled. To feel strong in your own life. We didn't want you in that hospital thinking you didn't have a normal home to come home to."

"You've been thinking about it that long?"

Arthur nodded.

And then I said what I'd known all along. "Are you in love with someone else?"

Arthur was immobile for a moment, and then he said, in that kind of voice men use when they recite oaths, "With all my heart."

"Who is it? Is it someone I know?"

"You never met her. Her name is Barbara Sherwood. She works as a court stenographer. You know that's a very good job and a very difficult one. She's been married. Her husband died five years ago. She lives in our neighborhood. Two children. And she's black."

I folded my hands. "Are you moving in with her?"

"I'll stay at her house in the meanwhile. Barbara's in the hospital right now. I'll help look after the kids and after she gets out we shall see." He poured the last of the beer into our glasses. Most of the food was still on his plate; it had been cut and pushed around, as if he'd been looking for something inside of it.

"I don't blame you, you know," I said. "I don't think that's a big issue or anything, but I want to tell you I don't blame you for doing this."

"It's what I would expect," said Arthur. "You of all people."

"Wait. Don't say that. I love Mom. I don't care what it looks like. Our relationship is what we've made it but I'm always going to love her."

"I know that. That's not what I mean. You of all people know what it's like to be so much in love that everything else falls away. Everyone else I know would probably think I'm acting like a bastard or just an idiot. Leaving Rose. Leaving behind all those years. You know a man my age has more of a past than a future, and when you leave the past you only have a few years to call your own. They'd think I was acting irresponsibly. People believe in our marriage, Rose's and mine. Did you know that?"

"No."

"They do. Of course, no one knows what's happened. And when they find out, they'll all regroup around Rose. I'll be the villain. They're really her friends anyhow, always have been. The old comrades. In a lot of ways, I was sick of that crew ever since I got back from the war."

"When I was born."

"They're not going to understand, but you are. I guess a

father has no business saying this to a son, no matter how old the son is." His gaze passed over me, as if I was just one member of an enormous jury. "You were my inspiration. Seeing you in love reminded me."

"Of what?"

"Of how I once felt about Rose and how she never ever felt about me, until I didn't feel that way about her either. But you reminded me of how it feels. A lot of people never have it, that feeling, not even once. You know that, don't you? But you had it—"

"With Jade."

"And you reminded me that I once had it and that I never felt so large and important as I did when being in love was *everything*. I saw you walking a foot above the earth and I remembered that was where *I* used to walk, for a few months. Right after I helped Rose get her divorce and we were together every minute of the day. Before it came out how much she was in love with that Courtney and I had to realize it was going to take a while for her to get over it. I knew she'd get over it but it was going to take time. The magic in her heart was with him, not with me, even though she would have chosen me over him a hundred times. I understood that, but I wasn't walking in the air anymore. I had to be too intelligent for that; you make a few reasonable decisions and you can't make a fool of yourself any longer."

"I never knew that's what you wanted."

"I didn't either. I'd forgotten. You made me remember and then Barbara showed me I hadn't missed my chance. It was like waking up twenty years younger. Not that all of a sudden my hair was thick and I didn't need glasses and my death was far away. But I have an appetite for every single second of the day. I want you to meet Barbara. You're going to know what I mean. I never thought this would happen. I never thought I'd be able to believe in all of this a second time. But I do. And I don't have to be embarrassed."

"I know," I said. My heart was pounding.

"I know you know. You know it every second of your life
and you won't let yourself forget. It's why you sneaked out of
the house that night of your party to go to my office. And it's
why every time you come to my office to meet me for lunch you
manage to take a look at those letters of yours and it's why I
always make sure to let you."

Barbara Sherwood was in the same hospital I was taken to after
the fire and the room she occupied was next door to the room in
which I confessed—insisted—that it had been me who'd ignited
that huge, tender house. My father and I walked down the faded
corridors, with the bleary overhead lights that made everything
look the way it does when you haven't really slept in nights,
past the nurses who nodded at Arthur as if they knew him, past
an empty stretcher with dried blood on its safety straps, past a
metal table piled with food trays, breathing that high-pitched
medicinal odor which some people find reassuring but which
struck me as the smell of utter desperation, past the ringing
phones and the Dr. Abrams Dr. Abrams please report to 404,
through a little knot of visitors too nervous and distracted to
move out of our way, doing little confused dances, moving left
when we moved left and right when we moved right and finally
frowning at Arthur's touch and standing with their backs close
to the grayish wall, which I would not have wanted to touch
because it looked somehow slippery, but that was only the light.
My father carried the evening paper and five Ian Fleming paper-
backs tied together by a piece of yellow yarn; I kept my hands
in my pockets, counting and recounting eight dimes and a
quarter.

Barbara Sherwood had the most feline face I'd ever seen on
a human being. Her black hair was cut short and combed down
over her high broad forehead. She had those kind of over-
defined cheekbones that girls doodle in their notebooks when

they are dreaming of looking like an exotic model. Her eyebrows were carefully shaped and even though she was in the hospital and probably suffering, she'd put on eye makeup that made her eyes look even larger and more slanted than they were. I didn't know that she'd lost a lot of weight over the past months; her leanness seemed voluntary and fashionable. Her bed was cranked up so she was practically sitting. Her hospital gown was a little large; she looked like a teenager wearing her father's shirt, though she didn't look at all young. While her hair was black and her skin was smooth, her years lived beneath her surface, as if time had been sublimated, repressed, and was taking its due invisibly.

"Well, here he is," said Arthur, ushering me to her bedside. There were two chairs set up for us; the curtain separating Barbara's bed from her roommate's was drawn; everything had been arranged.

I wanted to take the first initiative. I thrust out my hand. "Hello, pleased to meet you," I said, in a bright, ringing voice, as if I was a boy who'd been taught to behave very elegantly around strangers.

She placed her hand in mine; her fingers were cold and when I shook her hand they felt colder.

Arthur stood there with his folded hands resting on his hard, round stomach, expressing the bliss of a figure on a Tarot card. He breathed out slowly and made a small musical sigh, as if choral music filled his head.

"It's good," said Barbara. I couldn't tell if she was nervous and had forgotten to complete her sentence or if this was her personal style. It's good? It's good? I mean really! I felt instantly ironical; I'd come fully prepared to make small judgments about my father's new lover.

"Are they treating you all right here?" I said, the extremely influential gentleman from out of town. I glanced over my shoulder, as if to make certain that my footman was in place, holding the gigantic bouquet of long-stem American Beauties.

"It's homey here," Barbara said. "Not like that other place."

"She was in All Saints last year," said Arthur.

"What a place that was," Barbara said. "That was a place to give you the creeps. Those sisters gliding around in their long black robes and all those baby-faced priests pacing up and down the halls with the purple ribbons around their necks, wondering who they could give last rites to." She smiled; she was missing a tooth near the front. She saw I'd noticed and said, "I fell," and touched her mouth, remembering.

We spoke for a few moments, with the bewildered caution of strangers who can break each other's hearts. Barbara said my father had told her all about me, which is of course what people say in those situations, but Barbara seemed to blush for a moment, so maybe he really had. Somehow I was gotten to talk about my classes, my job for the union, and the offer from Harold Stern to leave the picket line and work part-time as a researcher for the union's educational department. I was congratulated, encouraged, and if Barbara was half so bored as I was with the details of my life she must have feared slipping into a coma.

She gave Arthur an impish look, like an incorrigible, truth-telling girl in a Victorian novel. But there was no little jolt of tension in the air, and no release; Arthur sat in his place, perfectly calm. He knew she was going to say that; it had probably been planned.

"Well. Has Arthur told you about . . . *us?*"

"He did," I said. I cleared my throat.

Barbara nodded, looking at me. "So? What do you think?"

"You don't need my permission." I felt my father's hand touching me with some delicacy on my elbow.

"We'd like to know how you feel about it, though," said Barbara. She folded her hands in her half-formed lap. Her fingers were bare and very black; the plastic identification bracelet was too large on her wrist.

"I feel a lot of ways about it," I said. "I feel scared for my mother." I paused. Arthur shifted in his seat; Barbara nodded approvingly. "And I think I'm scared for my father, too."

"Why?" said Barbara. "Because of . . ." she gestured, indicating the hospital and her place inside of it.

"I don't know why. Because he's changing. Because he's different now, and he'll get more and more different. It doesn't make much sense. I just feel it."

"I won't change," my father said.

"You will. You want to. And you should. You won't be an unhappy man anymore. That has to change you. You'll be living right in the center of your best and bravest self and maybe it's not right for me to say this but I know, I really do know exactly what that's like." I felt more than a little puffed up and ridiculous but not one word of my tremulous oration came easily or fast. For all the inappropriateness of a son making a speech about his father's romantic leap, I felt everything I said as if the words had claws that dragged along my throat as I spoke them.

"I'm glad you feel that way," Barbara said. "I knew you would because that's how your daddy told me about you. You know, when I was waiting for you to come to see me this evening I was getting so nervous. I've got two children of my own and I know that when it comes to their parents, children are the rock-ribbed Republicans of the world. Isn't that right?"

"That's so true," said Arthur.

"My own children asked some pretty tough questions. Maybe I made it tougher on myself than I had to because I never wanted to lie to them. So they wanted to know how Arthur could come and be with us when he had a wife living less than a mile away. They wanted to know what kind of woman their mother was who let a man into her bedroom without the blessing of marriage. You see, their father was a religious man and though I am not, I have never interfered with their beliefs. It's their way of keeping their father with them; when they pray to God they're really talking to their own daddy who died when they were so small. Oh, and you know how it is with life in this city being what it is. They wanted to know how I could be with a white man."

"A Jew," said Arthur. "I don't think that helped matters along."

"Nothing helped matters along. They were starting to treat me as if I were an evil woman. Not doing their schoolwork, not doing their chores, not looking at me when I was speaking. You know they say you have never been chastised until you have felt the wrath of a child. I didn't know what to do. It was getting so bad I thought I might have to stop everything with Arthur and return to my life the way it was before I met him, no matter how alone and scared I was. That's when your daddy stepped in and made everything better when I thought nothing could. He sat with my children, my boy Wayne who's sixteen and my girl Della who was thirteen just last week, and he told those children that he loved their mother from the bottom of his heart and with all the care and nobility that any man ever loved a woman with. He said more than anything in the world he wanted to look after me and look after them. And he opened his arms up to my children and my children opened their arms to him, and that was that. We're a family again. You're too old, David, you're a man, and I won't tell you that I'm going to look after you because you don't need looking after. But I want to tell you what your father told to my children and that is I love your daddy. I wanted to tell you that the man who is your father, the man who gave you life, has found a woman who is in heaven when she's in his arms."

Barbara fell silent. Whoever lay sick on the other side of the curtain had visitors now; I heard their quarrelsome, unhappy voices. A doctor was being paged over the public address. And I realized, with a sense of real panic, that I was about to burst into tears. Like an icy pond whose thickness you've misjudged, my composure gave way beneath the weight of my feelings—and I was stranded. I stared hard at the curtain that divided the room and I listened to the voices. "Now what?" a man's voice was saying. "Another one and another one and another one?"

There was a light tap on the open door. It was Barbara's sister Rita and Barbara's children, Wayne and Della. Rita looked old. Her hair was white and uncared for and she was partly crippled. Though she was skinny, she used a big black cane thick enough to aid an enormous man. Her raincoat was open; the lining was coming out. She looked embarrassed and annoyed.

"I'm sorry," she said. "They would not listen. I told them they couldn't see you tonight but—"

"Hi, Mom," said Wayne. His hair could not have been cut any shorter. He wore huge, brown-framed glasses and a white shirt with buttons on the collar points. His was the kind of face they put on posters urging people to contribute to the Negro College Fund. Della seemed to be staking her emotional territory on the other side of the spectrum. Her hair was in an Afro, she wore a red scoop-necked tee shirt, blue jeans, and torn sneakers. It looked as if she'd had lipstick on and somebody had at the last minute scrubbed it off.

"We swore on the Bible," Della said. "We said to God every night we will come to see you, Mama." She went to the bedside and laid her head against Barbara's shoulder. As she did, she looked back at me and smiled.

My father introduced me to Rita, Wayne, and Della. Rita held only my fingertips when I offered my hand. Wayne was cool and businesslike. And when I offered my hand to Della, she clasped her arms behind her back and said, "No!" It was only a child's foolishness and teasing, but it made me feel very awkward.

Barbara was allowed only a half hour of visitors and most of it was already gone. I thought her children would want to be alone with her for a while. And now that they were a family, I didn't feel I belonged there any longer. I announced that I was leaving. Barbara tried to convince me to stay and then Arthur said he'd leave with me. But it seemed he wanted to stay for the last few minutes to be near Barbara and to be near the children and go home with them when the nurse said it was time to leave. I made up an excuse of having someone to meet. I said goodbye to everyone with a clumsy wave and walked into the corridor, moving quickly and hoping I was heading toward an exit. My hands were shaking. I thought it was only the strangeness of being with my father's new family, but when I was waiting at the elevator and had a moment to consider the evening I realized that for the past half hour I'd been remembering it had been in this very hospital and perhaps on this very floor that three and a half years ago all of the Butterfields had been treated for the smoke and the flame and the shock and the terror I had inflicted on them.

A few weeks later it was Thanksgiving. Every year my parents had the same group of friends to their house for Thanksgiving dinner, and as the day approached my original certainty that this year's dinner was canceled gave way to a growing dread that my mother was going ahead with the party, even though her life had snapped in half. Finally, at two o'clock on Thanksgiving, I put aside the long letter I was writing to Ann and called my mother.

"Hello?" Rose said. Her voice sounded soft and girlish.

"Hi. It's me. What's up?" I'd seen her a few days before, but she never called me and when I called her she usually seemed indifferent.

"What do you mean, what's up? I'm cooking."

"So the party's on for this year?"

"Of course it is. Why? Do you have other plans?"

"No. It's just that you never called me. I didn't know if you were going to have it this year."

"And so you made other plans."

"No. I said I didn't. What time should I be over?"

Rose was silent and then, sounding a little uncertain, she said, "Oh, four. Isn't that when we always have it?"

I showered, washed my hair, and shaved, because Rose was always annoyed if I was less than extremely clean and it wasn't something I wanted to hear that day.

My letter to Ann lay in fragments on the kitchen table, scrawled on notebook paper, scraps of shopping bag, and onion-skin paper that absorbed the ink from my pen and made every word blurry and soft, like lights through the fog. I had already received my second letter from her—in response, more or less, to mine to her in which I'd begged her to tell me where Jade lived:

Hugh appeared yesterday. Dressed in the uniform of his new ego—jeans, blue work shirt with red embroidered heart, tan boots with pointy toes: Ya-Hugh! He stunk to high heaven of some brain-damaged strawberry perfume which he readily confessed was his new girl's, Ingrid. "You wear her perfume?" asked I, waltzing into a nice left hook. "No," said Hugh. "It rubs off on me." He'd just spent some time with Keith and their fake obsession is The New Case against you. No new evidence, naturally, just new arguments, new and deeper logic. They jaw on and on about this New Case with the same vacant dreami-ness that the little kids on Blackstone used to talk about buying an ounce of pot, when they had no idea where to get it and no money to pay for it.

I walked the seven long blocks to Ellis Avenue. I arrived at my mother's apartment and was going to ring the doorbell to get buzzed in, but I *did* have the keys and by the time I was in that much too familiar entranceway I had lost the spirit of in-dependence. My mouth had a peculiar taste in it and it connected me to the huge dead center of my childhood. I let myself in and walked the three flights of stairs, and then let myself in to the apartment, knocking softly as I opened the door.

The atmosphere was brocaded by the smells of cooking. Thick, nostalgic, and eternal, the aroma of turkey and sweet potato struck me like some pathetic irony—a welcome mat in front of a bombed-out house. I closed the door behind me and listened for voices. I had hoped not to be the first to arrive. I walked down the long narrow hall toward the living room.

Rose was on the sofa, reading *The National Guardian* and listening to the radio. She wore glasses with round lacquered frames, a green pants suits and a gray shirt, and she sat with her small legs crossed. The room was in its customary wreath of shadows and the only light burned from the lamp positioned right behind Rose's shoulder.

"Hello," I said. "Looks like I'm early."

"That's because you were so anxious to come," said Rose. She didn't look up from her newspaper but I could tell she wasn't reading. The FM station was drifting in and out; static bit at the edges of Beethoven's Third.

I unzipped my Army surplus jacket and threw it on a chair.

"Hang it up please," said Rose.

"In a second. Who's supposed to be here?"

"I decided not to invite anyone," said Rose, folding her paper.

"How come?" I sat next to her on the sofa.

"I don't think people are very interested in showing their faces at my house right now," said Rose. "And I'm not exactly in the mood to work like a dog so they can eat me out of house and home."

"I thought you invited everyone," I said.

"Maybe you'd like to have dinner with your father's new family? I'm sure they'll have a full house. That is, if you're invited."

"I want to be here."

"Were you? Invited?"

I shook my head and my mother's eyes registered a dim, injured pleasure. It was clear to me that my father hadn't invited me to dinner because he knew my mother needed me more than he did—and it unnerved me to see what an effort it was not to make that very point.

"Well, don't feel bad," she said, with mock consolation. "Your father's very busy now. You can't blame him for not having much time for you."

"It'll be nice having dinner, just the two of us," I said.

Rose nodded and looked away, into the soft, formless darkness of the living room.

"I'm tired of inviting the same people to this house, year after year," she said. "The same broken-down crew. I'm tired of the same old . . . I don't know what. No one's ever understood my marriage to Arthur and I'm not going to degrade myself with a lot of explanations. I don't want to see their silly faces when the turkey comes out and Arthur's not here to carve it. And what if I have trouble pulling the cork out of the wine? That was Arthur's job."

"I could do that," I said.

"No. That's not the point."

Slowly, I made my way around the apartment, turning on the lights. My mother wanted to eat in the kitchen but I set the dining room table with a tablecloth and the best dishes. I lit candles and took the fern that hung in the apartment's sunniest window and made it the centerpiece. Rose called out to announce the turkey was done and I helped her remove the enormous bird from the oven—a turkey that could have easily fed a dozen famished guests. The vegetables were still cooking in a huge enameled pot: slowly, peas and pearled onions bobbed and jiggled in the dark water. There was a basket full of warm rolls and raisin bread and a purée of sweet potatoes with a crust of small colored marshmallows. Standing next to the stove were five bottles of Côtes du Rhône, one with the foil stripped away and a corkscrew turned into the cork, awaiting someone's hands to pull it out.

"God, Mom," I said, "you made so much."

"I know all about it. Just eat as much as you want and don't worry about the rest."

It took us a long while to get all the food onto the table. The candles were burning much too quickly. The turkey was before us, with the chestnut stuffing simmering in its cavity, and we served everything else while waiting to see who would be given the responsibility of carving. The symmetry of playing my father's abandoned role made me shy to touch the long gleaming knife. But finally Rose said, "You don't want any meat?" and I pulled myself out of my chair and began to cut at the bird. I'd never carved in my life. The small chickens I occasionally prepared for myself—or bought precooked from the supermarket—I was quite content to hack and pull apart in the solitude of my apartment. I felt a hesitance almost as intense as despair as I imagined the mess I was about to make of our meal. But the knife was wonderfully sharp and there was enough soft white meat on the breasts for me to avoid cutting through any bones.

"Very nice," said Rose.

I put a couple of pieces of turkey on her plate. Then I served myself. And finally I uncorked the wine and we concentrated on the meal.

Near the end, Rose put down her knife and fork and the sharpness of the noise proved how silent we'd been.

"I had no idea I'd made so much food," she said.

"It doesn't matter. We'll have leftovers."

"You can't find small turkeys. That's the problem. They make them for large parties. A waste . . ."

"We'll have sandwiches. It'll be great for me. I won't have to cook for a while."

"I wish I didn't have to worry about money. All my life . . ."

she stopped herself and fixed me with a severe, proud stare. "Let's get something straight, David."

I nodded, feeling the pressure of a vast, content-less anxiety, an anxiety that suddenly seemed as much a part of my emotional universe as gravity was of the universe at large.

"I'm aware that your father has told you I was married before I married him. And I'm also aware of how he portrayed my situation. Poor, naïve, poverty-struck little Rose marrying a rich playboy who dragged her through the slime and made a fool of her. I hope you know your father well enough to realize that his . . . well I don't know what—his ego! His *ego* makes him believe—or at least *say*, that's how it went between Carl Courtney and me. He needs to think of me that way. Defenseless. Sad. And maybe a little stupid? Maybe. But what really happened is different and I think I can be the judge of *that*.

"Carl was rich and spoiled and maybe he didn't have a totally honest bone in his body—but he adored me. He worshipped the ground I walked on. Some people said he was the handsomest man in Philadelphia. You know how long we knew each other before we drove out to Bucks County and got married? Twenty-five days. I'll bet your father didn't tell you that. And I'll bet he didn't tell you that Carl was crazy about me. And I loved him.

"What Carl really was was a poet but he was too rich for that and so he ended up looking like a fool. He tried to work as a newspaperman but it wasn't serious. Nothing was. That was the trouble. Not what your father likes to believe, about Carl committing adultery. The adultery we made up to get the divorce and Carl was too much of a gentleman to argue. I had to leave him."

"Dad helped you get the divorce?"

"He made sure I wasn't given a penny of Carl's money. No settlement. No alimony. Nothing. The Courtneys would have been *glad* to pay me to get out of their family. They would have laughed all the way to the bank, as the saying goes. Not that I

wanted his money. But Arthur! Arthur had no right to negotiate that kind of settlement. Carl's brother, Dennis—his wife
was a dope addict and the family gave her an annuity for life to
divorce Dennis!"

"Dad wanted you all for himself. He didn't want some other
man's money involved. And you were Communists, after all.
What did the Courtneys' money come from?"

"That's not the point!"

"Maybe Dad was worried if you had alimony you wouldn't
marry him."

"No. That's not the *point*."

"What is the point?"

"No one understood. I *loved* Carl. He was a beautiful man.
I had never seen such beauty in a man. Ever! I could never feel
the way with Arthur that I did with Carl. And it wasn't just the
physical thing, though what's the use in pretending that wasn't
important. No one will ever know how *beautiful* I was when I
was with Carl. Everybody fell in love with me when I was with
Carl."

I was frightened. I suspected that Rose wanted to imply she
had never altogether loved my father, that his thick, earnest body
had never pleased her. I didn't want to hear it. In Rockville there
was a boy named Paul Schulte whose mother had told him that
she'd never had an orgasm. "Your papa's tool is unusually
slender," she'd told him, and Paul was obsessed with the information. He often threatened to castrate himself and send his
cock to his mother so she could see it was no grander than his
father's, and for all I knew he'd gone through with it. He was
still in Rockville when I left. Of course it was wrongheaded to
blame his mania on his mother's one remark, but Paul served to
remind me that it is not for nothing that sons shrink from too
precise an understanding of their mothers' unhappiness. I could
tolerate hints and I could absorb my own speculations, but if
Rose were to come right out and say that my father had been

an incompetent lover I feared the knowledge would pierce something deep and defenseless in me and change me in ways I wouldn't know how to control.

Dutifully, I stood up to slice our second helpings when the phone began to ring. Generally, Rose was unusually responsive to the telephone; often if she was just a few steps from it, she'd run toward it when it rang. But now, with the phone on its third, its fourth, its fifth ring, she made no motion to get up and I, feeling it was somehow expected of me, put the knife down and went into the kitchen to answer.

It was Alberto Nicolosi, one of my mother's oldest friends. Along with the Rinzlers, the Sterns, and the Davises, the Nicolosis were inevitable Thanksgiving guests at our house.

"Hello," said Alberto, "is this David?"

"Yes. Alberto?"

"Hello, David. I'm not used to your voice over the telephone. Forgive me."

"It's OK. How are you?"

"Just fine. Are you there with your mother?"

"Yes."

"Ah, good. And others? There are others?"

"Not this year. It's just the two of us."

"I suspected. You know, every year Rose makes us dinner on Thanksgiving. Now we have just finished our own not too traditional I'm afraid dinner and we were thinking of your mother . . ."

"Yes?"

"Tell me. Do you think it would be worthwhile if we came for a visit? We have a cake. We could bring it over and Rose could make her coffee."

"I think that would be wonderful, Alberto."

"You're sure? We were going to go to the opera. My brother is with us. But it seems so strange not to see Rose today."

"Come right over. I'll tell my mother you're on your way."

Rose was clearing the table when I returned. She had placed the slice of breast I'd just taken off back onto the frame of the bird, and she'd poured the wine out of her glass and into mine.

"That was Alberto," I said. "He and Irene want to come over."

"But we're finished with dinner."

"So are they. They're bringing over a cake so we can all have dessert together."

Rose was silent.

"Al's brother is with them. They're bringing him, too."

She walked quickly into the kitchen with a load of dishes. When she came back she said, "They're coming now?"

"Yes."

"Well, I suppose I better wash my face." She pressed her hand against her cheek.

"You look fine."

"Oh, I know what I look like. Oh well. Here come Irene and Al, coming to eat me out of house and home. Irene's a terrible cook and I'm sure they're starved. I hope you'll be nice to them, David. Your father loves to make fun of them. But they watched you grow up. They love you and you should treat them with respect."

"But I think they're wonderful."

"Yes. I know all about it. Just remember they're human beings with as many feelings as you. They're two of my oldest friends, David. And they're precious to me."

The Nicolosis arrived while Rose was in the bathroom. Alberto wore a herringbone overcoat and a Russian fur cap. His hair was long and silvery and his eyes were a dark, purplish blue. He smelled of pipe tobacco and cologne. Irene, erect, thin, and getting brittle, wore a black cape. Her lipstick was fire-engine red and her white hair swept back in two large waves. Arthur once said that Irene's hair was so well trained she could probably make it stand up and bark. Alberto's younger brother looked chilled and deferential. He shook hands and nodded and smiled shyly as Alberto explained that he spoke no English.

As I took their coats, Rose emerged from the bathroom.

"Well, look who's here," she called, in a crazy, gay voice. She extended both of her hands like a tea room hostess. "Will you look what the cat dragged in?"

"And you must be Alberto's brother," Rose was saying, even before she reached them.

"His name is Carlo," said Alberto, "but I'm afraid he has no English."

"Oooo," said Rose, furrowing her brow and tilting her head, as if the news was very sad. "Oh well. At least he can eat cake and drink my good coffee."

If she could only be quiet and calm herself, I thought, and stop forcing people away from her. I hung the coats in the closet and when I closed the door and looked down the hall, Alberto had Rose in his arms. He held her tightly and seemed to be rocking her back and forth. Rose was on her tip-toes and as Alberto continued in his embrace she patted him lightly on the back, as if it were she who was comforting him.

7

Early the next year, I made contact with two more Butterfields. The first was Keith, whose name I found in the Bellows Falls, Vermont, telephone directory. It was a number I'd tried a few times before, but I'd never gotten an answer. I kept it on my list, though, and even put a check next to it because Vermont seemed like a place Keith would live—Vermont, or Oregon, somewhere you could paddle a canoe, backpack, and not have to compete, a clean isolated place with a tradition of loneliness and family history. And one evening, one manic blizzardy night, I called that

Vermont number again and a voice that was unmistakably Keith's answered on the eighth ring.

"Hello, Keith," I said. I wanted to hear more, to make certain.

"Hello? Who is this?" He was a perfect, clear tenor; he should heve been a folklorist, a collector of nineteenth-century American mountain songs, but he was too awkward to play the banjo and a thousand times too shy to sing even to himself.

"It's me." I heard a dog barking behind him; Keith clapped his hand over the phone and said, "Shush, Ambroise." Then, in a sharper voice, he said to me, "Who *is* this?"

"It's me. It's David Axelrod."

"I thought so."

Then I said a stupid thing. I said, "Don't hang up," which made him do exactly that. I called him right back but he just let it ring. That same night I wrote him a short letter, apologizing for calling him and asking if I could someday—not necessarily soon—come to see him and talk with him. He sent my letter back torn into pieces, though when I inspected my envelope I thought I detected that it had been opened. He put it all into another envelope and added a note of his own saying, "I know for a fact that you are on parole and you are not allowed to bother me or anyone in my family. If I ever hear from you again you may as well know I'll be calling the police here and in Chicago."

Then in March I learned where Sammy Butterfield was. When I'd thought about it without any clues I had guessed he was in some respectable prep school, on his way to Harvard, and then Harvard Law, and then Congress. I still took entirely seriously the ambitions he held when he was twelve years old. In fact, when I hunted around for traces of Sammy I called Choate and Exeter and a few other upper-class schools, but I got nowhere with that and I simply didn't know enough about those kinds of schools to try many others. As it turned out, he was in upstate New York in a place called the Beaumont School. There was a story about him that I read on the bus one evening coming home from work. It was a UPI wire story and when I checked in the library a couple days later, I saw the same story in papers from New York to Los Angeles.

STUDENT REJECTS ENDOWMENT;
DONOR LIFELONG FRIEND OF AGNEW

Beaumont, New York . . . Roman Domenitz, a prominent Maryland businessman and longtime associate of Vice-President Agnew, came to the Beaumont School to present the exclusive New York boys preparatory school with a half million dollars. Mr. Domenitz, president of Rodom Industries, was making the donation in memory of his son Laurence Domenitz, who died of leukemia last year while in his senior year at the Beaumont School.

Samuel Butterfield, president of the junior class, was chosen by the Beaumont students to accept the check from Mr. Domenitz, in a ceremony marking the prestigious school's 100th anniversary. Speaking on a stage that included Vice-President Agnew, young Mr. Butterfield stated, "We don't need Domenitz's money." As he tore up the check, Mr. Butterfield recounted charges recently leveled against Domenitz by such organizations as the National Urban League, the Congress on Racial Equality, and the NAACP.

The presentation ceremonies were held in Bigelow Auditorium on the spacious Beaumont campus. In attendance were the families of the Beaumont student body as well as Beaumont School alumni, including General Meryle Woods and Roger V. Addison, founder of Addison International. When Butterfield tore up the half-million-dollar check, there was an uproar in the auditorium and police and school officials were forced to cancel the proceedings and evacuate the hall. "We had the beginnings of an incident on our hands," remarked Dana Mason, the Headmaster of the School.

Samuel Butterfield was not available for questioning. His father, Dr. Hugh Butterfield of Camden, New Jersey, when asked to comment on his son's actions, said, "Sammy always does what he believes in."

Until now, Beaumont School has not been touched by the tide of student protest that has swept American schools and colleges over the past several years. In his remarks preceding the presentation ceremonies, Vice-President Agnew commended the school for its reputation for "scholarship, sportsmanship, and citizenship." Earlier on, Agnew described the student protest movement as "the most prolonged panty raid in the history of America."

Along with the story was a picture of Sammy, such as you would find in a school yearbook. His light hair was cut Sir Lancelot style and his face had the opacity of someone who can conceal everything but his features themselves from the camera. With his blue eyes, silky eyebrows, abrupt nose, and a polite, practically vacant smile, he had a face worthy of a film star, except his was as devoid of vanity as it was of whiskers— which is to say, vanity may have been beneath the surface but he had yet to cultivate it. I did my best to follow up on the story, but no one at any of the newspapers could tell me if Sammy had been expelled. I called Ann to tell her news of Sammy had reached Chicago—"And if they're printing it here," I said, "that means it's everywhere, probably even China"—and to ask her if Sammy had gotten kicked out of school.

"I know what you're getting at," Ann said. Her voice sounded dreamy, a little stoned. It was snowing everywhere north of Florida but she sounded like someone lying in the sun. "I don't like you calling me, David. It's too strange and it's always unexpected. It's not fair. It always means you're prepared to talk and I'm not. But if you have to call me, at least make sure you're not calling to trick me out of information about my kids."

I wrote Sammy in care of the Beaumont School, congratulating him on tearing up Agnew's pal's check. When I was a novelty to the Butterfields, I used to trade on the fact of my parents' political past. As far as I was concerned, I'd absorbed enough Marxism through osmosis to teach them all quite a bit about left-wing politics. But, as I wrote to Sammy, "here you are committing acts of real courage and I haven't made a political gesture since high school, and even that was a silent vigil outside of a military installation in Evanston when I was with five hundred other people and no possible harm (or blame) could have befallen me." Sammy didn't answer my letter, or acknowledge it, but neither did he send it back torn into eighths. I knew I was beguiling myself, but I took this as a kind of encouragement. A week later, I sent him a letter to Jade and asked him to forward it to her.

A letter from Ann.

Dear David,

Poor you. First to have me hang up on you and then having to trudge down to the post office to get my letters which don't fit into your mailbox. I've always helped myself to the privilege of irresolution when it came to you. You always seemed to revel in my ambivalence while the others tore out their hair. You were so certain that beneath my capriciousness I was a typical Yankee lady, as sure of her emotional priorities as she is of her lineage. I wonder if you still feel that. I would hope so. I'm certain no one *else* does. But now with yourself on the receiving end of my whimfulness, you'll want to forget the pleasure you once took in the odd syncopation of my feelings.

Syncopated feelings? God, there is no one on either side of the grave upon whom I'd inflict *that* little phrase, except you. I realize you'll put up with anything and you would do nothing to threaten this correspondence of ours. I finally understand why some women—or are they all just girls?—answer those box-numbered pleas from prisoners that run in the underground papers and write letters to some total stranger serving time in a penitentiary. Our history being what it's been, there's something about a bird in a cage that appeals to women.

Hugh was back in town—speaking of what appeals to women. His girl of the moment, Ingrid Ochester, is about twenty-seven, though she looks as old as Hugh. God only knows what's aged her. She doesn't really seem to *do* anything and her only worries are if the glaze will hold on her pots and vases and if her eight-year-old son will land safely in one of his constant shuttles between Ingrid and his father, a Pepsi exec in Saudi Arabia. Ingrid is the sort of woman I could never know, under any circumstances. Comfortable, vague, she seems to come out of nowhere, from nothing. Her past is full of towns like Camden, New Jersey; her parents summered in Easton, Maryland. They made their money selling sofas.

Hugh and I came from very different worlds, but in our case there was, at least, a pleasing polarity. He was from New Orleans and I was from New York, but our families both were faded rich (*very* faded) and they haunted and nagged at us in similar ways. But Ingrid and Hugh? Who could say what they hold in common; I can never even keep it straight how they met. There was somebody's cousin, a flat tire . . . But clearly Ingrid is smitten—all of the kids say so—and Hugh revels in it like a cat on his fifth canary.

That's what is so absurd about him. He is still amazed women fall in love with him and his ego is so weak (yet so insatiable) that he treats every dalliance as the affair of the century. Each time he feels himself the object of some lady's affections, Hugh will seize the moment with all the rashness and power of his heart. For a man as dead-on attractive as Hugh, he has been dumped by an extraordinary number of women. He holds on with such intensity that your average young lady—who like your average young man simply wishes to *enjoy* life, for God's sake—beats a hasty retreat. You know nearly as well as I do how wildly serious Hugh can be. How deeply he likes to think, how exactly he likes to remember, how fine and painful the calibrations of his emotions. A brooder, the silent type, Hugh's liable to do things like get up in the middle of dinner, come to your chair and stand you up, and then put his arms around you and embrace you with great strength and solemnity, while you try not to chew your mouthful of food. Well, most women can't *take* that kind of stuff.

There comes a certain point in one's courtship with Hugh when one realizes this is not just something Hugh does to *woo* you, but this is actually the way he *is*. The cataloguing of events—our tenth paella dinner, the fifth anniversary of finding the house, our fifth anniversary of signing the papers for the house, our fifth anniversary of moving into the house. It doesn't stop, it's not some stunt, it goes on and on. Seventeen years of marriage and I'd put down my book and have to confront Hugh's earnest blue eyes, staring silently at me from across the room, trying to fathom me. "Do you want to talk?" I'd say. But he didn't; he wanted to "communicate." Coming from a world of *The Autocrat at the Breakfast Table*, and adding to the general conversational din all my life, Hugh's over-whelmingly significant silences had for me a deep sonority. And while my relationship to them gradually became ironic and subversive, I never truly tired of them. I never ceased to believe that *his way* was a higher path and that he had something crucial to teach me.

I used to believe that it was Hugh who pursued me, but the truth is that even his Cambridge pursuit was incurably diffident. Hugh sought me out after I published a story in a local lit. magazine called "Birth Pains." The magazine was printed in blue ink on yellow paper and my contribution was so arch and pretentious—the usual twaddle about a me-ish young woman dying from her own cultivation and refinement—that I stayed out of sight for a week afterwards. But Hugh managed to find my piece enchanting and tracked me down. A stranger, he wrote me a formal note and asked to meet me for a daiquiri—in my story, the heroine drinks dozens and dozens of daiquiries—at the Parker House. The idea of meeting this well-mannered and apparently well-meaning stranger was too seductive to resist and I appeared at the Parker House wearing a black dress and a string of lilac-tinted glass beads. Hugh was in a double-breasted wheat-colored suit, holding a copy of "Birth Pains," and drawling to beat the band. (He sensed I would respond to the cliché of the Southern Gentleman.) He advised me as to the extent of his admiration for my story, asked me how I had achieved my anemic, third-hand effects, and, on the whole, interviewed me rather as you yourself did many years later when you came home with those photocopies of my *New Yorker* stories. Except then I was a young, ornery girl in a hotel with a stranger, and a half hour into our conversation (and halfway through my second daiquiri—a perfectly horrid drink, of course) I was hoping that Hugh would make his praise complete by suggesting we take a room.

If I'd known then what I soon enough learned, it wouldn't have been any more complicated than my saying, "Oh Hugh, I need to be with you"—Hugh would have been at the front desk in an instant, gulping so hard that his adam's apple would be leaping forth like a cuckoo clock. I had no idea of the depths of his shyness and susceptibility: in matters of the flesh, Hugh has always needed permission. The permission granted, he can be the goat of all goats, but before then he is withdrawn, or so tepidly flirtatious that it becomes inconceivable that a real libido lurks beneath. If it hadn't been for his great good looks, Hugh would have been miserable: all he could do was make himself available; he could not reach out and take. But how was I to know? It took weeks of thought and frustration before I realized that if I was going to have Hugh, then I must initiate it. Thus the famous dinner party in which I announced as I lit the candles: "Abandon all hope of leaving, ye who enter here."

God, I must be just a little bit lonelier than I thought. Going on about Hugh like this. It's near the first anniversary of our divorce. That must be it. We sold the house, sold the ten scabby acres in Mississippi that Hugh's father gave us on our wedding, and stood like waifs in a divorce court in Chicago, lying through our straight white teeth to the judge so our story would be less complicated and unseemly. Hugh's girl waited outside, double-parked in her infernal van, and I splurged on a taxi to O'Hare so I could get the hell out as quickly as possible.

The divorce was inevitable once the house was gone, just as precious papers get tattered and lost if you don't have anyplace to store them. That big house on Dorchester had a domestic magnetism at its core that could keep us together—and even in a kind of ramshackle balance. It was our homeland, our space station—well, you remember the magic of that house. We were so lucky to find it and losing it was terrible for us—especially coming at a time in our lives when we needed walls more than ever before, needed the feel of familiar wood, the low comforting groans of our old house's cellar, the mélange of sky and branch that hung so peacefully before our front window.

The house was a touchstone, the progenitor of memory; it had a quality of preservation, of preserving us, our lives, our promises. Driving us out of there was like driving a tribe from its ancestral home: the rituals of community dried up like empty pods. Without the familiar doors to walk through and slam, quarrels went on and on, deepened in import and acrimoniousness. Ah, the arguments in hotels, with the maids in the next room and the Kiwanis Club in the hall. The late-night whispers in my brother's house in Maine—even with my brother and his family in Boston and we Butterfields on our own for a few days, we tiptoed and mumbled, washing our cups as soon as we used them. We were refugees without a cause, more interested in blame than in bonds.

It's our link, you know, mine and yours. The blame. I suppose that's why you feel so free to contact me and why, to me, speaking to you again seems so natural and inevitable. We are, I would suppose, karmic twins. It was you—and you alone—who set the fire, but we'll never know what could have been saved if it hadn't been for my cousin's Care Package from California. When my cousin's package arrived with ten trips, ten 250-microgram doses of pharmaceutically pure LSD . . . Well, as *I* remember it, we all felt excited and privileged. We had all been curious—no, more than that: we all were committed to taking it. The only trouble had been our fear of buying it from some lunatic on the street, some flaky teen just as liable to sell us strychnine or horse tranquilizer. But with the genuine article at hand—and the weird blessing of having it come from a lab—we were set. It was my cousin, my letter, and the package had been addressed to me. But we all discussed it, all decided it would work best—be less divisive, less strange and exclusive—if we took it as a family. We were all prepared to learn something miraculous and transforming, and it was a measure, I thought, of our enduring commitment to remain a family that we wanted to take the journey together.

Yet, as it happened, we were as helpless as rabbits on a highway when the time came for us to act swiftly and well. We turned this way and that and learned something that turned out to be impossible to absorb: with life seeming to totter on the edge of oblivion, we were not a family at all—it was each for himself, in a state of panic, fear, and terrible isolation. We were not any of us really capable of holding a thought, but I'm sure all of us felt, to one degree or another, that we were being punished for our transgression against the brain's holy chemistry, that the fire was a foretaste of the hell we had condemned ourselves to. I've often wondered (and lamented) why we were so godawful bloody helpless to get ourselves out of the house in good order and I keep coming back to the emotional memory of *deserving* the worst.

Speaking of blame. I think I'd like to defend myself against *your* accusation. I quote: ". . . when I began spending nights at your house you decided that Jade wasn't getting enough sleep and your solution was to get us a double bed, a used bed from the Salvation Army which we sprayed for bugs and drenched in Chanel No. 5."

My idea? Perhaps the Chanel No. 5 was my idea—it was certainly *my* Chanel. But the bed was Jade's idea—and, I daresay, yours. Does it seem at all likely to you that it was *me* who dreamed up the idea of getting a double bed? Do you have any memory of my proposing it to you? Or are you calling my lack of objection to the idea a form of advocacy? You don't understand. I realized you two were hardly sleeping—but that seemed connected to the bizarre power of your love for each other. You made me crave sleeplessness because I recognized what it was in you two—a refusal to be separated. It was the *privacy* of sleep that horrified you. You didn't want to sleep. Those long late-night walks. We thought you were trying to tire yourselves out but now I realize the purpose of those two-mile strolls. You were reviving yourselves, probably stopping at the Medici for a cup of espresso before coming home.

Jade had always been such a deep sleeper. On weekends, it would be nothing unusual for her to sleep until four in the afternoon. She slept in school, she slept on buses, on family outings. Like an old man, she'd doze off at the movies. Naturally, we noted her semi-narcolepsy and realized it was an escape—from her too-rapid growing up, from all of the countless details of life that displeased her, and from us. Once, when she was nine or ten, I found her asleep in the bathtub and I shook her awake, partly because I was afraid she could drown herself like that and partly because I'd been waiting an hour for her to get out of the bathroom. She looked at me with all the defiance she could muster—which was considerable, even then—and said, "I need my sleep." She was very possessive about her sleep and she defended it as if it were property. If she could have hidden it the way I hid my chocolates there would have been dreams and packets of unconsciousness stashed everywhere. In a household where everything was shared and talked about and where there was much more need than there was ability to satisfy needs, Jade dug her heels into a universe in which she was unapproachable, uncriticizable, and unknowable.

So after years of accommodating her semi-narcolepsy, we then, with you on the scene, had to adjust to Jade's sleeplessness. When the first symptoms appeared—a certain icing-like quality to her eyes, as well as her own direct testimony that she was getting about twenty hours of sleep a week—Hugh took the homeopathic route and began giving her infinitesimal doses of stimulants. Herbal stimulants to begin with, brewed in with her tea, and then, relaxing his principles, he even crushed in a little bit of dexadrine. Hugh assumed that her body was keeping itself awake because of some internal crisis, some need for wakefulness, and following the homeopathic edict of treating like with like, Hugh attempted to relieve her body of its need to create these symptoms by creating them artificially—thus, he hoped, defusing the control center of her insomnia. Then he set off on homeopathic chase number two, which is a kind of folksy psychoanalysis—usually Hugh's strongsuit, for some odd reason.

Hugh developed the suspicion that your lovemaking was leaving Jade in a perpetually excited, that is to say unsatisfied, state. This didn't go very far in explaining *your* sleeplessness, but your sleeplessness wasn't awfully much in question. This continual sexual incompleteness may have been sheer fantasy on Hugh's part, a kind of compromise virginity, but nevertheless he tried to delicately draw her out about her "night life," as he called it. Jade spared him the realization that he had overstepped his actual courage, that he was not a WASP Freud, willing to face the truth no matter what its content or consequence, and she simply dummied up on the topic of your sex life. She knew, I think, that Hugh wanted to hear that each night you left her dangling, yearning, and whether it was true or not it was more than she could say—her loyalty to you and the world you both now lived in was too fierce—she was virtually patriotic about the emotional ground you'd portioned off for yourselves: My love affair right or wrong! So she sidestepped his questions, the subtle ones, that is, and when he resorted to frontal attack, she screamed, "You're taking things away from me. You're making mine into yours." It was Jade's genius to use Hugh's own language when she fought him. Jade dressed in the uniform of Hugh's troops and fought him from the trees and bushes, whereas I fought him like the colonial British army, straight up and down in a clearing and decked out in red.

And the sleeplessness continued. The nights when you weren't with us were no better. Jade would go to bed early, clearly anxious for an uninterrupted night, but then there would have to be at least one phonecall to you and as often as not, after an hour or two of sleep, she'd be at her desk composing a letter to you, or drawing your face, or writing a poem to you—sometimes even trying to catch up in her schoolwork. Hugh was convinced that Jade's short-term memory was unraveling, that she had gotten paler by two full shades. He was even waffling on the question of whether or not to subtly dose her with barbiturates—he was slower to use drugs medically than he was socially.

Well, *this* was the climate when Jade approached us and asked for a real bed for her room, a double bed as would befit a lady who shared her sleeping quarters with a lover. It's strange that our compliance in this small matter is what you chose to rattle in my face—and not the far more significant matter of our allowing you into our daughter's room in the first place. You approve, it would seem, of our belief in the sexual rights of young people, but raise an eyebrow at our choice of furniture. And what about your own terribly moral parents? What was on their minds when they failed to stop you from virtually moving into our house? At least Hugh and I knew where our daughter was—could actually hear her in her room, if we listened closely enough. The truth is that no one had the heart to keep you two from being everything to each

other, and the energy of your connection was strangely
overpowering. Since we did not believe that making love
is a sin or a crime, all we could have objected to was that
you and Jade weren't yet ready somehow for the pleasures
of the flesh—but how could we say that when we were
nearly mad with envy over your love for each other? You
were all of our half-forgotten romantic fantasies suddenly
incarnate; denying you would have been like denying
ourselves.

And so, yes, I *did* agree to it, the bed. I believed in you
two, in your gestures and in the world you created. It
wasn't until the bed arrived in that Salvation Army truck
and was installed in Jade's little room that I realized Jade's
arguments were wholly based on trickery. Having a
double bed didn't make a dent in her sleeplessness. Nothing
could have put you two to sleep. Love—or is it only
romance?—is a psychedelic. It's the flying carpet, the rope
trick. It is *that* singular, and no one who sees it—which
means, of course, *believing* it—can ever hope to be the
same. You two stoned-out beasts reigning up there in your
used bed. There have been times, David, when I think that
just that, just the fact of you two, never minding what it
all led to, but just seeing you two and feeling what you
meant to each other, and knowing that love is a state of
altered consciousness, has been more than I can honestly
absorb. And that in certain ways it has destroyed my life.

Ann

8

January is when time begins, and spring is when life begins and,
for me, the first day of spring was the day I sneaked into a travel

agency on Jackson and State to buy a plane ticket to New York.
It was a cold April day, gray, slushy, but the most extravagant
promises turned slowly in the belly of the wind. I paid for the
ticket with a new hundred-dollar bill, feeling as furtive as a spy.
I bought the ticket under a false name and kept the day of
departure open. I felt brilliant, brave, and absolutely imperiled.
The act of stepping outside the law provoked my imagination
and released torrents of fearful criminal passion. I wondered if
there was a permanent all-points bulletin out on me and if the
sweet-faced woman who sold me the ticket wasn't in fact looking
at a newswire photo of me taped beneath the Formica ledge of
the counter. I shoved the ticket into my coat pocket and quick-
stepped out with my head down.

I hid my ticket in my apartment and dreamed of my departure. I thought I was going to be quite a bit braver than I turned
out to be. Like a person doomed to fail, I thought of the hundred
things that could go wrong. I thought of my parole officer Eddie
Watanabe making a surprise visit to my school and finding me
vanished. I thought of being arrested for jaywalking on 42nd and
Broadway and having it discovered I was in New York breaking
parole. I thought of Ann slamming her door in my face and
calling the police. These were the variables and I was right to
think about them, but I could not stop myself. My imagination
of disaster tormented me as if it were a separate, vicious self. I
longed to stop thinking of consequences, just as we must do
when we dive from high boards, leap on our skis down steep
sunblind slopes, or play any of the other daredevil games we've
invented as metaphors for love.

I tried to prepare myself. I packed my suitcase. I bought *The
New York Times* and *The Village Voice*. I leafed through books
of photographs of New York. When I heard a jet pass overhead,
I searched the skies for it. I methodically withdrew money from
my small savings account, as if it were being monitored by federal agents. I said to Dr. Ecrest, "You know what? I'd like to go
to New York." He asked why and I quickly shrugged, cursing

myself for so profitlessly risking detection. I really liked him and it had been difficult all along to keep from confessing the dozens of long-distance phonecalls I'd made and the letters I'd written and the huge, nourishing letters I'd received from Ann. It was an agony often to think how I wasted my time and Ecrest's, especially when I felt stuck and fed up with my own character. I didn't much believe in psychiatry, but the fact was that I'd been given a chance to talk for years to highly trained, expensive doctors and I'd made very little of it because of my commitment to keep my secrets safe.

The clothing workers union had taken me off the picket line and into their regional offices, where I worked for a fellow named Guy Parker. Guy was a few years older than me and had convinced the Amalgamated to hire him to make a thirty-minute film "depicting the Union's struggle, from the sweatshops of the past to the challenge of the future." Parker's approach to the film clips and snapshots in the union's informal archives was wholly passionate. Looking at a picture of women leaping to their death during the Triangle Factory fire, Guy would tap his big ivory finger against his high, slightly flushed brow and muse, "Each one of these gals had a family. You know, parents, husbands, boyfriends, maybe kids. Each one. A life. And then out the window. Think of it." Guy wanted every incident to work into a Big Scene. Negotiations bored him, cooperative housing projects made him practically whinny with impatience: he needed strikes, boycotts, fires, goons, death tolls. Parker's vision of union history was one of unstinting hysteria; I suggested we call his movie *Oh My God! Here Come the Bosses!*

However, working for Guy was a lot better than pacing in front of a store, and since I was Parker's researcher there was an implicit understanding that sooner or later my work would take me to New York, where the national office of the union had a "treasure trove" of photographs and documents and where such early union heroes as Alma Hillman and Jacob Potofsky still lived.

Guy knew nothing and cared less about my personal life—though he liked the way I listened and often asked me out for dinner or drinks. Nevertheless, because fate is not only fickle but also flirtatious, Guy incessantly referred to my upcoming New York trip, alluding to it one day, postponing it the next, until I was half-convinced that the whole deal was an elaborate trap and I refused to react to his promises any more. However, I did use the possible opportunity as a means of putting my toe into the water of consequence if I were to suddenly use my own ticket to fly east. Meeting with Eddie Watanabe, I casually mentioned that "my work" might send me to New York for a week or so. And Eddie, answering so quickly that I wondered if he hadn't been expecting me to say this, said, "No way, David. No way on earth."

"Why not?" I said. "Even if I got a written statement from my boss that I *had* to go to New York?"

"No way, no how."

Two weeks later, I met again with Eddie. It was evening and spring had receded. A chilly rain was falling and the sky was a dark porcelain blue and looked as if a thunderclap might shatter it into a thousand pieces. Rather than meet at Eddie's office, we were going to have our talk at the Wimpy's in the shopping center near my apartment. Eddie was already seated in a booth when I came in. He wore a suburban car coat of a slightly gauzy wool, with long narrow wooden buttons. He'd just gotten a haircut. He was wearing his hair like a businessman now and his practically translucent golden ears looked larval and vulnerable. He smelled of peppermint and new car. As I sat down, he thrust his hand out for me to shake.

"Don't worry," he said. "You're not late. I was early." He snapped his fingers to get the waitress's attention, like a clumsy boy trying to act tough and worldly for his date. The waitress came over and took out her order pad, making it a point not to look at us. Eddie ordered coffee and I asked for a root beer.

"How come you wanted to meet here?" I asked. Wimpy's

had been one of the principal Hyde Park hangouts for years and
Jade and I had eaten a hundred hamburgers there, some of them
while seated in the very booth Eddie and I now occupied.

"I like meeting outside of my office. I get depressed sitting
in my office all day. And I get the idea that the place puts you
up tight. I'd like you to really relax and get loose with me and
maybe, just maybe, you understand, you'd have a bit more luck
being honest with me if we were to have our meeting in a nicer
place."

There were not many things in the world I despised more
than listening to Eddie Watanabe.

The waitress brought our order and placed it before us. Eddie
dropped a saccharine tablet into his coffee and stirred it from
the bottom up, as if ladling the sediment from the bottom of
a pot of soup.

"You still dreaming about going to New York?" he asked.

In a moment's confusion, I forgot I'd spoken to him about
it last time and I felt exposed, panicked. But then I recalled our
discussion and I shrugged.

"What's that mean?" he asked. "A shrug could mean yes or
it could mean no or maybe it means you don't feel like answering. So?"

"It means I haven't been thinking about it. What's the use?"

"That's the spirit. What's the use is exactly how you should
look at it. I was getting worried about you, if you don't mind
hearing the truth. You're an intelligent guy, you know."

"What's that got to do with it?"

"Oh, a lot. That's been one of my theories since I got into
this business, that the system doesn't work for the guy with the
higher than average intelligence. Either it breaks him into bits or
he figures out a way to scout around it, but there's no blessed
way on earth the system we've got now, as it exists I mean, at
the present time, is going to meet the punishment needs of the
guy with the higher than average intelligence. That's why a guy
like yourself, David, is a personal challenge for me, profession-

ally speaking. I can learn ten times as much about penology from an intelligent guy like yourself than I can from some goofball who gets busted trying to rob Mr. Goldberg's grocery store."

"Ah, do I detect a bit of anti-Semitism?"

"Screw. I'm not anti anything. If anything, I'm anti-anti and you know it. Jesus, David, you don't know when you've got a good thing. Especially seeing as you've got a parole officer whose been doing his share of standing up for you lately."

"What's that supposed to mean?"

"OK," said Watanabe with a rather theatrical sigh, "I wasn't going to tell you, but I may as well." This was his customary preamble when he wanted to inform me of my lack of rights.

"Tell me," I said.

"All right. The father was in town this week."

"The father? Whose?"

"Butterfield's."

"Hugh was here?"

"That's right.

"You saw him?"

"No way. I'm not interested in him. My thing is you, not him. *You.*"

"How do you know he was here if you didn't see him? Did he call you?"

"OK. I'll tell you. I wasn't sure I was going to, but since you're asking. Butterfield is tight with Kevin DeSoto. You know, the D.A. who prosecuted you. DeSoto's into that weird kind of medicine Butterfield specializes in. So Butterfield blows into town and—"

"From where?"

"I don't know. From nowhere. What's the difference? Anyhow, he shows up at DeSoto's office and he says he has new information for a case against you."

"What kind of case? My case is over. I can't be put on trial again."

"Butterfield wants to have your parole revoked."

"What's he saying? What's his reason?"

"Who knows? DeSoto won't say. It's probably nothing, right?"

I nodded.

"But Butterfield is hot and bothered that you're not locked up in a dungeon and getting nothing but bread and water. De-Soto lets him know that you're on a tight parole and then DeSoto calls my boss and talks it over and then my boss meets with Butterfield.

"This Butterfield thinks you're going to get mixed up with his family again. He's pretty damn emotional, the way I hear it. You'd think it was yesterday, the fire you set. When my boss said we had no intention of revoking your parole, Butterfield practically went nuts. He said you hadn't been punished. That the hospital we had you in was like a country club. He said you were free to do whatever you wanted. And then you know what he said?"

I shook my head, but I knew.

"He said you wrote his son a letter."

"That's a total lie," I said, quickly and with great feeling.

"I figured. In fact, that's what I called it when my boss asked my opinion. A lie. I said Butterfield was underestimating your intelligence. The guy was a little nuts, the way he was going on. There he is in my boss's office, taking up my boss's valuable time and just standing there beating himself on the chest and saying that he's made himself a promise that you'll never see his daughter or anyone else in his family for as long as he lives. My boss says, 'That's our job, Mr. Butterfield, not your job.' And Butterfield screams that we're not doing our job and that makes it his job."

Eddie finished his coffee and shrugged. "Whew," he said, shaking his head. "Just thinking about how the man hates you makes me worried."

"Why does it make *you* worry?"

"I'm not sure. It just does. Doesn't it you? Doesn't it make you worry?"

I shook my head.

"Well, I wish I was that cool. It gives me the creeps."

The next day was Saturday and I awoke in tears. The dream that usually woke me was one of meeting Jade. She would see me, turn, and flee, and I would race after her, sometimes through Hyde Park, sometimes through a forest. Soon she'd outrun me and disappear but my running never slackened.

This time, however, I dreamed I was weeping in my old room at Rockville. It was sunny and warm and I sat at my childish wooden desk with my head in my hands, crying. There was a knock at the door and I woke up, alone and in the dark because my bedroom was in the back and never got any sunlight. As I came awake, I heard my sobs like the bark of a lonely dog a country mile away.

The tears I shed that morning, rigid in the banal discomfort of my own personal neglect (the lumpy mattress, the stale sheets, the uncovered foam-rubber pillow with its refrigerated zipper), were all I could make of the catastrophic hunger I felt for Jade.

From the moment I set the fire, all of my life was an argument against keeping my love alive. I tried to hold on to what I believed was uniquely mine, fearing that when I lost it I would be nothing at all. But now, I could feel how much of my resolve was already gone. And I could also feel a part of me beginning to wish that my love would finally start to recede. It lay on me like an intolerable heat; it pressed my thoughts like a fever that wouldn't break. It was worse than mourning because grief was corrupted by hope; I could not even turn my love into memory.

I couldn't stop myself from longing for her. The feel of her small hard toes as I knelt before her with the tarnished-nickel nail clipper, the oak-colored birthmark on her inner thigh, the double orbit of platinum hairs that circled her belly button. "Trust me," she said the time we made love and she wouldn't let me come and she was on top with her hands on my shoulders, moving slower and slower like all human time running down and I was kicking at the mattress as if I were being electrocuted, and the way she said my name as if it were a secret, not softly, yet sometimes in a roomful of people only I'd hear it, which was just one of the thousand things we could never explain—all of these images I thought I was preserving so we could still have them when we were reunited, but now they came unbidden, they did with me whatever they wanted, and they ruled me with their limitless command.

Part Two

9

Six days later, I stopped all my careful planning and boarded a 10 a.m. American Airlines flight to New York City. I hadn't informed my parents, my employer, my school, my doctor, or my parole officer, and now that I was acting in the true bent spirit of utter incaution—admitting, I suppose, that nothing could camouflage the obsessive nature of my trip—I strolled through the great awesome airport, buying magazines, treating myself to a shoe shine, and never venturing a frantic glance over my shoulder. I was the first one on the plane and I took my seat as near to the front of the jet as I could get without sneaking into first class. I'd read somewhere that the nearer to the cockpit you traveled the better your chance of surviving a crash and, though I'd given up the dread of being apprehended in Chicago, my impending reunion with Ann was still so strange and terrifying that I wondered if fate might intervene after all and pluck the long silver plane from the sky and dash it onto some flat unpopulated stretch of Ohio.

Soon enough, the plane filled with passengers to New York. I was sufficiently drunk on the music of my own mission to believe I wasn't the only passenger off to run one of the heart's unreasonable errands. A woman in her middle age wearing opaque green sunglasses and asking for a cocktail before take-off, a soldier holding an innocent bouquet of daisies, an un-shaved man in his thirties carrying a shopping bag filled with clothes—who could say what crucial connections depended on this flight? It was only vanity and discouragement that some-times made me feel alone with my endless love, but now that I was taking one of the risks my heart had urged upon me I could also feel I was not alone. If endless love was a dream, then it was a dream we all shared, even more than we all shared the dream of never dying or of traveling through time, and if anything set me apart it was not my impulses but my stubbornness, my willing-ness to take the dream past what had been agreed upon as the reasonable limits, to declare that this dream was not a feverish trick of the mind but was an actuality at least as real as that other, thinner, more unhappy illusion we call normal life. After all, the intimations of endless love were the same now as they were thousands of years before, while normal life had changed a thousand times and in a thousand different ways. Which, then, was more real? In love, and willing to sacrifice anything for it, I felt myself connected to all of human time, to slaves weeping on the auction block, to musicians strumming beneath moon-bright balconies, and, whether she wanted me or not, to Jade. But if I were to turn away from love, if I were to put it at arm's length and do what was expected of me, who would be my companions then? Newscasters, Rose, and the chief of police.

I watched the ground crew checking beneath the wing. They peered at something for a few moments, nodded to each other, and walked away. One of the men gave the wing a little pat, as if it were his big silver pet. The gesture struck me as being so unconsciously tender, it made me want to know him. I turned away from the window. I'd sensed someone had sat next to me, and when I nodded hello I noticed that it was a fellow my own age and he was grinning broadly right in my face.

"I thought it was you," he said. "David Axelrod, right?"

I had what I like to think is a normal impulse to deny my identity but force of habit had me nodding.

"You don't recognize me?" he said, touching his dark mustache as if to remove it. "Hyde Park High. I'm Stu." He was, of course. He was Stu Neihardt. His forehead was high and as uncreased as the inside of his arm. His hair was dark brown and curly and his eyes swam cheerfully behind his thick glasses. He was, to me, one of those people you know in school but never think of. He'd had, until now, no reality outside of the classes we'd endured together: sitting at the edge of a chlorine-bright swimming pool, diagramming a sentence on the blackboard, banging a tray against a lunchroom table on the day of the schoolwide protest against civil defense drills.

"I can't *believe* this!" Stu said, taking my elbow and shaking it a few times.

"Small world, small plane," I said.

"Going to New York?"

"New York?" I said. "I'm supposed to be going to Denver!" I made a move as if to get up.

Stu smiled openly, with his quickness of feeling and his complete willingness to be amused. "You haven't changed, Axelrod." Even when people mean to be pleasant when they say that, the phrase can't escape its censorious overtones. But far more than the implication that I somehow hadn't managed to mature enough, I wondered if his remark carried the knowledge of what I'd done and where I'd been since the last time we'd seen each other. Our graduation class had been enormous and divided into at least two dozen cliques. I didn't remember who Stu's crowd was and the few people who considered me a friend didn't know Stu. If I was lucky, the last thing he had heard about my life was that I was planning to go to the University of California—I didn't recall what school Stu had chosen; the name Bates College came to mind for some reason.

"So," said Stu, fastening his seat belt and squashing out his cigarette, "what have you been doing?"

"I'm working for a union. I do historical research for the Amalgamated Clothing Workers."

Stu nodded. "Same old Axelrod," he said, with apparent (if not enthusiastic) approval. He placed a new cigarette between his large, dry lips, noticed the No Smoking sign was lit on the panel above our seats, took it out of his mouth and placed it carefully back in the pack.

"You were always into causes," Stu said. "Back then."

"Back then? What are you, Stu? Sixty years old." I made a kind of laugh. "Anyhow, unions isn't a cause." I turned away and looked out the window. We were beginning to roll toward the runway. Is this really happening? I asked myself.

The stewardesses were in the aisles demonstrating how to use the supplementary oxygen, pointing out the emergency exits, and generally preparing us for a tranquil journey. The jet picked up speed, little muted bells rang, and one stewardess raced up the aisle making certain everyone's seat was in the upright position.

"She's not wearing a girdle," Stu told me through the side of his mouth when the stewardess passed. "And the little bitch up there with the oxygen mask isn't wearing a bra. I've been on fifty planes this year and this is the first I've seen of this—no bras, no girdles. They must be fucking the pilots up in the cockpit and didn't have time to get dressed."

"Women don't wear bras and girdles anymore," I said.

"Look. Here comes the midget again. Look at that ass go. That's my favorite."

We were airborne. The jets roared, the windows shook in their moldings, and the altitude turned the world below into a joke.

"So," said Stu, after the take-off, "why you going to New York?"

"Visiting."

"Isn't that where you go to school? You got into Columbia, right?"

"No. Berkeley." I glanced at him. Was he really in the dark or was he merely inviting me to confess? "But I didn't go."

"No shit?"

"No shit. How about you? You go to Bates College or what?"

"Where's that?" Stu asked.

"Oh, I thought that's where you got in."

"No. I'm at Downstate."

This was how Chicagoans referred to the University of Illinois in Urbana. Urbana was only a half hour's drive from my alma mater in Wyon—in fact, some of the Rockville staff took courses at the University. Once, on one of our outings, my parents took me to Urbana to hear Oscar Peterson play in an auditorium that looked like a cross between a gymnasium and a space station. We were of course surrounded by students my own age. They were a serene lot, for the times—Urbana had more fuzzy sweaters and plaid pants than most college towns in the late sixties. I did my best to enjoy the music but my sense of isolation finally degenerated into feelings of true hatred. Rose frowned at me and shook her head and I realized I was scowling so outrageously my face hurt. We left during the intermission, stalking up the inclined aisle like a defeated minority caucus leaving a convention. The trip back to Rockville was a screamer, with me making my parents feel guilty for submitting me to the humiliation of viewing two thousand unencumbered college students, Arthur shouting his apology that was mixed with the implication that he'd known all along it was a bad idea, and Rose exploding into a fury of human pain—accusing me of making the day more difficult than it needed to be, accusing Arthur of hypocritically avoiding responsibility, and accusing the both of us of using any opportunity to conspire against her. "I'm always on the outside. You two want me to feel like a piece of dirt." Sitting next to Stu, with the nose of the jet still pointed up, I heard Rose's voice so clearly it made me shudder. It was summer and her school was closed. I knew she was feeling monstrously alone.

"How come you fly around so much?" I asked. I threw the conversation back to Stu, like a medicine ball.

"Summer job. I work for this guy named Dr. Schaeffer. Ever hear of him? He's the best dentist in Chicago."

"No."

"I mean he's famous. He's been on Kup's show, there's been stuff about him in the papers. He's fantastic." Stu pulled a large attaché case from beneath his seat. "He has his crowns and inlays made by this terrific place in New York. It's right above an art gallery and they're the best in the world." Stu snapped open the case and revealed a dozen or so plaster molds of Dr. Schaeffer's patients' mouths. "I drop these off and they do the rest. While I'm there they give me the crowns they made the week before. Each one comes in a little box, lined with purple felt, like you'd buy a diamond."

I tried to think of something to say and we drifted into silence. Clouds and vapor rushed by the windows as if we were flying through fire. Stu tapped my knee and cocked his head toward the front of the plane. A stewardess wheeled a cart filled with plastic cups, ice, soft drinks, and miniature liquor bottles.

"You like?" he asked with a friendly smile. I wished I knew him better so I could tell him to shut up. I shrugged, creating the impression, I suppose, that I didn't know what to make of the stewardess.

"Say," Stu said, "what ever happened to that chick you were going with? She was the best-looking flat-chested girl I ever saw."

I noticed a slight tension in the muscles around his scrupulously shaved jaw and it struck me with great, sickening force that Stu knew full well where I'd been the past years, knew all about the fire and the trial, and was for some reason teasing me with it. Maybe he was too shy, or too embarrassed for me and the wreck I'd made of my life, to simply admit his knowledge. Or perhaps some old adolescent score was being settled, some slight I'd forgotten. He'd never been treated as if he were terribly interesting or important and I was now conceivably ensnared in his dreary revenge.

"I don't know where she is these days," I said.

"Jade," Neihardt said.

"What about her?"

"That was her name, right? Jade Butterfield. She had that whole weird family. Her father was some kind of faith healer or something."

"No. He was a doctor. He had an MD. He just was into a different kind of medicine."

Stu shrugged, as if I were splitting hairs. "I knew her brother Keith. He was a brainy one. What's he doing now?"

"I don't know."

"He was weird, too. He never wanted to be friends with anyone but then he'd come up to you and say, 'I've been thinking about you. Can we talk after school?' He actually pulled that on me, if you can believe it. And I was stupid enough to go along with it." Stu smiled and shook his head.

"What did he say?" I asked. I felt caught in the logic and momentum of our conversation: it was like being accosted by one of the black kids after school and being taunted and misunderstood into insulting him, at which point you'd have to fight.

"Oh, I don't know. Psychological bullshit. You knew him better than I did. But the weird thing was it made me think he'd been studying up on me behind my back and all I knew about him was he never raised his hand in class but every time he got called on he knew the answer. Where'd you say he was now?"

"I said I didn't know."

"That's how it goes," Stu said, with satisfaction. He looked at me and raised his large eyebrows, inviting me to ask him to share his wisdom.

"That's how what goes?"

"All the great high-school romances. I always thought I was missing out on the best but you see I wasn't missing a thing. You and Jade were such a big deal, right? And now—poof—you don't even know where she lives. Am I right?"

"That I don't know where she lives?"

"No, David. The whole thing. Did you know Kenny Fox?"

"Slightly."

"Well, I see him around. Remember him and Arlene Kirsch? They went steady for two years, she had an abortion because of him, the whole bit. So what does Kenny do when I mention Arlene? He smiles. He can hardly even *remember* her. She goes to college in Florida and they don't even write each other."

"You sound pleased."

"No, it's just interesting. Here's me feeling like Mr. Asshole all through high school because I'm not part of some big romance. Never knowing what I'll be doing on New Year's Eve. Everyone and his brother losing their cherry and me going steady with Mrs. Thumb and her four skinny daughters."

"Sounds pretty normal to me," I said.

"Hey," said Neihardt, his voice sharpening. His aggressions were beginning to show more clearly; it was like ice melting off a pond, exposing the dark, brackish water beneath. "*I* know it was normal. I don't need you to tell me what's normal, for Christ's sake. I'm just telling you what it feels like for someone like me. Who felt so out of it. And who now sees all that shit he felt left out of didn't mean so much after all. I can't believe you're not getting what I'm saying because I'm really being honest with you."

The stewardess was next to us now, asking what we'd like to drink. I asked for an orange juice and Stu said, "Make that two, honey." As she poured our juices, Stu said, "What else you have today, huh?" The stewardess, who was at least five years older than us, began to rattle off the various fruit juices and soft drinks available, but Stu broke in, saying, "No, I was just kidding."

Stu finished his juice in one swallow and pushed back in his seat as far as it would recline. "I remember you two walking around the halls of old Hyde Park High," he said. "Couple of first-class hand-holders. Jesus Christ, you hand-holders used to drive me nuts. I mean, what was it? A school or a fucking lover's lane? You know what I mean? Kenny and Arlene were the same way—worse! One day I'm walking out of trig and goddamned Kenny whips his finger under my nose and says, 'Breathe deep, old pal. I just finger-fucked Arlene.'" Stu made one of those old-fashioned rueful laughs. "High school. Four years of torture. You know the only girl's tits I ever saw for that whole time were Jade's? And that was an accident. It was at the science fair. We were both looking at Marsha Bercovitch's water-pressure project and Jade—I didn't even know her, except she was your chick— leans over to get a closer look and I see her blouse hanging away from her body. So I say to myself, 'Peek in, Stuie, and maybe you'll get lucky.' So I take a quick look and there they are, what there was of them. Like two fried eggs shaking on a plate. And you know the pink part, you know whatever you fucking call that part that goes around the nipple—it was no bigger than a dime and it was wrinkled and tight. Christ. That's the famous Stu Neihardt sex life in four years of high school. You know if—"

I don't know what he was about to add to his little tale. I'd been wondering if I should punch him in the face, but I felt too vulnerable because of my broken parole. Still, if I let him go on, the whole purpose of my flight to New York would be weakened—the reunion with the best part of myself would be that much more unlikely. And so I leaned toward Stu and as quickly as you'd move your hand to catch a housefly I grabbed his lower lip between my thumb and forefinger. He tried to jerk his head back but I had him too tightly. "Why are you telling me this?" I whispered. I turned his lip like the key in the back of a mechanical toy—90 degrees, 120 degrees, a full 180.

He screamed and he grabbed my hand and pulled it loose, but it only hurt him more. He tried to rear back to hit at me but all motion increased the painfulness of my grip. My thumb was slipping a little on his saliva and his noises were attracting attention. I let him go, wondering what he would do to retaliate. But he merely sat back, rubbing his mouth and muttering. He had nothing at stake in fighting me or even knowing me and I'd frightened him.

"Are you crazy?" he asked.

"Could be," I said. The only people who gave any indication of having noticed the flare-up were three nicely dressed old women sitting across the aisle from us. But when I glanced at them, they averted their eyes, moving in unison the way young best friends or sisters sometimes do. Repeatedly, a little obsessively, I wiped my fingers on my pants, trying to fix my attention on the Antarctica of clouds that streamed beneath the silver and orange wing of the jet. My pulse was racing; the violence of my impulses toward Neihardt was still within me, like the sharp end of a splinter improperly removed. I didn't yet know if his remarks were merely gross or if they proved some cunning foreknowledge of my life's condition. But what was worse was the sudden plummet into a fact of my life that I'd been able to absorb up until this point but that was now grown in its immensity: tearing at Stu's lip had been yet another instance of my war with all the world since Hugh Butterfield told me in 1967 that I couldn't see his daughter for thirty days.

And now here I was on yet another desperate mission and what possible reason did I have for not believing that it would lead to more disaster? I'd violated parole, deserted my parents, ditched out on my doctor, and was probably going to lose my job. Was it all for the delirium of love? Was the path I walked flanked by ruin on one side and emptiness on the other? Or was there no path at all and was ruination and emptiness where I was really heading all along? I'm sure it is only the very wicked who think of themselves as Good, but sitting in that seat two miles above somewhere or other, I doubted myself as never before—not my prospects, not my sanity, but the nature of my ineffable, essential self: I was beginning to feel that at my root I was not at all good. It wasn't guilt and it wasn't really shame. I felt trapped and repelled by the person I was.

. . .

We were late arriving in New York, though I don't know why. Perhaps a headwind slowed us down. Stu was still next to me when we landed. Out of his incomprehension of my behavior, or perhaps out of simple boredom, he'd resumed speaking to me and I was grateful for this. Stu's conversation increasingly revolved around his mildly pornographic fantasies—the numberless girls he slept with at the University of Illinois, the dental technician he brought to orgasm by blowing on her clitoris with that forced-air contraption dentists use to dry out your mouth, and all the bars and massage parlors where he persistently tried to heal the erotic wounds of adolescence. He sounded half like a liar and half like a middle-aged man gone mad from too many nights alone, but it was somehow agreed upon that I was obliged to listen to him

As we waited for our luggage, Stu was still with me. He was at the next stage of his approach, which was to invite me to come with him and sample the paid-for pleasures of a certain New York whorehouse. "I haven't been there myself," Stu said, "but a friend tells me it's the best deal in New York. Thirty bucks for everything and no tipping. If you try to give the girls anything extra, they get pissed off at you. It's really supposed to be nice."

Our suitcases came out on the conveyor belt at the same time, his big blue American Tourister right next to my smaller wheat-colored case, an early inheritance from Arthur. My senses were at once blurred and jittery. Why of all the luggage in the belly of that plane did mine have to gravitate next to Stu's? Our bags glided toward us. Stu grabbed his with a possessive snap and I picked up mine gingerly because the night before, when I was stuffing it with as much clothing as it would take, I'd somehow yanked the handle loose and now it was affixed to the case only by a few feet of kite string.

"An antique," said Stu.

"Not yet." I was slipping into a kind of despair. I didn't regret causing him the small pain an hour before but the immediacy of my impulse still frightened me. I hadn't any real idea whether or not Stu knew all about my three years in Rockville—I hadn't had enough control over the conversation or myself to find out. And if he was in the habit of talking about me—his loneliness and sense of revenge made him a likely type to gossip about anyone who'd passed through his life—then it remained to be seen whether my meeting him was another instance of my generally crummy luck. I didn't think he was going to call the department of corrections to report seeing me, but his knowledge made my eventual apprehension just that much more likely. He was, at the least, an eyewitness.

We walked out of the baggage area, slowly, as if we were afraid to part. "Where you staying?" Stu asked.

My plan was no more developed than to go someplace central and find an affordable hotel. "With friends," I said.

"Oh yeah? Who?"

"This guy I know."

"Someone from Chicago?"

"No."

"What's his name?"

I stopped. We were in the lower level of La Guardia. The world beyond the glass doors looked to be the color blue of a gas flame. There was a line of cabs waiting and a few enormous buses.

"What's with all the questions?" I asked.

"In case I want to call you," Stu said with an uncle-ish shrug. "Look. I'm staying at the Taft Hotel. It's near everything."

I nodded. "The guy I'm staying with is named Ben Ecrest."

"What's the phone?"

"I don't remember. He's in the book, though. He lives in the Village."

"The Village sucks," said Stu. "Look. You want to share a cab? It'll be about three bucks each. It's worth it."

"No thanks." I waited for him to do something but he just stood there. "Ben's coming to pick me up."

"Oh yeah? OK. Would it be OK if he dropped me off in Manhattan? Then I could scoot up to my hotel on the subway. I could use the extra money to have fun with."

"If you don't mind waiting," I said.

"What do you mean?"

"He's going to be late. Maybe about two o'clock."

"Well that fucks that. I've got a two o'clock appointment on Fifty-seventh Street. Why's he coming so late?"

"He works."

"Well, why don't you give him a call and tell him you'll come in yourself and save him the trip out here?"

My anxiety was giving way to a great weariness. It seemed that no matter what I said, Stu would have another maddening idea. I was growing comfortable with my lies and my made-up friend; I could have imagined standing there lying to Stu and dodging his questions for hours. "He works. I have no way of getting in touch with him."

"He doesn't have an office?"

"No."

"What's he do?"

"He's a cop."

"A cop? A New York City cop?"

"That's right. Weird, isn't it?"

"Weird? Are you nuts? That's very weird. And he's a friend of yours?"

"He's a great guy. Not what you'd think. He smokes pot. He's a socialist, too."

"Leave it to Axelrod to know the one hippy cop."

I was outfoxing myself, I realized. My phantom pal was sounding glamorous enough for Stu to forget about the plaster-of-Paris teeth waiting for him in their plush cases. I could see him considering waiting with me, pacing before the idea like a guilty man pacing in front of a porno theater, leaning toward the ticket window, pulling away. He looked out through the glass doors. The long line of people who'd been boarding the bus was almost gone now. The driver was boarding.

"I'm going to take that bus," Stu blurted out. He grabbed my arm. "Remember. Taft Hotel. You remember my last name?"

"Neihardt."

Stu looked pleased, even a little touched. "So call me," he said, turning away. "Call me and we'll do something."

I waited a few minutes before leaving. I found a phonebook and looked up Ann's number and address, though I knew them by heart and had also written them down on the back of my library card, which was in my pocket. But it made me feel better to see her name and I went out to hail a taxi with a portion of my confidence and determination beginning to return. I asked the driver to take me to Macy's. I'd never been to New York and had no idea where to look for a hotel—the only hotels I knew were the fancy ones I'd read about and I knew just enough to realize they were way out of my price range. Macy's, I thought, was central and I felt certain there'd be plenty of hotels around. The driver navigated his cab as if he were more accustomed to driving a motorcycle. We sped practically up to the bumpers of the cars in front of us, darted in and out of lanes, and managed to pass nearly everyone on the crowded Long Island Expressway. "You want the tunnel?" he called to me over his shoulder. I didn't exactly know what he meant but I had a foolish horror of being taken for a total out-of-towner so I said yes. At one point, we were entangled in a knot of traffic that the driver could not pass through. To our right was one of those infinite graveyards that cause in us strangers something very close to disapproval—as if so many dead people reflected darkly on the city. And to our left was a big silver bus, its motors roaring, its sides splattered with mud.

After some tiresome, typical mishaps, I finally checked into the Hotel McAlpin. The lobby had quite a few people who looked even more awkward and on the loose than I felt—men

in green pants and string ties, an Oriental woman with a hairdo
that must have been two feet tall, a furtive pair of aging teens
carrying filthy knapsacks, eating Snickers and trying not to be
noticed—they looked more like siblings than lovers; they were
probably part of the last wave of mass runaways and they paced
the lobby not to get away from the elements (it was a balmy
day) but to relieve the foreverness of being outside. In a huge
conference room off the main lobby, the Scientologists were
conducting a personality test for people they'd spirited off the
streets. Shoppers, wanderers, and businessmen who didn't care
to return to their offices sat in folding chairs and answered questions pertaining to their emotional lives while a few grim-looking
Scientology employees paced the room like proctors at a college
board examination.

My room seemed like as good a place as any to commit suicide. I turned on the TV and unpacked. The phone rang and I
lunged for it, my hopes wild and unformed. It was the front
desk. A woman's voice apologized: wrong number. I hung up,
my desolation laced with little threads of paranoia. I took a
shower and while I stood beneath the powerful hot spray, the
thought that finally I was in the same city as Ann Butterfield
took on a new vividness and my heart began to slam so fiercely
that I pressed my hands against the wet tile wall to keep from
falling. "What am I going to say to her?" I heard a voice say,
and I was in a sufficient state of confusion to take a full moment
before realizing the voice was my own.

It hadn't been my plan to waste so many hours but I couldn't
control it. Sitting in my hotel room and staring at the telephone
I was closer to Ann, and to Jade, than I had been in nearly four
years and I was afraid that the wrong response from Ann would
break the spell. Then I was seized by the idea that calling her
would be totally wrong and what I should do was simply appear
at her door. Her apartment was on 22nd Street.

I walked from the hotel on 34th, downtown on Avenue of the Americas. It was not the New York of movies or my imagination. Small stores, some of them permanently closed, others with plain old junk pressed against their sooty windows; Jewish cafeterias mixed in with hardware stores, old men's saloons, and wholesale linen outlets; the streets filled with taxis and phenomenally noisy trucks; the sunlight white, blurry, and warm; the odors of cardboard and gasoline suddenly giving way to eucalyptus and carnation as I passed three solid blocks of flower shops.

I turned the wrong way on 22nd Street and walked west for a while, past handbag and ladies' clothing factories and tiny restaurants with Spanish names lit up in green and red neon. I asked some truckers the way and they pointed me east. My shirt was wet with perspiration, but only partially from the heat. I crossed Fifth Avenue—not the Fifth Avenue of fashion models but the street of toy manufacturers—and continued down 22nd Street, past an occasional young tree and huge, stately buildings that were either empty or filled with small factories. There were no Chicago industries here, no sausages, no steel. Here they made corrugated boxes, flags and banners, and junior miss raincoats. Mixed in was an occasional townhouse with window boxes filled with geraniums and kingly grillwork on the slender windows to keep out the burglars. There was a grubby little sandwich shop and an Indian restaurant slightly below sidewalk level—it was empty except for the staff who sat reading newspapers and drinking tea at a front table. I was at Park Avenue now (and, for me, an utterly perplexing Park Avenue), standing next to a savings bank such as an early socialist balladeer might have sung about—bricks the size of mattresses, the tinkling glow of chandeliers in the high arched windows—and the addresses were climbing quickly and neatly toward Ann's. Looking east, I saw a dark green canvas awning reaching across the sidewalk with her address printed in white. For the entire walk, I'd done my best to keep myself at bay, but now my pulse was racing and I felt a mixture of yearning and dread I hadn't experienced since the day I stood in Judge Rogers's chambers waiting to hear what he planned to do with me as punishment for starting the fire.

Posted in front of Ann's building was a middle-aged man with long graying hair and thick, wire-framed glasses. He was hosing down the sidewalk, and when I passed him he redirected the stream of water just enough to allow me to walk by without getting wet. I was dizzy with anxiety; everything felt dangerous and unstable. The heavy doors leading to the lobby were covered with thick decorative grillwork, the sort I would now call Art Deco-ish but which then seemed creepily fancy. Of course those doors had been opened and closed for decades by young children and enfeebled old people, but that day it took all my strength to push them open—my arms felt as if all the bones had been removed and my blood had been exchanged for scalding weak tea. The lobby was small, cool, and lined with green marble. There were a hundred or so buzzers next to a locked glass door. As I searched for Ann's name, my eyes moving sporadically from column to column, the glass door suddenly opened. It was a beautiful young woman. Her face was at once pale and Egyptian. Prancing excitedly at her side were two largish dogs, an Airedale of sorts and a German shepherd. The shepherd sniffed passionately at my thighs. "Judy!" the woman whispered and yanked the dog's leash. Then, to me, she said, "Are you all right?"

I nodded but a large part of me must have been looking for help because involuntarily I placed my hand on the back of my neck and squeezed.

The woman snapped her fingers and her dogs sat. They were both panting deliriously. "You sure?" she said. "You've got that look."

"What look?"

She raised her hand and cupped it the way you would to swim. Then, as she lowered it again, she made a whistling sound that ended in an explosion.

"I'm all right," I said, glancing away. My eyes landed on Ramsey—7G.

"You're sure? I don't want to come back from the park and find you lying on your back."

Oh my God she's so beautiful, I thought. What's happening to me? She wore wheat-colored pants and a sheer blue shirt with the sleeves rolled to the elbow. Her arms were narrow and hard —long muscles, prominent veins and tendons: you'd have to be half mad not to want those arms to hold you.

"Is there a phonebooth around here?" I asked. It was clear I couldn't just ring Ann's bell; I would have to warn her, give her a chance to avoid me.

"Yes. Right on the corner." She glanced down at her dogs and they stood up, their tails straight up and wagging. I struggled to open the heavy door and we walked out. The superintendent was still hosing the sidewalk. He had the water aimed at a peanut shell, which he powered along the sidewalk and finally off the curb and into the gutter. The dogs quickly licked the wet pavement. "Hello, Rolf," said my companion.

Rolf nodded. "Hello, Miss LaFarge."

She walked with me to the corner and stopped at an old phonebooth. "Sit Judy, sit Steve," she said. She reached into her pocket and pulled out a dime. "Here," she said, putting it in my hand. "Do you want me to stay here while you make your call?"

"No. I'm fine. Thanks, though."

She walked across Park Avenue with her dogs. I watched her walk away, repeating her name to myself and wanting to know her. Though loneliness and aimlessness had led me into a languid, circular friendship with a woman in Warren Hawkes's set of friends, this Miss LaFarge awakened in me an intimation of desire that in an instant made her totally distinct from anyone I'd met or even noticed since the beginning of my exile from Jade. I felt her presence drifting within me like sunlight in a dark wood and I knew that she felt my thoughts as they followed her. It was life as dream, afternoons as eternity, it was all manner of leaps of meaning, all varieties of mental magic, it was the world luminous and transparent once again—just as it was when I fell asleep in Jade's embrace and woke with her hair on my pillow. I dropped the dime into the slot and broke off the dial tone with the first digit of Ann's number. I was still shaking, still sweating and dizzy, but now it didn't seem like dread or confusion; it was the change in gravity as I entered now the first and soon the second ring of the only world I believed in, the only reality I wanted to call my own. It hardly mattered if I should quake or faint dead away; I was in a field of force, of emotion raised to the pitch of physics, and it was rhapsodically larger and more powerful than anything else I'd known, finally and at last.

I didn't remember dialing the rest of her number and didn't hear the phone ring but there was Ann's voice. "Hello?" She always said it as a question, a secret, slightly embarrassing question.

"It's me," I said. It never occurred to me that she wouldn't recognize my voice. "I'm twenty-five feet away from your house. Can I come up? Or would you like to go out for coffee?"

There was silence on her end of the line. I heard classical music in the background and a police car siren that was just then racing north past me, throwing its stuttering red light against the glass of the phonebooth. "Is this who I think it is?" Ann finally said. Her voice was casual. I knew she recognized me and the lack of emotion in her voice both disappointed and reassured me. Clearly, she was not about to weep with joy over my appearance, but neither was she treating me like some armored insect found beneath a rock.

"Can I come up?" I said. "I just came in today. I'm staying at a hotel. I'd like to see you. We can talk."

"I've been having so many *visitors*," Ann said. "Keith's been camping out on the sofa."

"He's there now?"

"No, he went home this morning."

"Can I come to see you, Ann?"

She paused for a moment. "If you like," she said. She waited an instant for my reply and then hung up.

I went back to her building, rang her bell, and Ann buzzed me in. A small wood-paneled elevator took me to the seventh floor. A conventional sense of anticipation told me I should be busy imagining what it would be like to finally be with Ann, or what I would say, but the future stood with its back to me, warning me not to even try to look in its face. The elevator stopped with a slight lurch and I stepped into a wide hall— white ceiling, faded pink walls, brightly polished black floors. Ann's apartment was at the very end. The door was freshly painted white and the doorknob was intricately textured lead, round and as large as a croquet ball. I knocked and waited. There was a knot in my leg muscle, painful I suppose, but I barely noticed; it rose through me like a bubble up the stem of a syringe. I knocked again and finally there was the sound of Ann's footsteps.

She was dressed in a floor-length pale green robe, bordered in a darker green, with those medieval hanging sleeves. Her dark hair was pulled back and she looked at me through large, faintly tinted eyeglasses. She smelled of perfume and her painted toenails poked out of gold-braided slippers. In one hand she held a copy of *Ariel* by Sylvia Plath and her other hand was clamped on her hip. She looked totally self-possessed.

"You know I don't like surprises," Ann said. "And you won't stop surprising me." She didn't ask me in but she moved to the side so I came forward. We were in a long, narrow corridor. The walls were covered with prints and drawings, including a Dutch railway poster that used to hang in the second-floor hallway on Dorchester, between Ann and Hugh's bedroom and Sammy's. That it had survived the fire amazed me.

"You still have this," I said, gesturing toward the poster— it showed a Peter Lorre-ish man opening the door of an olive-colored railway car.

"No. It's not the same one. I found it in an antique store on Second Avenue. One hundred and fifty dollars. I starved for a month but I wanted it."

The hall got lighter as I walked toward the front of Ann's apartment, and when I was in the living room the light was almost overwhelming. The entire south wall was casement windows and most of the west wall was glass as well. The bamboo shades were raised and Ann had hung small prisms that dangled on thin threads and blazed red and green as sunlight passed through them. The floors were wooden and bare. There was a white sofa and three director's chairs grouped around a glass-topped table. Off to one side of the room was a small yellow desk, such as you might find in a college dorm. A red manual typewriter and an open box of typing paper. Bookshelves, mostly empty. It was hard to say where the kitchen was, or if it even existed. Perhaps behind the closed double doors.

"Where should I sit?" I said.

"Assuming you should," she said.

"Yes. Assuming."

"Why don't you look out the windows first? I like to show my view when newcomers arrive."

The view was of a series of slate peaks, the roof of a church. The black slate looked liquid in the sunlight. Beyond the church was a tall white stone and glass loft building with scallop shells and coats of arms carved in beneath each tier of windows. A photographer's strobe flashed like summer lightning from the top floor. Ann stood next to me; she'd always liked showing things to people and then trying to see the familiar through new eyes. Long strands of down stood up on her cheekbones, caught in the light. I felt the beginnings of an overpowering shyness in myself.

Ann glided across the room and sat on the white sofa, drawing her feet up and leaning her chin onto her open palm.

"It's nice here," I said. "Your new home."

"Three hundred and ten dollars and eight cents a month,"

she said. "For this, a pullman kitchen, and a small bedroom. It's insane. I'm always broke. A friend has a place on the West Side, six enormous rooms, for less than I'm paying here. But I'm too timid to live on the West Side. It's so ridiculous, but that's how I was raised, to be afraid to live on the West Side. Do you know Mother used to make a point of telling people she hadn't been west of Fifth Avenue in twenty years? 'I went to hear that Jewish violinist at Carnegie Hall. My, what an adventure *that* was.'" Ann laughed, shortly. "But oh if only we'd had the dough to justify our little eccentricities. But without money it was all so stupid and awkward, like chimpanzees dressed up in formal gowns."

"Ann . . ."

"Sitting at little toy pianos."

"Ann," I said, "do you mind if I sit down?"

She pointed to one of the director's chairs. "Brand new," she said.

"Tell me if you want me to leave," I said.

Ann shook her head. "You're still doing it? Still giving people permission to say what's on their mind?"

I sat down. The chair seemed to give a little beneath me and its fragility made me feel huge, clumsy, and potentially destructive.

"If there's one thing wonderful about you—I mean, just one —it's that I can say anything at all to you, David, and never have to feel the slightest degree of guilt."

"That's true," I said. "Not only now but always."

We sat in silence. I wanted to look directly into Ann's eyes but I knew she found that sort of gesture more pressuring than frank. ("People invade your privacy as if they were helping you overcome a fault.") I fixed my gaze on a section of quilt, blue and pink pyramids in a row, burned at the edges, and hanging above Ann in a rough wooden frame.

"Look familiar?" Ann asked.

I shook my head.

"It's from the house. Maybe we weren't using it during your tenure. It's part of a quilt—all that's left of it—Grandmother gave me when I set off for Bryn Mawr. Very sentimental. I've been defending it like the Grail these past couple years. From Keith. I told you Keith just left here, didn't I? Yesterday."

"Is Keith still the Butterfield historian?" My voice cracked slightly.

"Of course. He brings a portable tape recorder on his visits now and attempts to interview me. I feel like a perfect idiot speaking into the microphone. Immortality without revision? Who needs it?"

I felt my cheeks go hot. Every word she said made her more familiar to me and I was struck with the image of myself falling to my knees before Ann and pressing her hand to my lips—a knight returned to his Queen.

She turned around and patted the glass that covered the quilt. "Don't feel *too* bad about it being burned. It was on its way to oblivion anyhow, like most of what we owned. The only thing was that this was the quilt I had on my bed when Hugh got back from the war. The night he just appeared. He'd been in Baltimore recovering and I hadn't even gone down to visit him. I didn't know *what* our relationship was, or what it was supposed to be. But when he appeared I knew *something*. We didn't even get under the covers and that was the night that sealed all of our fates because that's when Keith was conceived."

"Is that why he wants it? The quilt?"

"Naturally. Evidence. Talisman. Keith's theory is that if I hadn't gotten myself pregnant, then Hugh and I would never have married. And according to Keith this gives me a tripartite role: part son, part father, part husband. Proving, I suppose, that all gall *is* divided into three parts."

A laugh exploded out of me like a sneeze. "That's wonderful," I said.

"I've used it a hundred times, the line, that is. Is that what you meant?"

"Ann," I said. I could think of nothing else to say; my mind was dull gray light.

She allowed the silence to continue. Then: "What brings you to New York, David?"

"You."

What did I expect? For her to hold her hand out to me? To confess that she'd hoped for my arrival? She nodded, as if my declaration concerned only me. Ann's opaque gestures had always, in my eyes, been a sign of her elegance and artfulness. Yet now with my life breaking beneath the weight of my vast load of unexpressed feeling, I wanted her to be less herself and more what I needed. I looked at her and felt myself sinking— and it was like waiting for a cat to rescue you from drowning.

"How could I bring you to New York?" she said, finally.

"I wanted to see you, talk to you."

"Ah. But that's not *me*: that's *you*."

"I don't try and fool myself. I wasn't sitting on the plane thinking you were going to find it easy, seeing me. I've been here since one trying to get the courage to call you."

"That's because you're not in love with me and so you still can remind yourself there's a difference between *you* and *me*. If you were in love with me, if you felt something you'd just assume I did, too."

I bowed my head. I thought I was just lowering my eyes to collect my thoughts but when my head tilted down it stayed there.

"Have you come to quiz me about the others?" Ann asked.

There was no place to be polite and so I said, "Partly."

"And what else, then?"

"To be with you. I miss you all the time and hearing from you makes me miss you more." Finally, I could look up again. Ann's features had softened. She touched her glasses as if to remove them and reveal herself to me, but her hand dropped into her lap and she sighed.

"I'm being mean to you. I feel it," she said. "Covering for

myself. This way if anyone finds out you were here and asks any questions I can recall all the mean and teasing things I said and I'll get their approval. The last thing I'd want to say is I was glad to see you."

"But is that it? How do you feel?"

"Let's see. You already know where Sammy is. You should see him, David. What a solid oak. He's literally the most responsible person I know. I suppose that story about him tearing up the check makes him out to be a hothead . . . but that's not Sammy at all. Sammy always negotiates from a position of strength—quiet strength. He's so obviously blessed; very few people feel as at *home* on earth as he does. Compared to him, the rest of us are like freaky little wayfarers, hangers-on. Sometimes I think the world was made for Sammy and maybe five thousand others to exercise their intelligence in."

"What's Beaumont, New York, like?" I asked. I don't know why I chose to ask that—probably nervousness. I leaned forward, my folded hands dangling between my knees.

"A prep-school town. Dirty river, red brick factory, slanting houses, townies, orchards. And Keith. You know where Keith is, too. I'm not telling you anything you don't know, or half-know. In Bellows Falls. He's got a job in a furniture factory and he's learning a lot and mashing his fingertips as well. He makes chairs, rocking chairs. Strange, from Keith. He never had much interest in building things. I think he started trying to build something when he was a little boy, but Hugh—old helpful Hugh—tore the hammer out of his hands, to show him an easier way, of course, and I suppose it was a symbolic castration since that's my last memory of Keith building anything."

But he was building a stereo receiver the night I looked in from the porch, the night I saw you all . . . the night I set the fire. I looked away, uncertain if Ann remembered this or not, wondering if she was teasing me deliberately.

"Electronic things, once in a while," she went on. "But no birdhouses or rabbit traps, or anything that took saws and hammers. But now he's quite adept. He's built most of his own furniture, too. He lives in a rotten but really beautiful old farmhouse. Keith's idea was to make it the new family headquarters but so far none of us have taken him up on it. He's got a few chickens running around out back complaining about anything and everything and also, wonder of wonders, a full-time lady, a girl from town. Sort of an Ingrid Ochester type, you know, Hugh's girl. Passive, compliant, a little sad, but satisfied with herself and stubborn as a wart. I shouldn't say that. It sounds as if I resent her and I don't, not Keith's girl, I mean. She's very good for Keith and if she's a little drab then so is he, as I've always known. He's very lucky to have someone who cares about him.

"And Jade is well, in school, studying ethology, as of the last time, that is. She's given to changes of mind, threatens constantly to drop out of school and, receiving no objections from me or Hugh, decides each time to stay on."

"What school?"

"*And*," continued Ann, raising a finger to silence me, "Hugh. Hugh is still off rattling around the USA, leading a life of utterly *passé* bohemianism. It's in its last stages, however. Come September they go to live in Utah with this fellow named Whitney St. Martin—or who calls himself that, at least. I'm sure it's a made-up name. He probably has a long and very tacky police record, Whitney. It's an experimental community, set in a hundred or so barren acres. Hugh will be the doctor. The place is called Autonomy House. Did I already say that? Autonomy House. It's for professional people only, drug-free, no alcohol. Teachers, lawyers, doctors, architects, writers, I suppose writers. I think Hugh mentioned there would be writers. Maybe he was including poor Ingrid in that category, though I should think doctor's mistress would be profession enough.

"They'll all live in those Buckminster Fuller–type domes and live the life of professionals in an ideal community. According to Hugh, it's not a think tank but . . . a *do*-tank. Do-tank! It makes me want to commit serious acts of terrorism. Not only the goopiness of it, but Hugh's actually paying for this. That's Whitney St. Martin for you. Each of the carefully chosen and screened professionals is assessed thirty-five thousand dollars for the privilege of living in this white-collar utopia. Supposedly, Hugh will be able to charge people who use his services, but only nominally. And there's a lot of expense besides the thirty-five thousand, which is only an entrance fee. The economics are terribly complicated and I promised myself not to learn much more about it since the little I already know turns my intestines into Belgian lace.

"You see? Everyone is doing quite well. Our independence is—I don't know what to call it. Staggering. I think I'm turning into a Keith; I can't *believe* how seldom we need each other."

"What school does Jade go to?"

"David."

"OK. I'm sorry. I know I shouldn't ask."

"That's right."

"I can't exactly *help* it."

"How convenient."

"It's not that."

"It doesn't matter. I just don't want you to ask. I don't want you to hint or pry. I don't want you poking around or trying to trick me or playing on my thoroughly mixed feelings about you. It's . . . it's very likely that if I did tell you about Jade you wouldn't feel very good about it. But you must realize that, don't you?"

I felt her words like a blow to the face. Injury and humiliation. The helplessness of my circumstances never failed to astonish me; the life of constant emotional peril never lost its peculiar terror. I felt abruptly close to tears. Here at last with Ann, I realized I was only half capable of listening to her. If the deliberate meanness of the sudden mystery she'd created could cause me such pain, where did I ever get the idea that I could listen rationally to the truth?

10

It was understood that my life was not to be discussed. It was, after all, only a mass of loneliness and the least attractive kind of solitude, whereas Ann's was alive with struggle and readjustment.

I had always been more than eager to extend myself and show avid interest in every detail of Ann's life—her first sexual encounter (a young doorman in her parents' apartment house), what she did with the money she made from the first story she sold to *The New Yorker*, why she got the willies whenever she shopped at Marshall Field, and the gauzy waking dreams she had when she was stoned and listening to Vivaldi, some of which inspired her to write haikus onto notecards, notecards that would end up in the trash but not before I was given a chance to read them. I never felt neglected or taken too lightly. In a world filled with people, in a house bursting with visitors, she had chosen to lay out the pieces of her life (delicately, artfully, coyly) in front of me. It was my reactions she courted, my fledgling sensibilities she had selected to interpret the mysteries of her character. I felt immensely privileged; I was certain there were things she told me that no one else knew—she confided in me not so much the depth of her private thoughts as their *tone*. Hugh and others might have known her secrets in more detail, but I was given a chance to learn the exact pitch in which she spoke to herself.

There was nothing about her, nothing that she said (or didn't say) that struck me as anything less than vital. And I didn't study Ann because I was in love with her daughter. I didn't devote myself to understanding Ann as a way of foreseeing the future of my lover's character. I don't think it ever really occurred to me that Jade was going to be like Ann, any more than I thought

I would be like Arthur or Rose. Ann was unique, unduplicatable, wry, secure, haughty, vulnerable, and so explicitly calculating that her every word and gesture, in my eyes at least, was incandescent with significance.

That afternoon and into the evening we talked about her life alone in New York. Until it went bankrupt, her family had run a charity called the United States Foundling Homes, a kind of combination orphanage and vocational school that would have seemed more at home in a Dickens novel than in the sunny USA. It was Ann's father who sped the dissolution of the Foundling Homes—he awarded himself a salary high enough to verge on embezzlement—but it turned out to be fortunate for Ann because it was the recently dead Mr. Ramsey's money she lived on now. Her legacy afforded her $850 a month, and she talked about living on a finite sum, of buying her clothes in thrift shops, pilfering sugar from restaurants, and of living with a general overall material pessimism that turned out to be justified—though $850 every month seemed like a more than adequate sum to me, Ann claimed that she never made it through a month with anything left over. "I haven't eaten on the last day of a month since I moved here." We talked about the prices of things, of shopping at Saks Fifth Avenue and then taking the bus down to the "Jewish Lower East Side" to see if she could find something similar, of sitting in the stratosphere in Carnegie Hall, and having to keep up her payments to Blue Cross. (I interjected that my father's lover had been hospitalized for weeks and that I hated to think what her bills were, but Ann let it pass without a curious tilt of her head.) She talked about the price of typing paper, the price of ribbons, the cost of Xeroxing and postage, and I said I was glad she was writing again.

"I'm glad too," she said. "I've gotten close to selling two of them to *The New Yorker*. They send a very sweet rejection letter. Full of encouragement and such. I would be encouraged, too, if they hadn't grabbed what I sent them twenty-five years ago. It's true what they say about early success: it *is* a jinx."

"That's a comfort to me, at least," I said.

"One of the little quote unquote literary magazines printed a story of mine last month. But no money. Enough glory to stuff a hummingbird, but they didn't even refund my postage."

"Still," I said, "it's great to be published. What magazine? Do you have a copy? Let me see it."

"No. I don't want to. It's not a very good magazine. I don't know why I sent them a story. And it's a terrible story. I did it all wrong. From now on, once *The New Yorker* turns a story down I'm going to either redo it or throw it away. They publish stories that are written the way I want to write."

"I'd still like to read the story."

"But I'm not going to show it to you. I don't even know if I kept my copy of the magazine. They send *one* copy, by the way."

"Can you at least tell me what it's about?" I asked.

"OK. You finally asked the right question. The title of the story is 'Meyer' and it's about you."

I felt a nervous laugh hatch at the top of my throat but I held it down. I suppose I thought she was just making fun of me, but Ann's only form of deception was omission. I covered my mouth with my hand, sick with triumph, electric with hope.

Evening. Ann asked me if I wanted to go out for supper.

"I've got a date at nine thirty," she said. "But it's decidedly not for dinner. I never invite men over to cook for them."

"I'll buy you dinner if we go to a place I can afford," I said.

Ann left me in the front of her apartment while she went to her room to dress. Though the apartment had only two real rooms, her bedroom was separated from the front by a long hall and I felt quite alone. I paced. I looked through one of the hanging prisms in the west windows, trying to catch the flat red rays of the sinking sun. I looked at the books in her shelves, noticed her compact little stereo set and her two dozen records: Vivaldi, Bach, Joni Mitchell, the Beatles, the Fauré *Requiem*. The small table in front of the sofa had a few issues of *The*

Village Voice and an old paperback copy of *To the Lighthouse.*
I tried to absorb the facts of that room. Who was she when she'd
chosen that little Chinese flowered rug? How had she come to
purchase those distinctly non-Butterfieldian director's chairs?
Where did she sit when she read my letters? Where did Jade sit?
Did human presence leave a kind of dust in its wake? Did the
sound of Jade's voice hang like little threads of spider weavings
in the corners of the high ceiling? Were strands of her hair
curled beneath the sofa cushion? If I were a bloodhound or a
werewolf, wouldn't I be able to taste her presence, drink it in
through my omniverous sense organs, even if it had been months
since she'd last breathed in this room?

In my pacings I passed the small kitchen. A beige telephone
was on the wall and hanging next to it a blue leather book. I
stared at it for a moment, without quite knowing why, until I
fully realized this was Ann's address and telephone book and that
within it was undoubtedly Jade's whereabouts, waiting to be
memorized like the combination of a safe. I reached for the
telephone book but thought I heard footsteps behind me. I
stopped and turned—but there was no one behind me and the
apartment, though humming with the noise of the city, was
innocent of footsteps.

"Be with you in a minute!" called Ann from her bedroom.
A new politeness (engendered by the anxiety of bachelorhood?
I wondered).

"Take your time," I said. I occupied one of the wobbly
director's chairs, and crossed my legs. All ready when you are,
C.B.! The punchline of my father's favorite joke. But in my
parents' set they weren't called jokes: they called them "stories."
More dignity in a story. This particular story was about the
third-string cameraman in a Cecil B. DeMille spectacular, and
when Arthur delivered the All ready when you are punchline he
laughed so eagerly, so instructively, squinting his dark brown
eyes, raising his wild eyebrows, and as often as not coughing up
the vapors of a half dozen Pall Malls. Oh gentle geezer!

Ann had changed into a floor-length peach and purple dress, turtle-necked and sleeveless, with a zipper up the back. The material was satiny and the pattern looked like those pictures of crystals taken by an electron microscope. Her hair, shoulder-length and absolutely straight, was parted girlishly in the center. She wore dark blue eye makeup, lipstick, and small gold earrings done to resemble the smiling, beneficent sun in a medieval woodcut. She looked at once spectacular and strange, cheerful and uncomfortable.

"The *nouveau moi*," she said, with the very beginnings of a satirical bow.

"I'm not wearing the right clothes," I said. I was in loafers, black corduroy pants, and a pale green shirt I had to wear with the sleeves rolled because of a stain on the cuff.

"No, don't worry. I'm dressed for later, not for dinner."

She took me to a bar called Pete's Tavern, which O'Henry used to patronize. On the short walk over, Ann pointed out other literary landmarks—the apartment building where one of the editors of *The New Yorker* lived, a small carriage house once occupied by a novelist I'd never heard of, and the former home of Washington Irving.

We sat at a booth in Pete's. A thirty-ish-looking man with thin black hair nodded at Ann from the next table and Ann nodded back, evasively. The waiter was a young Italian wearing fancy tight trousers, a body shirt, pointed shoes, and an old apron. He said hello to Ann and asked, with what seemed to me a touch of irony, "You thirsty or what?"

"Oh, always, Carlo, always," Ann said. "Bring me a glass of your cheapest Scotch and your coldest water."

The waiter looked at me. "I'll have the same," I said.

We finished our drinks, asked for two more, then ordered broiled chicken and a bottle of white wine for dinner. Ann talked about a wine tasting she'd been brought to at the Essex House a few weeks before, commenting on the incredible prices of the wine and the hysteria of the well-appointed patrons as they crushed forward for free samples of rare vintages. "They were like desperate pilgrims competing for blessings," Ann said. Then she raised her glass and I raised mine and we clicked them together with an exquisite *ping* that somehow went right through me.

"I'm nervous about tonight," Ann said.

I nodded, thinking she meant it was because of our reunion.

But she went on: "This fellow I'm seeing later. I have this bleak feeling that he's another dead end. It's a little embarrassing to talk about, but I think it's absurd to keep it a secret. I mean how goddamned *hard* it is for a woman who isn't young but who feels young to put together any kind of decent, satisfying life. Younger men are seldom interested in women my age and I know I don't look a minute younger than I really am—but the things I'm interested in and what I'm capable of put me outside of the men who are of a more suitable age. It's a total mess. And I suppose I've been, well, I don't know what to call it, getting around, yes I think that will do, getting around more than I should. Tonight's gent is an NYU professor and he was born three days after me. But his wife left him a year ago and he's very shaky. He takes *so* much work. I think of him as my part-time job." Ann drank quickly and I kept pace; somehow a second bottle of wine appeared on our table.

"Do you have a girl now?" she asked.

"No. I sometimes see a girl, but it's nothing. It's just for company."

"You don't sleep with her?"

I shook my head.

"Or with anyone else?"

"No one. I want to be with Jade. Being with someone else would be giving up."

"That's so simple-minded."

"I don't care."

"And hopeless."

"No it's not. And even if it was . . . I don't have a choice. My feelings haven't changed."

"I wrote a story—or tried to—about the first time you two made love. But it's much too compromising to submit *anywhere*. I came very close to sending it to you a few months ago. I don't have anyone else to show it to."

"Not Jade?"

"Oh no. She'd never forgive me. Maybe Hugh. But he hates to read my stuff. He says it depresses him." She called to the waiter. "Carlo? What time is it?" It was eight thirty. "We have a little more time," Ann said to me. "Would you like me to tell you the story?"

I nodded.

Ann smiled. "You're not even thinking, but I'm going to take advantage and tell you anyhow. You're not allowed to interrupt me, either."

"I won't."

"OK," said Ann, pouring wine into both our glasses. "It was a Saturday. Early June, 1966. Hugh and I had been out—a rare occasion, as you probably remember. We didn't have friends and we were always too broke to treat ourselves to the standard entertainments like restaurants and shows. We loved music but the only concerts we heard were those free ones in Grant Park, sitting on an old Army blanket under a few smudgy stars with the Chicago Symphony Orchestra fiddling like mad about a half mile away in the bandshell. But this night, your night, Hugh and I had gone to a party on Woodlawn, thrown by an architect who was one of Hugh's classier patients. A pot party, as we used to say. Thanks to you, we were both smoking like pros, so we managed to get very high and hold our own—even though everyone was younger than us. Everyone was always younger than us, it seemed.

"There was a lovely rain falling by the time we reached home. I found you two in the living room, listening to the radio.

You both were in jeans and Oxford blue shirts—you were in the stage of dressing like each other. You sat on the floor, both of you, and a fire was going in the fireplace. Jade in particular was wrapped in the orange and blue light. I remember thinking: Jade reflects the light and David absorbs it. I was still feeling the lovely euphoria of the party and the grass and the two of you looked unbearably beautiful. I stood in the living room grinning, shaking the rain out of my hair, and wanting, I must admit, for you to guess I was stoned.

"Enter Hugh, looking as pensive as a monk in a spiritual crisis. He was wearing his gray suit, the one that was an inch short in the sleeve. God, wasn't he the handsomest man? Shame there wasn't money to dress him properly. Whatever *you* might have thought of him, Hugh looked like a hero—his hair the color of buckwheat honey and his beautiful eyes the color of a bluejay in the sun. But he was no pretty boy and certainly he wasn't chic. His features were broken, but in a good way; he looked like one of those rare men who know right from wrong. My war hero. Well, you read them, the stories I wrote about Hugh when I was in college. Loving Hugh, and even betraying him, made me more a part of my times than ever before—or since. He never spoke about being a war hero and hardly ever complained about what he took out of that prisoner-of-war camp. But that night, that night of the party on Wood-lawn—maybe it was the grass or being with fifty people, all of them younger than us, but Hugh couldn't shut up about his war experiences, like an old man in a VA hospital. He didn't so much talk about his heroism as the discomfort, the fear, and the injuries. Maybe he wanted us to organize a charity ball in his honor.

"Anyhow, in comes Hugh, still feeling mighty herbal. Jade turns and gives him a 'Hi Pappy' with much more nuance than any fifteen-year-old girl has a right to."

"Then Hugh started in on us about having a fire going," I said.

"That's right. He was furious you'd made a fire and you knew no one but Hugh was allowed to work the fireplace but you pretended to be so bewildered. 'I'm in charge of the fireplace,' Hugh said. He thumped his chest—his gestures were so basic. A real man. He made no attempt to hide the nature of his complaint. He didn't say it was June and too late for fires; he didn't say we were almost out of wood; he didn't even mention you guys forgot to put up the screen. He was at the end of a long, loose night and you know he always had a taste for the bare, unpleasant truth—little embarrassing admissions were Hugh's hidden chocolates. So there he is, flat-footed and red-eyed, saying, 'I don't like people making fires in *my* fireplace. The fireplace is the one thing in this goddamned house that *I'm* completely in charge of.' "

"Jade said we were cold," I said.

"And Hugh said you should wear gloves, or sweaters, or go someplace else."

"He was staring at me when he said that. He meant *I* should go someplace else. Home."

"Oh, I'm glad you said that, David. I always wondered if you noticed things like that."

"Of course I did."

"I'm glad. It seemed you didn't."

"Then I said I would leave after the fire burnt out."

"Yes, searching for your advantage and pressing it at the same time. You two did a little more clumsy emotional fencing— you were a lot less agile than you imagined, you know, David— and at one point Hugh put his arm around me, the way men on dates will suddenly make physical contact when they think you might be getting bored. Hugh warned you to be quick getting home and then he and I walked upstairs. God, I loved that house at night, when the windows were black and the children were asleep.

"I turned on the reading lamp on my side of the bed and

Hugh asked me if I planned to stay up. I was reading *The Wap-shot Scandal* and I wanted some time with Cheever and some time to think. My mind was blown from being with so many people and I needed to regroup. Hugh slipped into our enormous bed wearing his shorts, a signal that he was insulted I'd chosen to read. His way of saying I was unworthy of intimacy. I asked him what was wrong and touched the elastic band on his shorts beneath the blanket. He inched away. 'Nothing's wrong,' he said and how I hated to hear his poor injured voice. He turned over and folded his hands over his big chest. He hardly had any hair under his arms and his chest and belly were as smooth as Sammy's. 'I'm lonely around you,' he said. And I said, 'I'm a lonely person. It's contagious.' But what I was thinking was Oh go to sleep, please go to sleep so I can have fifteen minutes alone.

"Hugh started reviewing the people at the party but he was yawning too and I relaxed. I knew it wouldn't be long. Some-where in there, I heard the front door open and then close and I assumed it was you, making your exit. Then I heard Jade come upstairs and go to the bathroom down the hall and I assumed she was preparing for bed."

I had a powerful impulse to stop Ann at that moment. I re-membered myself opening and closing that door, with Jade at my side and both of us giggling like the children we still half were, and creeping back to the living room certain our sound effects had been foolproof. And I remembered taking off my shoes and my shirt as Jade went upstairs, thinking to myself that I would never be so immense and would never forget an instant of that night, and being so right.

"I fell asleep for a few minutes," Ann said, "with the book on my belly and the lamp on. But suddenly I was up, as if a shadow had passed over my face. I heard noises from downstairs. I clicked off the lamp and listened. Twittering floorboards. Squeaks and ticks that seemed more purposeful than the simple breathing of the house. I wonder what I thought it was. Did I really think a thief had found his way into our house? And if he had, what would he take? The magazines? The radio? My chocolates?"

"Stop, Ann," I said, finally. "You're getting too . . ."

"Close?"

"No. Strange. You're hurting me."

"This shouldn't hurt. You remember it all anyhow. I'm telling you what I remember. I remember being in my bed and hearing noises from the downstairs of a house that I don't live in anymore."

Her eyes were bright, alert, but she didn't seem to be using them. They shone like those lights people leave on in empty houses to fool burglars.

"I slipped out of bed and put on my robe, that blue-quilted robe, a winter robe but it was all I had. In one of Hugh's dresser drawers there was an old hickory-handled buck knife—one of his many many boyhood souvenirs—and I thought I'd grab it in case I needed to stab someone. What a laugh. I was making no noise at all, less than a cloud, floating through the bedroom, into the hall, onto the landing of the stairs. It was more like an acid high than marijuana. I could see everything. I had the night vision of an electric cat. The ripples in the wallpaper, the scratches on the banister, everything."

"Including you, the both of you."

"Please don't, Ann," I said. I could feel her dismantling my memory of that night, tilting it, enlarging it, until it was no longer mine.

"Oh stop, don't be so damned squeamish. There's nothing in this that's going to hurt you. And you know there's no one else to tell it to. Are you embarrassed? You explode like a bomb in the middle of my life and *you're* embarrassed? I didn't get very close, you know. I was much too surprised, and scared. I only made it halfway down the stairs and if it wasn't for the fireplace I might not have even known you two were making love. I saw Jade's hands on your shoulders and the tops of her knees, the way they were raised . . ."

I lowered my head onto the table and my arm knocked over my wineglass. Ann righted the glass and continued.

"But the thing I noticed most was your clothes. They weren't strewn all over the place. They were nicely folded. Which meant you both knew exactly what you wanted and didn't have to pretend to mindlessness. Oh, I was so touched by that, you have no idea. I honestly was.

"So up I went and crept back into bed. You never knew I was there. Isn't that so?"

I raised my head. My eyes felt fifty degrees warmer than the rest of my body. I reached out for Ann's hand. "I'm sorry," I said.

"Sorry? What for?"

I shook my head. "For everything. For being at your house that night, making too much noise, making you see us. I don't know."

"Then listen to me, if you are. And think of me getting into bed with Hugh after seeing you and Jade downstairs. I was shaking and my mind was a tornado. I moved so close to him and God did I feel bad he hadn't stripped down because I would have given a lot to feel his nakedness just then. I didn't want to be alone. But you see I must have been radiating desire. Because suddenly Hugh stirred. His snoring stopped and he turned toward me and his eyes were slowly coming open. I touched his smooth, smooth face and he kissed me and when he kissed me I held my breath and I heard the floors squeaking downstairs. Hugh put his hands between my legs and that certainly finished the job of waking him up. I felt ready. For him. We'd been making love for eighteen years and we knew each other's signals like high-wire acrobats—only we were low-wirers and we weren't acrobats. Anyhow, I said I'd be right back and Hugh smiled because this meant I was going to put in my diaphragm.

I walked across the bedroom and down the hall to the bathroom, listening for you two downstairs, and trying not to, and feeling slightly crazy and close to tears.

"And the bathroom was freezing. I was naked and shivering and those glass shelves Hugh put up looked to be bursting with the life of my family—deodorants and foot powders, shampoos, bubble bath, brushes and combs, Stimudents, a plastic frog, those hand-muscle flexers Sammy liked to squeeze when he soaked in the tub. It all looked so immense and beautiful; I stared at it with my mouth open, like a miser gawking at his gold. I *never* felt that way about the family; I wasn't in my normal mind. My diaphragm always was on the second shelf, next to the shampoos, and there it was, as always. Encased in a maroon plastic pouch. I zipped it open, and my heart flipped out. My diaphragm was missing.

"I wasn't confused over this, at least for not longer than a moment. I remembered hearing Jade going to the bathroom earlier and I realized that she'd gone and taken my diaphragm. Before you came along and relations got a little strained between me and Jade, we used to talk about how alike our bodies were and I suppose she figured what was good enough for me would hold the fort for her. And you, Jewish-radical-rock-and-roll-pot-head, you didn't even have the brains or the cunning to carry a Trojan in your wallet. God, David, even Sammy was carrying a rubber around, and he was eleven. Look, I was proud of you, even if you were too stupid to plan. At least you were both too steady to risk her getting knocked up. Good for them! I thought, like a ruddy camp counselor. Yet I had to wince. Quite a world of difference separated my battle-weary cervix from Jade's. It must have hurt like hell and done her no good at all. I mean it was obscene, hilarious, but mostly it was pathetic. I zippered up my little case and then I felt a flash of resentment: how dare she assume I wouldn't be using my birth control! I ran the water over my hands, dried my hands, and I was trembling with the cold and the damp and from everything I was feeling. I made my way back to bed, wondering what I'd tell Hugh.

"If I'd told him the diaphragm was missing, he would have wanted to know why, and then there was every chance of him thundering down the stairs and doing something about it. And maybe that would have been the best thing. Don't think I don't often wonder. If I'd let Hugh in on what I knew about you two, I mean right from the beginning, then maybe everything would have been different. Maybe he would have chased you out of the house. Maybe he could have organized his feelings better when you slowly started moving in with us. He wouldn't have had to wait until it was too late to take control and then suddenly become a father figure and ban you from our house. Then it was too late, but that night if I'd told him—who knows what would have changed? But all I thought about was the preciousness of what I'd seen, the two of you holding each other in the corny glow of the fireplace. I wanted that memory and I wanted it to myself. I didn't want Hugh charging down the stairs. I wanted Hugh to make love to me.

"Which is what he did. We made love and I risked getting pregnant, just as you and Jade made love without any useful protection. What a night of risks! How the souls of the unborn must have hovered over that old house, waiting for the act of inception."

"I wish she *had* gotten pregnant that night," I said and then, surprised by the sound of my own voice and surprised at what I'd said, I let out a sob and covered my eyes. The room was moving, not with drunken abandon but slowly, as if the room really *was* moving, through space and time, as all things of course do but which only mad people see.

"I'm sure you do," said Ann. "But that's your story and this is mine. It changed everything, that night, everything I believed about making love and Hugh. Because it was never complete, you know. I never ever came and mostly I never got close. Only when I masturbated, but never with Hugh. And of course I blamed him—blamed men, not just Hugh, but the boys I slept with before him and when he was away making the world safe for democracy, all of them, and myself too, but Hugh, mostly I blamed Hugh. For being too small, too fast, too eager, too gentle, too selfish. What difference does it make? I didn't even try. But that night, I was on fire. And the image of the two of you downstairs burned behind my eyes. Oh God, I was pornographic, moving beneath Hugh and knowing that beneath the two of us were the two of you. I knew I was going to make it and I'd never be able to blame Hugh again because he was perfect. He wasn't doing anything different; I don't even know if he was fully awake, but he was perfect. There was no hurry. I knew I was going to come. My legs were turning to water and stone at the same time. For the first time in my life, I was truly indiscreet."

Abruptly, Ann was silent. She finished the little bit of wine that was left in her glass and then took mine, but it was empty. She looked exhausted. A slight film of perspiration made the powder on her face look porous. For all the fineness of her features, the straightness of her posture, and the persistent delicacy of her gestures, she looked like an abandoned middle-aged woman in a dark warm bar, known by the bartenders and the waiters, short on cash, lonely, garrulous, and letting go.

"There's a simple law," she said, leaning forward on one elbow and tossing her napkin onto the table. "Whenever you tell the truth, you're also confessing. No confession, no truth."

The waiter had probably been watching us, waiting for a drop in Ann's intensity. He was at our table now, clearing the dishes and making a point out of checking if any wine had been left at the bottom of either bottle.

"Coffee, dessert?" he said. He was looking at me.

"What time is it, Carlo?" Ann said.

His hands were filled with our dishes but he turned his wrist so Ann could read his watch.

"Oh. Ten to ten. I've stood up my date." She looked worried, even a little scared, but then she said: "Good for me! I haven't stood anyone up since I was sixteen years old!"

We walked back to her apartment on the chance that her friend was waiting. When we were beneath the awning in front of her building, Ann said, "I'll faint if he's still here," but I couldn't tell if that would mean joy, surprise, or disappointment. As for me, my own preferences lay buried beneath fatigue and a familiar, yet exhausting, self-envy: the boy who had lived through the evening Ann had described at Pete's Tavern still reigned within me, but, increasingly, he was *not* me. While I still believed the self who had made love to Jade that night was my best self, it also existed as a kind of younger brother whose exploits, whose flights of ecstasy I was condemned to admire with a kind of brittle, helpless awe.

"Well, he's not in the lobby," Ann said. She was walking with a very faint wobble. Every once in a while she touched my arm, as if to right her balance, but there was a shyness in those touches that made each of them noticeable. There was no doorman in sight. Ann opened the door and glanced once over her shoulder. It disturbed me that the habits of caution were now second nature to her. I'd always thought of her as being so safe.

I was feeling lopsided from the wine as well. In the elevator—we stood very far apart—I said, "When we first started smoking grass we never would drink and we put down people who did."

"That's when we were Puritans," Ann said.

"We were Puritans?" I asked.

"Now we'll do anything to get through a night. You know, I don't know *why* I'm going up to my apartment. There's no chance that my friend's going to be awaiting my return. He's not the type—that's the kind of thing *you'd* do." The elevator stopped; the doors hesitated before sliding open. "We should be out somewhere listening to music," Ann said.

The hallway was empty, silent. I was a little disappointed her friend wasn't waiting in front of her door—I would have liked to see him. But my principal emotion was relief. I wouldn't be sent back to the Hotel McAlpin right away.

"I suppose I should call him," Ann said, as she let us in. We walked to the front of the apartment and I sat on the sofa while Ann opened her telephone book to find her friend's number. The sight of that book and knowing that Jade's number was in it agitated me, but by now I'd been agitated for so long and in so many different ways I was scarcely able to notice it. "One ring," said Ann, tilting the phone an inch from her ear so I could hear the ringing as a distant purr. "Two rings. Three rings. And . . ." she hung up the phone. "Free." She reached into a kitchen cabinet and brought down a pint bottle of tequila and two of those thick, narrow orange-juice glasses you see in old-fashioned diners. "The cleanest of all alcohols," she said, placing bottle and glasses onto the table. She sat in one of the director's chairs. "And the most psychedelic. From whiskey comes dreams, from tequila comes visions. It's liquid hashish." She poured a modest, reverential amount into both glasses, picked up hers and left mine on the table.

We drank quite a bit of her tequila. Each time she poured some, Ann screwed the cap back onto the bottle, giving it a good hard twist as if she were going to be storing it away for months. I didn't know if this gesture reflected her material caution or if it was a self-teasing game played by someone with a drinking problem. We also smoked a joint of Ann's grass—specially grown for her in Vermont by Keith, using top-grade Colombian seeds—and I suppose if she'd had LSD or mescaline on hand we would have taken that, too. It was eleven in the night and the more familiar we became with each other the more solemn and mysterious our connection felt.

"Are you still a fledgling astronomer?" Ann asked me.

"I guess not. I'm just in college, finally. I studied a little astronomy when I was in the hospital but there was a limit how much I could get on my own. It's complicated."

"Oh, I know."

"Sometimes I think I'll still be an astronomer. But mostly I don't think about the future."

"Jade used to be so enchanted with you and your astronomy. She really did believe that you were going to name a star after her. I, on the other hand, didn't believe in it for a minute. I thought you were taking her to the Planetarium just to have a place to feel her up and not pay for a movie ticket."

I felt something touch my arm. I looked down but it was just the nerves ticking at the surface of my skin. When I looked back at Ann, her eyes were hazy and a high, warm color was in her face.

We were silent, totally, almost unendurably silent.

Ann poured two more drinks. She smiled and said, "I knew you'd sit in that chair."

"How?"

She sipped from her glass. "Because you knew I'd sit on the sofa and you don't think it would be safe to sit next to me."

"Safe?"

Ann nodded. Her lips were pressed tightly closed, narrowing her face and deepening the lines at the corners of her mouth. "Sit next to me," she said. "I want you to."

I didn't say anything, nor did I move.

"I think about you," Ann said. "All the time. I return to my thoughts of you, my memories, my *ideas*, like a secret vice. You're my hidden imported chocolates. Hugh used to have these old, I mean really old pictures of naked girls he picked up in Europe during the war, and he kept them—who knows? Somewhere in his underwear drawer. He had a yen for those pictures, even with a wife and a houseful of kids. They were his private sex life. After a tough day or a disappointment in the sack with me, he'd fish out those pictures. Never in front of me. Part of the thrill was sneaking it. It was like a kid and his rag-tag security blanket, but much sadder and more desperate, because the older you get the more sad and desperate everything is—not more *serious*, mind you, but more irrevocable." She took another swallow of tequila, a longer one, almost emptying the glass. "I'm rattled," she said. "I don't know what I'm talking about." She closed her eyes. "And it feels so *good*."

"Ann," I said, leaning forward and raising my voice to drown the pounding of my heart and the dark frantic sloshing of my blood, "you have to tell me if Jade—" I stopped; anxiety coated my eyes and I looked at Ann as if through the far end of a telescope. She was shaking her head.

"Sit next to me," she said. "I don't want to sit here all alone."

I stood up. It was like wearing someone else's glasses, those thick spectacles that flash rainbows when the sun hits them from the side. My legs were long and stringy and my head was a balloon nuzzling the ceiling. Ann was a perfect miniature curled with remarkably human expectations on a sofa rendered in all its simplicity.

Yet when I sat next to her she was as large as ever, even a shade or two larger.

"The only things I regret," she said, "and the only things I'll ever regret are things I didn't do. In the end, that's what we mourn. The paths we didn't take. The people we didn't touch."

That's not true, I thought to myself, but I could barely feel my thoughts. I experienced my consciousness as a drowning man sees the shadows on the surface of the water.

"You seem frightened," Ann said.

I nodded, but thinking of it now I realize that nod could have been taken to mean anything.

"I made love to a young man," Ann said. "Younger than you. Not long ago. He chewed his nails. He was thin. He wore a white muslin shirt from India, see-through. I seduced him. Very expertly, if I can be allowed . . ." Her voice trailed off and then she glanced quickly at the black windows, as if she'd seen something. "He was terribly thin and terribly gentle. It was like making love to a butterfly. Too gentle. I hardly knew he was with me. He left in the middle of the night. It was like an erotic dream, except for the little half moons of fingernail in my bed the next morning." She took my hand. The gesture was neither slow nor sudden. It was like someone engrossed in thought picking up a familiar object and absently feeling its weight, its texture. She skimmed her thumb along the side of my hand. "Are you terribly soft and gentle and careful when you make love, David?"

I waited in silence, hoping something would happen that would make none of this true. The scent of Ann's perfume rushed toward me, as if she'd just put it on. "I don't know," I said.

"Of course you know. It's absurd for you to be shy. Not at this point."

"What point?" I said. "I don't know what point we're at."

"We're at the point where I'm asking you if you're one of those terribly gentle lovers. And we're also at the point where we say anything we care to. The mere fact that you're here, David. For so many hours. We're at the point where we admit the only reason we're together is we need someone whom we hold nothing back with. Right now, David, I'm admitting that to you right now."

She carried my hand to her face and pressed it to her cheek. She closed her eyes and nuzzled against my hand and I leaned toward her and kissed her half on the forehead and half on her hair.

"I need to be with you, Ann."

"I knew this would happen," she said. She opened her eyes and I took my hand away from her face. "I think that night, the night I came down and saw you with Jade and then made love with Hugh, I was making love with you, wasn't I? You know, everyone thought we were lovers, you and I. Not then, not from the very start, but later. I often ached with curiosity to know how you explained yourself to poor Jade."

"She asked me once. She asked me and I said it wasn't true."

"Well, I was flattered," said Ann. "That the others were finally recognizing I could do such a thing. And that a boy like yourself, you know, certifiably insane with love for such a pretty little girl, that you'd want me. You know, whatever you said to Jade about it didn't stop her believing it. It must have been a very tepid denial. And that made me believe you liked the others to suspect us and I was glad for that."

"But Jade knew I could never be with anyone but her."

"But that's not so at all, David. She always believed you and I made love. Sometimes she thought it only happened once and other times she was sure we sneaked away together whenever we had the chance."

"No," I said. "She never believed that about us. She brought it up only once. It was nothing. I remember it very clearly. It was a beautiful day. We were sitting on the Midway. Jade was wearing sandals, brown shorts, and a sleeveless blouse that buttoned in the back, big tan buttons just the color of her hair. I was a little nervous because you could see in her blouse from the side, at the bottom of the armholes."

"I'm sure you remember everything," Ann said.

"No, wait. Listen to me. Jade had her head on my shoulder and when a breeze came up, her hair touched my face. We started talking, about what it would be like when we had kids and I said I'd be very jealous of the baby for having its whole body inside of her. And then she said—and this was so casual, it was right off the top of her head, it seemed—'What's going on between you and Mom?' And I said I liked you, or something like that. Then she lifted her head off my shoulder and looked me right in the eyes and she smiled and said, 'Did you ever fuck her?' And I said, 'Fuck her?' but really loud so it made us nervous and we laughed. Then Jade said, 'Well, did you?' and I said, 'You've got to be out of your gourd. You better tell me what you've been smoking because I'm going to try some as soon as we go home.' And then, and this was the last of it, this was all she said, she said, 'So you never made love with her or saw her naked or anything?' I don't even know why I answered her seriously, but I did. I shook my head and said no, never. And that was the end of it."

"Except it wasn't," said Ann. "It never ended. Jade still believes we were lovers. Even the last time I saw her with the whole family together, or what we call being together these days, which is something very odd and altogether . . ." Ann fell silent and rubbed her eyes. "Oh God," she muttered to herself. Then fixing her reddening eyes on me, she said, "I'm sorry. I'm unraveling. What I'm trying to say is Jade still believes we were lovers. At Keith's a couple of months ago she brought it up in the most remarkably naked and ugly way. It all hinges on the fact that you and I had a secret bond. We were emotional conspirators. Lovers. Whatever Jade thinks of you, David, and I don't know and don't want to, but when she said she knew what was going on between us, I mean a few months ago, it was like living in Chicago, standing in the old kitchen. Only now, with everybody a little more bruised and callused, no one tried to smooth things over. They all joined in and they all let me know that they believed *then* that you and I were lovers and they believe it *now*. Jade was so relieved she actually wept—and you know how she is about tears, how hard it is for her to cry. It meant she wasn't crazy, that the whole terror wasn't the work of her imagination and her unconscious. They *all* agreed." Ann took my hand again, gently now, with nothing casual or accidental, and absolutely nothing unconscious; she moved my thumb away from the bulk of my heavy, moist hand, moved it until the tendon stretched and began to hurt.

"Don't misunderstand me," she said.

"I don't want to misunderstand you," I said.

"Everyone thinks we're lovers, or were, so maybe we ought to do them the favor of making them right," Ann said. She waited for me to say something. Then she said, "I'd love to go to bed with you. I'd love to feel you in me."

She was so close to me and her bravery alone made me want to hold her. And hearing that she wanted me inside of her made me want to make love. Yet it was alien for me to think of a woman so much older than me in sexual terms. I had never loved an older woman. I was not one of those eight-year-old boys who want to marry their mother. I had never had a crush on a teacher, never stared longingly at a friend's older sister, and wasn't interested in movie stars or even those naked models in the skin magazines. They were too old and I was blind to them. The most erotic photograph of my early adolescence was from a *National Geographic* article about the Seychelle Islands and it was of a half-naked African girl walking along the beach—she was just my age or perhaps a year younger.

"I could never go to bed with you, Ann. I could never do that."

I shook my head. I wanted to put my arms around her and I wanted her arms around me: I was in terror and I wanted her to protect me.

"I think you're misunderstanding me," Ann said. "I'm not doing this because of what they said. It's you. I want you. I want this night with you."

"I want to be with you," I said. "I've been in agony for half this night but it's heaven anyhow because it's here, with you, and this is my real and only life. But I can't do the other. Don't laugh at me for saying this, please, but I can't make love with anyone until I see Jade again, until I can be with her. It's very difficult but it's the only way I can do it. It would be worse if I ever went with anyone else. It would put me further from Jade than ever. You know, it's not even loyalty, probably, it's fear. I have to wait."

Ann's hands were closed into fists and she rested one on

either leg. She was flushed, no longer looking at me. If she wanted to hurt me, it was the perfect time to tell me of Jade's lovers, and I waited for the worst, already telling myself that it wasn't necessarily true, that Ann was only speaking out of spite.

"I should be angry," Ann said.

"No."

"Yes. I should be. I should be furious. It's elementary, my dear Watson." She stopped, closed her eyes, amazed she had made light of herself. "This is what all anger is. Being denied. Not being held. Not being satisfied. This is war and mayhem and I should be in a rage. I'm so sick of myself. I'm *still* waiting for life to begin."

"I better go," I said. My heart was pounding; it felt frail and absolutely out of control. I felt very close to dying on the spot and not at all concerned.

Ann got up and went to the windows. I wondered if she was going to do something horrible but she seemed calm.

"I'll go," I said, standing. The blood that raced to my head was thick with stars and slashes of colored light. "I'm sorry about tonight. I'd like to call you tomorrow. That's what I'll do. But I'll understand if you don't let me—"

"It's late," Ann said. I could see she was looking at my reflection in the window. "And you don't know your way around." She turned toward me, her arms folded over her chest. "Sit down," she said, and when I did she walked past me and down the hall.

She was back in a moment carrying a pillow, sheets, and a pale blue blanket. "Get up," she said.

Ann smoothed the sheets onto the sofa. She was squinting, furrowing her forehead, and poking savagely at the corners of the sheets. I stood by, saying nothing. She was finished in a minute. "That's where you'll sleep. You'll be in good company. We've all put in our nights on this sofa." She stepped back and looked down at the sofa, remembering the people who'd slept on it.

"I've got pajamas. They belong to Keith and they'll fit you. Do you need them?"

I shook my head.

"One rule. When I get up, you get up. I write in the morning so it'll be toast, coffee, and goodbye."

"OK."

She nodded. The circles beneath her eyes were royal blue and the texture of crushed velvet. She was looking directly at me now, inviting me to meet her steady, open gaze and come to some silent understanding of what we'd just been through. But I didn't have the strength to fight my evasive impulses. I glanced from side to side and when I did fix my eyes on hers I wasn't really seeing anything. The only part of me that was worth calling alive was by now seething with a very simple thought: in moments I would be lying on a spot upon which Jade had lain.

Ann went to her bedroom. I couldn't tell if she'd closed the door or not. I heard a long unzipping sound but not much else. I turned off the lamps and sat on the edge of the sofa and undressed in the dark. The sheets were cool and softer than any I'd ever touched. The blanket felt like cashmere and when I pulled it over my shoulders the feel of its satiny border touched off a memory of a cell meeting at my parents'. I was very young and on my parents' bed, where the comrades had dropped their coats. I was caressing the satin lining of someone's coat. I'd just learned the word *grand* and I repeated to myself, "This is grand." Other memories. Coming fast and unbeckoned. Glimpses of things I'd seen years ago. The view from my room in Rockville. Christmas decorations on State Street. The images came in no order and I wasn't trying to remember or understand. It felt as if a part of my brain was shorting out.

I didn't want to think, yet I didn't want to fall asleep too quickly. I wanted to be awake on the sofa Jade had slept on. I rolled onto my stomach and held the pillow close, so it touched me from my lips to my belly. The blanket had slipped half off me but I wasn't cold. The room was very warm and the only reason Ann gave me a blanket was she remembered I liked to sleep with some weight covering my body. And how Jade sweated through summer nights with me, steaming with me beneath the blanket through a long martyring July.

I was crushing my genitals as hard as I could against the sofa and I turned onto my back. The room was slowly brightening and I wondered if it was getting near dawn. No. The windows were still slate black. I got up on one elbow and looked down the corridor toward Ann's room. I couldn't see the door but I saw the light from her room, coming out in a thin, pale wedge and stopping about ten feet from where I lay.

Like any visitor, I'd heard a hundred strange, small sounds since I'd turned off the lights. Sounds from the street, from the wall, and I knew enough to pay no attention. But now, I heard a sound from Ann's room. She was dialing her telephone. Slowly at first, with pauses between each digit, and then faster and louder. The clicking of the dial was like tiny footsteps racing from her to me. My first thought was that Ann was calling the police. She was going to tell them that someone who the court had ordered to keep away from her had broken his parole and was now sleeping in the living room.

I held my breath. There was silence in her room. Silence and more silence. The phone was ringing on the other end of the line. It couldn't be the police; they pick up right away. I heard Ann shift in her bed and then I heard her murmur:

"Hello, Jonathan. It's Ann. I'm waking you."

A few moment's silence, and then Ann's voice again.

"I know it's late. But I'm still awake. I am very much awake. . . . Please. I'm sorry. I didn't call up to argue with you. I know it's very late. You know I don't do these things. You should know that I was worried about you. . . . I didn't know if you came when I was out. Or maybe you decided not to show up after all. . . . It is? Oh. Well, I'm sorry-glad. . . . Jonathan. You're way off target. I'm going to show you how uncomplex

I am. Are you listening? I want you to get in a cab and come down here and make love to me. . . . Yes. . . . Do I *sound* drunk? . . . No. I'm not scared, I'm just lonely. But I didn't call because I'm lonely. I called— . . . Oh Jonathan. You're so well trained. Everybody knows what time it is, Jonathan. And we are all acutely aware of your commitments tomorrow morning."

She hung up. A moment after that she turned off the light.

But a minute or two later Ann turned the light on again. She picked up the phone and began dialing what I guessed was Jonathan's number. Don't do it, Ann, I said to myself. Please don't do it.

In the middle of the fourth or fifth digit, with the dial still clicking in its arc, she dropped the receiver into the cradle and turned off the light, this time for good.

A moment after that, I was unconscious. The last thing I saw was the change in the windows: the glass had turned a flat grayish blue.

II

The next morning I was up long before Ann. The windows were brilliant with sunlight; the dust on their outside looked like a kind of electrical gauze. I crept about like a burglar, wondering if I should leave immediately. The bathroom was halfway between her bed and the living room and as foul, discolored, and weak as I felt I didn't want to take even one step in her direction. I dressed and slunk into the small kitchen to wash.

I'd forgotten that Ann's personal phonebook was hanging next to the kitchen phone. Next to that was a pad of notepaper and a felt-tipped pen. I gave myself a moment to reconsider the small social treachery I was about to commit and then, after turning on the hot water and adjusting the faucet so the cloudy steam would hit on the quietest part of the sink, I opened the beige leather phonebook and paged it open to B. There were no Butterfields. I turned to J and there it was, Jade, your phone, your address, my first new knowledge of you in four years. I tore off a page of the notepaper and wrote using my hand as a desk. My handwriting was almost illegible; it looked as if it were reflected in a broken mirror. But in scrawl, in pieces, in lunatic peaks and valleys I recorded what I needed. Had any jewel thief with a bagful of diamonds felt greater exhilaration than mine? Had any skydiver tumbling free through the sweet ether of space felt less subject to the normal rules of life on earth? You were in Stoughton, Vermont, living on a street called West. There were three phone numbers next to your name, all written in different pens, at different times. Even then I realized this meant that you were often away from your home, but the agitation this caused me was nothing to the exhilaration of being closer to you than I'd been since the last time we touched.

I wondered if Ann was staying in her room because she was waiting for me to leave. I couldn't tell from the sun what time it was but I was sure it was at least noon. I stripped the sheets and blanket off the sofa and folded everything as best I could. Then I looked through *The New Yorker*, pretending to myself that I was looking for a good jazz club or a terrific play. Next to my return ticket to Chicago, my only assets were ninety dollars. I owed the hotel at least twenty and though I already had much more than I'd expected the trip to bring me, I was quickly plunged into despair at the thought of having to leave New York because I was out of money. I continued to flip through the magazine, glancing at the cartoons and squinting at the ads: fur coats, ruby bracelets, Scotch that advertised itself as the most expensive in the world. It amazed me how much money other people had—truly astonished me, as if it was the first I'd heard of it.

I must have drifted. My fatigue had been pretty much untouched by my few restless hours of sleep so perhaps I dozed off for a moment. I remember thinking of what it would be like if Jade and I had a lot of money. Would we spend it all on ourselves? Give it away? Start a foundation that would award grants to people who wanted to stop everything else in their lives and live by the most romantic, unreasonable impulses of their hearts? A monastery for lovers, though of course not at all monastic. The thought was, to be sure, far from profound, but it had a great many tributaries and perhaps I was paddling my way down one of those when Ann entered the room. I hadn't heard her wake, hadn't heard her footsteps, but when I turned away from the glarey windows she was standing at the foot of the sofa, dressed in blue jeans and a red silk shirt.

"How long have you been up?" Ann asked, in a rather sharp voice.

I was certain for a moment that if I'd had any sense, any real idea of how the world worked, then I would have damn well made sure that I was out of there before Ann woke up.

"A few minutes," I said.

"About last night . . ." said Ann.

Don't say it, I thought.

"It's OK, really," I said, too quickly.

"Look, if I was Hugh's new girl I'd write it all off on the stars. Ingrid likes the astrological explanation. Venus goes into one phase and she's unfaithful. Mars bumps into the moon and she throws a stapler at Hugh." Suddenly, Ann sneezed, a most diminutive sneeze, gentler than a cat's. "Oh God, my head. I doubt I got three hours sleep."

"You don't feel well?"

"I'm not involved with how I'm feeling." She covered her face and rubbed her eyes with her fingertips. "I was a harpie last night, no, a Medusa. Finally, I owe *you* an apology."

"No. We don't need to explain to each other."

"I was being mean. I want to explain one thing. About Jade.

I think I wanted you to believe that she never thinks about you, never mentions you. For some reason, I thought I wanted you to feel absolutely shipwrecked. But the truth is she does think about you still. Don't take this in the wrong way, David. I mean I'm quite sure she wouldn't want me to talk about it with *you*, but I think it's fair that you know. You haven't faded from her . . . her memory. And maybe that will be consolation for last night, for me putting you on the spot like that."

I struggled to get up from the couch; my legs were wayward and weak. My deepest impulse was to put my arms around her, in gratitude, in fellowship, but instead I placed my hand on the side of her face. Her skin was soft, amazingly soft, and my fingernails were uneven and lined with dirt. She almost pulled away from my touch but she stopped herself.

"I'm going to kick you out now," she said.

"For good?"

"For the day anyhow. It's ten o'clock. I'm going to work." She gestured with her eyes to the table that held her typewriter.

"Can I call you later?"

"I can't imagine where we can go from here."

"We can have dinner."

"We had dinner yesterday." She shook her head. "OK. Call me. At six. I want you to. But be prepared for me to give you the brush, OK? I'm still half catatonic and I don't know what I'm going to feel about last night after my tenth cup of coffee."

As soon as I was back in my hotel I took off my dirty clothes, brushed my teeth, and sat naked on the bumpy white bedspread with Jade's phone numbers in front of me. I picked up the phone and gave the operator the first number on the list. I didn't want to waste any time. I was still sluggish from the night and absolutely high from finding the numbers: there would be no time when I'd be less apprehensive about making the call, less capable of a second thought. I heard whoever ran the phone in the lobby of the McAlpin dialing the Vermont number and the throaty clicking of the turning dial filled me with rapture.

Her phone began to ring. In a panic, I almost hung up, thinking *You must be out of your mind*. Someone picked up the phone on the third ring, a woman, and said hello with a cheerfulness as vivid as the taste of an orange.

"Is Jade Butterfield home?" I asked.

This is Jade, the woman answered in my imagination, and the thought of it sent my heart soaring upward: my throat throbbed like a bullfrog's.

"She isn't here," the woman said. "Can I take a message?"

I called the second number and let it ring a dozen times before acknowledging it was trilling away in an empty house. Then came the third number, and this time I was answered by a young man who sounded as handsome and relaxed as the first woman had sounded friendly.

"I'm calling Jade," I said. "Is she there?"

There was a pause—memory of heartbreak? cuckold's aphasia?—and then he said, "I don't *think* she's here. You want to hang on? So I can check?"

"Please." He seemed genuinely doubtful whether or not she was there, though I couldn't say if this meant her presence was in question or if she might not be accepting calls.

"Who's this?" he asked, the voice friendly and motiveless.

I hesitated. "This is Dave," I said. Dave? Who was that supposed to befuddle? That wasn't a mask; it was a false nose. I listened to my intermediary's footsteps disappear on the other end of the line and imagined him walking through an enormous slipping-away Victorian house, not unlike the Butterfield house in Chicago but much larger, and intersected by drafts, with mattresses on the floor, Marx Brothers posters on the walls, and cartons of milk name-tagged in the Korean War refrigerator. Ah: one of those informal, nonideological college communes. A bunch of great guys and gals pitching in and saving on the rent.

"She's not here," said handsome Sean, or Philip, the commune's champion kyacker. "I didn't *think* she was, but you never know with Jade."

"Oh," I said, in an amazingly dead voice, as if my throat was lined in brick. "When will she be in? Do you know where I could reach her?"

"She *might* be at the music barn. I don't know. She was *supposed* to go to that thing at Sophie's farm but I *think* it was canceled."

"God." It was too amazing: music barn, Sophie's farm, the boy's voice. I was hovering over Jade's life like an errant, misled ghost, rattling the shutters in the wrong window. How could I have made this arduous journey and still be without her?

"Do you want to leave a message or something?" he asked.

"Yes," I said, but left it at that.

He waited—I don't know how long. He had a healthy respect for the unspeakable.

"This is a friend of hers," I said. I seemed to have wandered back to the beginning of the conversation, like a nervous rat in a maze. I was sprawled on my back, holding the phone with both hands and staring at the texture of the paint on the ceiling. It looked like chicken skin. "You have no idea when she'll be back?"

"No," he said softly.

"But this is where she usually stays, isn't it? At this number?"

"Who *is* this?"

"Dave. I told you. This is Dave."

"But who *are* you?" Well, I knew those long tender sessions that must have taken place at the commune, just as they did at Rockville, those conversations that alternated between anecdote and lament, and it was my foregone conclusion that the name David Axelrod was familiar to that handsome sentinel at heaven's oak door.

"Oh, I'm an old friend of hers. A friend of the family." It seemed both risky and unkind to leave a true message. I didn't want her to come home and find my name thumb-tacked to the communal bulletin board. "I'll get in touch with her later."

"I'll tell her you called, Dave."

"No, that's all right." I wanted to warn him not to, but seizing on a bit of strategy with all the subtlety of an opera tenor plunging a knife into his breast, I said, "It's no big deal. I'll catch up with her."

"OK," he said.

"Don't even mention anything," I said.

"OK, Dave. A friend of the family."

"No! That's the whole thing. Don't even mention it." I thought for a moment and was seized from behind by what seemed a rather brilliant idea. "Dave's not even my name," I said.

"OK. Who *is* this?"

I very quietly hung up and kept my hands on the phone, just as I did when I was in Chicago and allowing myself just a few calls a day from my list of Butterfields. A wave of futility came over me, followed by an equally powerful wave of humiliation. It wasn't until I placed the phone on the bedside table and buried my face in the cool, barely yielding pillow that I remembered this hadn't been one of my ordinary long-shot phonecalls: I'd just been very close to Jade; I still had the phone numbers; I still had an address; and I was loose in the world and unstoppable.

I showered and rang up room service and had them send me French toast (what Hugh called "lost bread"), ham, orange juice, and a pot of coffee. I had a wedge-shaped view from my window and I watched the Saturday shoppers ten floors below streaming past me like the world viewed from a box camera. How beautiful it all seemed . . .

I read the newspaper as I ate breakfast like a man with a stable life. Despite the agonies of expectation, I felt I sat in the lap of towering luxury. I ate as slowly as I could, read as slowly as I could, and would have liked to have tied sandbags to the hands of time. Since the day of the fire I had wanted no more of time than for it to move swiftly and humbly along, like a nun in the rain, but now my life had texture again.

I noticed in the newspaper that *Krapp's Last Tape* was being performed that night in a small theater on the East Side. It was my favorite Beckett play and I remembered that Ann liked it, too. Tickets only cost four dollars and I could actually afford to attend. Impulsively, I called Ann.

"Sorry to interrupt," I said. "But I was wondering if you'd like to see a play tonight?"

"Not really. Hugh called."

"That's good," I said. I don't know what I meant. I might have been feeling all of us coming together again.

"Hugh's in town with his new girl," Ann said. "They went to Chinatown. They're buying spices and oils. She's also going to introduce Hugh to a healer, a Chinaman much older than the century, who's going to divulge certain secrets of herbal teas. She's so much better for him than I am."

"So are you going to see Hugh tonight?"

"No. They're going back to New Jersey. Where I'm sure they belong." Ann laughed; she sounded edgy and she was poking around trying to locate the exact dimensions of her sadness, jabbing at her feelings as if with a stick.

"And you don't want to see *Krapp's Last Tape?*"

"I don't think so."

"My treat?"

"I said *no.*"

We were silent for a moment.

"So should I still give you a call around six?" I said.

"Only if you want to," answered Ann.

Suddenly restless, I left the hotel and headed for the streets.

I wandered uptown on Fifth Avenue starting at 34th, gazing into the generous-looking windows of electronics shops that featured pocket cameras, battery-operated tape recorders, and short-wave radios. While somewhere near, across the street, or perhaps next door, Hugh and Ingrid were smiling uncertainly at a small circular window with eight-inch glass behind which stood a miniature red wagon that held a pair of diamond and emerald earrings. It was their mild misfortune to have the tastes and appetites of the rich and to suffer the wanting of things they couldn't even remotely afford—whereas I walked the same street and noted that the carved Mexican chess set could be mine if I wanted it, likewise the Austrian binoculars, and likewise the Japanese setting for eight, with soup bowls and a covered dish, painted my favorite shades of blue and yellow, and marked down from thirty-five dollars to nine.

I could explain this so much better if I'd lived in some other time, if the story of my love was a true ballad, if I could shake my fist at the sky and believe *not* that I was gesturing at layers of ozone and oxygen, at chunks of mineral and pockets of gas, but at *heaven*, at a real heaven, alive with intelligence, churning out time and circumstance.

I was walking up Fifth Avenue to pass an hour or two before it was time to call Ann. Hugh was with his new lover remembering the things he'd been taught to want when he was young. Who knows how many people were out there with us? A million seems a fair guess. New York is the place in America where you're most likely to meet someone you know; it's our capital of surprise encounters. If you stay there long enough you might see everyone you ever knew.

I'm thinking of a skeleton bent expectantly over a radar screen and Hugh and I are blips of light heading into each other's path with the blind imperiousness of comets.

We are blind to the future. We can barely hold on to our strange versions of the past. We see only a little of what is directly before us. We know almost nothing. The only way we can stand it is not to care. I care and I can't stand it.

I should just breathe in and out and be brave. But not know-ing what is going to happen next and living with the hope that whatever it is it won't be too difficult to understand is like driving at top speed with the windshield completely painted over with a picture of where you used to live.

I had been looking in the window of the Doubleday Book-store. I was thinking of going in to buy Ann a book. It had once been a common thing for me to bring her things to read, trading her a copy of *Jews Without Money* for *The Good Soldier* or *The Subterraneans* for *Strait Is the Gate*. We were so entertained by our differences. And I was thinking that a part of that pleasure might be recaptured if I brought her a book. But nothing on display in the window seemed right for Ann and I couldn't think of anything I'd read recently that I wanted to give her. I turned around and I saw that across the street and a little to the north was Tiffany's. Jade and I once saw the movie *Breakfast at Tiffany's*. We'd skipped school and watched it at the Clark Theater in downtown Chicago, and when Audrey Hepburn went searching for her cat in the rain Jade and I sat sobbing in that empty theater, squandering our emotions with the abandon of drunken pirates reeling through port with a sack full of gold.

I thought that I would go and take a close look at Tiffany's. If I saw Jade soon, it would be something I could tell her about. I walked to the corner and waited with about fifty other people for the light to change. I was folded into the crowd and feeling poorly dressed. In Chicago, a city of blondes, I always felt dash-ingly Semitic, but here in New York, surrounded by men in dark suits and inkwell eyes, by women with huge spreading mantles of electrified black hair, in that mass of silk ties and jewelry, I was overwhelmed by the classiness of Manhattan and had the hick's reflexive comeback: Are these people *for real?* It was in the middle of the day and I could have been standing in the lobby of the Opera House. As subtly as I could, I glanced from face to serious face, at the large noses that were displayed like genetic trophies, at the furry eyebrows and four o'clock shadows, at a powder blue beret, a shaved head, a teenager with a red velvet yarmulke.

And then I happened to let my glance drift to the other side of the street where a knot of pedestrians just like the one I stood in was waiting for the light to change. And there was Hugh, standing at the edge of the curb and staring directly at me. Next to him was a tall woman with reddish braids wearing a sleeveless shirt and a denim skirt. She was holding a shopping bag and looking straight up into the sky. I followed her gaze and saw a small plane expelling gauzy smoke and sky-writing a message: and H, an O, a V . . .

There were so many responses available to me.

The light governing north-south traffic was still green. I cut through the crowd and crossed 57th Street, heading toward the fragrant green blur of Central Park. Though I knew, essentially, it wasn't so, I told myself that Hugh hadn't seen me and that I'd be doing us both a favor if I got out of his way. I moved with my head down and I moved quickly. I was almost running.

Hugh bolted after me, cutting diagonally across Fifth Avenue and 57th Street, coming at me like an arrow. Ingrid shouted out to him, as she would tell us later: "Hugh! What are you doing?"

And here comes the taxi cab, gunning ahead to make it through the yellow light, because cab drivers are always in an acute hurry. That's how they make a living.

I glanced back once to see if Hugh was following me. He was, of course, and I tried to make myself stop but I couldn't. My legs were committed to cowardice. I told myself not to look back again, just to keep going straight and fast. The sidewalk was crowded; it was like a Christmas crowd.

Everything was noisy and dense but the sound of those brakes couldn't have been more penetrating if I'd heard them in a concert hall. I stopped in my tracks and turned around and saw Hugh just the moment after the taxi struck him.

He was in the air, sailing backwards in a northwesterly direction. It looked like a stunt. The taxi cab was going up an inch, back an inch, starting and stopping and bobbing up and down as if in seizure. No one was saying anything and Hugh was in the air.

Then he was on his back, but still moving, shooting along as if he were on a sled. His arms were spread at his side and his tan jacket was riding up and bunching at the shoulders. He was turning over, in a broken, graceless motion—now, for the first moment, it looked serious and out of control. He turned on his right shoulder but his head didn't move and his legs were going in two different directions. It looked like he might break into pieces. And now another car was slamming on its brakes and another and another. For the first moments after the cab hit Hugh, his body had been skidding in its own lane, between the east-west traffic on 57th Street, but now that was no longer the case.

It probably didn't matter. The taxi that hit him was going fast and it hit him direct. Hugh was probably already dead, or on his way toward death. But a green florist's van hit him a second time. It wasn't even a hit. The little truck rolled over Hugh and ruined the top part of his lifeless body.

Did the sky turn red? Did the sun even hesitate in its stiff rounds? The world, even along the dense strip of Manhattan, seemed utterly calm. People turned slowly, quietly; faces wore that perplexed, slightly absent expression you see in the lobby after an *avant garde* play. *This* is it? You tell *me* what it means. It was as if we needed a second look to confirm what had happened. And then the image of that man being tossed like a sack of meal by that cab completed its frantic loop through our senses and we did see it again. The long moments of waiting were over, the synaptic reprieve canceled, and now the first screams, the first shouts, the first hands clapped over unwilling eyes—we were suddenly a terror-struck herd staggering toward the street, stepping on each other's heels, elbowing each other, afraid to look too carefully at any stranger, and each of us hoping that someone would know what to do.

But no one knew what to do. No one ever does. We were just moving toward the point of impact. Then I saw Hugh get up, but that didn't happen. Someone in front of me dropped a pretzel, one of those big brain-sized New York pretzels, and I stepped on it accidentally. Someone else dropped a newspaper. People were dropping things.

"Oh Jesus," I heard someone say, "don't look. Please, sweetheart. Don't look."

I was half on the curb, half in the street. All traffic was stopped. Five blocks down, cars were blowing their horns. There were dozens and dozens of people in front of me. No one was screaming "I'm a doctor!" No one was asking us to make a path. It was all right just to be standing around like a total idiot.

I felt for a moment as if I might lose consciousness and I could imagine in that instant what it would be like to be beneath the feet of the crowd. I thought of a high heel in my throat's hollow.

It was not even Hugh anymore. Hugh had passed out of that ruined body and . . . he was standing next to me. No, but the man standing to my side, leaning into and not feeling me, wearing one of those straw hats you expect to see only at racetracks and a yachtsman's blazer, had a bit of Hugh in him, it seemed to me. An earnestness in the sea green eyes, an impassiveness that allowed you to project your most heroic fantasies. Maybe Hugh's spirit was everywhere around us, floating through the air like debris after an explosion, and we were all absorbing parts of it. But that's what you always want to think when someone dies.

I moved closer. No one put up much resistance. Those who were closer than I to Hugh's body had no will to defend their position.

From the other side of the street, Ingrid Ochester was making

her way. "He's mine," she said, in a voice far behind her grief—
the tone was declarative, slightly embarrassed. She seemed to be
apologizing for her connection to the disturbance, like a baby-
sitter whose ward has toppled a department store display. "He's
mine," she said over and over. She was waving her large hands
in front of her, slapping abstractly at anyone who didn't make
way for her. She looked like someone in a garden who is being
attacked by a swarm of black flies. As she staggered over the
curb and was almost upon Hugh's body, Ingrid's knees gave way
and, making no effort to stop her fall, she landed on her palms
and knees. She was planted five or ten feet from Hugh, though
by now the pool of blood beneath him had spread out and she
was on its rim, staring down into it as if to see her reflection. I
was standing on Hugh's other side, ten or so feet from his body.
Three other strangers had also made it through the crowd and
we existed now within that dazed sphere of onlookers, as if
caught in some ritual dance, surrounded by faces.

"Don't touch him," a voice said to Ingrid. But when I turned
to look at the cop who'd made it through the crowd and was
now taking control, I saw nothing but pedestrians, and when I
turned back to Ingrid she was kneeling in Hugh's blood, stroking
his hair back from his eyes. Her loosely braided red hair dangled
in front of her and her denim skirt was red and wet with Hugh's
blood and now her hands were red too and her face when she
touched it. She was saying something—to Hugh, to me, to
everyone—but I don't know what. I was watching Hugh run
after me. I was Hugh. The cab hit me in the chest and I fell
forward onto the hood, but the cab kept coming and the velocity
threw me backward. I went flying and when I hit the street I
kept moving. The bones in my chest were broken, and when my
head hit the street a piece of it fell away, like a chunk of an old
jack-o'-lantern. But the worst part was the skidding backward,
the tearing of my skin: it was the most familiar pain, the
stupidest and the most ordinary. It was like rolling in hot shat-

tered glass, though I don't actually know what that would be, and I knew this, this pain that filled the last instants of my life like a fierce hideous chord at the end of a symphony.

The driver of the florist's van that had run over Hugh got out of his truck. He was a huge fellow, a muscle man, in a white undershirt and tapered black pants and an Elvis Presley hair cut. He pressed a handkerchief onto his forehead, blotting at the little pinpoints of blood that seeped through the scrape he'd suffered when his large head knocked into the windshield. He was stopped a full hundred feet beyond Hugh; it had taken that long to stop after running him over. The driver walked in an odd mincing gait, as if he were wearing his little brother's shoes. He was looking at Hugh and shaking his head: it seemed so inconceivable to him that he'd suddenly been thrust at the center of a man's death.

"Look what happened!" Ingrid was saying to the driver.

"Stand back, stand back," someone else was saying.

Hugh moved slightly, though probably not. I was crying fairly hard by now and the world trembled before me like so much jelly on a spoon.

"Oh look," said Ingrid, in the voice of a mother showing her child a nest of newborn sparrows. The driver of the van had stopped his advance toward the body. He was shaking his head and glaring at Hugh's body, wondering, I suppose, how that alien sack of blood could have been dropped before his wheels, exploding in the center of his consciousness, threatening his job, taking food off his family's table.

"Don't touch him, don't touch him," someone was saying. I turned around. A tall bearded black man wearing a sailor's cap was pushing his way through the crowd. "Make way, goddamnit, make way." He looked terribly competent, relaxed, trustworthy—perhaps someone who'd learned first aid in the Navy, or the mysteries of ancient healing on a distant island. The black man placed his hands on my shoulders and gently moved me out of his way. He pointed to Ingrid and said, "You got to give him room to breathe, darling."

Ingrid shook her head and smiled at the man. "How can I?" she said. She indicated Hugh's body with a shrug and now for the first time I looked closely at what it had endured. The length of it was covered in blood; it looked more like a casualty of war than an auto accident. In the center of his body, Hugh's clothes seemed to float, like leaves in a stream. His arms were thrown over his head in angles that unbroken bones could never have described. The darkest strip of blood was right at his throat; it seemed that the wheels had run over his neck, and if we were to try to lift him we'd risk separating his head from his body.

The black man trod workman-like through the blood and crouched at Hugh's corpse. Ingrid held onto this stranger's arm, half to keep him away from Hugh, half to connect herself to something living.

"He's dead," the driver of the van said. He was standing next to me.

"He was dead when you hit him," I said. "A cab hit him first."

The driver of the van nodded.

"He's breathing," the black man said, looking up with a radiant smile. It had never even occurred to me, until that moment, that he was out of his mind. "Does anyone here have a silver dollar? Or anything that's unalloyed silver?" He thrust his long bony hand out. "Give me silver," he said in an entirely reasonable voice.

Ingrid got up slowly. Her eyes were half-lidded and her lips were parted: a combination of shock and nausea.

"This man is alive and I can save him," the black man said.

Ingrid shuffled away, shaking her head. When she turned to face the black man again, she was standing next to me. Sweat was pouring off her; her breath wheezed at the back of her throat.

"Be careful," I said. "That guy seems crazy."

"That man," she said, pointing to Hugh. "That man is my husband." She closed her eyes and I took her arm.

"Life is eternal," the black man was saying. "It cannot be terminated. It dies from neglect because we are ignorant. The spark of life is an electrical charge that can be rejuvenated over and over if we act with God's speed." He was kneeling in Hugh's blood, supporting himself with one hand resting on Hugh's hip bone, and emptying out his own pockets. "I have no silver coins. I'll use three dimes." He placed a dime on both of Hugh's eyes and a third dime in the center of Hugh's forehead. Though the top part of Hugh's face was unmarked, he was bleeding from the skull and his honey-colored hair was growing dark, from the center out, like those flowers that are stained most vividly at the stamen.

In fifteen minutes it was over. An ambulance finally arrived and took Hugh's body to a hospital where it could be pronounced dead officially. Newspaper photographers arrived and took pictures. There were a couple of reporters from a radio station, a TV station. Two cops arrived on scooters. The driver of the taxi—who hadn't ventured out of his cab yet—and the driver of the van were both put into the back seat of a police car, though I couldn't tell if they were being arrested or simply questioned. Ingrid rode with Hugh in the ambulance. Passers-by were asking the original witnesses to fill them in on what had happened. Someone in a baggy suit was marking off in chalk the area on 57th Street where Hugh had lain. Within a minute car wheels were rolling right through Hugh's blood. It was a busy time of the day and there wasn't time to clean it up.

I heard what the witnesses were telling the police and there wasn't anything I could say that made any more sense. The person to worry about was that fellow driving the cab, but everyone said that Hugh bolted out into the street and it was clear that the cab driver wasn't going to be blamed.

One of the cops asked if any of us had a statement to make, if we'd like to step forward as witnesses. One woman wanted to talk about the black man who'd put the dimes on Hugh, but that poor fellow had disappeared when the sirens were upon us and the police weren't interested in him. Someone else wanted to complain about how long it had taken either a squad car or an ambulance to arrive. I was shaking quite a bit. I don't know if tears were on my face but my eyes were full enough with them to make it hard to see. When the cop looked in my direction I glanced down and as subtly as I could turned around so that my back would be to him, as if I was looking for a friend or a public clock.

I set myself adrift through the crowd of onlookers and then into the stream of people walking up 57th Street who hadn't seen Hugh lying on the street and who had other things on their mind: I joined the incurious who had better things to think about than those squad cars and their flashing lights.

There was nowhere to sit down. If I tried to stand still and catch my breath I'd be hit from behind, walked over. I was walking west; there were too many people for me to see what was in the shop windows.

I wondered if he'd said anything to Ingrid before setting off after me. Had he said, "There's David Axelrod"? She hadn't even looked at me; she didn't seem to know who I was.

I had, I suppose, already decided to keep my part in Hugh's death a secret. I hadn't worked out any of the details. I wasn't even thinking about it directly. My only calculation concerned Ingrid: I was a stranger to her and she hadn't really looked directly into my face. Even if we were to meet at some future time, there was, I thought, every reason for me to hope that she would never be able to retrieve the image of me standing on that corner as all the life drained out of Hugh.

I was walking down the Avenue of the Americas. I stepped off the curb and raised my arm for a taxi. It was five thirty. I was going to call Ann in half an hour.

12

"Am I calling too early?" I asked, as soon as Ann picked up the phone.

I had the air conditioning running in my room and I was under the bed covers with my clothes on.

"No," Ann said. "I'm glad for an excuse to stop. What's wrong? You sound strange."

"I fell asleep," I said. "I'm just getting up."

"Well, you sound dead. Why don't you ring back when you've finished waking?"

"I'm up," I said.

"Believe me, you're not. I'm going to smoke a joint and listen to one side of my Erik Satie record. That gives you twenty minutes to take a cold shower or do some calisthenics. How long were you asleep?"

"Most of the afternoon," I said. The first lie was complete now. I sat up in bed and looked around the room. I had committed myself to a mean and dicey strategy and I felt that lie as if it were a weight tied to my leg and dropped into a bottomless pit: you wait at the edge and watch the rope uncurl.

"Good," said Ann. "I rested too. We can make it a late night if we want to."

"I'll come over in about an hour," I said. I didn't want her to suggest we meet somewhere else. I wanted Ann at home so someone could call and tell her about Hugh. The police? Ingrid?

But by the time I reached Ann's, she still didn't know. It was seven in the evening and the darkness's only presence was in the lengthening shadows. Ann was dressed in striped seersucker pants and a boyish shirt. Her hair was wet and combed straight back and her face was paler than before and her lipstick darker. She'd been writing all day and that's what we talked about.

"I can feel myself getting better," Ann said. "I can hear my own voice now. I mean, I sound like myself when I write, and later on I recognize myself in a way that pleases me and surprises me, too."

"Would you show me something you've written?" I asked. I was sitting on the sofa, rocking back and forth.

"You seem so nervous," Ann said. "It's about last night?"

"No."

"Maybe we should talk about it, though. I'd like to let it rest, but you seem . . ."

"No," I said, but it didn't matter because now, finally, the phone was ringing.

"Ah!" said Ann, rising. "Opportunity. Fame. Romance."

Ingrid. She was calling from a phonebooth. There was something she needed to discuss with Ann and she didn't want to do it over the telephone. Could she come over? Right away? Yes, right away.

"What a peculiar mystery," Ann said. "My guess is she wants to look me over, which is, if I recall, a common symptom of the matrimonial virus. Listen to me! I feel so cocktail-in-hand ex-wifey. But I feel such an advantage over Hugh's new girl. With her hushed little voice and the bogus drama: she *so* wants to make an impression."

I made a move to get up and Ann started in her chair as if she'd just remembered I was there. I wondered if she had any idea how nervous she was.

"Where are you going?" she asked.

"I'll come back later. I'll call in an hour or so."

"No. Stay right where you are. We'll make up a name for you, if that's what you're worried about. I like my little illusion of superiority and I don't intend to cancel it out by letting Hugh's girl find me all alone on a Saturday night. My generation places great mystical emphasis on Saturday nights and I know that's the first thing Hugh will ask her, if I was alone. Let him think I was with some young hip man. It'll do us all a lot of good."

And so I waited with Ann, in a position so profoundly false that the highest pitch of madness could not have felt more strange. Of course, it was not the first lie I'd told in my short, evasive life, but it was by far the most enormous. This was no social lie, no defense of my privacy, and this was in no way on a par with the careful deletions I made in my monologues with Dr. Ecrest, or my upbeat progress reports to Eddie Watanabe. The lie I'd told to Ann loomed over, darkened, and then devoured all the truth that was in me. The popular expression is "living a lie" but you don't live it, you live *in* it, the way you might live in a cave.

I thought suddenly, sickeningly, with that sense of relief that slows the racing heart by stepping on it, that there was a good chance no one would ever guess my part in Hugh's death. Only Ingrid could connect me to that moment, and with a gambler's feverish keening prayer—it moaned through me in a fretful, spacy tone, chanting like a man at the top of a mosque—I begged the future to make Ingrid innocent of all knowledge of me. Of all she'd seen that afternoon—Hugh's race into the path of that cab, the black man with his dimes, the driver of the florist's van dabbing at his forehead, the refraction of the sun off the policeman's spiral notebook—I hoped that my face existed in her memory only as so much kindly vapor. My lie, my need to remain near the wounded core of the Butterfields' life, my slow way back to Jade—everything finally depended on Ingrid's not recognizing me, the way a smuggler's run, months in the planning, depends finally on a heavy fog for its success.

Ann seemed so adamant that I meet Ingrid and so oblivious to my terror in waiting with her that thirty times in as many minutes the thought came revolving into my consciousness that Ann knew everything I was trying to hide, that her talkativeness and her coyness were only bizarre and costly strategies, like those deadpan psychological gambits private eyes run in movies to force a suspect's hidden hand. She drank a glass of white wine and placed one on the table in front of me.

"What shall we call you?" she asked.

"My name?"

"We'll make one up." She reached behind her and switched on a delicate wooden floor lamp with a small flowered shade. "I know I'm bullying you, David, and believe me I know this is sick, but I do want to handle it this way. I have this terrible feeling Hugh's led his new girl to believe I'm some frosty old celibate, and even if I'm correcting the image under *false* pretenses—" she overemphasized the word *false*, or so it seemed— "I think I have that right." Her glass was already empty; the wine seemed to have disappeared without her having once raised the glass to her lips. "We'll call you Tony. That's a good one. It sounds well bred *and* frightfully proletarian. Hugh will turn it over in his mind, I think. And really, David, you don't have to say anything. I'll just introduce you and you can leave. But say you'll be back. I mean, don't make it appear that you're off somewhere. I'll owe you a favor, if you want. Will you do it?"

Ann got the jug of white wine from the kitchen and began to pour it into my glass before she noticed I hadn't drunk any yet. A little oily puddle formed around the stem of my glass as the wine overflowed.

"Oh, I *am* nervous," she said. "Ingrid coming to see me. Our little charade. I *always* get caught in my lies, too. I admire successful liars—I mean right up and over the edge of envy. My stories would be so much better if I could lie more easily. But I drag the actual facts of my life around like that poor man in *Madame Bovary* with the metal foot."

The living room was dense with dead heat; the open casement windows brought in the noise of traffic and a faint gassy breeze. The down above Ann's lips was shiny from the heat; her skin looked moist, stimulated; her hair refused to dry. I felt coated in sweat from my scalp to my legs; when I touched my throat, my hand came away wet.

And then, finally, the buzzer was rung from the downstairs lobby and it fired off in the long hallway of Ann's apartment. The bulk of my fear had passed. My nerves seemed to have collapsed from exhaustion. When I heard the buzzer I sat forward and took hold of my wineglass. I had an impulse to ask Ann not to answer the door. But that was all: my decisions were made; my life was going on without me.

"Horrible thought," Ann said, getting up. She put her hand over her mouth and looked at me. "What if she's brought Hugh along? Or if he's bullied his way in." She shook her head. "That's all we need. Right?"

She picked up the old-fashioned black intercom and said, "Who is it?" I took a small sip of the wine. "It's her," Ann said to me. "Sit where you are. When I come back, I'll sit next to you." She shook her head and said, "I'm positive I'm going to regret this."

In a few moments, the elevator brought Ingrid to the seventh floor and Ann was waiting for her with the door open, leaning against it with her hands behind her back like a teenager. Ingrid wore clothes nearly identical to those she'd worn that afternoon: a sleeveless white shirt with pearlized buttons and a denim skirt. Her legs were bare and she wore sandals that had been repaired with string and tape. She carried a huge leather shoulder bag embossed with the face of a smiling avuncular moon. Her hair was no longer in braids but hung straight down to the middle of her back; indoors, it didn't look nearly so red.

"Come in, come in," Ann was saying, in a voice that meant to be cheerful but sounded merely insistent.

There's a moment in Joseph Conrad's *The Secret Agent* in which an anarchist explains that he has wired his entire body to an enormous charge of explosives and if any policeman tries to bring him in he will detonate himself, avoiding the dangers of arrest and interrogation and killing a cop or two as well. All that is involved is tripping a simple mechanism, and in five or ten seconds—a fatal explosion. But the time waiting for the explosion, the listener wonders, the long heavy seconds—wouldn't you go mad just waiting? Yes, the anarchist says, thoughtfully. Yes. But what difference will it make? As Ann and Ingrid made their way to the front of the apartment and I sat rigidly perspiring on the sofa, I felt as if the lever had been pressed that would explode my life—not in five seconds but at some elusive point in the future, and I would be waiting until then with fate ticking away in my belly. Would I even know when my life had finally been ruined? Ingrid pointing at me would not fully accomplish it—after all, I hadn't seen Jade in years and I still thought of us as inseparable. All the blame I deserved and a good measure of what I didn't would not end my life, would not even—and this is what was most fearful—change it. I would still be the same person and still want the same things—I would only have much less of a chance of ever having them. The same passion and no real chance: that was the kind of madness I seemed to be heading toward.

Ann sat next to me and Ingrid took the seat Ann had been occupying before.

"Can I get you a glass of wine?" Ann asked, after making herself comfortable.

I was looking straight at Ingrid. If she was going to recognize me, I wanted that moment now. Her eyes were dark brown, with tan and lavender hollows beneath them. She had the withdrawn, composed look of someone who is easily offended, someone who must prepare herself to meet people, someone who suspects others wish to cheat her. Ingrid's nose was narrow and direct, red at the flares, and the freckled hands that she folded into her lap trembled uncontrollably.

"This is my friend, Tony," Ann said. Her voice held a measure of uncertainty suspended in its center like a haze in a gem. Ann was poised for some balletic contest of wits and the letdown of seeing Ingrid in that chair, exhaling wet, broken breaths and searching for words as if for childhood memories, the sight of her would-be adversary in an already vanquished state left Ann in confusion and agitation. Yes, Ann's voice faltered and thickened and took on a poignancy that had nothing to do with the impression she had wanted to create—I think that in all the most important ways she already knew that Ingrid had come to her with vile news.

"I guess I'd better be going," I said. Ann took a deep breath, as a way of reminding me. "I'll be back in half an hour," I added. I was going to say something on the order of "I know you two have a lot to say to each other," or some such social piffle, but I knew full well that everything I would say and hear would be in my memory permanently. I turned to Ingrid and nodded, then reached down and laid my hand on Ann's shoulder. "I'll let myself out."

"No," she said, springing up. "I'll let you out. I have to, oh, lock the door." She touched me lightly—and I suppose conspiratorially—on the elbow and we walked down the hallway to her door. Ann followed me out and pressed the button to summon the elevator for me.

"Whew," she said. "Not at *all* what I expected. Hugh talks about her as if she's something out of the Tarot and then he sends me *this*. Tell me, really, the truth I mean: aren't you getting very *down* vibes from her?"

"She's upset," I said. The elevator appeared. "I'll call in a little while," I said. The elevator doors closed behind me. The small car started with a lurch, and then foot by foot I was sinking.

I walked down Park Avenue. I thought I would go six blocks and then turn around. By then, surely, Ann would have known and maybe I could be of use. Walking quickly, my mind a fearful void, I kept as far from the street as possible. The sound of the traffic was petrifying: more than once I had the impulse to simply sit on the sidewalk and cover my ears. The taxis in particular seemed not only dangerous but sinister. I couldn't understand how they drove so far through the heavy traffic, passing on the left and right, breezing through stoplights, using their horns instead of their brakes. I was standing in front of Max's Kansas City, a restaurant and bar a few blocks down from Ann's apartment. I remembered hearing or reading something about Max's, but I couldn't remember what. Mick Jagger, Andy Warhol. Something like that . . . I thought of going in, ordering a drink, but the largest part of me had already decided differently. I was turned around and heading back toward Ann's, first at a slow trot, then I was running.

I pressed the little black button next to Ann's name with my full hand and may have buzzed a half dozen other apartments, but it was Ann's voice that came through the intercom.

"Hello?" I could tell nothing from her voice.

"I'm early," I said. "I came back early. Is it OK to come up?"

"But only for a minute," Ann said. She buzzed the locked glass door open and I pushed my way through, leaving a perfect handprint on the glass. With a crook's instinct, I wanted to stop to wipe it clean. I made a passing swipe at it with my shirtsleeve and then I resolved to tell the truth to Ann about my part—my small or large part—in Hugh's death. I would tell the truth and escape from my lie, I thought, just as a prisoner might daily resolve to grab the guard by the throat and steal the keys to freedom.

She was waiting for me at the elevator and her eyes were swollen like bubbles. Irregular red streaks covered her face and her hands were closed into tight fists. "Hugh was hit by a car," Ann said, just as soon as the elevator doors opened.

I stood where I was. I placed one hand on the top of my head and covered my eyes with the other. If I was trying to manufacture a reaction I'd gone too far, because she hadn't told me the worst yet. But I wasn't acting at all; the shock I felt was real. It was the first time I had heard the truth of what happened that afternoon said in a voice that was not my own. Hearing what happened from Ann was like the difference between seeing your face in a mirror and seeing it in a photograph.

The elevator doors began to close; I hit them with my fist and they hesitated, wavered, and opened again. I came forward and took Ann by the elbows. "Oh God, Ann."

"This afternoon. He's dead. Killed. Dead on arrival. He never knew what happened. No suffering. All that heart and vanity gone in an instant."

"Oh, Ann."

"Well come in, OK? Ingrid just left. She went to the hospital to make a death mask of him. I felt like spitting on her but I suppose she has more of a right than I do. A death mask. Who wants a death mask? I mean what sort of person? But he was more her business than mine, when he died. Christ, David. Come in. Sit with me, OK? Be my witness."

She let me into her house, slammed the door behind us, and burst into tears. "Oh shit," she said. "Here I go, here I go." We were standing in her narrow hallway and I put my arms around her. "Everything's giving way. I don't want to feel this, I don't. Hugh. My Hugh. Hit by a car. The poor thing, David. Shit. He didn't want this to happen. He was still so damned *interested* in everything. That's what I feel so sad about. It's not for me. But poor Hugh enjoyed his life so much. It's like a child's death. No, worse." As she spoke her voice became clearer, as if she were climbing a summit of reason. But now, perched atop it, she flung herself off in one grand, perilous phrase: "And you know I loved him so much, still. There'll never be a man I can love like Hugh." And with that, Ann sealed herself into an atmosphere of wild grief that held us both through the evening and into the night.

Ann's grief was like what I had known of love: it increased itself; it wound its way to its very source. She wrung her hands and her sobs cracked in her throat with the sound of great falling trees. "I am unequal to this," she said, more than once, but of course she wasn't at all: she was immense in it. I had, until then, loved and admired her with an incompleteness that bordered on blindness. I had been idolizing her evasiveness, her control, and the soft satin distance she seemed to keep between her feelings and her responses. I was already too old not to know the difference between personality and character, but seeing Ann at the peak of her towering sadness I realized I was seeing her for the first time. The revelations of the night before—the confession of having watched me make love to Jade; the wobbly attempt at seduction in this very room—were immediately reduced to anecdotes. This, now, was Ann as she really was: savage, helpless, eternal.

Ann wept and I wept along—for her, with her, and for and with myself. I was too dominated by my secrets to be set free by grief: I remained always aware of the hierarchy of sorrow and knew that it would be wrong if my tears exceeded Ann's, or even drew attention to themselves. But Ann spiraled only deeper into her feelings and I knew my own sobs would not intrude on hers. I lowered my face into my hands and cupped my hands to keep the tears from falling on the floor. I don't know why. The weeping was like ceremonial breaths, such as might be used by a Taoist, and the afterburn of all those tears filled me with a vapor. My sobs grew louder; the tears overflowed my hands and ran down my shirtsleeves. And then I was sitting next to Ann on the sofa, sitting close to her with my arms around her, holding her to me and letting her cry on me, with my cheek against the back of her hair and my tears falling drop by drop onto her shirt. She held my forearm, and as the sobs broke inside her, she dug her fingernails into my arm: it was as if she were in labor. But as tightly as she held me, I don't think she really knew who I was or if it mattered at all. Her hold on me was contact at its most true and elemental: like two lone wolves huddling together in a blizzard, we grabbed each other and held on to life.

"Such a stupid stupid death," Ann said. "They were standing on the corner of Fifth Avenue waiting for the light to change and then Ingrid said he bolted off—not even across the street. Diagonally. It was like a suicide but I'm sure it wasn't. He resented waiting with everyone else in the crowd. It was Hugh's terrible, infantile arrogance. A free spirit. That was his idea of independence—you know, leaping over fences, walking on the grass, picking the flowers in the park and burying his big nose in them, ordering things that weren't on the menu. That was always Hugh's special stupidity, this doing things his own way. Remember how he used to say, 'I'd rather do something *my* way than the right way'? He hated customs and rules and he hated stop lights. And so that's what happens. Goddamnit. It's not a man's death. A man doesn't get knocked on his ass crossing the street. And now I have to call his children and tell them that their father didn't know enough to keep himself out of traffic. And now his mistress is at the hospital trying to talk someone into letting her make a death mask. I'm sure they won't let her. They're waiting for someone official to come in and make arrangements. That'll have to be me, I suppose. The ex-wife. This would be a lot easier if we were still married.

"I didn't want the divorce in the first place. I told him I'd give him one in a minute if he wanted to get married but there was no reason to do it just to live separately. I would like to go to that hospital as his wife and take care of everything. I don't know if they'll even listen to me. I might have to get his brother Robert up here from New Orleans. I can't ask Keith to do it— he wouldn't be able to. Maybe Jade. I don't even know where she is right now. Off camping. Lake Champlain. Oh Christ. What I really want to do is go to bed. Or throw myself out of the window. I don't want to know what this is going to feel like tomorrow."

I sat there almost immobile, breathing deeply, with my eyes attentive through a film of tears. I wanted only to be solid, to be a wall between Ann and the chaos. All the guilt was mine to feel, every excess of self-loathing and self-pity was available to me. But guilt would be an indulgence in my case, a way of wriggling partially free of the hook of circumstance, the terrifying logic of my life, and, above all, guilt would be a gesture of obsequence to the future, a way of striking a bargain with the day when Ann and everyone else learned that Hugh was racing after me when his life was taken away.

Guilt would have been a swoon of feeling in my own behalf; I owed it to Ann to put all of that away, for now. My guilt, the eruption of my conscience, my inability to understand how I fitted into the fate of the Butterfields, all of that would have been a second assault on Ann. It was time for me to shut up and just be there with her. Nothing I had to confess was as important as Hugh's death; the truth of the day was inappropriate for the while. That confession would only interfere with the larger fact of Hugh's death and the grief of the woman who adored him, who joined her body with his and created new lives, who once saw in his eyes the whole of her life. After all the lunges I'd made at the separate universe of feeling, at the uniqueness of perception that stands at the center of endless love, sitting there with Ann and realizing that for the time I was a witness to Ann's levitation over the plane of normal feelings, I felt the reality—the shifting, unnameable reality—of love, and so as Ann began to sob again and I took her in my arms and held her, I loved her and all of life with the full raging power of my reconsecrated heart.

Sometime later I got up and poured us both a drink. Ann took it in her hand and smiled at me. "You're a good friend, David. It's good that you're here. I wish I could say it was what Hugh would have wanted, but really I can't think of anyone else in the world who could be in this room right now. None of my new friends. Only you. The children. Sammy. This is a time for Sammy. Oh God, I have to call them. It has to be me."

"I would do it for you."

"I know." She placed her glass on the table, still full. "And then what?"

"Then the hospital. I should be there. And find out what I have to do."

"Everyone will help."

"I hope so."

"They will."

"I'd better call them."

"Do you want me to leave?"

"I don't really, but I think it would be right. You shouldn't be here while I'm telling the kids."

I nodded.

"You better go home, David. You should be on your way back to Chicago. You'll get in a lot of trouble. You told me so yourself."

"It doesn't matter."

"I know it feels like that right now, but it matters. We all have to look out for ourselves now. That's how it's working out. Hugh said the same thing: No more dreams of paradise; every man for himself."

"It can't be done."

"You should go home."

"I am home."

"No. Don't. I know what you're feeling. And I thank you. But there's nothing to be done. I'm going to start taking care of everything. I'm practical now. I have the rest of my life to live with what happened but now I've got to make arrangements. I have to make telephone calls and be strong for the kids, even if they don't expect me to. I'm going to do that. You have to go back to Chicago. And I have to make these calls and forget for a while that it was you who was here for me during the worst—" her voice suddenly broke and she lowered her eyes and began to sob. "I've got to make these calls," she said. "And you've got to go. That's all there is to it."

I wanted to protest. I wanted never to leave her, but I knew it would be wrong for her to make the calls to Keith, Sammy, and Jade with me sitting with her; they would find out and it would add a measure of foolishness and deceit where only sorrow belonged. Without question, they would all learn that I'd been in New York when Hugh was killed, and it was hard to imagine they wouldn't speculate on the meaning of that. Perhaps by the time they began to solve the unknown in the terrible algebra of circumstance I would have already found the moment to make my own part in Hugh's death known.

I left Ann's apartment. I don't know if she expected me to go back to my hotel or call American Airlines and make a reservation back to Chicago. It didn't matter. I knew I wasn't going anywhere. The night was starless and warm. There was a restaurant in the ground floor of her building and customers walked in and out of it. I looked in through the bright open windows; the people inside looked so terribly happy. They sat at tables with little marble-based lamps and painted shades that showed street scenes of old New York: moons over church steeples, buggies drawn by proud high-stepping horses. I felt a sudden surge of desire to be in that restaurant, to be drinking wine and talking with people I knew. I wanted to be in the company of friends such as Charles Dickens imagined, people to whom I could tell my story in all its detail and who would shed tears of pity, neither judging nor forgiving me. But as quickly as the desire appeared, it receded and I turned away from the windows, shaking a little, my head beating like a huge bony heart and the taste of my body's most appalling recesses rising to the roof of my mouth.

Across the street from Ann's apartment were the offices of the Children's Aid Society. The steps to the side entrance faced the entrance to her building and I sat down. The Children's Aid Society was locked and utterly dark for the weekend, with jail-house bars on the windows. The metal banisters were peeled and rusted, and beneath the steps, going down to a chained cellar entrance, were a number of empty pint bottles showing the labels of cheap vodka and port. The steps themselves were filthy, with chicken bones, spittle, and a kind of general refuse that city life creates the way an engine creates smoke. It was a quiet street and I knew that doorways such as these were used as safe harbors by men who had no homes, but I sat down anyway. I didn't dare pass the time by walking the streets. I wanted to be right there when Ann left her apartment. The next stop was the hospital and she might need me.

I sat where I could watch the street, west to Park Avenue and east almost to Lexington. I sat for a very long time and the night got cooler, degree by degree, ticking them off like a clock. Maybe it was because I was waiting for some homeless, tormented man to claim my perch for his bedroom, but all I could think of was that man who had placed the dimes on Hugh's eyes and tried to bring him back to life. He had long fingers and the tips were disproportionately broad. There was a certain disease that did that to you, but I couldn't think of which one. When he crouched down to administer his magic, the cuffs to his light gray trousers rode up and I saw his bare, scratched ankles. He had no accent; he had traded his racial cadences for psychological ones.

By now, the calls would have been made. I could feel the knowledge spreading. New tears were being shed, bags packed. By the morning they would all be here.

In a very short while I would see Jade.

But it was impossible to think of it, dangerous. To have our reunion take place at Hugh's funeral, to present myself soaked in his blood. It was hopeless and it was my only hope. Tomorrow: Jade.

And now Ann was pushing the door out and emerging from her building. She had a long fringed blue shawl around her shoulders and she looked down the street toward Park and straight across at me. I was sitting with my elbows on my knees, my head resting in my hands. She looked at me for a few long moments, tightened the shawl around her, and then raised her hand.

We were silent in the taxi on the way to the hospital and we only glanced at each other once, when Ann took my hand and I moved close to her so she could rest her head on my shoulder.

13

The Butterfields were filing into town one at a time, first Keith
and then Hugh's older brother Robert, who'd flown in with
one of his nine children, a middle son named after Hugh. They
gathered at Ann's; there was nowhere else to go and even Ingrid,
her sister, and a few of Ingrid's friends went to Ann's.

I stayed away, utterly isolated in my hotel room. I remember
that room better than myself on that day. When I conjure it up
in memory, I see an empty room, a ladder of sunlight rising and
falling on one wall, a pigeon lighting on a window sill and peering in through the glass, a dead fly resting in the convex glass
shade covering the overhead light, a fraying light cord oozing
brown fuzz, the rattle of room-service trays in the halls, voices,
hundreds of voices and none of them mine. If I concentrate with
all my might, I can just barely picture myself in that room: on
the bed, my hands behind my head, my feet crossed, fully
clothed. I see myself at the window, looking down at the street.
I see myself in tears. Yet even these memories are dim and somehow unreal. All I truly know is that I stayed in my hotel, waiting for someone to call me, and, for the most part, I had ceased
to exist.

I also remember writing and I think I was writing a letter to
Jade. But I never found any evidence of any writing at all. I picture myself tearing some hotel stationery into shreds and watching it drift into the tin wastepaper basket, but that feels more
like logic than memory. An anesthetized patient will awaken and
remember being wheeled to the operating room, the overhead
lights flashing by, the masked attendants, the squeak of rubber
gloves. But it's difficult to say if these images are retrieved from

the unconscious or if they are invented, drawn from our sense of what the world without us must be like.

I never think of the life I'll miss after I'm dead, or all that I missed before I was born. It's the time I'm as good as dead during this, my one and only life, that makes me tear at my hair. It seems to me that if I carefully gathered all of the time I was entirely alive I would have amassed perhaps two years of life so far . . .

At four o'clock Ann called.

"You belong here," she said. "As much as anyone. You belong with us."

I was sitting on the edge of the bed with my hand over my eyes.

"Do you . . ." I stopped. "How do the others feel about me being . . . ? I want to be with you."

"David, I don't know how the laws of karma work. But for some reason you were here when I needed someone. When I needed you. And today that seems bigger than anything else, the past. And everyone here agrees. I wasn't sure you hadn't gone back to Chicago. But really I knew you'd still be here. I can't figure it out now but this is right and really, David, you should be here."

"I want to."

"Then come. Now. Right away."

"It really is all right?"

"Yes. It's a lot more than all right. It's . . . essential. We're getting righteously drunk. We're gathering our forces and I need you here. If you're worried about Keith, well, he knows I need you here, too. Also, by the way, Ingrid knows."

"Ingrid knows what?"

"All about you."

"What do you mean?"

"She knows you're you and why we did that act in front of her last night. And as a citizen of Jupiter, she couldn't care less.

Anyway, you don't have to worry about that. Look, David, I'm not giving you a choice about this. I don't want you sitting in that hotel room all alone while this is happening. When the sun sets you won't even turn on the lights. There's no choice. Just come over right now."

"I will. I want to."

"I know you do. OK. Oh, one thing. If you pass an open deli, pick up some mixers—tonic, club soda, you know. We have to make highballs. If we keep drinking everything straight, we're going to be dry way before Monday morning."

Ann hung up and I held on to the phone.

When Sam Butterfield opened the door to me, I was sobbing. I didn't want it to be that way and I'd been fighting off my tears from the time I left the hotel. It was a stupid thing that broke my defenses: when I rang the buzzer in the lobby, no one asked who it was through the intercom. It was as if it hardly mattered who was there because it would never be Hugh. The locked glass door was buzzed open and I burst into tears. I didn't ring for the elevator. There was a bench in the lobby and I sat down, shaking my head and saying "Stop it" to myself, but it seemed I would have to be one of those mystics who can stop a bleeding wound through the powers of the mind to wrest the control of my tears from the spacious, anarchic part of myself that ruled them now. Suddenly, the elevator appeared. I staggered in and rode up to the seventh floor. I was still crying when I knocked on Ann's door.

"Hello, David," Sammy said. "It's nice of you to come."

His voice was deep, much deeper than mine. His egg-sized Adam's apple quavered at the center of his long tanned throat: at seventeen he was already over six feet tall and though I was just an inch shorter than him, I felt him looming over me. His light brown hair was parted in the middle and gathered in back in a small Thomas Jefferson pony tail. His blue eyes looked at me through a red mist. He extended his hand and I took it. I bowed my head, ashamed to be crying and helpless to stop.

"I'm sorry, it's a terrible thing," I said, but I doubt it was clear. I thought I should turn around and compose myself. I felt like a huge emotional pig to be inflicting my sorrow and confusion on them. I'd been summoned to be strong and my tears were a violation of trust.

"We expected you," Sammy was saying. "Jade's not here yet. Mom just hooked up with her a couple hours ago."

There was a measure of relief in learning that the moment I'd been waiting for had been moved forward a notch or two. With any luck I would have control over myself by the time Jade arrived. But the real deliverance from the ruination of my feelings was Sammy's telling me. I knew there was no particular reason for him to let me know that Jade wasn't there yet, no purpose except to ease the pressure on me. Sammy was comforting me, really, and I swallowed hard and tried to be worthy of it.

I looked at him and said, "I've missed you, Sammy, but I would have rather gone through my whole life without ever seeing you again than have to see you on a day like this." I waited for him to say something but he just gazed mildly into my eyes and suddenly I realized I hadn't actually said anything: my thoughts were loud and out of control, but I hadn't even moved my lips.

When I reached the front room, Keith was sitting on the arm of the sofa holding that framed square of pink and blue quilt. His hair had darkened to a deep, opaque brown and his once frail body had a kind of obstinacy to it now. He drummed his squarish fingertips on the raw wooden frame; his sandals sank into the sofa cushion; his feet were creased and powerful-looking, and his toenails were grown out long.

"This is mine, OK?" he was saying, in his high, reasonable voice.

"Not now, Keith," Ann said.

"But I'm the one who wants it. I'm the only one." He stared hard at the piece of quilt. He knew I was in the room but he gave no indication.

"Hello, David," Ann said. "Thank—"

But what she was saying was lost to me; I was listening to Keith.

"You don't hang something like this up on your wall," Keith was saying. "This isn't a picture, you know. It's not something to add *color* to your house. This quilt is our flag. This is the Butterfield flag. Pink and blue pyramids and the most beautiful one in the world, I think."

"That quilt comes from *my* family, Keith," Ann said. "It was made by Beatrice Ramsey and if it reminds me of anything, it's my grandmother's house in Hillsboro, New Hampshire."

Keith kept his eyes fixed on the quilt and he was shaking his head. "That's not it and you know it. That's like saying . . ." his voice dropped off and suddenly he lifted his head and looked at me. He returned his attentions to the quilt in an instant. "That's like saying . . . Well, I was born on this quilt."

"No, you were not," Ann said.

Ingrid and her sister Nancy were seated in the director's chairs, talking to Hugh's brother Robert. Ingrid kept her hand on Robert's wrist and spoke to him in a rapid whisper; Robert, who was standing with his son Hugh slightly behind him, looked down at Ingrid with a kind of glassy, compromised compassion. He was an enormous man; the wineglass he held in his massive hand looked absurdly delicate, and though Ann's ceilings were ten feet high Robert stood with his back slightly curved, out of a combination of caution and shyness. He had Hugh's slightly worried expression when he listened, that kind of mild tightening of the forehead, that slight narrowing of the eyes that seemed to be asking, no matter what the circumstances, "Are you all right?"

"When Pap got out of the Army and he came to see you at Bryn Mawr," Keith was saying, "you had this quilt on your bed.

And then you got pregnant, with me. And that's how we all began. All right? Now do you know what I mean?" He tapped his finger on the glass and seemed to glance at me again. "Even you said if you hadn't gotten pregnant you might not have gotten married to Pap."

"Not this again," Sammy said, with no particular emotion.

"You're getting to be an old man on this subject, Keith," Ann said.

Keith shook his head to tell them he wasn't listening. "And so if it wasn't for getting pregnant with me, on this quilt, then Pap would have married that other girl and you'd be married to someone else too, or maybe not married at all."

"But I'm *not* married," said Ann, with a kind of faltering gaiety. She looked at me and shrugged, inviting me to join her in an askew angle of vision, taking refuge in the slight aloofness she assumed I was capable of.

"And if you hadn't gotten married, then none of us would have been born," Keith said. He had moved his face even closer to the quilt, increasing his concentration. He was saying something everyone in his family had heard on innumerable occasions but he had no way of stopping himself: he was trapped within his sense of the truth of his family and it was an everlasting mystery to him that the others found his passions meaningless. Long ago he was faced with the choice of either abandoning his obsession with origins or becoming an object of occasional ridicule, and he had made the more honorable choice of following the curve of his impulses, deepening his loyalty to the truth as it became less welcome.

Ingrid was looking directly at me, even as she held onto Robert Butterfield. She wore a dark blue skirt and those kind of sandals that have rawhide laces you wrap around your legs. She held a ball of facial tissue in her fist and cocked her head first to the left and then to the right as she looked at me: I knew that in some inarticulate way she was now remembering me. I had slipped through the net of recollection the first time because I'd been falsely identified as Ann's young lover, but now that my identity had shifted, it was alive within Ingrid's consciousness, and I could sense her following the drift of her thoughts like a cat intently watching the ellipses of a moth.

"That's why I say, in a way, that I'm not only a son but the father too," Keith said. "Because it started with me."

"Then you must be dead," Sammy said. His voice was so naturally deep; he didn't have to touch it with his personality in order to give it its meanings. "They must be putting you in the furnace right about now so they can put your ashes in the old urn. Right? Because *my* father's dead and you can only have one father. So you must be dead."

"Do I really have to be a referee?" Ann said. "I'm going to be so worried about everyone else I'm not going to have my own feelings."

"I don't like it when he goes on like that," Sammy said.

"I don't much care for it, either. But Keith likes it, and I don't want to have to draw the line one place or another."

"Can I take this home with me?" Keith said, holding the framed piece of quilt away from him, offering it to Ann.

"As far as I'm concerned, yes. If you want it so damned badly. But you'll have to square it with Jade and Sammy."

Robert Butterfield walked across the room and stood in front of me. "You're David?" he asked, careful to make his voice unmistakably accepting. When I nodded, he put his hand out to me. "I'm Hugh's brother, Robert. Ann told me what a help you've been. You stepped in when the family couldn't be here. It means a great deal." When Hugh was feeling wilful or lonely, we all used to say, his southern accent would sprout, like those wonderful mushrooms that come out after every rain. But here was Hugh's older brother, still living in New Orleans, with less of an accent than David Brinkley. Straight on, his face was rectangular, at once open and shy, massive and vulnerable. He shook my hand with a gentleness that nearly tipped the fragile balance I'd achieved. Here was all of the gigantic sweetness of Hugh looking at me.

"I'm aware of the complications involved in your participation in this sad ceremony," Robert was saying. "But as our father said, 'When you get above the lowest vegetable orders, life turns into a holy mess.' David, I'd like you to meet my son Hugh." Robert reached around and draped his immense arm over his son's shoulders. Hugh was dressed in a light blue suit and wore a tie decorated with tiny flowers. His hair was pure yellow, from tip to root, front to back, and his eyes were gray and blue. At fifteen, he was only a few inches shorter than his father, and from the size of his hands and feet it was probable that, one day, he too would be enormous. I wondered if the elder Hugh, my Hugh, conventionally large, had been small for his family.

"It's nice to meet you," said Robert's son, with a shy, formal half smile. He seemed absolutely ill at ease and had probably considered affixing himself to each of us who had gathered at Ann's, even me. I put my hand forward and solemnly he shook it. I gazed into his open, slightly frightened face and was aware of (or imagined) the other eyes that were upon me: Keith's, Ingrid's.

"Hugh's one of our middle sons," Robert said. "We're eleven in all. Six boys and three young ladies, Christine and me. The rest arrive tonight." He let out a low sigh. It was as if the thought of his arriving family had touched off a quiver of happiness in him before he remembered the occasion of their journey.

I had been clutching a brown paper bag filled with three large bottles of club soda and three of tonic water. I felt the weight only as a general numbness, and when Ann asked me if I'd remembered to pick up mixers I had to think for a moment.

"Oh, they're right here," I said.

"I was *wondering* what you were holding in there," she said, with a kind of embryonic brightness that made me fear all the others might turn on us. I knew that Ann was asking me to con-

spire with her, to move back with her a step or two and view
everything with a kind of private, wounded mirth. Surrounded
by tragedy, overcome by everyone else's grief as well as her
own, Ann was nostalgic for her irony: she longed for a taste of
it, as if that small space that irony places between consciousness
and emotion contained the only air she could comfortably
breathe. She waited for me to say something, but I only looked
at her and then at the bag I was holding, which was dark with
moisture. "Well, good," Ann said. "You brought it. I'll put it
all in the kitchen."

"No, I will," I said.

"No, I will," said Keith. He was at my side in an instant and
took the bag from my arms. "I'd like to talk to you," he said,
just above a whisper.

I nodded. "Good."

"I'll put this shit away and then we'll go to Mom's room and
talk."

"Ann, Ann," Ingrid was saying, "we have to be clear about
everything." She was rubbing the side of her face and holding
her sister's hand. "We have to make ground rules."

Ann folded her arms in front of her and nodded. "You've
been saying that all afternoon, Ingrid. As far as I can see, there's
nothing to be decided. You chose the chapel. The ashes are being
divided up. What more is there?"

"There's a lot. Everything. Everything." Ingrid looked at
her sister—a chubby, mild, nunnish-looking woman—and her
sister closed her eyes in that way that means "Go ahead and
say it."

Keith brushed my arm with the back of his hand. "Come on.
We'll talk."

"Where you going?" Sammy asked.

"We'll be right back. Stay here," said Keith.

Sammy shook his head and looked disgusted.

I followed Keith into Ann's bedroom and he closed the door
behind us. I felt that gesture of closing the door was the begin-

ning of a reprimand—we were certainly not here to exchange confidences as equals—and the dull bloated thud of the heat-warped door felt like one of those ambiguous affronts to your dignity, a hearty slap on the back or a pinch on the cheek.

The windows in Ann's bedroom, framed by sheer white curtains, looked out onto a reddish brick wall. The glass in the windows had the clean look windows have in houses that haven't been occupied yet, and you could see the wall with such vivid clarity that it became beautiful, strangely exciting. I turned and saw that Keith was staring at me, his mouth refined down to a thin, pale line.

"So," said Keith. "Mom tells me you materialized Friday afternoon. Is that true?"

I felt, acutely, that Keith was doing wrong to check my version against what Ann had said, but I nodded. "Late Friday afternoon."

"Mom says it was about three."

I paused. "I don't know. Probably it was."

"Was she real surprised to see you?"

"What do you think?"

Keith shrugged, and lifted one of the corners of his mouth in a little twitchy smile. "I don't know. That's why I'm asking you. If I knew . . ." his voice was absorbed by his largest instinct, which was to say nothing to me.

"She was surprised."

"Well," Keith said, drawing out the word, like a small-town cop on television, that long drawl of folksy menace, "I guess it was the next step."

"I don't know what you're going after, Keith. Tell me what you want to know and I'll tell you."

"All I'm saying is I guess it was the next step. I mean, if you were busy writing *me* letters—I mean to *me*, and you know how I feel—then I guess Mom got quite a few of them. Quite a few. Is that right?"

I had a suspicion that Ann had said something to the contrary. Perhaps she'd confessed only to a note; likely as not, she'd said she never replied. "I found out where you lived in the telephone book."

"I know. But that's not how you found Mom. She's not listed under her name."

"She's under her maiden name. Ramsey. I remembered it."

"You remembered it?" He seemed disturbed that I knew his mother's family name. I had once again put my fingerprints on his past. "OK," he said, as much to himself as to me, "so you remembered it. And you wrote her. And you told her how sorry you were, and how lonely, and how it wasn't fair what happened to you—"

"I never said it wasn't fair, Keith. What happened to me, I mean to *all* of us, can't be touched by words like fair."

He dismissed what I was saying with a wave. "So you wrote her and said how sorry you were and she wrote you back. What did she say in her letters? That she knew you were sorry and it was time to let bygones be bygones?"

I felt, and was, trapped. It wasn't a question of whether I should lie to Keith in order to protect Ann, but whether she had already confessed to answering my letters.

"She answered my letters. But she never said she was sorry for me, and you know Ann would never say it was time to let bygones be bygones."

Keith's face creased in that sort of smile one makes when the triumph is proving you've been betrayed. I knew I'd lost the maneuver, but it was hard to care.

"I thought so," he said.

I made no reply; there was no point in inviting him to illustrate the deceit he'd uncovered. I'd taken a chance and it flopped: I knew now that Ann had told him she'd never answered my letters.

"I don't want to argue with you, Keith," I said. "None of this is important today."

"Bygones?" He was lifting his spirits. His life was more than a little berserk and it gave him a feeling of control to poke butterfly pins through whatever I said.

"No. I'm not talking about forgetting anything. I don't believe in forgetting any more than you do."

"That's funny," he said. "I think if I were you there'd be a lot I would want to forget."

We were standing in the center of Ann's bedroom. Her bed, covered by an Indian print spread, was on one side of us and a painted dresser and an upholstered chair were on the other. I took a step back so that if Keith tried to hit me, I wouldn't catch it full force.

"You obviously don't want me here," I said. "What did you say when Ann said she wanted to ask me to come?"

Keith stepped forward and I readied myself for defense, but he was moving past me now, toward Ann's bed. He gazed at it and then softly, as if it were a living thing, set his open hand down upon it. He turned around and sat on the edge of the bed and then, with an abrupt, clumsy motion, he lay down, propped against the simple wooden headboard, with his sandals on the colorful spread. He kept his hands beside him and drummed his fingers slowly, one at a time, as if he were counting down. Then he reached behind him and pulled a pillow from under the bedspread and placed it on his belly.

"You came here to see my sister?"

"Your mother asked me to come."

Keith was silent, his face flushed momentarily and his eyes seemed to recede. He took a slow, deep breath.

"She doesn't want to see you. She hates you. She knows what you are. You're using my mother. You're just using her to get to Jade, but Jade would rather still be trapped in that burning house than see you."

"Keith, if—"

"And Jade has a lover, you know. She's had plenty. Terrific appetite on that girl. She has a *female* lover. Did you know that?"

He waited for me to answer and finally I shook my head.

"Oh? So it's news? Good. I'm glad I'm the one to tell you. Her name is Susan Henry, Jade's girlfriend. They sometimes stay at my house in Bellows Falls." He unfolded his hands and squeezed the pillow he'd lain over his belly. He was flexing his long, perfectly articulated toes against the bottoms of his sandals, in and out like the beating of a heart.

"You don't have to prove how much you hate me," I said.

"The reason we couldn't find Jade is she's with Susan right now. Camping trip. They love camping trips. They like doing it outside. They do all that woodsy stuff—camping, canoeing, twenty-mile hikes." Keith smiled, a disassociated grin, deliberately unreal.

I was standing over him now. I reached down, grabbed his shoulders, and with one motion literally lifted him out of bed.

"You don't have to do this," I said, holding him, with my face an inch from his. "You really don't. If you hate me so much you shouldn't have let your mother ask me over."

Keith shook loose of my grip and pushed me back with his hard, blunt fingertips. "I said it was all right," he said, showing his small, squared teeth, "only because Mom wants you. Mom needs to believe in some kind of life outside of the family, even though she knows there isn't any." His face flushed red again and he closed his eyes for a moment. If he had lost his composure, broken down and wept, then I would have put my arms around him . . .

"Keith," I said. My mouth was dry and filled with a strong, arid taste. "I like you," I said. "I don't suppose it's what you want to hear, but I liked you from the start, when we met, and whenever I think about you, which is a lot, I think . . . I just like you and respect . . . And I feel horrible about your father, about Hugh." I stopped; I was starting to tremble. I could feel my emotions toppling out of me.

"It was me you wanted to kill, wasn't it?" he said, softly. "When you set the fire, it was me. And I know why."

"That's not true. You know—"

"Because I knew you for what you were." He drew himself up. "I don't want to talk about it. What you did. Ruined everything. I don't . . . My father is *dead*."

"Keith—"

"Don't say my name!" he said, his voice rising. "None of this would be happening if it wasn't . . ." He closed his eyes, tightly, and swung out. My arm went up to deflect his blow. He swung again and missed, but scratched the side of my face. He tried to hit me again but I caught his wrist and held it.

"Don't touch me. Keep your hands off me, you fucking dirty creep." He pulled away from me, but in fear I held on to him. "Let me *go*." He swung at me with his free arm and I let him go. He put his hand on my shoulder and moved me aside. Then he walked by me, brushing into me with his shoulder, and headed back into the front of the apartment.

I waited in Ann's room for a minute or so, not knowing what to do. Finally, I decided there were really no more decisions to be made: for good or for ill, I belonged with the others.

Ann sat next to Sammy on the sofa, her legs curled, holding him with both arms and resting her head on his shoulder. Ingrid was standing above them, trembling so terribly that the ice chattered in her glass and the carbonated water worked itself into a foam. She was glaring at Ann, and Ann was doing her best to pay no attention; it was Sammy who looked back at Ingrid, fastening his eyes on her with a kind of piercing incredulity.

"All right, all right," Robert was saying, holding up his huge hands with ceremonial patience. "This is no way to carry on. For Hugh's sake. Hugh, my God, he was a peaceful man. He'd be scandalized to hear us snarling at each other." He glanced at his son and then gathered him in, draping his arm around him and holding him close. When Robert kissed his son's hair, they both momentarily closed their eyes.

"It's five o'clock," Keith said, holding up his watch. "Pap's ashes now. It's all done."

"Thank you very much," said Ingrid's sister. "We would have perished without the information." She sensed sides were being drawn up and she wanted to assure Ingrid of her support.

Robert unbuttoned his green and white seersucker jacket. His chest was massive and there were ellipses of sweat on his jacket. He took a folded sheet of air-mail paper out of his inside pocket. He handed his drink to his son and Hugh strode over to the table to place it down, clearly pleased to be serving his father.

"What's this?" asked Ingrid. "A will?"

"No," said Robert. "It's not. This is a letter from our Hugh. He sent it to us a little more than a year ago." He unfolded it; it was typed in blue. "I took it along. It's a rare thing, a letter from Hugh." Robert looked down at the letter and smiled, as if he saw Hugh's face looking out from it.

"Read it to us, Uncle Bob," Sammy said.

"I thought I would pass it around."

"No. Read it to us."

"God. Then I suppose it'll be time to drag out the old pictures, too," said Ann. She didn't sound displeased.

"I wish I could do this in Hugh's voice," said Robert. "It was his voice that made everything so special." He looked at Sammy and nodded. "Like yours."

"Read it, Uncle Bob."

" 'Dear Bobbo.' " Robert stopped, looked up at Ingrid. "That's my family name," he said. He wiped sweat from his forehead and squinted uncertainly at the page, as if it had suddenly become less legible. " 'By now you've heard about the divorce and you've had a chance to get used to it. I feel like Cousin Derek, the time he wrecked Granddaddy's Packard and simply moved to Charlotte for a year. Sometimes a man has got to lay low. I remember about eight years ago you and I were having a crayfish pig-out in that little place with the folding chairs right on the Ponchatrain, and you were carrying on a little about Billy Corona because he'd just walked out on Alison and you said something to the effect of what kind of shitass would leave a wife of a decade and a half and I shook my head and clucked like an old gossip on a verandah—say, the summer of '38 with the trees in full bloom and all our values intact. Do you know what I mean? Those times in our life when everything is simple. And now here I am, doing Billy Corona one better because he left with only two children and I'm leaving three. Fairly grown children, I would say, and they've got more of an idea what they'd like to do with their lives than their poor old father has. Gosh, here we are, as always, in our baggy olive shorts and strawberry preserves sticking to the webs of our fingers, and calling ourselves poor old father, registered Republican. It seems so damned unlikely, doesn't it?' " Robert's voice broke and he turned the page over. His face was growing darker, a deep orderly flush that began at his neck and moved up, filling his face with color like wine in a glass.

"It's *so* Hugh," said Ann.

"I have a letter Pap sent me," Sammy said. "I should have brought it."

"I have poems, a hundred things," said Ingrid. She covered her eyes, in grief and perhaps, in part, in shame: she had no choice but to angle for her rightful position, yet it humiliated her.

I was standing with my back to the wall, holding a glass of whiskey and soda. My legs ached and with everyone in that room weaving on the brink, I was terrified that my own tears would break free first. The sight of each face seemed to light another fuse that went leaping and hissing toward the impacted, volatile center of my consciousness: each sorrow was separate and unbearably specific, but each was finding its way to that part of me that was ready to detonate. Robert was going on with Hugh's letter.

" 'What you heads of unbroken families don't realize is how

we wandering fathers love our children,' " Robert read, and I could tell from the way he nodded that he wanted to look at Sammy and Keith to make sure they'd heard that line, but he resisted. Then he read something else, but I don't know what. I heard Robert's voice as a dull, wordless murmur and I stared at his open, suffering face with an utterly improper fixity: I simply poured my attentions into the overwhelming reality of his large brown eyes, his dry grayish hair, his closely shaved, slightly jowly cheeks, and his massive chin.

Robert was committed to keeping the peace in the wake of death. He had stepped between Ann and Ingrid and had probably intervened in peace's behalf when the squabble began about my arrival. He believed in the alchemy that turned all passions into sorrow—all jealousy, all rage, all sickness and fear transformed and laid at the silent altar of the dead. For now, he would not interrupt the rhythms of mourning to express his feeling about me: such emotions were mere luxuries of the living, and to parade them now would violate all the decorum proper to survivors. It would be later for me. Then I would feel the heavy hand on my shoulder, see the steel woven into the wool of Robert's soft brown eyes. Later, he would judge me as Hugh would have; later, I would be put painfully in my place, accused, and disposed of.

I turned away from Robert and looked at Ingrid: she was sobbing openly now and looking back at me, her eyes puzzled behind the tears. I was certain that the memory of me standing not ten feet from Hugh was stirring within her, straining to become articulate, like those voices some people claim to hear at a séance: the windows of memory rattle, the curtains blow, the table shakes, but no one is there. She cocked her head and parted her full, colorless lips. There was disapproval in her stare and for a moment I was sure that the first layer of her memory of me had come into focus, but then I realized she was asking me to take my eyes off of her, to give her her sorrow in the artificial privacy of averted eyes. I shifted my gaze to Ingrid's sister, a large-boned, heavy-set woman in a shapeless gray dress, dark stockings, and shiny black shoes.

It was at that moment that Keith, sitting perhaps twenty feet from where I stood, threw his tall, fragile glass at me. I don't know if he meant to hit me or terrify me, or even if he'd considered anything at all, but the glass exploded against the wall, a foot, or perhaps even less, from my head. I thought it was glass spraying into my face but there were no cuts so I suppose it was only crushed ice. The clear base on the glass came to rest on my shoulder and later I found chunks of glass in my shirt pocket. It took a long moment to realize what had happened. I heard the crash and even had a shadowy, peripheral vision of Keith sitting forward and letting the glass fly. But it took a moment to understand that it all had to do with me. I felt the spray of liquor on my hair, my face, my shirt, and noticed, as dimly as a film projected on a black cloth, that everyone was looking at me. Robert stopped reading and Nancy clutched Ingrid's shoulder as both of them gasped. I covered my face, finally, and turned away, stooping and shaking my head.

"Oh, Keith," said Ann. "Keith." Her voice sounded exhausted, more hurt than disapproving.

"He's out! He is out of here!" Keith was shouting. I turned to face him, shaking my hands to get the moisture off of them, still half crouched as if to ward off subsequent blows. Keith was standing up and panting like a racehorse. It was awesome to see the passion and intensity of his respiration. His ribcage moved up and down like enormous wings and I don't think I was the only one wondering what I would do if Keith suddenly keeled over. "I can't feel anything with him here. It's only him back again to do more harm. Jesus, it is incredible. He can't stay. He's out." And then, pointing at me, he repeated: "Out, out."

I looked at Ann. "I'll go," I said.

"Out, out," said Keith. "Out, out, out."

"Shut up," said Sammy. He grabbed for Keith's arm but when he missed, he didn't try a second time.

Ann covered her eyes and shook her head. Don't leave? Don't stay?

"I'll leave," I said, as much to myself as to Keith.

I looked around the room; no one quite dared to return my gaze. I nodded, stupidly trying to act normal. In a feverish blur I saw that Keith had picked up another glass from the table and then it was sailing toward me, slowly, horizontally, the ice and whiskey cascading out, the glass capturing the lamplight. This time it collided with the wall a good distance from me. A hanging curtain of moisture appeared on the white wall. I stepped forward and crushed a large piece of glass beneath my foot; the shards scratched against the wooden floor and made a miserable, tearing noise. I covered my face—I thought I'd seen yet another glass flying at me, but Keith was standing still, his hands slightly in front of him, holding them as if I might attack him.

I turned quickly and walked down the long hall and let myself out. No one, of course, called to stop me. I closed the door behind me but the latch didn't catch and it remained ajar. I didn't dare wait for the elevator and I found the stairs in the center of the floor. I ran down a couple of flights and then had to sit down because I found that my legs weren't really responding to me anymore. It felt as if a cluster of nerves had been severed, and I sat on the marble steps and pinched at my calves and pounded my knees for quite some time before any feeling came back.

As I left Ann's building a taxi cab was pulling up. Its tires whined against the curb and the next thing I remember is the back door opening and Jade standing in front of me. She was larger, though not very much. Her long hair was gone. Now she had a short, athletic cut, perfectly straight, parted in the center and combed to the sides, shored off from the wind by a dark blue plastic headband. She wore a yellow blouse, opened two buttons worth at the top. Her neck was creased, three deep grooves, and then a small gold chain. Khaki pants, high-waisted and billowing. A black overnight bag, nylon. She was tan, tanned all over. Staring at me.

The cab pulled away. Jade took one step forward. Her lips parted and then came tightly together. I came slowly forward, and when I stopped, the points of my shoes were practically touching hers.

"Mom told me you were here," Jade said.

"I am. I'm here." And then I placed my hands on her shoulders and drew her close to me. I could feel the stutter of her resistance but it was faint. I put my arms around her, and just as I'd imagined ten thousand times, I embraced her. I wondered—fleetingly—if I was forcing myself on her. I felt her breasts against me, smelled the brilliance of her perfumes, immortalized the architecture of her bones. She rested her hands on my arms. Did not return my embrace. Did not push me away.

I held her for as long as I dared, and when I let her go I didn't look at her because I knew she didn't want me to. I faced straight ahead and listened first to her breathing, then to that ruminative silence as she struggled for one simple thing to say, and finally to the soft, jittery click of her footsteps as she walked toward the door to Ann's building. I didn't move until she was gone and then I still resisted turning around. I walked at full speed, squeezing my hands and talking to myself, running, stopping, walking again, and finally just sitting on the corner of 29th and Park, on the sidewalk with my back against a mailbox, waiting.

14

Twenty-eight hours later, the telephone rang in my hotel room and I picked it up in the middle of the first ring. It was the front desk.

"Mr. Axelrod?"

"Yes."

"You have a visitor." He paused. "May I send her up?"

"Let me speak to her, please."

"Just one moment."

"Hello?" said Jade. Her voice was husky. It always made me think of sand and sun, and smoke.

"I just wanted you to hear it from me," I said. "Come up. You have my room number?"

"Yes. I have it."

"Or do you want me to come down? Would that be better?"

"No. I'll come up." She paused. "OK?"

"Yes. Please."

I met her at the elevator; she got off with two women wearing short leather skirts and cowgirl hats. Jade was dressed in gray and carried her black nylon travel bag. She smelled of cigarettes and alcohol, and riding on top of those scents like light on a wave was the aroma of lilac water: she must have put it on moments before arriving at the McAlpin.

We stood looking at each other for a very long while. I heard a high-pitched whoosh, such as aviators must have heard when they flew in uncovered cockpits. The impetuousness that allowed me to grab for her as I had yesterday afternoon was absent now. It was all I could do to look into her eyes, though, of course, I couldn't have possibly turned my gaze anywhere else.

She looked exhausted. Her eyes were enormous, injured, and unfocused. Her lips were parched. She wore makeup and streaks of it showed up in the bleak, watery light of the hotel corridor. Her short hair was tucked behind her ears and the tops of her ears, with their hard, broad rims, were red. She had a gold stud in only one earlobe.

"You're missing an earring," I said.

She touched her right ear. "Oh," she said. She touched the empty lobe a few times. "Damn."

I shrugged. "We'll get you another," I said. I winced. It was such an idiotic remark. It was worse than idiotic: it was arrogant and desperate and I wouldn't have been surprised if she'd laughed in my face.

But Jade was looking at me as if she hadn't heard. My heart pawed at my chest like a huge dog behind a door.

"Are you surprised?" Jade said. "That I'm here."

I shook my head. "You had to come."

She narrowed her eyes a little. "No. I chose to. I decided."

"Well, I'm glad."

She nodded. Her eyes moved as she looked me over. She was noting the ways I'd changed. As her attention flickered over me I felt it like a human touch: it was clear to me that no one had looked at me in years. All of the other attentions had been fleeting, partial, obstructed: now, at a moment's notice, now and at last, I was seen as I was.

"Do you want to come into my room?" I asked.

Jade nodded. "For a minute. I'm on my way to the bus station. The last bus up to Vermont leaves in half an hour."

I closed the door and turned on the overhead light. I'd been propped up on the bed, rereading the newspaper by the table lamplight: the bedspread tortuously imitated my form; papers were askew; the tableau was one of disorganization and a certain grubbiness.

"I wish I could have greeted you in one of those silk smoking jackets with a glass of champagne," I said.

She looked as if she didn't understand why I was saying that. But I knew she did. There was something deliberate in the glance she gave me, something that wanted to insist she was missing the context of my remark. But Jade always could fill in the silence that flanked whatever I said, could picture what I'd seen without my having to describe it. It had been her intuitiveness that first tempted us toward the belief that soon overran every other thought: that we lived together in a world separate and superior to ordinary life. And now, the act of feigning confusion only told me that she still knew exactly what I meant, knew it as she always had and probably always would, for Jade understood me at my source, could trace the genealogy of my words back to their origins: as shifting tides of blood, drives, preconscious terrors.

"Should I call and have something brought up?" I said, walking across the room and sweeping the newspaper off the bed. "Some coffee, or wine?"

"If they bring it fast." She was casting her attention around the room, memorizing it, looking for a place to sit.

"Wine's all right?" I said.

"Yes. Though something's happened to my enamel and wine stains my teeth now." She showed me her lower teeth.

I sat on the edge of the bed and asked for room service. "Would you bring up two glasses of red wine, please?" I said.

"We're all getting old," I said when I hung up.

"The lucky ones."

She seated herself with a purposeful lack of grace, sighed, and zipped open her travel bag. She poked around in her bag and finally withdrew her hand.

"You have any aspirin?" she asked.

I shook my head.

"Damn," said Jade.

"What's wrong?" I asked. A mistake.

She sat slightly more erect, drawing herself away from me. "My father was killed. I was at his funeral. *With* my fucked-up family. I'm in my period. And I'm on a special all-protein diet to lose ten pounds." She raised her eyebrows and nodded, as if to ask: Enough?

I waited to say something but no words came forth. I thought of offering to rub her temples and the base of her neck but that gesture was clearly not mine. And then I made the stupid, compulsive error of thinking of her in her period, of envisioning the inch of Tampax string curled in her pubic hair and that was followed by a memory of me plucking at the string with the nails of my thumb and forefinger and then wrapping the string once around my finger as if for a yo-yo loop and pulling the blood-streaked cotton tube out of her. It was not, for all of its deliberateness and detail, a welcome thought: it was enough to experience Jade in three dimensions; the pull of intimacy, even remembered intimacy, and its inevitable quick heat, practically made me squirm.

"I want to ask you about the funeral," I said. "But I don't know how."

"It was terrible, terrible. You know, *boring* in a crazy way. I couldn't get it through my head that that was Pappy in the jar. I think it's crazy, cremation. Or if you're going to do it, then let's do it right. A bonfire. *With* all of us there. How am I supposed to believe the guy's really dead? I get a goddamned phonecall, spend a few hours with a lot of hysterical drunks, and then sit on a folding chair with about fifty other people listening to organ music and staring at an urn. I don't have any proof that anything really happened. I mean, everyone *tells* me he's dead, but I'm not sure. They could have gotten those ashes anywhere." She shrugged and hooked her finger around her gold chain.

"Fifty people," I said.

"And a lot I didn't know. Also unreal. Ingrid's sloppy crowd. I like her, though. Probably for the same reason Pappy did. Her earnestness. Her sexiness. How much she cried. Mom was very cool. She seemed impatient with the whole business. Ingrid was crying so loud that it made a lot of other people cry, you know, people who might not have otherwise. But Mom leans over to me and says something like Why don't we get a bucket of ice water and pour it over the woman's head? She's a strange lady, my poor mother. Lonely. Getting a little bitter, I think. Uncle Bob spoke, about Pap and growing up. It was actually quite beautiful, to tell the truth. I didn't think Bob had it in him. But he was almost *singing* and I could see even from where I was sitting that he had tears in his eyes. It made me cry, but you always cry at funerals, no matter what's said. I looked over at Mom when Uncle Bob was talking. She held on to my hand and I looked at her. I could *see* she fucking wanted to cry but goddamn if she was going to let herself. The tears were Ingrid's, I suppose that's what she was thinking, let Ingrid cry. Like Mom knew Pappy too well to cry for him. That's how she swindles herself out of practically *everything*."

"I was with Ann when she found out," I said. I wondered if this would be the first that Jade had heard of it.

"I know. She told me." She narrowed her eyes for a moment.

"She cried then," I said. "A lot. I mean if that matters to you."

We went silent for a time. We were strangers and half terrified in each other's presence: we were seeing ghosts, both of us. How strange to be having a supernatural experience in that small hotel room. We should go out, I thought, we should be walking. But just as I was afraid to clear my throat, I was afraid to suggest anything.

There was a knock at the door. When I heard the knock I realized that Jade and I were staring at each other, quite boldly, and I had no idea how long our gazes had been locked.

I got up. "That's the wine, probably," I said.

"I have to go pretty soon."

I wanted to shake my head but I stopped myself. "It's good to be with you," I said.

"Like you expected?" There was a slight smirk in her voice, from shyness.

I paused, to emphasize that I wasn't just answering out of politeness. "Yes. Like I expected."

The wine came in a heavy glass carafe. Two wineglasses and a foil package of peanuts. I signed for it, like a man of the world, and gave the man who delivered it a dollar bill because I didn't want to ruffle the surface of the moment by digging in my pockets for change. I placed the tray on the table next to Jade.

"Shall I pour?" I said.

"The wine's so dark. It looks black."

"No. It's the light in this room." I poured some wine into her glass and held it in front of the light. It turned bright red. "See?"

Jade nodded and took the glass from me. I wondered if she would let her fingers touch mine accidentally, but she didn't. I was disappointed, sensually let down, because I wanted to feel her, but it was better, I knew, that we not permit ourselves coy gestures. What better way to emphasize our strangeness than to flirt?

I poured my wine and stood in front of Jade. I would have liked to propose a toast but I knew I wasn't going to. I returned to the edge of the bed. "I've been trying to find you," I said.

"I know."

"Your family protects you from me. I asked Keith and your mother, but they wouldn't give me a clue where you were. I sent Sammy a letter to pass on to you."

"I know, I know, David. I know."

"Did he?"

Jade nodded.

I waited for a moment and then I nodded, too. "You didn't answer."

"There was nothing to answer. They weren't your words, or don't you remember? You sent me someone else's letter. Charles Dickens."

"It was all I could say," I said. "I don't know why. I was afraid to send something in my own words. I needed someone else to talk for me."

"That's not how I remember you," Jade said.

"All I needed was one word from you," I said, "and I would have sent you a hundred letters. I wrote them but I didn't send them. I didn't know where to send them or if you wanted me to."

Jade sipped the wine and then ran her tongue over her top teeth, to wipe them clean. Each gesture drove the flag of her reality deeper into me; each movement made it seem more certain we could never be apart.

"I want to ask you a lot of things," she said. "And tell you things. It's too strange. I've just been to my father's funeral and I want to ask you how you've been doing. I can't handle it. This doesn't make any sense."

"How have I been?" I asked. "You can ask that. I mean, I can tell you. It's not very difficult because I'm just how you think of me."

"How do you know the way I think of you?"

"OK. I didn't mean that. I mean I'm just the way I was the last time we saw each other."

Jade looked away and rubbed her fingers together in that nervous way people do when they're used to reaching for a cigarette but they've given them up. I could see the picture she had of herself in that moment, lighting the cigarette, drawing on it and keeping the smoke in her lungs for three or four moments, and then expelling it along with her breath and a sigh.

"The last time we saw each other," she said, "was in Chicago and you were in my house after you set it on fire. Is that how you are now, too?"

I answered without hesitation. "Yes."

She immediately consulted her wristwatch. "It's time to go," she said. "I've got twelve minutes to get eight blocks. I'll be lucky if I make it."

I had already hit upon my plan. I would offer to go with her to the bus station. I didn't know where it was in New York but if it was like most cities it probably wasn't in a safe area. I would insist. She would accept. And then I would tamper with the pace of our journey and cause her to miss her bus. But instead of offering to accompany her, I leaned forward and said, "No. Don't go. Miss the bus. Stay. Stay with me. We haven't talked in so long and I don't know when I'll be able to see you again."

She stood up and it felt as if that gesture was duplicated by a replica of her within me, displacing the blood in my mid-section and sending it in a rush to the five outermost points of my body. I forgot I was holding a wineglass and it dropped out of my hands; it landed upright but then it fell down.

Jade watched the mustard-colored carpet absorb the wine. She was nodding her head in that way that sometimes accompanies thought and sometimes means a tentative yes.

"Please," I said, trying to impress my will on the moments as they flowed away from me, like a child lobbing stones into the sea.

She took a quick gulp of breath and then swallowed. She looked so tired and frightened. A pulse was beating in her forehead; her ears remained an astounding dark red.

"All right," Jade said, in a careful voice, a voice that only pronounced the words, such as you might do if you were making a recording to teach English. "I better call the bus station and see when the next bus is."

I thought she was going for the telephone but she took the three steps separating her from the edge of the bed and sat next to me.

I didn't want to touch her or look at her or do anything to confuse the impulse that had brought her so close to me. I looked straight ahead at the spot she'd been sitting in and I felt her weight shifting. I felt her looking at the side of my face and then she leaned over and rested her forehead on my shoulder.

I longed to return the gesture with a caress of my own, but I knew better. I knew she meant more than one thing by her touch. I was someone she used to know who she was seeing on the day of her father's funeral. It could have meant as little as that. It could have meant even less: exhaustion, sadness, that depletion of spirit that comes when we surrender to another's will. Ye I was sure it was otherwise. There was something specific and deliberate in her touch. She was not merely laying her head against me. There was life in her muscles, in her neck and shoulders; she was making certain not to lean on me too hard. She was touching me and holding back in a way that seemed wholly calibrated, judging where to touch me and how hard, and that meant that not only was the center of her brow touching me but all of her. It added the dimension of decision to her gesture, of measurement and risk, and that made leaning against me as intimate as touching my face or taking my hand and pressing it against her breast. Moments passed, moments and moments, and it felt as if the whole of her being was concentrated in that stretch of brow that homed in on me, just as the entirety of a singer seems concentrated in her mouth as she hits her highest note.

I couldn't put my arm around her without causing her to move her head, so I reached over and laid my hand on her leg, just above the knee. I laid it flat, without closing or even curling my fingers, so it wouldn't seem as if I were trying to take possession of her, or even hold her.

I took measured breaths and tried to ignore my mind's chaotic bursts of speculation and joy, but even so I was trembling.

Jade lifted her head and leaned away from me.

"I'm sorry," I said. "I should have known I couldn't touch you." I pulled my hand away from her, but I continued to quiver. I stood up and walked to the window. I felt my heart pounding, felt it at the back of my throat, in my stomach, the tip of my penis, my legs. I leaned against the window and looked out. Moving above me was a piece of the black and gray nighttime sky. It could all end here, I thought, my life, all life, it wouldn't matter. And the thought seemed so reasonable and did such justice to the wildness of my feelings that I almost said it aloud.

"Are you going to make trouble for yourself by coming here?" Jade asked.

"No."

"But you're not supposed to see any of us. You're on parole. I'll bet no one knows you're here."

"It doesn't matter. No one will find out. I've been gone some of Friday and today. The weekend doesn't count."

She looked at me skeptically but didn't want to pursue the thought: she had inherited from Ann the stylized belief that the best way to be *for* someone is not to show much concern over what they *do*.

"You know who I met on the plane coming out here?" I said. "Stuart Neihardt."

Jade shrugged.

"You don't remember him. He was in my class at Hyde Park High. He works for a dentist now and he's in New York having gold teeth made."

Jade nodded. She suspected I was inviting her to make an ironic remark about Neihardt and she wouldn't do it. She was either too close to other people to make fun of them, or too far above them to bother: it depended on her mood.

"He remembers us," I said. "He has this really sick grief over people he knew who were happy together. He was super lonely and got to hate all of us who weren't. It was strange hearing about us from him. I never think about him so it was weird being remembered."

"I don't remember that name. What does he look like?"

"It doesn't matter. I don't think you knew him. But he said ridiculous things about us. He said he looked in your blouse when you were leaning over some exhibit at the science fair."

"Thanks for telling me."

"It made me fantastically jealous. I grabbed his lip and twisted it."

Jade winced. "God, David. You're so violent and crazy."

"No I'm not."

"You are. You don't know it but you are."

"I'm not. What I feel, it isn't violence or craziness. I don't like violence, and craziness is sad and boring and frightening. I was with a lot of crazy people, you know, and was treated like one, too. I mean there were times when I wondered if I was insane, and then for a long while I *wanted* to be crazy, just for a way to be, a way to have it make sense being there. Something to occupy me, make me less the person I was, who was in so much pain, and more like some other person, someone unknown, whom I could watch. But I wasn't crazy. That was the thing. I wasn't crazy at all, though I know that's the best way to prove you are, saying you're not. All it took for me to get out—I don't know why it took me so long to catch on—all it took was pretending I was changing, that I was starting to feel differently about myself and—" I paused for a moment, to give her a chance to diminish her attention if she wanted to "—about you. All it took was pretending that I was getting over you, that was all." I was sitting next to her again.

"I don't know why I call the people there crazy," I said. "It's not what they are. It's a habit, a way of thinking about Rockville and keeping myself separate. You know what it is? All of us have two minds, a private one, which is usually strange, I guess, and symbolic, and a public one, a social one. Most of us stream back and forth between those two minds, drifting around in our private self and then coming forward into the public self whenever we need to. But sometimes you get a little slow making the transition, you drag out the private part of your life and people know you're doing it. They almost always catch on, knowing that someone is standing before them thinking about things that can't be shared, like the one monkey that knows where a freshwater pond is. And sometimes the public mind is such a total bummer and the private self is alive with beauty and danger and secrets and things that don't make any sense but that repeat and repeat and demand to be listened to, and you find it harder and harder to come forward. The pathway between those two states of mind suddenly seems very steep, a hell of a lot of work and not really worth it. Then I think it becomes a matter of what side of the great divide you get caught on. Some people get stuck on the public, approved side and they're all right, for what it's worth. And some people get stuck on the completely strange and private side of the divide, and that's what we call crazy and its not really completely wrong to call it that but it doesn't say it as it truly is. It's more like a lack of mobility, a transportation problem, getting stuck, being the us we are in private but not stopping, like those kids you'd know who would continue to curse and point and say the secret things even in school or in front of your parents. They wouldn't know when to stop; they wouldn't be the way people wanted them to be. And the thing that made it so terrible for us is that they'd be getting knocked out for doing things that we ourselves did—but we knew when not to do them, we could actually pretend we never ever did that kind of thing, and when it came down to the sticking point, we'd kick them in the ass just as hard as anyone else."

"Like you and me," said Jade. "How *we* used to be."

"What do you mean? Crazy?"

"Living in our own world. Believing what we felt was separate from everything else. We couldn't do anything except be together and nothing else was real."

"That's right."

"Well, that's crazy. And you just said it was, even you."

"No," I said, "not when we both believe it. Crazy people are alone and no one understands what they mean. But that's not our way. We both know and it makes complete sense. It's not crazy when you both believe it, when you make it true by living it. And other people believe it, too, remember. Believe it about us. Everyone who knows us, sees us together. We have that effect."

"Don't."

"Don't?"

"Don't talk about it as if it were still happening. It's not. It's a long time ago."

"A long time ago. But now I'm with you and it doesn't seem that long. I think I could forget all the time in between."

Jade shook her head and lowered her eyes; her fingers were spread out on her lap, the thumbnails touching, the fingers rising and lowering. "Don't," she said. "You don't know who you're talking to. You're walking in air."

"I know you," I said, and the statement took on a weight far greater than I expected, as if the simple claim had within it an emotional magnetism that attracted everything that was unknown, unspoken, everything that was vague and hoped for and dreaded as well. I told her that I knew her and the atmosphere between us became as charged as if I'd finally gotten the courage to lean over and kiss her. Yet I had no choice but to come more and more forward, like someone pursuing a ghost: either the vision would recede into light and dust or it would take on weight and substance.

"You don't know me," Jade said, finally. "You just remember me."

"No. You can't call it remembering. You remember something that's past, over, but if you want to call it remembering, then I remember you the way you remember how to walk if you're bedridden. I mean it's not just looking back, it's returning."

"To being crazy together?"

"It wouldn't matter."

"To you."

"To me."

Jade closed her eyes and shook her head, as if to dislodge an image. "I don't know what we're talking about," she said. "We shouldn't. It's painful, isn't it?"

"For me?"

"That's what I'm thinking—for you. It must be."

"No. You?"

She shook her head. "It's different for me. I'm not a part of this, not in the same way. You've been trying to hold on to what we had and I let it go. It's one of those things when you drop it, it doesn't bounce back, it just falls away, and falls and falls."

"But inside."

"What do you mean?"

"When you drop it, us, it falls but it falls inside you, so no matter how far away it seems, it still is there, close. We're sealed, tighter than space capsules. We can't really forget anything."

"Oh, I think about you," she said, in a voice that was meant to be casual.

"I think about you all the time," I said. "When I was in that fucking hospital, and at my parents', and now in my own apartment."

"Where do you live?"

"Fifty-three eighteen Kimbark. Two and a half rooms. Second floor."

Jade nodded. "Kimbark," she said. "I miss the old neighborhood. We're lucky to be from there, believe me. Especially when you come east. They really give you hell for being a midwesterner out here, but it helps if you're from Hyde Park. You can keep up with things."

"Like what?"

"Talk." She shrugged. "Stuff. Is the Medici Coffeehouse still open?"

"I think so."

"Good. When I was in Chicago last time they were saying it might close."

"When was that? When were you in Chicago?"

"In the winter. The worst time. Worse than Vermont."

"This winter?"

Jade nodded.

"But *I* was there!" I almost stood up.

"I know. I was there with a friend. I thought about calling you. I really did. I almost called your parents to find you. I dropped the dime in the phone but I changed my mind. When I hung up, the dime didn't come back. Scared me."

"You should have. It's so terrible that this is the first time we see each other. Your father's funeral."

"It fits," she said. And then, "Sorry. That was stupid. Anyhow, I said I was with a friend. It wouldn't have worked out very well."

"It wouldn't have mattered. I mean it would be worth it. I'd see you under any circumstances."

"We were on our way to California, Santa Barbara, her home town. So we stopped to see mine."

"Susan."

"What?"

"Her name is Susan. Keith told me about her. Your friend."

Jade was silent, shrugged, her lips pressed tight, jaw tightened: she'd learned the silent warnings people give who don't want to be asked certain questions. She had heard more than she could bear about Susan, about being with a woman and loving her. But the stab of jealousy I felt sunk into dead tissue: I'd bled the wounds a thousand times already and there was nothing more to feel and certainly nothing to say.

"Did you go to your house?" I asked.

Jade nodded. "Yes. It was hard but I owed it. It was a good thing, though. It didn't look as bad in person as it does in dreams. In dreams it's still on fire—just a little, like out of one window, or on the roof, but burning, always. It was good to see it as it really is. Have you?"

"For me it's the opposite. It looks so much like it used to. It makes it harder, as if the whole thing comes close to never having happened. You know how it is when you play an event over and over in your mind and you see all the things that could have happened that would have made everything so different?"

We went toward the silence, sitting close to each other.

"I wanted to write to you when you were in the hospital," Jade said, looking away from me. "To see how you were, you know, and tell you where I was going. But everything was so confusing, then. And I thought I might make trouble for you. There was no right thing to do, for me. It seemed wrong to write you after what happened and it felt wrong not to. I don't approve, you know, I don't approve of letting things drift. I hate that. But—" and then her voice broke, with a soft, furry click, and the color came rushing into her face. She lowered her head and hunched her shoulders.

I took her hand. No. I laid my hand on top of hers and then, one at a time, I curled my fingers around the heel of her hand until they touched the outer border of her palm. "Tell me," I said.

"I feel so alone," she whispered. She'd begun to cry.

"You're not. I'm with you. I'm always with you."

Suddenly we were no longer next to each other. Jade was standing, walking across the room, seating herself in the armchair and blotting her eyes with the backs of her hands. "I'm in my senior year at Stoughton," she said, crossing her legs. She tucked her hair behind her ears. "Next five months I'm going . . ." she trailed off for a moment; her tears had left a web of moisture on her voice. "Next five months is all independent study. I've got two pregnant golden retrievers, one blind. They're both going to drop their pups in a few more days and I'm going to study how the litters develop, how the ones with the blind mother do compared to the ones with the normal mother. Then do a paper and that's it."

"Then you'll be through with school?"

"Just about."

"I go to Roosevelt."

Jade made a face.

"I hardly go. But I have to be enrolled. I have to do a lot to show I'm back in the swim of things."

"Swim of things? That doesn't sound like you."

"It's my parole officer's phrase. Or maybe my mother's. Thank you."

"For what?"

"For remembering what doesn't sound like me, not forgetting."

"I remember. We were sweet together."

"We were," I said.

"I know. It's a once in a lifetime thing. I hate to think it but I bet it's true. It's too bad for us that our once in a lifetime happened when we were too young to handle it."

"Probably no one handles it very well. I mean it's big, isn't it? It's like an emergency. All the rules are canceled."

"Are they? Ever? I know that's what we used to think, all that living in our own world stuff. But we were young. We're still young but we were really young then. I don't want to talk about it, anyhow. All that arrogance, craziness, and what it led up to. When I think about it. All the stuff that you said and I believed. I don't even remember all the stuff *I* said and made you believe. I'm not blaming it on you. But it makes me feel strange to hear about it, like someone telling you everything you said when you were drunk."

"I haven't changed," I said.

"There's no way, it's impossible."

"There's nothing I said then that I couldn't say now. I want to, to tell the truth. But I'm afraid. Not of exposing myself because I know that you know I love you—"

"I don't know that. How can I know that?"

"I love you. I still love you. I love you."

"It's an idea. You've held on to it."

"No. It's real. It's the only real thing. It stands by itself and it hasn't changed. Don't be afraid. You don't have to do anything about it."

"It's not that. It's just I know it can't be true. It's been too long and too much has changed."

"I haven't changed."

"Then you need to believe that," Jade said. She folded her hands onto her lap and then squeezed them together so tightly that the color left them for a moment. "You need to pick the thread up where it was broken. Maybe as a way of forgiving yourself for what happened. At the end."

"No."

"You don't love me, David. I never came to see you."

"You couldn't."

"I never wrote you."

"You couldn't."

"But when you got out. Then."

"It doesn't matter. It's something that can't be changed."

"It can be."

"No."

"When you give your love to other people. When you find out you can feel the same way about them."

"I didn't give love to anyone else."

"But when you try to."

"No. Never. There's one girl, a sculptor, I see her now and then. I just fell into it through friends but we don't try, we don't touch."

Jade shook her head.

"You're all I care about," I said. "No. And me. The person I am when I'm with you, the way I see myself and know myself. That person who lives only when I'm with you."

I stood up. The blood came up into my skull like a wave splashing on the shore. The room softened, moved a little; I didn't know why I was on my feet. I was touching my shirt, poking my fingers in the spaces in between the buttons, discovering the little pool of sweat that had gathered in my chest's hollow. "We're together again," I said. I heard my voice as if it came from another part of the room, perceived it with a kind of woozy clarity: its texture, timbre, its faintly hypnotic monotone.

"I may as well tell you," Jade said. Teasing?

"What?"

"I knew it would be too late to catch that bus. I was counting on you asking me to stay. For a while."

I nodded. I walked toward her. The room was so small. I was already next to her, but I still needed to move. I stepped back, forward, and then, finally, down on my knees. Kneeling before her broke open a deep, unexpected store of feeling; I felt it spreading within me like warm gel. I took her hands and held them on her lap.

"Is this all right?" I asked.

She fixed her eyes onto mine. I could see her sinking into her feelings and she knew she held the silence between us—a silence that sung in perfect pitch—could hold it forever and I would not interrupt it, would not lose faith and question it. I held on to her and her pulse was so powerful that I felt its reverberations in her hand.

"Yes," she said. "It's all right."

I didn't say anything. I lowered my eyes for a moment and then looked back at her.

"I love you," I said.

She leaned forward and I tugged at her hands until she was out of the armchair and kneeling, her bent knees touching mine. We embraced and I felt a sudden terror, more total and enormous than any I'd ever felt before. It filled me as the sound of an explosion would fill a room and then just as suddenly it was gone. I had let go of my past and it receded from me like an open balloon. We lay on the worn smooth mustard rug, as clumsy and disjointed as invalids who have fallen out of their beds, and I was no longer holding on to anything at all except what was directly before me, except for Jade. Like a horse breaking from the gate, my life had begun.

"You've got to hold me," Jade whispered. "I feel like I'm just about to faint but like I've taken a dexadrine too. I'm going in so many directions. Seeing you. Pappy. God. It's too strange. I can't even begin to explain it all, but if you'd only hold me. I broke up with my friend over the weekend. Susan. It was ending for a while but the camping trip finished it. I left her in a place called the Green Mountain Café. I stuck my spoon in a bowl of disgusting oatmeal and hitched home, seventy-five miles.

The message to call Mom. And then finding out and then seeing you and being here. No. Really hold me. Not just a little." She squeezed the back of my hair as if wringing it out.

I held her as tight as I could; it didn't feel as if my arms had much strength. She arched her back and pressed herself against me. Her head was on a dark stain in the carpet that someone else had left. It surprised me for a moment to notice that, but with Jade I always noticed things that were outside of us—cracks in the wall, the smell of wet maples coming through the window screens—and by registering them I made everything a part of us. It had been the same for Jade. We were both of us impossible to distract. Our consciousnesses, having found their perfect human keys, swung wide open and admitted everything. I stroked the side of her face and pressed my mouth to hers.

I could feel she had kissed many times since our time together. Her lips strange. Flat where they had once protruded. Parted much wider, not out of the moment's impulse but out of newly acquired reflexes. I wondered if my own lips betrayed how many times I had kissed the pillow, how many times, lost in fantasy, I'd tasted the back of my own hand. I expected no praise or privilege for my long fidelity. It gave me no moral advantage. The fact was I hadn't been tempted, hadn't been capable. A kind of hysteria, perhaps. A chance to realize some monastic impulse, the negative erotic drive, the inevitable polarity of my conscious, ceaseless yearnings. Looked at another way it was all quite laughable. Or wilful: a temper tantrum. A chance to sit on the jury in my own trial. Almost never—*never*—masturbated. It was lunacy and I'd known it all along. The doctors, in this instance, were absolutely right. Dr. Clark had spoken to Rose and Arthur about my need for sexual outlet. Embarrassed, they kept it to themselves. A decent impulse, their respect for my privacy, but perverted by their shame. And Dr. Ecrest going so far as to threaten to terminate treatment unless I began to release my sexual energies. How I hooted at that one! "Now, let me get this straight. If I don't see you, it's back to

Rockville, right? So what you're saying is that if I don't jerk off, you're going to have me locked up. Right?" I saved my jissom as a prisoner might hoard scraps of cloth—the edges of sheets, shirt collars, cuffs—with the idea of one day making a long cotton chain and lowering himself from the only unprotected stretch of wall.

Suddenly Jade's body went taut. She straightened her back and a space between us snapped open like a parachute. She rolled onto her back and stared up at the ceiling with the concentration of a child watching her life reflected in the moving clouds.

"I feel like I'm being pushed," she said.

"By me?"

"No. Not you. Not only you. Everything. One thing I've learned about myself is it's easy for me to forget who I am. I let things happen. I go along. It's wrong."

"I don't know."

"It is."

She scrambled up. I remained still and looked up at her. I suddenly wanted to smile. What had we been doing on the floor? It made no sense—I was encouraged by our lack of thought. I was sure a quotient of mindlessness was required if we were to reconnect.

Jade opened her nylon bag and extracted a little brown envelope, such as banks use to give you your change when you cash your paycheck. I lifted myself up on my elbows and then stood. Jade squeezed the edges of the envelope so it opened into a kind of cup and she peered in.

"Look," she said, thrusting it toward me. "What's left."

It was a small portion of Hugh's ashes. They were coarse, like broken pieces of peanut brittle. Not altogether black. Silvery and white here and there.

"Everyone took some," said Jade. "You know, like favors at a wedding. We're all supposed to scatter our share in some place Pappy loved. I'm supposed to bring mine to the Green Mountains, even though he never went there. But he loved mountains, especially the Alps. Ingrid's throwing hers all over New Jersey and keeping a little in a leather pouch in her van. Keith's bringing some to Cambridge. Uncle Robert's bringing really a lot down south with him. Isn't it the stupidest thing?"

"No. It's all right."

Jade watched me look at the ashes and when my gaze ticked away from them, she released the pressure from the sides of the envelope and withdrew it.

"Everything's happening at once. Ending this long-term thing with my friend. You know, even seeing my family, I mean just on a nothing occasion, takes its toll. One at a time is hard. In a group—murder. Really. It takes so much out of me. I have to fight for everything. I feel so thick in the past. Everything's exhausting. The family politics don't stop for death, you know. If anything, they get more nasty and frantic, like a chicken running around with its head cut off. And now you. Of all times, right? When I can handle it least. Everything happens at the wrong time—especially between me and you."

"I'm not rushing you. I know what I want, to be near you, but I know it's not simple. I act like I don't know anything except what I want, but I do know more than that."

"I don't feel pushed by you," Jade said. "I don't even know if you can reach me yet. You understand? And I'm exhausted. I can feel little parts of me going to sleep. I'm going to call Vermont Transit and they're going to tell me there's not another bus until about seven next morning. And then I'm going to have to go to sleep. We're going to talk about one of us sleeping in this chair, or camping out on the floor. But that's not going to happen. We're both going to fall asleep in that double bed and it makes no sense for it to be happening like this. If we are going to reinstate our friendship, won't this put another hex on it? I was wrong to stay. We should have arranged to meet some other time."

"I *will* sleep on the floor," I said. "I do that a lot anyhow."

"Why?" Jade asked.

"Sometimes I can't stand being in a bed."

"I've got to sleep." She closed the envelope and pushed her portion of Hugh's ashes into her overnight bag with the impatience of filing a bill you have no intention of paying but don't dare throw away. It was how she treated the mimeographed multiple-choice test papers she'd done poorly on: Jade's talents as a student were ones of accumulation and exposition; she had no skill for filling in the blanks. An associative intelligence, deep, transforming, but not quite specific. She saved the examinations to study her mistakes, shoved them into a sideways folder at the bottom of her little yellow desk. A hoarder of debts, mapping out elaborate voyages of self-improvement. Evelyn Woods Speed Reading. The articles razored out of *Scientific American*. *Twenty-five Ways to a Better Memory*. Sprigs and leaves gathered on walks and stored in a cigar box for future identification. A collection of snapshots, ticket stubs, matchbooks, and menus shoved into a Woolworth's bag with her diary, along with scraps of paper inscribed with key words—"Sammy's stolen bicycle," "examining breasts," "rainwalk"—and all waiting for the ideal time to be inscribed in those empty oblong pages: her life as it happened, viewed from the *outside*. Her great task was to build an intellectual bridge from the universe of insight and feeling to the universe of quantifiable, reportable facts. To be a little more like Keith, able to rattle off her reasons one two three. She could have lived indefinitely in the fertile haze of her instincts and perceptions, but she wanted to learn the outward signals. She was tired of people not realizing exactly how rich and complex her mind was.

But now she was a senior at a good college. She must have learned any number of mental tricks, pared down her thoughts, organized them. Learned how to present herself. Learned how to pass.

She zippered up the bag and slung it over her shoulder. I had a moment's panic that awakened a bit of cloddishness in me: I thought of throwing myself against the door. But she turned away from me, away from the door out, and faced the bathroom.

"I'll change in there," she said.

"OK," I said. "That's fine." I tried to make my voice light but I don't think I got very close.

She hefted the bag once or twice as if she could tell by the weight if everything was in place.

"You want to use the bathroom first?" she said.

"No. Go ahead."

She shrugged, as if I'd refused to take her business advice. "OK," she said, "but I'll be a while."

I was on the floor, so rigid that most of my spine did not touch the rug. In my underwear, covered by a thin, butterscotch-colored blanket (butterscotch-Butterfield: the meaningless association Ping-Ponged in my head) and a cushion from the armchair serving as my pillow. I left the two real pillows on the bed for Jade—her luxury. When I'd slept nightly with her we needed three pillows, the third for her to embrace in those private, essential hours of sleep when her back was to me and her life was as closed as an oyster. Sometimes she kept the pillow pressed to her small breasts, but most often it ended tucked between her thighs. That third pillow was often hard to keep hold of; the other kids appropriated it for their hard, monastic beds. A way of stealing our magic, subtly defacing us. Coal-dusted hands reaching through the iron grille and swiping irises from the rich man's lawn. "I bought that pillow with my own money," Jade had fairly whined, patrolling the house in her robe and not being as careful as she could have been to keep it belted. Even then I realized the teasing arrogance of much that she did, but I never minded: I'd helped to make it possible by whisking her into happiness. Changed her position in the family from one of ambiguous status to a wild card.

Jade got into bed and noticed both pillows were there. I saw her notice. There was always a physical response to information: a nod, a blink, a subtle realignment of posture. But then I thought that she'd made something different out of it. She guessed that I'd left the pillow there because I planned sooner or later to work myself into bed.

I'd folded down the blanket and smoothed the border of sheet so it would look like the bed was new. The lamp with its little tea-colored shade was on next to her bed. Its switch was made to look like an old-fashioned farmhouse key.

When she first came out of the bathroom she was wearing a light green robe, the color of her eyes. She'd walked right by me without pausing, swiftly, as if she needed to cover a great distance. I had my hands behind my head, flexing my biceps so they'd look reasonably large. I tried not to follow her obviously with my eyes. Her feet looked brutal: hiking boots, cross-country skis, inexpensive tennis shoes all had squeezed, reddened, and allowed her feet to callus and spread.

I realized when she slipped into bed that I'd placed my head in such a way that even though I was camped like a dog at the foot of the bed I could still enjoy a perfect angle of her face. As long as she came to rest on the side of the bed the lamp was on— which she did.

She tucked the edge of the pillow into the space between the mattress and the headboard. That hadn't changed. Then she turned off the light. The room didn't go particularly dark; it was maybe 70 percent dark. It was lit by the lights of the city, the dome of diffusion that was above the city, and my own desire to see. Jade unbuttoned her robe and took it off. She wore pajamas underneath, pajamas cut in an Oriental style. They looked wet and shiny in the weak light. It was a modest gesture, finishing her undressing in the bed under cover of darkness, modest and unnecessary, and it gave evidence of a certain kind and intensity of awareness—awareness of *me*, that is.

She let the robe drop to the floor and I went dizzy with hope.

"Well, good night," she said, after a few moments.

I didn't want to say good night; the word would draw the curtain on the evening. "Sleep deeply," I said. I was surprised to hear myself say that, disconcerted. Sleep deeply? A reasonable phrase but foreign to me. And seeming to hold within it—now that I thought about it—some lascivious little worm. Sleep deeply and I'll undress you without your knowing it.

I could sense Jade musing, wondering if there was something more she could say. I thought I heard her lips part; she shifted in bed as if preparing to speak. But then, quite suddenly, I felt her intelligence leave the room like a cat out of the window. She was asleep. The air conditioning hummed louder, making Jade's breaths inaudible. More of my backbone was touching the floor now and I began to relax into a heavy, sullen sleeplessness. She'd left me with shocking abruptness and I would have liked to chase after her in sleep. But I seemed bound to wakefulness and what I had to do was decide what *kind* of insomnia it would be: a vacant, open-eyed cousin to sleep or a clumsy, distorted version of waking. It was a question of coming forward and making the most of it or lagging back as close to the border of sleep as I could, hoping to accidentally fall in.

My thoughts raged. I experienced myself as if I were living before the invention of language. Emotions spurted up but I couldn't name them and without a name they couldn't be modified or controlled. Emotions presented themselves as colors, as spasms, indecipherable voices: if I'd lived at an earlier time, I would have thought I was possessed; I would have strained to decode the instructions of my surging blood, just as ancient warriors bent their ears toward white rivers to learn their orders.

I sat up and wrapped my arms around my knees. My breath felt strained, as if the familiar passageways had been removed and replaced by bright aluminum tubing, perfectly unobstructed but a little too small. Clear thought returned in the form of lavish self-pity. I thought, Here she is after so much time and here I am on the floor. It felt as if this night—with the dawn already sailing in over the Atlantic—would be our only time together, my last chance. That I had read it wrong. Some daring had been required of me and I hadn't figured it out. A lunge. Or perhaps strategy. Flirtation, accusation, cartwheels of wit. My opinions on death. The last role I wanted was that of the woeful tenor standing on the apron of a dark, empty stage, clutching at the brocade of his antique costume.

I wanted to stand up, walk to the bedside, and gaze at her sleeping face. But what if she awakened? A scream of fright? Or perhaps she'd grab me and pull me on top of her.

My desire was heavy, feverish. I knew if I wasn't careful I would elevate my instincts, appoint them to the command.

People make fun of Catholics for confessing to impure thoughts but my own thoughts, reflecting my overcooked passions, were worth confessing to. I would have liked to neatly categorize them into Sin, to gather them in like that and hand them over to someone else. To be absolved. A father confessor.

I had none, of course. The closest I came to a spiritual life was the worship of the very feelings that plagued me now, that closed in on me the way the body does when your temperature is soaring.

Confession. The word stood up in my consciousness, like a monster, a ghost, and every other thought shrank back. Then slowly this one puzzling, unfamiliar word stripped itself down, casting off layers of meaning and association, all the moldy trappings that made it an *idea*, reflex, a duty. And the more the word *confession* divested itself of familiar meanings, the larger and brighter it stood within me. I felt I was being told to do something I had no idea how to begin. I couldn't even tell if my impulse to submit myself to the blind ritual of confession was evidence that somehow in the middle of all this I had taken a turn and wanted to be a different sort of person, or if it meant something much less important—a need to relieve the intense moral pressure, a way of talking myself out from beneath the rock that sat on my chest. Confession as negotiation; confession as show of good faith. Even the Communists had a form of it. They called it self-criticism. You discussed your mistakes and promised your friends you'd do better. They looked at you unpleasantly but forgave you—unless you really fucked up, in which case you were out. My father told me he never went in for self-criticism; he assumed his ideological shortcomings were discussed behind his back anyway. But Rose watched her politics like a sentinel, to the point where her detailed, minute self-criticisms became an expected part of every meeting and came close to becoming a kind of joke. (Rose confessing to white chauvinism and proving her point by reporting she'd given her seat on the bus to a Negro woman who was *younger* than her.)

Why had my father bothered to tell me that my mother was so committed to the act of self-criticism? Had he wanted to warn me not to be fooled by her sometimes monolithic nature? To remember that behind her small, set face, with its deep stubborn grooves and injured eyes, was a self that never lost the habit of measuring and doubting itself. That she was a critic of others but tougher on herself, etc. Or was he inviting me to share his ironic perceptions of her? He seemed to be fooling with his image of her, just as children watching a color TV will fiddle with the controls when they become bored with the show, turning the faces vermilion, royal blue, orange.

Without a priest or any ceremonies, my own father was my last possible confessor—but what deliverance from sin could I expect from that burly, compulsively kind man? Speaking to him about myself was like falling onto a huge sack of oats, neither comforting nor hard. Arthur's view of the world alternated between the grandiosely cosmic and the frigidly empty; either we lived in the warm pouch of a universe that loved us wholly and mysteriously or we were simply configurations of protein and water bubbling for an instant in the long curved beaker of time. In any case, judgment was impossible. The Butterfields were *for* you by examining and ordering your gestures, like cards in a game of solitaire. Arthur's mode of acceptance was flamboyantly blind. He believed in my *fate* as a man of passion and principle and wasn't concerned in amassing data for a proof.

A good boy! A fine son! Oh the joy! Every now and then he would stare at my face to see if I was beginning to look like him. I never came to resemble him but it was no cause for jealousy because I didn't look like Rose either. "He looks like a Russian— but an aristocrat," my father used to say of me. It was better, finally, that I resembled no one. He protected me from his fears of his own mediocrity and in the process withheld all of his majesty as well: the lump in his throat as he faced the scowling jury; the tears over the Rosenbergs; losing at poker with his new friends in the Army because they were destined to lives of manual labor. He considered himself corny, coarse, he was ignorant of the beginnings of his feelings and staggered beneath their weight when they were full grown. It was his wish that I not know him. He was someone to depend on, to take my nourishment from, someone to teach me language and rudimentary manners—the idea of fairness; the habits of pity. But not to know him: he quarantined me from his deepest self as if from a contagion, convincing himself that somehow he was a rooster who'd been given the responsibility of teaching a hawk how to fly.

He wanted to pass the torch—the torch of romance and heedlessness, the torch that could never ignite in his own hands. And when it was ablaze he shyly stole it back from me. He held it now, he displayed it like mating plumage before Barbara Sherwood, he waved it in Rose's face and accused her of being afraid of it. How could I confess to him? The process of his blind love had been reversed: now at this relatively late stage he had finally seized upon the idea that he and I were the same sort of people, and since he had never been less capable of judging himself than he was now, I could certainly not expect anything but the most partisan view of me. Now that we had, in his mind, fused into one person and that person was the man he had always wanted to be, I operated with a moral blank check—my mere signature was good *anywhere.*

Someone was blowing on his automobile horn, that shave and a haircut ditty, as if 34th Street was Elm Street in some midwestern summer town, teenagers out for a night of warm beer and starlight, calling for the class jock. Beep beep. Yo Ed-diiiiie. . . .

"David?" whispered Jade. Her voice was steady, but turned a bit on its side from the brief sleep.

I answered with a sound.

"You can't sleep on the floor?" she said. She stretched her legs, pointing her toes and urging them toward the edge of the bed. I heard it. She let out a low moan as she climbed further out of sleep. I sat up again and looked at her. Her head was half propped up on the pillow. Chin on her chest, reverberating out in a ring of flesh, more like an infant's than an old woman's. Her eyes closed again, shuddered, submitting their sightless wanderings to the curious hum of her intelligence. Opened. Looking down at me.

"I'm not trying to sleep," I said.

"Is the floor too hard?" she said.

I was going to say no but I caught myself, realizing she wanted a different answer. "No, it's OK," I said, in a polite voice, deliberately uncertain. What coyness, but easy to forgive. The formal little bow before the sweaty whirling ecstasy of a barn dance.

"It feels ridiculous, you on the floor," she said. Her neck swelled, lower lip fattened: she was suppressing a yawn, didn't want me to know she was still half gone.

"Always a gentleman," I said.

"Well," said Jade. A pause. It couldn't have been a more sultry silence if she'd practiced it for years—before the mirror, in the woods alone, spare moments. "May as well climb in."

Summer camp lingo. An older sister offering an hour's comfort to poor Peewee after his nightmare.

You're sure? I was going to say. But I had no hope of feigning such innocence. "I want to," I said. I clambered to my feet. A breeze from somewhere rippled across the room, a wavy line, an electrical current. My penis was erect and felt harder than any part of my body—my teeth, my skull. The tip of my cock poked through the fold of my Hanes underwear: it looked so clumsy, comic and frightened, like a stagehand caught on the wrong side of the curtain.

She tossed the second pillow onto what was now my side of the bed, the pillow she had embraced, anointed. The top buttons of her pajama jacket were unfastened; I could have glanced in and seen her breasts. Like Stu Neihardt. I got into bed carefully. She was right on the edge of her side. I settled myself near the edge of mine. On my back, staring at the ceiling, blinking often so she wouldn't fail to notice I was wide awake. She was on her side, turned away from me, arm around the pillow, left leg straight and the right bent at the knee. She was covered to the shoulder by the sheet, but the blanket on her side had been pulled down to her waist.

"Well, here we are again," said Jade.

There was a sense of humor somewhere in that. It confused me, put me on guard. I chose not to answer.

"It just seemed ridiculous, you on the floor," she said after a few moments.

We lay in silence, yet there is no question but that we engaged in deep cellular conversation and were in a sense already beginning to make love. I listened to Jade breathe, noted minute shiftings of her weight. I wanted to empty my mind so I could penetrate Jade's thoughts: I wasn't sure if I believed in trances and ESP but I wanted to be totally receptive to any message she might send me. I think my fantasy was that I would be able to decode her silent request, to make it explicit and encouraging:

that in the hush of my brain I would hear her voice saying, "David, touch me." I heard nothing of the sort; it wouldn't be that easy after all. But I did rid myself of the ceaseless nervous internal chatter. Frivolous, passing awareness was receding. I listened to her lungs fill, felt the oxygen balloon and press against the pink wet walls, then make an acrobat's turn on the exhale. I carefully touched my erection. It felt as if its root spanned my entire body, ganglia down through my thighs, the backs of my legs, clinging to the soles of my feet and up through my belly, shooting straight up to my throat. A fly slowly ticked against a windowshade, or a lampshade, something paper. Jade changed position, slightly. She rubbed the back of her foot against the sheet—nervousness? Or satisfying an itch? A signal of wakefulness, like my batting eyes.

I was on my side now, facing her back, the ends of her hair just over the satin collar of her pajamas, her body and its illusion of massiveness in the near dark.

I fixed my eyes and all their energies onto the back of her head. Psychic trick from fifth grade. Make someone turn around. Make Arlene Davenport blush by staring at the backs of her ears. Make Ira Millman scratch the back of his head by fixing the old beady eyes on his silky black hair. Works, too.

"It's so goddamned hot in here," mumbled Jade. As if to herself? Not sure. She squirmed beneath the covers, moved her arm. About to rip them off her. But no. "Like August," she said.

The heat. Did she mean I was moving too close to her? Pressing the warmth of my own blood in on her.

I thought of *her* blood and in a dizzy leap of hunger and exhaustion I longed to *be* her blood, to be the stuff that made the constant circuit through every inch of her.

Her menstrual blood.

The Tampax string curled into her pubic hair.

Her vagina. The lips yielding to my touch, moistening, opening. To look inside the body. To be inside her body. Joined.

The oak-colored birthmark on the inside of her thigh.

Covering her belly with kisses, lips cupped over her belly button, tongue touching the wrinkled recess, the twin orbits of down rising in excitement.

Her hand on the top of my head. Pushing me down. Gently. Further, oh a little further.

Jade rolled onto her back. Knees raised, feet flat on mattress, hands folded beneath the sheet, resting on her belly. Looking at me through the corners of her eyes.

"What are you thinking?" she said.

But she *hated* that question. She thought it pushed people apart, made it more difficult to speak the truth. A simultaneous violation of privacy and intimacy.

She'd *changed*.

I shrugged. "I don't know," I said.

She shook her head. Sighed. "Stupid question," she said. "Sorry." She turned her head away for a moment and then returned her open gaze to the ceiling.

Looking at her profile. Her narrow nose. ("The Jewish girls hate me for my nose.") The deep chin furrow. The large U-shaped forehead that always looked too delicate, like painted glass.

"I don't know, David," she whispered—the sudden whisper was like being pulled into an alcove. "One of us might have to sleep on the floor after all."

I reached across and touched her shoulder. She allowed herself no reaction and in my confusion of feelings I almost withdrew again, but I kept my touch upon her.

She turned her head. We were directly face to face.

"It's so strange, isn't it?" she said.

I nodded, but not in a way that meant I thought it was strange. It meant that I heard her. It only meant yes, a larger, inclusive yes. An intoxicated yes . . .

We were silent again. The silences were larger now, richer,

more familiar: there was no dead air in them. I felt her streaming toward me in the silence. We were suddenly and again at the
point where *not* making an effort brought us closer.

My touch became heavier. I didn't move closer to her but
the thought of it seemed to shift my weight.

"I wanted you to touch me," Jade said. She had an impulse
to turn away from me but she didn't.

"I wasn't sure," I said. My voice surprised me; it was thick,
unstable, something swollen out of its normal confines.

"But we better stop," she said. "I feel so restless. It's a sexual
thing. Hungry. That old desperate thing. You get to depend on
sex. Depend on coming, on a goddamned *release*, to be perfectly
frank. And there's a way in which you could be anyone, David.
I really feel it would be unfair." As she said it, she brought her
arm from beneath the sheet and laid the palm of her hand against
my chest. My heart, she must have heard it knocking away.
Touched it out of wonder. Or perhaps to silence it.

I knew, obscurely, that her saying I could be anyone was
something that could hurt me. Been meant to, possibly. But it
slid past me. Her ambivalence seemed to matter so little. A mere
problem of the mind . . . How to compare it to the soft dry
heat of her hand on my chest?

My fingers bent at the knuckle and opened out again, moving
further onto her shoulder, touching her collarbone. Her hand
on my chest stiffened and then relaxed.

One of our legs moved. I felt the loose cold satin of her pajamas. Withdrawn.

I rolled to her. My hands on her shoulders, not pulling her
toward me but clearly about to.

She moved her face nearer to me. A blurred darkness rifled
by the noise of her breath.

Her knee touched mine. Withdrew. Touched again.

Then her hand left my chest and was on my cheek. A kind
of sadness in her touch. An undercurrent of farewell. I gripped
her harder, holding on. Her forehead was against mine, the

bridges of our noses. Lips coming forward but stopping short of a kiss.

And then the kiss: light, shy, brief. Swimmers with one toe in the ocean, etc. We leaned away from each other. It was so hard to see and, I think, hard to want to. The closeness not only blocked the room's diffuse light but it encouraged us toward a kind of voluntary blindness. We had seen enough to take us this far. Like pilgrims who have to pass through countless rooms and withstand the most puzzling trials, we found ourselves now in the chamber of deep physical urgency and truth itself seemed of lesser importance, something that could wait. We kissed again. Our mouths were hot and slippery; our teeth climbed. My hand was on my underpants, starting to pull them down. Instinctually. I stopped myself, wrapped my arms around Jade, crushed myself against her.

"David, David," she said. An incantation. And proving to herself it was really me. Forcing herself to *admit* it.

A sigh. Hers or mine? Its edge of impatience told me it was Jade's. She wanted whatever was going to happen to declare itself.

"I've wanted you so badly," I said. "And all the time."

"I'll never sleep," she said.

"It doesn't matter." I was still holding her tight, looking out across to the wavy gray window.

Her breath caught.

"I want to make love," she said.

I loosened my hold on her. I wanted to look into her face. But she held me fast.

"No," she said. "I don't. I don't. We can't make love and it's not really what I want. I want to come. I want to have . . ."

I placed my leg between her legs.

"Will you help me?" she whispered. "Will you like you used to? First me, then you. We can do that." She slid down a few inches, so the top of my knee was flush against her. She moved back and forth two times and then a third, grinding, precise.

"I want to come," she whispered. "Help me. Please." There was something wild and a little cruel in her voice, like an escaped prisoner asking for water.

I pressed my leg higher, harder, felt her give way a little and then bear down on me. A breathy sound in her throat, like a ball rolling down a flight of stairs.

In one motion, I tore the sheet and blanket off of us. They hovered at the end of the bed for a moment and then sank onto the floor. Jade's toes were pointed, her foot tensed and arched like a ballerina's. I put my hand into her pajamas, covering her breast. The skin around the nipples puckered like fingertips left to soak in hot water. Nipples themselves had grown, though the breasts remained adolescent. She'd once been nearly hysterical with shame about her breasts: I'd several times put my fingers into her vagina before she finally allowed me to share the secret of her naked breasts, the revealed artifice of the padded bra. "Bee stings, right?" she'd said, folding her arms over her chest. Now she offered them freely, arching her back as I cupped my hand and then squeezed.

Her shirt was unbuttoned, folded itself into shadows along the line of her ribcage. She was flat on her back now and I was at her side, over her, dropped on one elbow. I touched her belly, slipped my hand beneath the elastic waistband. I suppose my heart was pounding; I suppose my mouth was dry.

"I told you," she said, as soon as I touched her underwear. Lined with a huge gauzy sanitary pad.

I withdrew, confused, startled. Then put my hand on her again, over her cotton underwear, and pressed uncertainly. She arched her back, took a deep breath, telling me that even this indirect contact would do.

I moved my hand back and forth. At one point I became aware I was losing the sensation in my right arm—the arm that supported all my weight as I leaned over Jade—but this aware-ness passed, along with the feeling. I rubbed her slowly, steadily, no variety of pace. She didn't seem to want surprises. Simple.

Direct. The comfort of it increased by the steadiness. The lack of play affirming that romance was kept at bay. The sanitary pad came loose and moved clumsily around. Jade reached into her underwear and removed it, quickly, tossing it overboard. I hooked my thumbs onto her waistband and pulled the pajama bottoms down. She lifted her ass, brought her legs together, made it easy. I turned around to throw them on a chair and she slipped out of her underwear.

"Come," she said, pulling me next to her again, placing my hand on her vagina, moving it back and forth for me once and then letting go, closing her eyes, holding her breath in anticipation.

Her pubic hair was thicker than before. Also dry. Along with the sanitary napkin, she wore a Tampax and it absorbed the moisture.

She reached up and lightly touched my shoulder. Head turned on the pillow, eyes away from me. She was whispering something, but I couldn't understand it. I leaned my ear closer to her but it upset the rhythm on my hand and her legs gave a flutter of impatience. I resumed my original position and pace and her thighs parted still wider. A low groan of encouragement. The whisper louder now: "I want to," she said.

My hand was on myself, my hardness, gripping it with imbecilic force. A drop of semen seeped out, quivering on the head of my cock like a drop of hot wax. Waves of hot and cold. A sense of phosphorescence, X-ray consciousness. I rubbed her mound. The lips opened at the pressure but very slightly. Her legs were open wider than seemed possible. Her willingness, her hunger—they terrified me. *She* terrified me.

"Want to," she said, her chin up, her head all the way back, pressed against the wooden headboard.

I twisted the string of her Tampax around my finger and began to remove it.

"No," she whispered, grabbing my hand. "Can't. Too much blood."

I nodded and continued to move my hand over her. I wanted to touch her everywhere but I didn't dare leave her sex and my other hand supported my weight. I leaned over her, kissed her breasts.

Her teeth chattered. A wave of coldness came over me. I thought of the lights coming on in a city viewed from the air. Then the darkness again. Warm and dense. The sound of her breathing, rapid now, frayed at the edge. Her knees were raised, wagging back and forth. Her moisture seeping through, mixing with the perspiration. Her pubic hair slick, though nothing compared to what I remembered.

She put her arms over her head. There was hair in her armpits now. Long. Curled at the bottom like the toe of a Turkish slipper.

The last time it had been time to shave, she'd let me do it. I took at least an hour, working at the biscuit-colored stubble with a care made up of equal parts of caution and sensuality. "From now on," I'd said, when it was over, "this is my job."

"That's it," said Jade. Her hands were tight fists. Her mouth twisted, grim: not that spacey, surprised look. She gripped my hand and pressed it harder against her, lifted herself up toward me, sawed back and forth. She made a "mmmmnn," sound, rising in pitch.

Her muscles were rigid and she held her breath. Ribcage turned into two parallel rollercoaster tracks. Rump puckered. You're not supposed to hold your breath when you have an orgasm. Jade learned that in a book and taught it to me. "It's living, not dying," she said, then.

She held her frozen pose and then collapsed. A light film of moisture appeared on her skin; her breaths reappeared, heavy and slow. Her eyes were closed.

She rolled over on her side for a moment but then remembered her manners and rolled onto her back.

"That sort of sneaked up on me," she said. "I thought I was further away."

I let myself down onto the mattress without bringing my head up to the pillow. I was eye level with her belly, rising and falling. She'd left her legs wide open but now she slowly brought them together again. Her pubic hair was much coarser than it had been before. The triangle had swollen, increased its domain.

A memory of Warren Hawkes persecuting me with his fantasies in Rockville: "Ah yes my brother, the sweet fuzz of a truly girlish cunt. We are evolving away from the great pleasures. When the sunlight can get through the hair. By the time we're out of here, we'll have to risk arrest to sample that sweet girlish cunt. Sweet, sweet, sweet girlish cunt . . ."

Jade placed her hand on top of my head. I thought she was going to guide my mouth onto her, but she stroked my hair and the pull of her magnetism was upward, away from her.

"I forced that, didn't I?" she said, when I was next to her.

"That? No."

"I did. I don't know why. It seemed logical and right but it always does, doesn't it? When you want something. A pleasure. Or anything, I guess. Now I feel a little . . ."

"I love you," I said. I stroked her cheek.

"I feel so much better. I have to admit." Suddenly, she sat up and patted the sheets.

"What's wrong?" I asked.

"Blood. I thought I felt myself leak. I'm not in the mood to bleed all over these sheets. Well, it's all right. For now. Shit. I'm going to have to get up anyhow and get in my monthly swaddling clothes. I've got the heaviest flow of anyone I've ever *heard* of." She slumped down and rolled onto her side, facing me, our noses almost touching.

"Don't worry," she said. "I'm not forgetting you." She reached down and laid her hand on my stomach. Kissed my chest. Then with a falsely light touch, a delicacy that was terribly exaggerated, she put her fingers over my erection.

"Not like that," I said.

"Yes. It's all right."

"I want to be in you."

"No. We can't. Don't worry, don't worry." She gripped me harder. She made a circle with her thumb and forefinger and slid it down the length of me. Gripped the base, and then pulled up.

"You're bigger," she whispered.

"No."

"I think so. But maybe it's just I . . ." she was probably going to say it had been a while since she'd made love with a man.

I felt suddenly annoyed, jealous, shy.

She moved up and down me, slowly, at the same pace I'd stroked her. I was trying not to come, trying to gather the courage to insist again that she let me enter her. But then she touched the side of my face and kissed me—lightly, like an infatuated stranger—and everything began to fall away. I felt myself coming without experiencing any real pleasure. I discharged a long unbroken ribbon of burning semen. It was shooting somewhere or other and then Jade turned my penis toward me and I felt the come against my belly, my biceps, my collarbone.

Now the pleasure, long moments after the release, seeped through me, honey from a broken jar.

"God," Jade said, "you got it all over me." She sounded vaguely pleased. She was still holding my cock. "But you're still hard."

"Yes," I said. I was on my back; I thought of a patient waking in the middle of an operation.

"You're still like that?" she said, letting go.

"I don't know. I'm with you, that's all."

She sank into her pillow, letting out a sigh and drawing it around her like a curtain. She folded her pillow in half, drew her knees up. "We've got to sleep," she said. "I'm so tired I can't even follow my own thoughts. Really."

Suddenly she slipped out of bed, gathered up her underwear and pajamas, and then got her travel bag and took it all into the bathroom. I lay there for a moment wondering what to do with the come that was all over me, but then I sprang up and before I could think my hand was on the bathroom door.

I turned it. Unlocked. I threw it open.

Jade had the tops of her pajamas draped over her shoulders. She held a rectangular sanitary napkin and her underwear. She stood with her thighs pressed together and her pubic hair grew out in long fern-like curls.

"This is it?" I said softly. I touched the door, to show I hadn't meant to make the frightening noise.

"What."

"We can't do this," I said. "I should have stayed on the floor. No. You should have stayed in the lobby, or caught your bus. We can't have this be the way we get back together. Jerking each other off? I can't do that."

She held her pajama bottoms in front of her. In the watery glare of the bathroom light I saw they were orange.

"We were just helping each other, David. Like old friends."

"Helping each other what. Go to sleep?"

"Yes."

"But I don't want to go to sleep. I want to be with you. It's been a while, right? It's been a long goddamned while."

"I couldn't sleep and *I* need to," said Jade. "Think of me for a change."

"I do think of you. All the time."

"I wonder."

"No, you don't. You know I do."

"I want to end this day, David. I want to pull the plug and let it all go down the drain."

"We're naked together," I said. I stepped forward, reached for her. My cock was absolutely erect. I remembered there was come all over my belly. Too bad. I reached for Jade's hand and got her wrist. The gesture seemed much too aggressive. Only her coming toward me, throwing her arms around me could have salvaged it.

"Please," I said. "Come back to bed. Don't put your clothes back on. Don't go to sleep yet. Be with me."

"You don't understand," she said.

I put my arms around her, kissed her hair, her forehead, the sides of her face. They were the most adulterated of all my embraces: I wanted to make her want me. I pressed myself against her, some distant surviving remnant of mating ritual. I presented myself to her.

"Go into bed," she said, as I tried to kiss her mouth. She put her lips onto mine, briefly. "I feel like you're forcing things. I want to think."

"Come with me," I said.

"In a minute. I'm scattered all over the place."

"It doesn't matter," I said. My knees puckered with impatience.

"In a minute. Just let me think. I want to decide. OK?" She moved out of my embrace, back a step.

I got into bed and turned on the lamp. I waited for Jade, but I don't know how long. It seemed like quite a while but there's no reason to trust myself in this. It could have been thirty seconds. It was its own time, separate, like the inestimable durations of dreams. I was at the bathroom door again, having spliced away those instants of consciousness I would have used for reflection. I opened the door carefully. Jade, naked, sat on the edge of the undersized tub, her head in her hands, weeping.

"I don't know what to do," she said. "I'm afraid of you. I've got too much to feel right now. I can't let myself go too far."

She looked up at me. There were white fingerprints on her face.

I thought: We *must* be out of our minds. Haven't seen each other in years. Standing naked in a hotel toilet, weeping, shivering, cock pointed straight up.

"It's all right," I said. "We can just go to sleep." I stepped forward, put my hand out to her. She took it, brought it to her moist, flushed face.

"I have this voice in me," Jade said, "and it's a very small, simple voice. It keeps on saying, 'My daddy's dead.' It doesn't even sound like my voice. I never called him Daddy." Her voice broke; she tried to smile but that broke too. "And I keep thinking of Keith and Sammy and what they're going through. And Ann, too, damn it. Ann, too. All of them are with me and I can't handle it. I've done everything to get out of this family and the smaller we get, the more I'm in it." She paused, covered her eyes. "I just wish my father were still alive," she said, sobbing.

I brought her to bed and kept my arms around her. She was trying not to cry. I could feel her impatience with herself, her exhaustion with her own grief. Soon she was quiet.

"I wonder what time it is," she said, just when I was wondering—with a certain dread—if she'd fallen asleep.

"I don't know. Late, I guess." My arm was beneath her shoulder and it had fallen asleep but nothing could have made me want to move it.

"Everyone knows all about you, you know," Jade said.

"Who?"

"Everyone I know. I tell everyone about you. What it was like for us. You know, stories about the house and Chicago and being like we were."

"I don't know that many people," I said.

"Everyone in Stoughton knows you. I'll bet—well, you look a little different but not that much—I'll bet if you walked across campus, all by yourself, a lot of people would know you were you."

"Honestly?"

"And I don't have pictures or anything. It's all from talk. Sheer description. I talk about you and remember, and when I want to I let myself feel what it was like to be me with you. But God, David, this is something I never thought would happen. It just never seemed like it could. Even when I was in the elevator coming up here, I didn't believe I'd actually see you. Do you know what I mean?"

"But I saw you yesterday."

"A dream. So fast, then poof. It didn't count. It seemed impossible to be with you ever again. And wrong."

"It's not, though," I said. "It's really not. I don't know why it's been so hard for us, everything going so wrong all the time. But I know we can't turn back. That's true. I'm sure of it. Whatever is being put in front of us, we have to walk through it."

"Everything's so different," Jade said.

I didn't know what to say. Jade didn't say anything and the silence continued. Jade took the lamp off the table and placed it on the floor, still burning. It toppled over and threw long flat shadows across the room like railroad tracks.

A little later, Jade sat up and pulled her Tampax out and dropped it beneath the bed. I stayed on what had become my side of the bed and she sidled next to me, pressing herself against my hip and squeezing my chest as if I had breasts. For some reason I tried to lift myself on my elbows but she pushed my shoulder to make me lie flat. She seemed to be looking down at me from an enormous height.

"I want to do this," she whispered. "But I don't want it to . . ." she trailed off.

"It'll mean whatever it means," I said. I reached up for her.

"Or nothing. It's just this night. Seeing you again on top of everything else. I don't want us to hurt each other, David."

I knew I didn't much care if we hurt each other. No pain could match the emptiness of separation, no agony rivaled the unreality of not being with her. But I didn't want to frighten her away. I nodded.

We kissed and stroked each other for a while. Jade straddled me and I thrust up to enter her, but missed. She took hold of me and guided me in. She felt a little dry and her discharge was thick, viscous—the result of her period, the blood mixed with her normal secretions. She winced as I entered her—it's awful, really, how stirring men find those small signs of pain. She lifted herself up a little and I popped loose of her. She came back down until the knobby bones of our hips touched and the bow-shaped curve of my cock pressed into the cushy heart of her genitals, sinking until it hit a ridge of cartilage. I pressed her at the small of her back; her hips were locked around mine now and I felt her pubic hair brushing against me, as soft as breath on my belly. I pulled her down, made her bend from the waist and crushed our chests together.

I whispered her name and when she didn't respond I felt a moment's panic.

I held her face and kissed her mouth. Her tongue felt huge, soft, and unbearably alive in my mouth. I breathed her breath. It was the night's first real kiss. Precise, enormous.

She was up on her knees, her small breasts dangling a little, the light on the floor illuminating each strand of down. I put my hand between her thighs and cupped her vagina and Jade opened herself to me, posing for my fingers. She was open at her center and it was at least ten degrees warmer there.

Then, suddenly, I was inside her. I would have wanted to stop, to absorb the moment. She was straddling me, her hands on either side of my head, her forehead pressed against mine. She moved slowly, with her eyes screwed tightly shut, until I was all the way inside of her, and then she rocked back and forth, pressing herself against me with such huge power that I thought I might cry out. Yet it was not pain, of course—the intention of her pressure was specifically sexual and so potentially ecstatic that my nerve ends could only disregard their habits of response. The power with which she ground herself against me was awesome; it was all I really felt. I could sense the division in her genitals yet I could feel myself inside her only indistinctly.

To keep her balance, Jade planted the heel of her hand in a wedge of soft muscles beneath my shoulder. I felt surrounded by a membrane of pleasure, a huge, incandescent cocoon, brilliant and opaque for the most part but diaphanous at this curve or that. And through those patches of pleasure from which the color had somehow drained, I was intermittently aware of the shadows on the wall, the creak of the bedsprings, the peevish nuzzle of one prominent mattress button. Then, like a slowly revolving dome, the pleasure surrounded me in all of its opacity and I was lost again.

I was covered in sweat; my muscles ached as if knotted by fever. Someone somewhere in the hotel flushed a toilet and the sound roared through the thicket of my senses.

Jade moved back and forth, back and forth. I could tell she was not altogether with me. I'd never remembered, never thought of making love as something so *private*. The only commitment was one of need, but it seemed to stop there.

Jade kept one hand on me to hold her balance and placed her free hand on her belly. I noticed it dimly and wondered if she were in pain—a menstrual spasm, perhaps. But her hand slipped down, led by her extended index finger, and headed straight for her clitoris, lodging itself in that small space that existed between my pudendum and hers. She stroked herself with a rapid, circular motion while she raised and lowered herself on me. It seemed devastatingly expert of her. I could imagine it diagrammed in a book, explained at a symposium. Perhaps that sounds humorous, but it wasn't at the time. Her up and down motions were steady but incomplete: she had somehow calculated the degree of withdrawal and repenetration that best accompanied her finger's masturbatory spiral.

She was even too expert to forget me. She fixed her eyes on mine for a moment and then closed them, as if in a swoon. She bent low to touch my face with her lips—so dry, as if she were lost in a sexual desert and my face was only a mirage. But she did kiss me, and when I captured her retreating mouth with my own kiss she lingered, breathing the air out of my lungs and exhaling into me the pungent blend of our combined redolence —the flat red wine, the long night, and the radiation of our nervous systems.

The dome of pleasure my senses had crouched beneath was

no less opaque but it seemed to have risen: it no longer enveloped me like a blanket but now sheltered like a tent. I could feel my own orgasm moving within me but it would suddenly dart in some new direction, like a fish hiding within a coral reef.

When her climax came—and it appeared suddenly, like an accident—Jade trembled and made a high whinny, as if in distress. Then she was absolutely still, like a startled animal etched in the brightening beam of speeding headlights. Her mouth was open; it seemed as if she might drool but she closed her lips and lifted her chin, breathing out so heavily that her belly swelled and made her look pregnant for a moment.

Of course when you love someone it is a tireless passion to experience their pleasure, especially sexual pleasure. Of all the many perversions, the one I found myself most capable of succumbing to was voyeurism—as long as the object of my voyeurism was Jade. I never failed to be moved by her expressions of sexual pleasure. When we were first learning to make love and I had some trouble in controlling myself, she had to be careful to keep as quiet as possible. Even heavy breathing would speed my climax, not to even mention moans. Later in our life together, when we were making love three, four, and five times a night (for our passion grew with our prowess), Jade would sometimes become impatient for my final orgasm—which would come with more difficulty than hers, because of the natural differences between the genders—and to bring us safely home so we both might fall asleep she would feign groans of pleasure with her lips right next to my ear, or say my name. It wouldn't really take anything more than that.

And so it was that night. As soon as her body began to jerk and shudder in response to her climax, I found myself astoundingly moved—as if by choral music that surprises you, or a kiss from behind bestowed by your lover on tiptoes. Jade let out her high keening call and I felt an abrupt rush of my semen, racing through me like twin rivers, turning with an acidic twist but not slowing down. I grabbed hold of her back, instinctually afraid she might leave me, and I arched myself toward her as I came. I could sense my pleasure passing through me almost unnoticed and I tried to fix my entire concentration on it. A perceptual lunge—like trying to discover the silver arc of a shooting star whose dive through the sky you've just caught out of the corner of your eye. When Jade felt the blurry warmth of my climax, she moved up a little and tightened herself for a slow, deliberate slide down. Whatever semen I had surrendered at the coaxing of Jade's fingers had left a prodigious storehouse behind—almost a *creepy* abundance. My scrotum, feet, hands went icy cold and my mouth—moments before filled with the slosh of desire—was dry as a wafer. My muscles were collapsing, my lungs shriveled like burst balloons, but I continued to come.

Jade looked down at me. Smiled. Her eyes were glassy, indistinct, like someone who has breathed in smoke. A burning room. She was about to say something but she didn't. She leaned forward until I was no longer inside her and then she was flat out beside me. She was breathing deep, easy breaths and I suppose I was too, but the silence between us was troublesome, dangerous. It lay coiled like a sleeping cat, graceful in its way but liable to claw if stroked indelicately. I could feel Jade considering and rejecting possible things to say. Her leg touched mine but then moved away. She sighed: relaxed, slightly pleased.

I began to plunge into the static blackness of sleep, like someone who is staggering along and walks into a ditch. But I pulled myself short, dug my nails into my palm.

Jade reached down and switched off the fallen table lamp.

Finally, she broke the silence: "My bones feel like lead."

I didn't say anything for a while. I had prodded myself into a state of wakefulness and I was just realizing how furious I was. Then I whispered, "That was the first time I made love since the last time I was with *you*, you know."

"Amazing," she said, rather quickly.

"Why?" Because it's so pointless? Because you've made love so many thousand times since?

"Because you're so *good*." She stretched her body and rubbed her eyes with the back of her hand. Propaganda for sleep. Getting me used to the idea; pointing everything toward it. It was how my parents used to put me to bed. Arthur would check the time. Eight o'clock and both of them would break into extravagant yawns . . .

"Good?" I said.

"Yes." She seemed to regret bringing it up.

"That's funny," I said. "I didn't feel like I had much to do with it. Where'd you ever learn to do that?"

"Do what?" There was a real edge on her voice now.

"That thing with your hand. You were making love to yourself, weren't you?"

"Oh God, David," Jade said in an older sister accent.

"Well, weren't you?" I loathed my voice. Consciousness roamed the circumference of my brain, turning like a lighthouse beam, stopping here and there when a dense patch of darkness threatened to swallow the light, extinguish it. Unexpectedly, I found myself wading through that stream of unconnected images that surrounds the heart of sleep like the rings of Saturn. I had only a slight hold on myself and I realized that Jade must be in much worse shape: it wouldn't take all that much to have us screaming at each other. "You weren't making love to me. You were just fingering yourself, for Christ's sake."

"Oh shut up, David. You don't know anything about it." She opened her eyes and looked up at the ceiling for a moment and then closed them again. I could feel her thinking: Why did I come here? But I didn't know if it was what she really felt or if she was just wondering if she might say it, for its effect. She needed to push me back, that much was certain. And I would rather have us end up with our hands on each other's throats than to drift apart now, to descend into the privacy of sleep with our makeshift pleasures clutched to our breasts. The kind of junk jewelry that turns you green.

"Jade . . ."

"Let me alone. *I've got to sleep.*"

I was silent. I put my hands on her.

"You make me feel really *stupid,*" she said, accusingly. "I could prove to myself backward and forward and inside out that it was fucking *stupid* to come here and really stupid to make love with you—but no one could prove it the way you are doing right now. You really prove it, David. How stupid I am. You really do." She was up on her elbows, looking at me.

"But that's not how we make love," I said. "We don't do that, that business with your hand. It's not our way."

She sighed as if finally realizing she was attempting to speak rationally to a madman. She fell back on her pillow and then said, "Oh, for Christ's sake," and sat up again. "I'm bleeding," she said into the darkness. "I almost forgot." She patted the mattress between her legs. "Oh God. I blew it."

She swung her legs out of bed, bent down, and turned on the light. The fallen lamp reflected directly into the grimy window, in that three inches of black glass between the hastily drawn curtains. Jade peeled the covers down to see what had happened. An oval of blood, bright and sticky, rather more brown than red, the color of an apple bruise. "Lovely," she said, shaking her head. There were little wisps of bloodstains here and there, but most of it was in that oval—the size of a bar of soap.

I happened to look down at myself. My cock was glistening and red with blood. There was a little blood on my belly and quite a bit of it on my thighs.

Jade shook her head.

"It's glorious," I said. I touched my fingers to the blood on my legs. Some of it came off and I brought my fingertips close to my eyes.

"We better strip the bed," Jade said. Her legs were close together and slowly she was beginning to fold her arms over her breasts: the blood was making her ashamed.

"No. We don't have to." I wanted to tell her I liked that

blood a lot more than the orgasm she'd given herself with her
finger when she was supposed to be making love to me.

"Well, *I'm* not going to sleep in that goo," she said.

"I will," I said, sliding over. I reached out for her, took her
around the waist. The hair around the opening to her vagina was
dark with blood; I pressed her close to me and kissed it. I was
leaning out of the bed in a twisted, uncomfortable position; my
erection was nuzzled right into my belly. Jade put her hands on
my head. I thought she might pull me away from her but she
gripped me with both hands and dug her fingers into my scalp
and then, moments later, discreetly yet unmistakably, she inched
her hips forward, moving herself closer to my mouth, opening
herself to me.

I pulled her into bed. I wanted to go into her immediately
but I was frightened and I could feel her fear, too. It wasn't a
matter of inhibitions, or shyness, or doubt. The resistance of our
bodies had already been broken down. The unfamiliarity of
nakedness—gone. Even Jade's twinge of embarrassment at her
own blood had been quieted by my drinking it. The fear we felt
was that terror you experience when the possibilities of your life
begin to match the full range of your desire. It was the great
fear the first pilots must have felt when their planes nosed slowly
off the ground, the blinding anticipation of a treasure hunter
with his hands finally trembling on the half-buried chest of gold.
I ran my hands lightly over her and she trembled: it was not, for
the most part, a shiver of pleasure. She stretched herself out,
arched, but it seemed almost involuntary. She said nothing;
her breath was not even loud. But I was certain that I was now
approaching her, the part of her that had remained alive to the
possibility of my return.

I kissed her. I felt the fog burning off within both of us, could
see the origins of her feelings, deeply into her, like those ten-mile
vistas in the farm country. Back, back so far, through the heart
of Illinois, following the fertile rows, hazeless, almost airless sky,

and where the vision finally ends is where there is simply nothing more to see. A pulse beat in her forehead; the veins along the inside of her arm were hard, almost like little delicate bones. Our mouths were open wide, as if we wanted to swallow each other. Cannibalism and kissing, I thought, trying to stand back from it for a moment, oddly theoretical, the way you might seize upon a passing fascination with blood after accidentally cutting yourself, choosing to concentrate on the bright gush rather than the pinwheels of pain. But this was not pain, and nothing like it; I sought refuge from softer feelings, softer and more vast. If it was only pain, then I would have been able to imagine its wretched conclusion, but what I felt with Jade seemed the beginning of something with no known limits, the unknown parts of the body and the spirit. Out of the perceptual prison! Storming the barricades! But really: *storming the barricades!* A journey into unexplored space. Not to the moon, not to Venus or Saturn, but outward toward the universe's most outward curve, up and around the horn of time.

"David," she said, when I put my finger inside of her, as if now, this instant, was the first time I'd touched her. Her arms were around my neck and she squeezed me with the unexpected strength of someone who is drowning. She brought our faces together, not in a kiss—our mouths were slippery inches apart—but in an indiscriminate crush. My forehead was on her cheekbone and I think if she'd pressed me against her with any more power I would have broken it.

I tasted blood in my mouth. It was Jade's and it was mine: I'd broken the flesh on the inside of my lip.

She held me down below and tried to push me into her. When I touched her near her opening, she let out a small cry. I slipped away from her.

We turned to face each other. Our bodies were fluttering. Birds caught in a cold chimney. I humped back and forth. My cock was against her belly but we were both so wet now that everything seemed a prelude to penetration. Our smell rose from the mattress, flapping like a wet sheet. The bedsprings were whistling, twittering, groaning. The sound of our bodies in all the wetness like footsteps in morning grass, crushing the tiny air bubbles of dew.

Down between her legs, on my knees, with my hands on her thighs, I licked her more like a dog than a lover. I ran my long lilac tongue over her thighs, the skirt of flesh at the bottom of her rump, her pubic hair, inside her vagina, her belly. She flexed her legs in and out as if treading water. I felt something lodge on my tongue. A pebble-sized clot of blood. I removed it and then wiped it off my hands onto my chest.

She was making a high-pitched moan. Distant. A voice locked in a box at the back of her throat. It became higher, more present. Her pubic hair was so wet that the skin around her opening was bare, unprotected; dilated enough for a premature birth. I kissed it fully as if it were a mouth. Her thighs were rigid now, trembling, ticking like a clock. Lifted herself toward me. Her legs were off the mattress now, lifted straight up. I crawled toward her on my knees, keeping my mouth on her. I was kneeling directly in the center of her blood now. Her breaths were coming fast, with a pneumatic wheeze at the end of each one. Her hands clawed at the mattress; though it pierced nothing but the air between us, I felt an enormous pressure in my sex. I heard the sheet rip beneath Jade's fingernails.

"David," she said, in that feverish, sliding way. She meant for me not to stop, or vary. Her opening was even larger now and it seemed to have a kind of undertow, a riptide. I remembered not to touch my mouth too hard against her tenderest parts but I increased the pressure, just a little. I felt something running down my chin; I didn't know if it was her blood or my spit, or a combination. I caught my breath by opening my mouth still wider. She came forward at the same time and my teeth accidentally knocked against her wet insides. Sweat was rolling into my eyes and I thought it was tears. She clapped her legs closed; her thighs covered my ears. I heard her moan as something eerily distant. But I heard its pitch rise again and I knew she was about to come. I didn't lift my mouth off of her but I held it still. The pace of her movements doubled as I stopped but I placed my hands on her hips to hold them still and then I moved away from her.

Her body quieted down but her breath came in explosions. Its sound filled the room like panic. Her legs thrashed; I looked at the smears of blood on her thighs, visible now through the first gray layer of dawn. I placed my hand on her, squeezing. She placed her hand on top of mine, closed her legs, and moved up and down.

"David," she said, "I'm so close."

"To me," I said. I was lying next to her now, with my arm around her shoulders. She drew her knees up, rolled over, pressed herself against me.

"Inside me," she said.

"No. I want to hold you." I thought to myself: I may never be with you again. A desperate idea but it flew by like something blown about in a storm. Thoughts, images—everything seemed to be moving away from me, as if the contents of my mind had been stuffed into a cannon and fired. Dr. Ecrest saying he had no intention of reading my files forwarded from Rockville, dropping them into the wastepaper basket right before me. Arthur's sad and anxious grin as he watched me talking to Barbara Sherwood at her bedside in Jackson Park Hospital. Chasing the ball, a big fat softball as pliant as dough, across the lawn at Rockville, rolling away, rolling rolling, coming to rest at the fence to The Outside, where two little blond townies stared at me, holding onto the fence but backing away as if I might try to grab them by their empty belt loops . . .

"David," Jade said, touching my face. She turned me toward her and put her mouth on mine.

I embraced her with all my strength; her vagina was against my knee, moving back and forth.

"I feel so much," she said. "It's scary."

"I know," I said. "I'm very frightened."

"Only with you." She ran her hand over my face. I caught one of her fingers in my mouth and sucked it blindly. It tasted of salt. "Only with you, David. It's so strange."

I rolled on top of her. Her legs flew apart; her hands gripped my slippery back and pressed me down.

"Don't wait," she said. "Come inside me. I want to feel you inside me."

"I don't want it to end," I said.

"Inside me."

I slipped in so easily. It was only when I pushed myself all the way in that I felt the tug of her flesh. She seemed to narrow, further in.

I came immediately. She was so wet and I didn't make anything of my orgasm—no particular interest in it; it was something occurring on the side—and I remained just as hard so Jade scarcely knew it had happened. I stopped to rest for a moment and she looked questioningly at me. Then I began to make love to her. I was clumsy, surprised by the limitation of our bodies. Only our nerves, our imagination, and our desire were infinite; our bodies remained beneath gravity's thumb, ruled by the stern congress of tendons and joints. More than once I misjudged how close together we were and our bodies slapped together with a hollow wet clap.

I could feel it getting a little out of control. Her arms were thrown out to either side, her legs opened wide, she was moving up and down and from side to side and we were slipping around quite a bit. There was no control. I held on to her and every now and then her hands would grab on to me. Then we'd be tilted to one side and in danger of falling out of bed altogether. The racket we must have been making. I wouldn't be surprised if the front desk got a few calls of complaint. And if any single, lonely guests found themselves with an ear to the wall and a hand on their middle, I would have to forgive them. We turned slowly in the bed as we made love. A clock with one hand. The bedsprings were the very soul of indiscretion and at a certain point the headboard began to thwack against the wall. Jade had begun her high warbling hum, a tone like a sad, unendurably erotic pitchpipe. I felt another orgasm taking shape within me, locating itself not so much in my genitals as in my belly, the backs of my legs. I slowed the pace and this time Jade didn't protest. She moved her head back and forth and said my name and I said hers.

Suddenly, I withdrew from her completely. She let out a whimper of surprise and, instinctually, brought her hand down onto herself and squeezed. I kissed that hand and then it moved away and I kissed her hair, her belly. I was straddling her, looking at her, knowing that my eyes looked glassy and half mad—like hers. She was panting and shivering and her body continued to move over the mattress, as if we were still joined.

"I love you," I said. "It's so much more, so much, but I don't know what to say. Nothing's changed. I remember everything, even the things that have changed. I love you, Jade. I love you."

"Come in me," she said. She lifted herself up with her hands around my neck and kissed me. Then she reached down for me and pressed the head of my penis into her. "I want to feel us," she said. And when I lowered myself upon her and sank as deep as I could go, her voice was replaced by that high keening hum. I watched her face as best I could. Those strange contortions that would be so horrible under any other circumstances. Her lips parting, stretching, her mouth opening in a silent howl. Eyes closed and then suddenly open, staring up at me with real helplessness, mixed with hunger and surprise. The heel of her hand hit my chest; it seemed for a moment as if she were going to try to push me off of her. But it passed. She was rising toward me, levitating, holding on with her hard competent hands. I could feel her reaching her climax and I almost stopped because I didn't want it to end. It was, after all, how we'd taught each other to make love: the sin of the Adamites; the psychedelia of the suppressed orgasm. Each time I stopped, the eventual come would be more powerful. Each interlude would send us streaming closer together. But as I slowed my pace she quickened hers and her grip had a sternness in its strength, an undertaste of fury. I thought that if I didn't carry through she might actually punch me in the mouth. And so I slipped my hands beneath her rump so no matter what our bodies did they would be touching and I would stay in her as deep as possible. The hum became a kind of toneless noise, like the loudest part of a yawn stretched out indefinitely. Sweat ran off her back and new threads of blood came out of her: I could feel it pooling in the spaces between my fingers. I was totally soaked. The cut on the inside of my mouth had opened again and spawned in my drool to create a dark pink torrent. Jade's eyes were wide open now and she was staring up at me: with her mouth turned down in an aspect of weeping, the stare seemed almost accusatory. She was shaking all over, not just her feet and legs, but tremors running like currents from her vagina, straight up her belly, and into her chest. I finally realized that half the noise I was hearing was my own: I was moaning like a dumbstruck giant, a low, clobbered, dizzy note. We were starting to slip off the bed, we were slick with sweat and blood. We were moving like mad and suddenly I could feel her inner walls in terrifying detail, as if I'd gotten fifty times thicker. We came, first Jade and then me, moments behind her, holding each other, and our voices joining, forming one wild and unbearably lonely cry.

The rest of that night is lost to me. I remember a slight, almost embarrassed silence, but it lasted only moments. Jade said her blood felt phosphorescent and at one point I burst into tears but I stopped myself fairly quickly. There was conversation but I don't remember about what. We just talked. I started to fall asleep but then Jade said something. I don't know what, but the sound of her voice made me roll on top of her and we made love again, for a long while. Jade said, "No, rest, rest," and rolled me over and we made love with her on top. She held my face in her hands and held my mouth in a long open kiss and made love very slowly until we both came. More conversation. The windows bright gray. Almost falling into sleep like slipping off the ledge of a cliff. She was on her belly, with one leg almost out of the bed and her soft, flattish rump high. I entered her vagina from behind and only when I cupped my hands on her breasts did I realize she had fallen asleep.

A few hours later, a chambermaid unlocked the door and opened it as far as the safety chain would allow. The sharp metal bang awakened us both and we sat up in bed. The door was open three or four inches. We could see the sherbet green sleeve of the woman's uniform.

"We're still sleeping," I called out.

Jade sank back down into the bed. The room was filled with dull white light now and I looked us over. We were both covered in dried blood. The sheets were stiff with it. If we hadn't put the chain on, the poor cleaning woman would have walked in on us and perhaps fainted. Immobile, we would have looked like the victims of a savage crime. There was blood on our legs, our thighs, our arms and fingers. There was blood in our hair and in the corners of our lips. Our lips themselves were caked with it.

15

There was nothing to discuss. The next day I went with Jade to the Port Authority Building and when the bus left for Stoughton I boarded it with her. Jade's overnight bag was bloated like a sick black fish: rather than leave the bloody linens behind, we'd stolen them. We did it to be polite, really, thinking that the small loss suffered by the hotel would be preferable to the experience of the chambermaid having to confront the stiff brown and red sheets. But even though our intentions were good, the moment we stuffed the sheets into Jade's bag was a shaky one. She said, "Stealing from a crummy hotel," and shook her head, as if this might reflect on us, our willingness to commit crimes both great and puny, our destiny to be always outside the proper way of doing things.

There were other shaky moments, of course. Paying my hotel bill took all my money and I didn't have enough cash to buy the ticket to Stoughton. What I wanted to do was cash in my return ticket to Chicago, which was worth about forty-five dollars, but Jade insisted on paying my bus fare. It wasn't a generous impulse, it seemed to me. The idea of my ticket to Chicago comforted her and her need of it galled me. It was things like that. Our coming into and going out of focus: constantly, we were reminded of how partial our reunion still was. The bus was crowded nearly to capacity, which astounded me. I looked up and down the aisles, shaking my head. "We were lucky to find a seat together," I said. "I had no idea so many people would be going to *Stoughton*. It's incredible."

Jade frowned at me, took her hand from me. "This bus goes to a lot of places, David," she said. "Albany, for instance. God. It's so much like you to think that just because *you're* going to Stoughton then *everyone* is." I smiled because I actually liked the way Jade speculated about the details of my character, how the net of her intelligence would unexpectedly dip into me, present me with something that had been living and breeding beneath my surface. It was a part of our romance to speculate about each other and I smiled to hear her now, smiled and held the smile, and then felt it die because it took me that long to realize she had been speaking not out of interest but annoyance. And mistrust.

It was a flat, glarey day. The bus seemed to be leaking exhaust, maybe a rusted-out patch of flooring, and a faint stink of gas filled the inside of the bus. Jade held my hand and looked out the window and I leaned back in my seat and looked over her shoulder at her reflection in the tinted glass. Then she leaned her head on my shoulder and dozed off, and I once in a while kissed her hair as lightly as I could, careful not to awaken her. I was never completely certain she was asleep; she was breathing deeply and her face was slack, but the pressure with which she held my hand never let up.

I was living far outside the law and now there was no chance to sneak back into Chicago, to slip back into my old life. The parole was shattered into a thousand pieces and it could never be put together again. The tyranny of parole is the illusion of trust, and I had violated that trust with all the vehemence and flamboyance of my truest self. The judgment of the court—if they captured me and brought me into their domain—would be harsher regarding the broken parole than it had been when faced with a house burned into ruins and five lives hurtled to the very edge of extinction. If that one act earned me three years of constant care and an indefinite period as a ward of the court, then my running away would surely result in a sentence far, far harsher. The truth was that the course I had taken was perfectly outlined in a thin red line of absolute danger, but the truth beyond that was I didn't much care.

My life over the past four years fell behind me and it was too early for memories or regrets. I was fleeing from one part of my life and toward another, and though I did not know with any certainty what this would finally mean, I nevertheless was wholeheartedly in flight: giddy, proud, and absolutely certain. The only longing I had for the life I was leaving behind was for Ann, and even there the regret was luminous with hope. It was not asking so awfully much of fate, I thought, that one day Ann might be a part of the world Jade and I were destined to create.

. . .

And so I moved up north to Stoughton, Vermont, with Jade and lived in her house the best I could, making friends with her friends, adjusting my impulses to her schedule, and trying, because it was what she wanted, to find a place for myself in that community, a reason for being there beyond my love for Jade.

The house she lived in was a grander version of the house on Dorchester in Chicago, a Victorian monstrosity but this time swollen to gigantic proportions. The porch itself could have been used for band concerts; the mahogany ball on the banister to the staircase leading to the second floor was as large as a child's skull. The house had been used for communal student living for at least ten years; it was a house with a reputation, legends, and even a name: Gertrude. People actually said, "I might rent a share in Gertrude next year," and were actually understood. The place was filled with furniture. It was not the done thing to take your belongings out of Gertrude once they'd become a fixture. The living room was claustrophobic with sofas, ottomans, New England rockers, and potted plants. The kitchen was bursting with the gadgets left behind by the occasional gourmet who drifted in and out of the house's spell. There were electric toothbrushes galore and, I later found out, even a communal supply of vibrators left behind by women who went on to presumably happier sex lives. One of the Gertrude legends was that on Sunday mornings the place sounded like the inside of an enormous hive from the collective hum of a half dozen vibrators.

Jade had one of the worst rooms in the house, a tiny, perfectly square lavender room with a small, too-soft bed and a dull view of the street from its single window. The room's saving grace was supposedly its close proximity to the second-floor bathroom. Jade herself said, "Well, at least it's near the bathroom," and when one of her housemates, Colleen MacKay, was discussing the situation with me one day, she said, "Well, at least Jade's room is near the john." This small consolation had probably been described in similar terms since the first student was stuck in that room—and perhaps when the house was occupied by a large, prosperous family man, the middle son who was forced to occupy that room was cajoled with the same shaky reasoning. Of course, I hardly cared what room we stayed in. I would have gladly slept in the tub, or outside, or hanging from my thumbs, for that matter. But it was made clear to me that Jade had been assigned that particular room because she was hardly ever at home anyhow and when our conjugality was recognized—and rewarded!—with a transfer to the attic bedroom, which was vast and private, I felt a deep, vindicated joy that had me literally biting my lip to stop from crying. How kind I thought they were to make new arrangements for us. It was Colleen MacKay who moved out of the attic bedroom. "Don't thank me now," she said. "Wait till winter when you're freezing your asses off up there. *Then* thank me." It was supposed to take the softness out of the gesture but it only further weakened my knees. Wait until winter? People were already treating us as if we obviously had a future.

Life was difficult, awkward; Jade and I experienced the confusion of people whose lives have moved on a faster course than their imaginations. There were lapses into silence that suddenly exposed how fragile our entire enterprise was, collisions of will that came from our unfamiliarity with each other in the practical world. There was the trouble with my panic at finding Jade up to her hips in a stream of people, friends and enemies, lovers, deadlines, private jokes, rivals, and debts. But for the most part, I was filled with wonder at how happy we managed to be. We made love on cool lawns at night. We bathed each other and sang in whispers into each other's ears. I cooked my half dozen specialties for her and flushed with pleasure when I noticed how pleased she was that I got along with her friends. We took rides in a borrowed Saab, played tennis on a private court owned by a professor of music theory, and when I got a job at a local men's clothing store Jade met me for lunch every day: tuna sandwiches and iced tea, which we ate on the lawn of an immense

Presbyterian church, a crazily huge Gothic structure that could have simultaneously baptized all the children of Vermont.

When I first loved Jade, I had dozens of friends and a good appetite for that orgy of hors d'oeuvres that passes for social life in adolescence. I had pals, confidants, playmates, and loyal co-workers in the clubs I belonged to—the high-school literary magazine, the Student Peace Union. No one knew—or perhaps they knew and didn't mind—that my gregariousness and slightly acidic cheer were the lucky manifestations of a character that remained essentially isolated. In the privacy of my room—"the privacy of my room" was a catch phrase of my adolescence, as if I felt the world outside submitted me to a constant scrutiny— I wrote, in a vaguely Allen Ginsberg tone of voice, long formless poems about my Loneliness, about my "shrouded self," which no one knew and which I perceived as a mass of cold fog. My loneliness was completely social then, and when I saw myself reflected in Jade, the first thing I did was to sever my ties with my peers and then my family. Six months with Jade left me virtually friendless—perhaps I was imitating Jade's own alienation. My world became only Jade and her family; even as I applied to college, I knew I wouldn't be going. The world, I thought, had been too content to listen to my lies, to fall for the facile tricks of character I'd learned, the world was both too simple and too cruel to claim my allegiance or even be taken seriously. In a sense, I betrayed Jade in this: she'd seen me as a way out of the gravitational swoon of Butterfield family life, but rather than lead her out I burrowed in, becoming, at least in my aspirations, as militantly Butterfieldian as Keith.

But this time in Stoughton, being with Jade had the opposite effect. After nearly five years of having nothing to do with the world, of carrying my inconsolable separateness around as prominently as a picket sign—"Please do not spend your attention and affection on me. I am *Unfair*"—I was finally finding my way back into the world. This time, rather than aping Jade's isolation, I adopted her friends as my own: housemates, classmates, shopkeepers, professors, virtually everyone she knew became a part of my life as well.

She never said as much, but I knew Jade wanted me to become a part of the world she shared with her friends. She used the phrase "neurotic patterns" to describe what she wanted to avoid with me, and isolation was the principal neurotic pattern to guard against. She knew, of course, that I would have been more than content never to see anyone but her, to spend every free hour in our attic, in bed, in each other's arms, admitting nothing into our world, and the adoration I offered her was tempting enough to make Jade afraid she might succumb to it. "I want to be with you but not like before. Not less but different." How could I argue? It would have been like crabbing about the size of our room, the texture of our bed. I had no heart to worry over the details of our being together; that we were together at all overwhelmed everything. I experienced occasional tremors of fear over what I perceived as the "slightly new Jade"—but even in Paradise it's impossible not to remember now and then that you like a slightly stiffer breeze and have never altogether cared for wisteria.

Friendship with Jade's friends was not what I wanted. When I had imagined our reunion, I hadn't bothered to fill in the human landscape. I had fantasized our living out our piece of eternity in some stark version of my grandfather's planned community in Florida: a window, a bed, a refrigerator, and a shelf of books. But when it became clear that knowing Jade's friends was going to be a necessary part of living with her, I found myself pursuing my new-found social life with surprising relish. It was nearly deranged how quick and ardent my affections were for virtual strangers. Jade took me to meet old Professor Asbury—Carlyle, after ten minutes; Corky midway through the first drink—who'd been laid up for nearly a year from spraining his back playing tennis on his dewy, shabby back yard court. White-haired, bony, and elegant, Asbury was such a profound campus favorite that students with no interest in music took his music theory course just for his company. I had a perverse impulse to resist his charms, but as we left his little gingerbread cottage I squeezed Jade's hand and said, "God, what a *nice guy*," and I don't know if I was primarily moved by Asbury or my response to him but I practically sobbed as I said it.

Jade took me to dinner at her friends Marcia and Trig's apartment. The place looked like an assassin's hideout, with slanted linoleum floors and a view over a tarpaper roof onto the back of a peeling garage. We sat on the floor. Marcia and Trig weren't hippies; they gave us no India print pillows to sit upon. They seemed utterly unconcerned with their personal comfort— or ours. But when they finally served up the meal, it was terrific and delicate. Fish with slivers of pistachio. Newly picked vegetables in a Japanese batter. That they had gone to so much effort with *my* poor pleasure even vaguely in mind touched me like a caress. I ate as slowly as I could and looked at them with warm swimmy eyes as they described the circumstances of their health food store being harassed out of business by thugs they believed to have been hired by the local grocers' association.

Gertrude had house meetings every Wednesday evening, and now that I was a member of the crew, I was invited to sit with the rest of them around the expansive Formica kitchen table, smoking Camels and drinking Almadén jug wine like all the rest—the Camels and Almadén were ceremonial and virtually required. We talked about chores, expenses, passed judgment on visitors (*I* was no visitor!), and as I looked from face to face—there was Jade, Oliver Jones, Colleen MacKay, Nina Sternberg, Miriam Kay, Boris Hyde, and Anemone Grommers— I often thought to myself: This is the best bunch of people in the world. I felt real patriotic love for Gertrude and its residents, as if we were all members of a gang or a cult or a revolutionary cadre. Of course we were nothing more complicated or grand than a handful of people sharing roof and rent, but all gestures of friendship—no, not even friendship, mere *friendliness*—heated my passion and imagination. In the world of normal discourse I was like a tourist—a *dying* tourist—on a twilight tour of Europe. Each sunset, each spire, each cobblestoned path, each lobby, each glass of local beer is monumental, tragic, and unparalleled.

I did manage to learn that a little more than a year before, Jade had lived in Gertrude with a student named Jon Widman. Jon—bald at twenty, toweringly tall, anemic—was a musical genius, played twelve different instruments, and composed music from blues to string quartets. I also learned of Jade's affair with a professor of English. This information was given to me—with a certain meanness of spirit, I thought—by one of my house-mates, who was ostensibly proving that an affair with a faculty member was an inevitable Stoughton ritual.

But it was Jade herself who talked to me about her love affair with Susan Henry. There were places we could not go, movies and concerts we could not attend, because Jade was worried about meeting Susan.

"It's my own doing," she said. "And so useless. I didn't end it the right way and didn't call her when we got back."

"But I thought, I mean the impression you gave me, was the break-up was mostly *her* doing," I said.

"We were too close for that to matter. At a certain point everything's mutual."

And then one day when we were walking down Main Street—I was on my lunch break from Main Street Clothiers and we were crossing the street to go to the stationery store for a notebook—Jade grabbed hold of my upper arm, turned me around, and walked quickly with me into a dime store, with its scent of wooden floors and candy corn.

"What is it?" I asked, though I fairly well knew.

"I can't believe how stupid this is," she said. "Susan. I saw her on the other side of the street and I just don't have the courage to run into her. It can't be like this. I have to call her."

We were inside that variety store and it was like being inside a different decade: old women in faded sweaters, with their eyeglasses hanging onto their bosoms from silvery chains; bins of loose chocolates, bridge mix, peanut brittle; the strange hush of a store lacking Muzak; displays of cheap underwear and thin, powder blue socks; coloring books and cap guns. Jade and I wandered aimlessly through the aisles. Her hands were in her pockets and she kept her eyes cast down. She was walking fast, pulling ahead of me, and I reached out to take her arm. She allowed me to stop her and then I turned her and put my arms around her.

"It seemed so perfectly natural to be with Susan when we were together," Jade said, as I held her. "But I don't think I'd be treating her like this if she was a man. It's because she's a woman and I loved her."

The difficulty inherent in choosing to love another woman and now the long pull of conscience in the affair's aftermath made the time with Susan more intimate and enviable than all of the other parts of Jade's life that I'd missed. As I held her in that antique dime store and watched the few customers circulating lazily throughout the store—the ten-year-old girls choosing party favors, an old man inspecting a tiny cactus plant—I thought of how the difficulty of a connection increases its intensity. I thought of how alive with courage and desire that love must have been to carry Jade past the boundary of her established sexuality.

We walked around the store. Jade almost took my hand; her fingers brushed against me and then she moved away.

"Susan's a powerful person," she said. "The most powerful person I've ever known. She lives inside her feelings like a queen in her castle. I admired her so much. Envy too, I guess. She could take herself so seriously and never seem stupid, or self-involved. I had such a case of hero-worship with her, God, it was months before I realized that it was also something more. That I . . ."

"I don't know how to be in this conversation," I said. "I think we have to stop. Just for now."

Jade nodded. We were in front of a bin of phonograph records.

"I want to know it," I said. "I just need a little breathing space. I know it was important to you and I suppose it was difficult, too, and maybe even scary. But I was feeling myself starting to get jealous. I know I don't have a right to—"

"It wasn't scary," Jade said. "The only love I've ever known that has scared me has been with you. Being with Susan wasn't frightening. It wasn't at all."

"It seems that it was very intense," I said.

"What else is there? I'm not casual."

"I know," I said, my voice slipping away.

"We don't have to talk about it."

"No. That's not what I mean. I just need to hear it in stages. It's stupid. I have no right to say this. Don't listen to me. Tell me the rest. Tell me it all."

"It's not necessary," said Jade. "It's mine."

And so we dropped all talk of Susan Henry and the silence hovered over us, as watchful as a bird of prey. I longed to ask Jade to speak to me about her love with Susan but, temporarily at least, I'd forfeited the right. We ate dinner at Gertrude that night and Jade didn't say a word at the table, though we ate with seven others. She went upstairs before me, and when I followed her up to the attic some fifteen minutes later, Jade was in bed and all the lights were off. I got undressed and lay next to her and after a while I put my hands on her breasts. She breathed heavily and didn't stir; I knew she wasn't really asleep.

The next morning we were hesitant with each other. It was our turn to do the weekly grocery shopping for the household. We shopped at a huge store called Price Chopper, and it didn't seem like a piece of remarkable coincidence at all that halfway through our nervous shopping we were once again confronted with Susan Henry.

This time, Jade had no opportunity to flee. Susan appeared from around an aisle corner. She looked tall, tan, willowy, and toothy, rather like Joni Mitchell. Her straight hair was almost white; she wore a loose, pale blue dress and little sandals. Her long arms were bare and she wore turquoise and silver bracelets. Her eyes remained mysterious behind brown-tinted sunglasses.

"Beep beep," said Susan, giving our cart a small jostle.

"Hello, Susan," said Jade, her voice a metaphor for nights of cigarettes and grain alcohol.

"Hello," said Susan. Her voice was lilting, a trifle cute—or trying to be. I could feel her effort and it drew me toward her for an instant.

Jade looked into Susan's cart. "Still buying junk food?" she said.

"That's right!" said Susan.

Jade shrugged. Then: "Susan Henry? David Axelrod." Pointing to us as she said our names.

I offered my handshake. As romantic victor I felt it was my place. Susan looked at me as if the handshake were some archaic salute and then, nodding as if remembering, took my hand and shook it with a certain irony.

"Hello, David," she said. She gave no indication of ever having heard of me.

"Hello," I said. I thought the confident thing to do was smile, but I learned later from Jade that it looked more like a leer.

Susan focused her attention on Jade and began telling her something about a friend of theirs named Dina who'd just left for Cologne to study philosophy with someone who'd studied under Wittgenstein. The tone of the anecdote was admiring and ironic. The victory celebration dinner was described. Dina got drunk and spoke German all the rest of the night. Professor

Asbury showed up for a while, moving gracefully on his aluminum walker. Et cetera. I wondered if the purpose of the story was to make Jade feel embarrassed at not being invited, but Jade didn't seem at all upset.

Then, suddenly, the anecdote was over and my wandering attention was stopped short by the silence. Susan dropped her gaze for a moment. She looked jittery, with those kind of raw nerves that you get when you feel doomed to be misunderstood.

"What are the chances of our having a talk?" she said to Jade.

Jade didn't answer right away—not out of indecision but as a way of acknowledging the difficulty of Susan's gesture.

"We should talk," said Jade.

"I'm going to Boston this evening," Susan said. "For five days."

Jade nodded. "To stay with Paula?"

"Yes."

"Say hello, OK?"

"I'd like to have that talk before I leave," Susan said. Her shyness had passed; she knew as well as I did that Jade would go along.

Jade almost turned toward me to see if that would be acceptable, but she stopped herself. "We can," she said, with somber, almost corny judiciousness.

The situation struck me as fairly intolerable, but I did my best with it. I slipped my arm around Jade's waist and pressed her to me for a moment. "Why don't I finish up with the shopping?" I said. "I'm the best shopper anyhow."

"OK. That would be fine," Jade said. She sounded uncertain, formal. Susan was staring off down the aisle, hurtling her attention far away for the moment. She was refusing to look at me. I engaged Jade in a conversation about groceries—did Anemone like creamy or chunky peanut butter? What was the name of that delicious breakfast cereal Oliver had made for us the day before?—and finally Susan backed her cart up and announced

she was going to finish her shopping and would meet Jade in a
few minutes at the front of the store.

"Well, that's Susan Henry," Jade said.

"That's all right. It had to happen. Running into her."

"She seems so nervous. It's not like her. Susan's totally confident *all* the time. It's scary seeing her like this."

"Well, people change," I said, trying to be inconsequential
but revealing more of my own resentment than I wanted to.

"You're upset about me having coffee with her?"

"Just as long as coffee is all," I said—I actually thought I was
being lighthearted in this. I produced a loopy grin.

"You said you'd never hound me," said Jade.

"I won't. You're going with her, aren't you?"

We had to move our shopping cart. We were standing in
front of the salad oils. A young mother with pink curlers in her
hair and a sleeping infant in a canvas pouch dangling from her
back put a giant bottle of Wesson Oil in her nearly overflowing
cart. The store manager's voice had replaced the Muzak on the
public address system; he was describing items on sale—chicken
breasts, Brillo pads, Folger's coffee, Duz detergent . . .

"I'll meet you back at the house," I said, taking control of our
cart.

Jade nodded. She was about to walk away and pretend that
we weren't going through anything particularly difficult or
strange. She still had a deep desire to pretend once in a while that
we, like everyone else, were essentially separate. But she stopped
herself and said, "I won't be long."

"You know what I think?" I said. "Here's what: if the world
ended right now, I'd be happy I got to spend as much time with
you as I have. I'm not modern or sophisticated, but I really do
want you to do what you want, what you think is best. Because
when you're most like yourself, something good always comes
of it."

I made it a point to be in the back of the Price Chopper when

Jade and Susan left. Jade had given me the keys to Colleen MacKay's Saab and when I thought of driving it home I had a flutter of apprehension. I knew how to drive but I didn't have a license. I thought of someone accidentally hitting me from behind. The police on the scene. No license? Then the call into headquarters. Finding out about my parole violation. Thrown into jail. Sent back to Illinois. No chance even to call Jade.

Back at the house, nearly everyone was in the kitchen as the groceries were unpacked. It was a Saturday, still early but very warm. Anemone spooned the peanut butter into her mouth. Nina Sternberg prepared a twelve-egg omelette. The kitchen was golden with sunlight and rather quiet considering there were six of us in it. I realized everyone noticed I hadn't returned with Jade. I was surprised; I didn't think things like that were noted.

"Jade and I met Susan Henry at the Price Chopper," I said to no one in particular. I was standing on a metal chair placing cans of baked beans and chicken stock onto the top shelf of a cabinet.

"Can I say something about Miss Henry?" Nina Sternberg said. "Miss Free Spirit borrowed fourteen dollars from me in *March* and now she hides behind trees when she sees me on campus."

"Really?" said Anemone, her voice sounding as if she had a cleft palate from all the peanut butter. "She owes me money, too. Ten dollars."

"Susan's not too good with other people's things," said Colleen. "I loaned her my car and she brought it back with an empty tank."

I felt weak and alone waiting for Jade and I was grateful when Colleen MacKay informed me that she was making sandwiches and I was invited to eat with her and Oliver Jones on the front porch. She'd set up an old wicker table, covered with an old linen cloth, graced by a Narragansett beer bottle filled with irises. She'd made cheese and cucumber sandwiches and I complimented her on the elegance of her meal. I'd never eaten a cucumber sandwich before. I sat on a little rocking chair and Oliver and Colleen shared a wicker loveseat.

Colleen was short, stocky, with powerful swimmer's legs and dark brown eyes that always seemed a little irritated, as if she'd just gotten out of a chlorinated pool. She dressed in overalls and checked shirts, or once in a while appeared in a dress of such stiff formality that even a stranger would have known she hadn't chosen it herself. Oliver had moved into Gertrude three years before, when he was in love with a Stoughton student named Sara Richards. He was at that time already in his mid-twenties and long out of school—he'd dropped out of Exeter in his junior year and hadn't been back to school since, though every so often he'd apply to do graduate work in Oriental Studies at someplace like Stanford or Harvard and wait for a letter of acceptance and a grant before deciding that his "un-schooling," as he called it, was not yet completed. Sara Richards was killed in a ski lift accident not six months after Oliver moved in, and his staying on in the house was a perfect Oliver Jones mixture of the tragic and the lazy. He had had love affairs with the majority of the women who had passed through the house, though none of the affairs ever lasted long. These affairs usually began in commemoration of one of Oliver's many personal days of remembrance: Mahler's birthday; the discovery of Uranus. (That was one of Oliver's comic bits, the homosexual astronomer discovering a planet and naming it after his lover's asshole. "Do you know what that is in the sky, you wonderful little monster? That's your anus.") The night Oliver and Jade took each other to bed was the anniversary of Sara's death, a stormy February night that turned all the windows in the house as opaque and white as gravestones. They remained lovers for a week and then one night Oliver got up in the dark complaining of a toothache. He went downstairs to make himself some warm milk and never returned to Jade's bed again . . .

We sat on the porch, the three of us, eating our sandwiches and drinking iced tea, like people in the 1920s, smelling the flowers and enjoying the breeze, watching the bluejays on their headstrong, raucous rounds. The sky was a deep, mild blue, as smooth as the inside of a shell except for one patch of rippled white cloud. I did my best not to think of Jade and Susan and what they might be doing. I was suffering, but what mild agony it was—as long as I remembered how much worse, how infinitely more dreary and without boundaries my unhappiness had been before. Here I was eating Christian delicacies on a shady Vermont porch. Blue skies. Bluejays. Oliver's sly blue eyes squinting at Colleen as she asked him if he enjoyed kyacking.

"David?" Colleen asked. "You here?" She mimed knocking at a door. "Hello?"

She leaned forward and put her small, slightly puffy hand on my knee. "If you're worried about Susan Henry, I can tell you you don't need to be, OK?"

"One always worries about the Susan Henrys of the world," intoned Oliver. "Just as one worries about influenza or, let's see, the steering column of your car snapping off."

"She didn't seem like a menace," I said. "The thing is I thought she looked nice."

"Nice?" Oliver said with a shrug, as if I'd used a discredited term.

"Nice-looking. As vulnerable as anyone else."

"It doesn't matter," said Colleen. She looked at her hand on my knee and smiled, as if she were pleasantly surprised to find it there. "You're who matters to Jade."

"I know that," I said.

"I wonder sometimes," Colleen said. She was glancing at Oliver now, and I could feel the core of her concentration turning toward him. "Men have a knack of being blind to what women feel about them. Men. I shouldn't say men. People."

Just then an orange VW pulled up in front of the house, with a black convertible top. I could see Jade's head on the passenger side, the hair touching the top of her white collar. I couldn't see further into the car but I knew Susan was facing Jade and they were talking and that the conversation was not an easy one. The little motor percolated and once Susan must have accidentally stepped on the accelerator because the engine raced for a moment, whirring like a power mower in tall grass.

"There. That didn't take long," said Colleen. She made a move as if to clear the lunch dishes away but thought better of it, and rested her hands on an arm of the wicker loveseat. She crossed her legs and peered out at the car, like a mother who's been waiting past curfew for her child's return.

"Is that Susan's car?" Oliver mused. "It looks new. Jersey plates, too. I wonder . . ."

I felt a panic of shyness. It seemed incredible that the two of them could be so near. It was a warm day but the windows of the car were rolled up: I saw the white skid of a sticker that had been only partially peeled away and the dim swaying reflection of an upside-down tree. All of the jealousy I'd been avoiding since leaving the supermarket fell through me now, like suitcases off the luggage rack in a train that's stopped too fast. My throat was tight, my fingers felt pink and cold. I stared at the car until my eyes glazed over. Oliver was going on about how it couldn't have been Susan's car, she must have borrowed if from someone, but who? I couldn't pay attention, but I was glad he was talking.

Finally, the door on Jade's side swung open and a few long moments later Jade got out of the car. There were dark streaks on her shirt where she'd sweated against the hot upholstery. Her brown cloth belt was twisted in back and I wondered, obscenely, if it had been like that in the morning. She closed the door. Susan pulled away—not with a roar, as I expected, but casually, hesitating before she swung into the middle of our street, even though there was no traffic. I watched the car leave. The back seat was filled with packages. A good sign: it meant they hadn't gone back to Susan's house.

Jade turned around. Expressionless. A passport photo. A memory. She was wearing jeans, Swedish clogs, a blue and white shirt with a white collar. The sun was perched on the chimney and shining directly in her eyes. She squinted toward the porch, noticing us for the first time.

Colleen waved.

Jade walked toward the house. The bushes were obese, making the sidewalk narrow; she ran her hand along the dark green brocade. Her gold chain necklace was gone. A Christmas gift from Susan. I rattled back the ice in my empty glass, tasting the old tea and the sugary sludge.

"Lunch on the porch?" said Jade, mounting the steps.

"A perfect day for it," said Colleen.

Jade nodded. She looked stern, heartbroken and beleaguered, like an Army medic. "And minding my business, too," she said.

"There's no business like Jade's business," Oliver half-sang.

Jade made a false smile in Oliver's direction and then walked by us and into the house, letting the screen door slam behind her.

We were silent for a couple moments. The sound of bees. Me rattling the ice in my glass.

"She has a power to make people feel like assholes," said Colleen, shaking her head at Oliver, comforting him.

"It's a power only the victim can bestow," Oliver said, crossing his long legs.

I got up and drifted lazily toward the door, still holding my glass. I placed my hand on the little cylindrical knob, but didn't open the door. I stared into the cool shadows on the house through the sagging mesh of screen, looking at the mahogany banister, the mirrored hatstand, the lantern-shaped chandelier, all crosshatched as if objects in an etching.

"I'll go see her," I said, and opened the door. I could hear her footsteps going up the third flight of stairs to the attic, the clogs made so goddamned much noise. I took the steps two at a time, chasing quietly after her. There was a pocket of hot, humid air on the second floor, like those little galaxies of warmth we come upon in cool lakes. Someone was taking a shower in the second-floor bathroom, the rush of water, that sweet white noise. Sunlight ignited the pale turquoise bubbles in the half-circular window on the landing—Jade said the world looks like memory through old glass. The staircase was not continuous. I walked down the hall half the width of house before mounting the steps to the attic, narrow, steep steps, wooden and uncovered, almost black except for the third, a plywood replacement the color of wheat.

Jade was standing before the huge, diamond-shaped window set in the lowest part of the attic and overlooking our back yard—with its maple trees and makeshift kennels. She was leaning forward, resting her hands on the window frame, her fingers almost touching the ceiling. She didn't turn around when I closed the door behind me, didn't even move, and I wondered if I'd made a mistake following her up. I walked halfway across our bedroom and then stopped, feeling awkward and imperiled. But I forced myself to continue, as I would have wanted Jade to if it had been me with my forehead against the window, and when I put my hands on her shoulders she turned quickly toward me and held me with such sudden fierceness that her strength broke my breath in two, snapping that column of air as if it were a twig.

We held each other. I heard the screen door slam downstairs. A bluejay flapped past the window, another, and then two more. I moved my hands down Jade's back but that was all. She was perfectly still, embracing me with unyielding strength. We went to bed and made love for a very long while. We didn't talk about Susan, or about anything. I had my mouth on her, pressing her with the insides of my lips and the back part of my tongue, where it is softer, and when she came I thought for a moment that I'd just imitated the way she and Susan made love. But that passed, quickly. I knew Jade was with me. Love, finally, isn't blind, and when I poured out into her I could feel how much she wanted me. Weren't we wonderful to each other when we made love? It was different from before, when we were beginning in Chicago. I think we were less happy. There was a death between us now and four years of separation, there were lovers and courts and hospitals and unsent letters and ten thousand hours of terror and doubt, but we were not less for it, just less happy. And perhaps not even less. It could have been that the light of consciousness struck our happiness from a different angle and it wasn't smaller but less brilliant, and it cast a shadow now, a shadow of itself that was chilling.

Finally, we fell asleep but it was still light when we woke. The dogs Jade was studying for her senior thesis were yipping out back. The reflection of the leaves moved like fast, cool water on the wooden plank floor.

"I'm sorry if that made you scared today," Jade said.

"It did. But not too much."

"It's funny, because when we were shopping today, I was thinking how of all the things about being with you again shopping is the thing I like the most. I like doing something so normal and everyday with you and, well, you know, to be going absolutely nuts inside because it's you and me doing it. It's like a great imposture. Wheeling our cart around looking as common as can be and knowing that in an hour's time we can be back here completely naked and doing something truly savage." She reached over and ran her hand over my chest. "I like just doing everyday things with you."

"I do too."

"What do you like about being with me?" Jade asked after a while.

"Everything."

"No. You know what I mean. Specifically what do you like."

"I like watching you get dressed, especially in the morning when you've just had a shower and you're off to go somewhere. I like the way you button your shirt in front of the mirror and watch your own fingers as you do it. Then you tuck it into your pants and smooth out all the material. You give yourself a nice feel-up before you go out. And if your hair's wet, it's even better. You pull it up in little clumps, shake it, so it'll dry, I guess, with real brisk professional motions like a hairdresser. Everything done with such energy. You seem so incredibly *on*."

That evening we went out to supper—my treat. I was making ninety dollars a week at the Main Street Clothiers, selling, among other things, the same Redman Pants I'd been picketing other stores for selling. It did nip at my conscience, but I couldn't live off Jade and the others and jobs, as usual, were scarce. I did my best to talk customers out of buying Redman Pants, but as much as I wanted the union to prevail, it was one of the very least of my worries. Once I sent ten dollars to the Amalgamated Clothing Workers with an unsigned note wishing the Redman workers well and asking that my contribution be put in a workers' relief fund, or strike fund. But after sending it I felt real panic. I felt somehow the money would be connected to me, the disappeared picket boy. The postmark deciphered. The police called . . . I knew it was terribly unlikely, bordering on impossible, but it was unendurable to have the false imagination of such a disaster whip through me. Anyhow, Jade and I went to dinner at a place called Rustler's, one of those restaurants that seem to encircle Stoughton, with heavy furniture, thick carpets, hamburgers, steaks, and pork chops, and a huge salad bar. Lights hung from a wagon wheel; the water glasses were dark gold; the menu was shaped like a covered wagon. It was for tourists, I suppose, the idea being that as soon as city people get out into the country they think about cowboys. Jade and I liked to eat there because we knew we'd never see anyone she knew. We ordered the cheapest things on the menu and it gave us the right to return as many times as we wanted to the salad bar and to eat more beets, onion rings, and canned chick peas than we would have under any other circumstances.

"Can we afford dessert?" Jade asked at the end of the meal.

I was still so moved when she said "we," especially when she said it casually.

"I want some of that apple pie with the melted cheese on it," she said.

"OK. Me too. Coffee?"

"No. Milk. A cold glass of milk. I want to be twelve years old."

I smiled. Twelve years old. A virgin. No: a "technical" virgin. Making pocket money staging nude dances for Keith's suddenly numerous friends. Mascara on the down between her legs. Second prize in a citywide children's painting competition sponsored by the *Tribune* and bursting into tears at the awards ceremony. Nabbed at Kroch's and Brentano's for stealing *Fanny Hill*. Where was I then? I could have been with her; we could even have been lovers. It would not have been wrong. I needed her then, not like now, but I needed her. I was living in the hush of my family. She was twelve. Keith had been caught in her bed, both of them in their underwear. Hugh dragged Keith out of the room by his hair. Jade was screaming, Hugh was bellowing, and Keith's face had that inanimate horror of a victim in a news photo.

The waitress appeared, dressed as a cowgirl. I ordered our desserts. The women in the elevator, I remembered, had been dressed as cowgirls, the elevator that had brought Jade to my room at the Hotel McAlpin.

"I like this restaurant," I said.

"I do too. Even though all the waitresses flirt with you."

"They do not."

"Oh, you poor, poor, poor, poor, poor naïve boy. Even tonight our waitress was leaning over you."

"A leaning violation?"

"I'm serious! Her breast was almost touching you. That kind of stuff's always going on."

"I wish."

"You don't need to wish. They all know, everyone does."

"Know what?"

"That you're you, who you are. Mr. Fuck-Machine."

The waitress came with our pie, a coffee for me, and milk for Jade. She got nowhere near me as she placed the cups and plates on the table.

"You see?" Jade said, when the waitress left.

"See what?"

"Oh, you're just going to argue. You don't see what I see. And it's just as well. I need a nonegotistical man. They're hard to find, you know."

"I'm not nonegotistical."

"Pretty much."

"Not at all. No matter what happened, and no matter what people said about me, I wanted to be with you."

"That's not egotism."

"Yes it is. Because I thought I deserved it. Me and no one else."

"You're going to make me cry."

"Why?"

"Because you touch me where it's always tender."

It was dark and starless when we left Rustler's. The parking lot was right off the highway and you had to nose your car out very carefully because everyone drove fifty or sixty miles per hour and there were no signs or lights to help you. It astonished me that something as planned and official as a restaurant parking lot could be so dangerous; it seemed to mean that life itself was so essentially dicey that there was a limit to how much you could do to make it safe. The high insecty whine of the cars speeding by. The smell of grass, fresh tar. The Beach Boys on the car radio. Jade at the wheel, waiting for an opening in the traffic, a place for us. Her eyes were hooded from the beers we had with dinner—she had no capacity for alcohol. Passing headlights cast strips of white across her face. Jade pressed the accelerator, I prepared for sudden death, and then we were out in traffic, our tires whistling.

It was a five-mile drive home. An old song by Bobby Hebb called "Sunny" came on the radio and I was going to ask Jade if she remembered it, but then I told myself of course she did. I was thinking about Susan Henry, with more ease now because no matter what happened it couldn't have made much difference, but I was thinking about her all the same. In the restaurant, I'd wanted to ask Jade if she'd ever eaten there with Susan. Ridiculous question. So annoying and without importance. I suppressed it, but it hovered within me, like a sneeze.

Jade turned off the radio when an ad for joining the Army came on.

"I want to thank you," she said. "I didn't want to talk about being with Susan today and you knew it."

"Was it hard?"

Jade nodded. "Very."

I felt my stomach turn.

We moved off Route 2, drove past an abandoned paper mill, and headed toward home. Jade was driving much too fast for narrow streets. It wasn't like her. She was a great believer in highway safety; she wouldn't even turn the ignition if you didn't fasten your safety belt. I thought about watching the back of her head when she was sitting in Susan's car, about Susan knocking into our shopping cart, and then an image, vaguely sexual, began to take shape in my mind—hands touching, an embrace. I let it recede. Jade continued to speed along. Her jaw was set forward; she seemed deliberately unblinking; her arms were straight and stiff. I didn't want to look at her because I didn't want to know what she was thinking. I put my hand out the window and cupped my fingers. The force of the sweet night air as we sped homeward was forceful, oppressive, something alive pressing against me.

"She frightened me," Jade said, suddenly. She touched the cigarette lighter with her fingertips and then grabbed the steering wheel again.

"How?"

"By what she thinks. About us. Me. It's so hard with Susan because she's always so convinced she's right. And she is right a lot, of course. She really is perceptive. But sometimes she doesn't know what the hell she's talking about, only you can't tell because she says it in the same super-convinced way. She takes aim and charges right at you, and if you resist it at all, she pushes that much harder. She's like Keith in a way. I mean she remembers everything. And she can take power with it. Keith doesn't do that. Keith will throw it in your face if he thinks you're trying to hurt him, but he doesn't try to take power. He doesn't want it, but Susan does."

"What did she say?"

"A lot of things. But the thing that made me . . . I don't know. Here's what: She says I use you."

"For what?"

"It's complicated. No. Not that. It's just hard to say. It all has to do with my fucked-up family and my feelings about them. She thinks I use you against my family," Jade said. "But in the most awful way. To really destroy them. She says you were acting as my agent when you set the fire. She says it was really me."

"No. It was me."

"I know. But it was you doing what I wanted. Reading my mind. We always do that anyhow. We always know each other right down to the bottom. I wanted something to happen and you made sure it did. I could have seen it in you from the beginning, the possibility. The way you charmed yourself into the middle of everything and then went wild. You know, even the fact that you could virtually become a member of the family galled me, if you want to know. There always seemed to be room for one more and in the meanwhile we got nothing. They took you right in—Ann did. And still does. But there was no room. There may have been room for me to have a lover but there wasn't any place for a new Butterfield. And that's what you were becoming. And I knew you would and I also knew that sooner or later the whole thing would explode."

"I don't think you knew that. You're blaming yourself."

"I think I did. And I wanted it. Even after it happened. I felt so strange. Grief and all that, but mixed up. I was glad, I think, that the family fell apart. I didn't know it would *end* the family, though I should have figured that out, I see now. But for a while I think I was genuinely relieved. The way you are when you finally say the most horrible thing that's ever wormed its way into your heart, or when you finally lose your favorite ring. The worst was out. The worst."

"Is this Susan talking or you? You sound convinced."

"I'm not convinced. I'm spinning. And you being in New York when Hugh got killed doesn't make it any easier, for obvious reasons. It's like you were the agent of my murderous spirit again."

I looked out the window. We'd just sped past our house. Every light was on except in the attic. I turned the side-view mirror and watched the house get smaller. A few hundred feet later, the blacktop turned to gravel; we were heading out toward where a few of the area's last real farms were. The tires hit the gravel, lifting a spray of stones that bounced and splattered against Colleen's car.

"Go easy," I said. But of course all that was really on my mind at that moment was the desire to tell Jade as much of the truth as I knew about Hugh's death. The pull of that confession was nearly hypnotic, like the urge to leap that sometimes overcomes you when you are on the balcony of a very high building; only now it didn't seem as if destruction was inevitable, or that it would take a miracle to save me, a violation of nature's law. It seemed that if I spoke truthfully now I would be doing what was best for both of us, drawing us closer, silencing that persistent hum of ambiguity that droned always between us.

We drove past the growing corn, an indistinct mass in the heavy night. A small farmhouse with the light shining behind gingham curtains. The piercing, suspenseful twitter of crickets. The last of the fireflies, their phosphorescence bleeding into the humid blackness. The gravel was gone now and the road was packed dirt, with ridges and holes. Jade was still pushing fifty and the old Saab rattled like a trayful of china. We came to a fork in the road and Jade veered to the right. She drove up another few hundred feet on a road that was getting progressively rougher and then suddenly she stepped on the brakes and we lurched to a stop. There was a cornfield on one side of us and on the other a vast, plowed field, which rolled gently toward a distant farmhouse, its tiny windows golden and alive. Accidentally, she let her foot off the clutch and the car bucked forward a few times and stalled out.

"I don't know where I'm going," said Jade. She leaned forward and rested her head on the steering wheel.

"It doesn't matter."

We were silent for a while and someone turned up the volume on the night around us. Then Jade said, "Sometimes I think we have an unhappiness all our own waiting for us. In some love affairs the people do each other in, but I really do think that we're too in love to do that, too much the same person, and what will do us in will be something quite a bit larger than just you or me. It's the special unhappiness of mutual love and it really scares the shit out of me."

I suppose I should have said something to the contrary, comforted her. But we believed we were deep enough to face anything, any sort of death, any shadow of fate. Yet even as I nodded slowly I felt a tightening inside, as if a doctor had just given me a fatal diagnosis.

"It's still possible for me to believe that it won't happen," I said. "And in the meanwhile . . ."

"In the meanwhile."

"Well, yes. In the meanwhile we can be together and I think we can promise each other all the future that's ours."

"Susan scared me, she really did."

"People like us are easy to scare. We're out on a limb." I moved closer to her but we were in bucket seats and the gearshift was between us. Jade put her head against the steering wheel again and when I touched her knee a teardrop, singular and warm, struck the back of my hand.

I knew I wouldn't tell her about Hugh and I knew also that if justice had anything to do with the unfolding of the human universe, then I no longer quite deserved to be with Jade. Loving her was not the perfect right of my birth but something I would have to get away with. And if love is a bridge that connects time to eternity, then I would have to slip across in some kind of disguise.

I wonder what—exactly—Jade was feeling then. It must have been something similar. She took my hand and pressed it to her, hard. "I want to make love," she said. "Now. Here. We can do that, can't we? Not in the car. In that field. I want to feel you. I want to be delirious again. David."

"I want to," I said, with my heart beginning to break.

16

Jade was going to be in a graduation class of one. Once she finished her senior thesis and made up the three courses she had dropped during her sophomore and junior years, it would be December. I don't know what plans had been made for awarding her her diploma—probably it was just going to casually arrive in the mail sometime later, delivered to an address she no longer occupied. We didn't know what Jade was going to do after graduation and we never really talked about it, except as fantasy.

Yet even with the end so clearly in sight, Jade often thought of quitting school and going somewhere else with me—somewhere of our own, a cabin in Maine, the southwest, a new city, Europe. I realized it was my place to say no to this, to help her keep her stamina up for the last months of formal education, but

I too dreamed of leaving Stoughton with her and living in a world more wholly our own. Sometimes I nodded when she threatened to quit school, but even when I told her she shouldn't my voice betrayed the true irresponsible depths of my longing to be alone with her and live a more adult life. I didn't want to live in Gertrude with a lot of people no matter how much I liked them. I didn't like the peacefulness of campus life and it really did gall me that Jade was forced to sit for hours in front of professors and allowed them to form her mind. I may have been plain and simple jealous of the hold that college had on her and of the worlds it made available, though I don't think it was that that bothered me.

I thought of us both going to school, together. When I was getting ready to graduate from high school, I'd been accepted by the University of California in Berkeley and I would have liked for us both to go there, get two desks, and turn them so we could face each other while we studied. Jade could do her graduate work in ethology and I might even take courses in astronomy. The energy and promise of my earlier life had worn a little thin, but I still believed that I might one day revive my old ambition.

But meanwhile it was daily life, the hasty Vermont summer —which even in July was autumnal in its dawns—and Jade's elaborate senior thesis.

I was Jade's lab assistant and worked every day—before setting out for the Main Street Clothiers and again in the evening— looking after the dogs in the makeshift kennels Jade had built in our back yard. The back yard was a small, patchy square, about seventy by seventy, and presided over by so many huge maples that grass could barely grow. Dandelions and dust, and where the lawn could sprout no one had the heart to cut it back. Jade made pens for the animals out of chicken wire, two-by-fours, tarpaper, and hay, and everyone in the house looked forward to the end of the experiment so the little canine shanty town might be eradicated. That Jade wouldn't allow any of them to pet or even coo at the pups made it all the worse for the others, but because she wanted to study the behavioral differences between the pups raised by the blind mother and the pups raised by the normal mother she was worried that injudiciously portioned affection might invalidate her findings. When she made her rounds, she carried a stopwatch and timed herself so she wouldn't spend an instant more (or less) than thirty seconds with each. She let me play with the puppies as well but she watched carefully over me with her stopwatch and said, in a dry, removed voice, "Next," whenever thirty seconds was up.

It was obvious pretty early on, however, that the experiment wouldn't yield any particularly clear results, let alone anything scientifically valid. Her professor, who had endorsed the project, seemed to have allowed Jade to wander into a dead end—but then perhaps that was the point of his agreeing. Jade was grief-stricken and ashamed when she realized that the experiment would yield no significant data—never had she been closer to dropping out of school and setting off to begin a new life with me. But I wouldn't let her quit, and soon enough she came up with the idea of recording all the experimental flaws in her design and making the anatomy of the fiasco her thesis—much like those reporters who are sent out to interview a reclusive celebrity and write a whole piece on *not* getting the interview.

Yet even this idea changed. When Jade finally set to work on her thesis, it was called "Watching Dogs/Myself," and it was perhaps the first confessional senior's thesis in ethology. Since all hope for hard data was lost, Jade went to the source of her inspiration and recorded her own reactions to the litters. "This is how Hugh would have done it," she said, the midnight she solved her dilemma.

"Dogs," wrote Jade, "are mirrors more telling than water or glass. In bright reflecting mirrors we see ego-bound versions of what we look like now and fearful apparitions of the future. But dogs can show us how we feel, our relationship to the life around us, and our past. Animals are us in our infancy. A hound baying at the moon is our true self . . ." Jade and I watched and tended and adored the dogs, and when something seemed to interrupt the flow of life we finally abandoned the last pretense of experimental rigor and stepped right in. A Tiny Tears milk bottle; an Ohio Blue Tip splint. How we loved those dogs and pups, and what a relief it was to have a different medium through which to romance each other. The pups were our first metaphor. We cradled them and looked at each other; we could wonder about ourselves by wondering about them. And every evening as Jade made a long entry into her "Watching Dogs/Myself" diary, I lay on our bed and watched her write—she rocked back and forth like a Talmudic scholar—and I too thought of my beginnings, the slow tortoise-like gropings of my childhood, the years like cool muck. No one's early life seemed so monolithically dull as my own, but I followed Jade's lead and did my best to think about it, trying to recover all the information I'd fed to psychiatrists and make it more honest.

"The blind mother," wrote Jade. "Sight without sight. Insight without looking. The numbing primacy of instinct. The blind mother eating the birth sack. Voracious. I almost screamed at Queenie to stop. I thought she might eat her first pup alive (Vladimir). An act of self-cannibalization. We are our mother's self, but what she wants back she takes, and what she can't admit she attempts to destroy, and what makes it through is what we are. Our first struggle: to get out of the mother. Our second (and lasting) struggle: to remain out, resist reabsorption. . . ."

"This is what I want to do," Jade announced one night. We were walking back into the house after weighing all the pups. "For the first time, I know. I really know. I want to study animals."

"I always thought that was what you wanted."

"No. I wanted to want it. But it never seemed right. All the scientific method got in my way. Someone else's shoes. And I'm not suited for it. I'm like Hugh in that way. I think that's why he became the kind of doctor he was. Homeopathy is more intuitive and personal." She took my hand and stopped me in my tracks. She pulled me closer to her. "That's exactly what I want. I want to watch the world; I want to see things that most other people don't notice. I'd like to go out into the woods for months at a time and do nothing but watch the world. Listen to owls, watch the deer get drunk on those old apples. And see everything for what it is and help myself see me for what I am. I'll go to graduate school and get all the education I need so people will take me seriously and maybe even pay me, but what I really want to talk about is what it feels like to be related to a grasshopper." She was smiling, squeezing my arm.

We went upstairs with a bottle of white wine. Jade wrote for a while and I drank and read from a book of stories by Isaac Babel. Then Jade joined me on the bed and helped finish the wine. Wine wants you to finish it, one of us said.

"Will you always be my assistant?" Jade asked.

"Will you pay me?"

"Half."

"A deal."

"And my husband?"

"We'll have to pay him, too," I said.

Jade smiled, laid down with her hands behind her head, her tee shirt tight against her breasts. Letting it pass.

"I'd love to be married to you," I said. It was the first time we'd talked about it in years.

"It doesn't make any difference. Marriage is probably unlucky, anyhow. It's not what I think about. It's something else. It's raising the puppies with you. Being so close to the beginnings of life and sharing it with you. I think you'd be a great father."

"I'd love to have children who looked like you," I said, almost in a whisper.

"All we'd have to do is . . . I mean there's nothing to it, really, then that would be that. No matter what happened, we would have done that. A child. God, I feel insane, but I really would like that. I want to do it. It seems that until you're a mother you're a daughter and it feels ridiculous being a daughter."

"That's true. I never felt very comfortable in the daughter role."

"Big joke. I'm offering you a chance at changing the universe and you're making jokes."

"Nerves."

"It's no excuse."

"Look, you want to have a baby then we'll do it."

"No. You can't make it mine. It can't be what *I* want to do. It has to be mutual, you know."

"It is. I'd love to be that baby growing inside you. It would be better than being married."

"It seems like the next step. We can fuck until we die but after a while it starts wearing thin, doesn't it?"

"Not for me."

"I don't mean *yet*. But it will. And I don't really know how I feel about childless couples. It seems like cheating."

"I could have nothing ever change again and I'd have a better life than I deserve."

"I think it's the normality of the whole thing that excites me," said Jade. "How simple and perfect and matter of fact. All I have to do is not put in my diaphragm and then we can do what we normally do and then just as simply as that the whole world is different. It really is exciting to me, David. It's like thinking about screwing for the first time, when all I had to go on was hearsay, one dirty picture, and my imagination."

As Ann would say, how the souls of the unborn hovered over us that night. Jade came to bed, her uterus unshielded, and we made love with a gravity and wholeness that exceeded anything we had ever known. It was what making love for the first time would be if we were born with sexual skills, yet even that doesn't faithfully describe the power of making love without contraception. We were playing long plaintive tunes on our bodies, trying to coax a human life out of the vast invisible jumble of chemistry and fate. A whole new vocabulary of instinct; my ejaculation seemed to hurtle itself deeper into Jade than ever before. The universe based on risk and effort. Sex no longer lifted us up and outside of time, but sent us streaming back and forth, into our own beginnings and toward the shrouded marker of someone's future.

"Again," said Jade after we came. "I feel like a dog. Never so out of control . . ."

It wasn't pleasure, it was destiny. We stared at each other as we made love and barely made a sound. Lovers used to believe that their souls rushed out of them when they made love and we did hold on to each other as if we were endangered. I don't know how many times we started from the beginning again, but we went on for hours that night. It was the energy, the obsession of our first month together, in Chicago, when Jade went through the days with lilac bruises on her spine and I'd be having dizzy spells. We petitioned the universe to make us a family, but it didn't work out. The next day we both felt we had acted more impulsively than we could sustain and we went back to using birth control. We waited the rest of the month to see if our one try at conception had taken. I was certain it had, but I was wrong. Ten days later, Jade got those pains in her lower back that herald her period. "I'm glad," she said. "We have too much to decide to have a baby now. You've got to straighten things out with the cops. My family doesn't even know we're together. I need to graduate and figure out my life. And so do you. You won't be selling pants all your life, I hope."

When her period finally began, we were having lunch on the lawn of the Presbyterian church near my work. "I have to get to a john," said Jade, putting down her egg salad sandwich. We looked at each other and shrugged. I got up, took Jade's hand, and pulled her up. We put our arms around each other. "I wasn't sure," Jade whispered. I didn't know if she meant she wasn't sure if she was going to actually have her period or if she wasn't sure about having a baby. I didn't ask. I wanted that baby without exactly knowing why. My desire for it couldn't refute all of the objections, yet the objections couldn't diminish the desire. I didn't know what to say. My heart was racing at twice its normal rate and I just held her.

August 12, 1973, was the sixth anniversary of the fire; every year on that day the Butterfields gathered at one or another of their homes. This year, they were expected at Keith's house in Bellows Falls—just ninety miles away. Up until the twelfth, Jade was decided not to go. She'd yet to stop concealing from Ann, Sammy, and Keith that she and I were together again—though I was certain that Ann somehow knew—and the anniversary of the fire seemed like the worst possible occasion to tell that particular truth. Yet on the other hand she didn't want to spend a whole day with what was left of her family in such a false position.

"I hate going to Keith's house," she said. "I hate that he lives so close. I hate the jobs he works to keep the place going. I hate all the photographs and little scraps of family memories. He must think we're the Romanovs. And I hate the place as much as he does. He makes you go on a tour each time so he can point out all the little things wrong with his house. The bricks crumbling around the fireplace, the wet spots in the wall, the rotting floorboards. I mean the guy is living in a house built in 1825 and we're supposed to be upset that it's not in perfect shape."

On the morning of the twelfth I woke to the clock radio and Jade was throwing a change of clothes into her black nylon travel bag. "I'll probably be back tonight but you never can tell with my family," she said. It made me late for work but I went with her to the bus station. We were both nervous. Our first separation since spring. The bus was headed toward Boston but it was completely empty. The driver was tall and silver-haired. He looked like an airline pilot and I wondered if some deep character flaw forced him to drive a bus instead. Jade stopped on the bottom step of the bus and hugged my head to her breasts. "I don't know what I'll do if they start talking about you," she said. "It makes me want to murder. I'll tell them right away that we're together and they can make anything they want to out of it."

Gertrude was empty when I got home from work. Colleen had taken Oliver to Fishkill, ostensibly so Oliver could be a carpenter for Colleen's mother, who was converting an old garage house into a guest apartment. Anemone Grommers was in Greece. Nina Sternberg was in Los Angeles. The others were simply out somewhere. I fed the dogs. In a few days, the puppies would be old enough to leave their mothers and we'd be taking the kennels down. I sat out in the back yard for a while and watched the pups gnaw on each other. I thought of how close they had brought Jade and me to starting our own family. It seemed truly lunatic to be influenced like that but I embraced our susceptibility.

I didn't realize it first off, but every thought I had was a part of a well-constructed unconscious argument in favor of my calling home. A couple of days after moving to Stoughton I'd sent Rose and Arthur short notes, telling them I was all right. I'd given both letters to Miriam Kay to mail for me, as she was on her way to visit her sister in Toronto and I didn't want a revealing postmark to give me away. Being outside the law bloats your self-importance and I sat for some time in the kitchen with my hand on the telephone, wondering if my call home would somehow be traced: like the hero of sentimental gangster story, I risked detection—death!—in order to get through to Mama. But finally the laws of civilization worked their way on me. Just as nature endows us with desire so that even the misogynist will reproduce, we bless ourselves with a sense of guilt so that even the heedless will sometimes do the correct, difficult thing. I dialed the Ellis Avenue number and Rose picked up on the fifth ring. She must have been taking a late afternoon nap; there was nowhere in the apartment that far from a phone. Her voice was small, meek, like a little girl who's been warned not to answer the phone.

"It's me," I said.

She was silent and the silence continued. The beginning of a word. And then she slammed the phone down and broke the connection.

I held on, shaking a little but not surprised. I pictured her with her small hands over her face. Then picking up the receiver to see if I was still there. Slamming it down again. Hoping I'd call back. It was like her to be more insulted than worried by the mystery of my whereabouts and hearing my voice—sounding so normal and untroubled—drew on that part of her that felt spurned by me, enraged that I missed the subtle points of her affection. What she offered me was loyalty and the chance to be a better person, and I, instead, took her reserve for coldness and fell for my father's sloppy love, choosing the overheated embrace over the guiding hand.

I picked up the phone and dialed her again. This time Arthur answered—I was surprised into silence when I heard his voice.

"Hello?" he said, two or three times.

"It's me," I said.

"David. Oh God. I can't . . . Where *are* you? No. That's OK. You don't have . . ."

"I'm all right. I'm better than all right. I'm fine."

"Are you near?"

"No. Not really. Is everyone looking for me?"

"We didn't know where to look. Your grandfather wanted to hire private detectives . . . We put ads in some of the newspapers, you know, the underground ones."

"I mean are the police and all that stuff looking for me?"

"It can be worked out. Are you coming home?"

"What's happened? How come you're at Mom's house?"

"I moved out of my apartment. Apartment! Hole, I should say."

"Where's Barbara?" I asked, and as I did I knew.

"Dead," said Arthur, after a silence. "Just a few days after you left. Three in the morning. In her sleep."

I started to stand but my legs warned me not to. The extension was picked up. Rose in the bedroom, sitting on the edge of the bed, near the air conditioner: I heard its hoarse, worn note.

"Where are you?" she asked.

"I'm all right. I just wanted to tell you."

"You're all right? Well, I'm very glad. But did it occur to you that *we* weren't all right? No. That would be asking too much."

"Rose," Arthur cautioned.

"You'd better get back here and I mean quick," Rose said. "Maybe it's not too late. Maybe there's still time."

"Time for what?" I said.

"To clean up the mess you've made. To be some help around here. To be a son, for once. Where are you, anyhow? You're with that little . . ." she left the epithet to my imagination.

"I'm happy for once," I said. "It's like before. I'm alive again."

"If you care so much about life then I think you'd better get home," Rose said. "If you follow my meaning."

"Please, Rose," said Arthur. "David? You don't have to come home. But maybe you can tell us where you are? It's terrible not knowing. We won't call, we won't bother you. You're old enough to make your own decisions and we respect that—"

"Shit," said Rose.

"—but it hurts not to know where you are, to know no matter how important it is we can't get ahold of you."

"He doesn't think about that," said Rose. "It's enough that he knows where *we* are and if he wants something he'll call and we'll come running."

"This is costing a lot of money," I said, "and I'm sort of broke."

"Not too broke to leave town and quit your job," said Rose.

"OK," I said. "I'll tell you. Write it down and keep it some-where safe, for obvious reasons. I'm in Stoughton, Vermont." I gave them the phone number.

"Are you OK, then?" Arthur said.

"You're only making it harder on yourself, not coming home and working this whole thing out," Rose said. Her voice had softened; she hadn't expected me to compromise.

We said our goodbyes in another few moments. I promised to call again but no one tried to pin me down as to when. After-wards, I went out back and played with Cora and Queenie, who were their old selves again now that the pups didn't need them very much. One of Queenie's pups had a cold, with little de-posits in the corners of his tiny blue eyes. I wiped them clean and held the pup to me, unaccountably worried over its health. I knew the pups were fine but even the minor imperfection made me tremble. "Poor Chetwin," I said, over and over. The pup nibbled at my thumb with his needle teeth and finally it was starting to hurt and I gave him back to his mother, who rolled him onto his fat back with a long sweep of her tongue.

The phone was ringing. I ran for it. Which is not something I do. It was only an hour and a few minutes after I'd called home, but when I heard Rose's voice on the other end, I wasn't sur-prised.

"David," she said, "your father's had a heart attack."

I waited until eight in the evening and then called Jade at Keith's, though I didn't want to. Keith answered. He knew it was me but he didn't show any particular reaction. "Just a minute," he said with a sigh, as if the phone had been ringing for Jade all day. I told her about Arthur and she said she'd call me right back. A few minutes later she called and said the next bus to Stoughton left at ten forty-five the next morning. I'd already made a reservation on the 9 a.m. flight to Chicago, which left from Albany. She gave me some names to call, hoping I could borrow a car and drive to Keith's and pick her up. But I couldn't focus on that. I said I wanted to go to sleep early and set out for Albany by six in the morning—it was only an hour's drive but I'd be hitching. We said goodbye. I said I'd be back in less than a week. Jade said if it looked like I'd have to stay longer, then she'd come to Chicago and be with me. We said goodbye; she couldn't say she loved me above a whisper because her family was near.

I packed a small suitcase. Most of my clothes were new, and nothing, for some reason, quite fitted me. Then I searched for and found my old return ticket to Chicago. I had about thirty dollars besides that. I called home before I went to bed to tell when I'd be arriving at O'Hare. My mother's friend Millicent Bell picked up the phone; she was taking care of the calls while Rose was at the hospital with Arthur.

It took a long time for me to fall asleep. I kept wondering if Jade was going to do something foolish. Specifically, I wondered if she would leave Keith's and try to hitchhike back home, to see me before I left. I kept myself awake waiting for her and when I dozed off I felt her lips on me, kissing me awake. But that didn't happen.

17

Rose met me at the airport, wearing dark blue high heels, dark nylons, and makeup, as if it were autumn. She hugged me briefly, with her face slightly averted.

"We have to hurry," she said. "My car's parked illegally and I don't feel like getting a citation." Her heels clicked across the hard gray floor, so loudly that a few people looked searchingly, curious about the noise.

I had to strain to keep up with her.

"How is he?" I asked.

"He's waiting for you. He's at Jackson Park Hospital. A terrible place. But . . ." she glanced at me: but that's where his lover died.

"How is he?"

"He's not a youngster. He's been working double duty to help support that woman's children. *And* you. Not just for the past few months, but for *years*. That woman played him for a sucker and this is the result. Not to mention . . ."

We pushed through the glass doors. The heat pounced on us, thick with gasoline and dust. Horns blaring. They were re-paving part of the airport road and the smell of tar was violently present. The sun pulsated behind a bank of low clouds. The parking lot was a long walk away but Rose had left her car right across from the terminal exit, in a space reserved for buses. A cop, looking incongruously military on his little blue and white Vespa, pulled up and began writing out a ticket.

"Officer! Officer!" called Rose, running toward her car. "Help!"

The cop looked up, his face impassive. He had blond eyebrows and freckles.

Rose waved her hands over her head. "That's my car," she called. "Please don't give me a citation." She darted recklessly out into the traffic and was by his side.

"It's too late," the cop said, turning his ticket booklet toward Rose. "See? I've already got your plates down. Once I do that it's out of my hands."

"But you don't understand," cried Rose. "My son's just gotten in from the East Coast. His father's suffered a massive heart attack. We're on the way to the hospital right now." She opened up her purse and extracted a ring with at least twenty keys on it. She held one up for the cop to inspect. "Here. I was just about to start my car."

"I'm sorry," the cop said. "But you're parked illegally. I've already started writing your ticket." He glanced at the tip of his ballpoint pen and began to write.

"But didn't you hear me!" said Rose. "This boy's father is in the hospital." She whirled around to look at me. I stood a few feet behind her, holding my suitcase and sweating. I thought of the cop looking at me and suddenly recognizing my face— did they have photo files of parole violators? But the cop didn't look at me; he hurried through writing the ticket and handed it to Rose with a brief, formal nod. Rose stared at the ticket and then turned it over. "Five dollars," she said. "I could have had valet parking for that."

I opened the back door and threw my suitcase in. It bounced off the seat and landed on the floor. Rose was still studying her parking ticket. She seemed to be checking the license plate number he'd written down against the number on her plate, hoping an error might invalidate the whole thing. A car pulled up next to Rose and the driver shouted through the window, asking her if she was leaving her space.

"You better not park here," she said to the man. "The police are giving out citations like there's no tomorrow." The man waved at Rose and drove off. Rose watched him go and then returned her attention to the parking ticket.

"Maybe we better set out," I said.

Rose folded the ticket into thirds and slipped it into her purse. There were beads of perspiration on her forehead, exquisite little drops as delicate as lace. I walked around to the passenger side and got in; a moment later, Rose was at the wheel. The seat was pushed back too far and she could only reach the accelerator and the brake with the tips of her toes.

"Of all the times to call," she said, as she turned the ignition, "you *had* to pick the twelfth. Did you think we wouldn't know it was the day of the fire? I struggle all my life for a decent existence and you change it all with one match." She swung the car into traffic.

"Would you please tell me how he is?" I said. "Was it a bad attack?"

"I said he was all right." She shook her head, as if my interest was somehow suspect. Did she resent my concern? Did she believe I'd care less if it were *her* in the hospital?

We drove in silence until we were out of O'Hare and on the Dan Ryan Expressway.

"I shouldn't say this," Rose said, "but you look nice." She drove with her eyes straight ahead, breaking her intense concentration every minute or so with a glance in the rear-view mirror. "You look better than you have in a long while. Apparently your new life agrees with you."

"I don't have a new life," I said with some vehemence.

Rose shrugged. "And you're with . . . ?"

"Yes." As I said it I felt a wave of doubt—perhaps I shouldn't have told the truth. And when the momentary panic subsided, I was left with a dense congestion of sadness. I could feel and identify all the parts of me that loved my mother, but all the passageways that connected what I felt about her to what I could express were in ruins, or had totally disappeared. My loyalty and instinctual affections crouched within me like ancient idols that preside over the thick silence of some tropical jungle. You can view them from the air but you cannot bring them forth.

"We knew you were," said Rose. "We tried to contact the family but we couldn't find any of them. Your father and I both looked through your apartment—you were evicted, by the way, for all you care—but we couldn't find a thing that told us anything about them. Weren't you in contact with any of them?"

"There were some letters, but I took them with me."

"Knowing you wouldn't be coming back."

"No. I just took them. I didn't think about why."

"We could have dug up one or another of them if we'd pushed harder but we had to be careful."

"I know. And I'm glad you were careful. I appreciate it."

"Well what did you expect? You're my son. I'm not going to have you thrown in jail."

We were silent again. My mother was driving slowly, and trucks and cars roared past us on either side. I looked at the speedometer; we were going exactly 40. I wanted to find out more about Arthur's condition but Rose began to speak.

"I've done a little snooping around on my own—you might be interested in this. Following your lead, and Arthur's too. You know who I've been looking for?"

"I don't know."

"Guess. Take a guess."

"You've been looking for Carl Courtney."

"And I found him. He's in Cherry Hill. That happens to be a nice Philadelphia suburb, though it sounds like a place you'd put a bunch of whorehouses. He's married to a gal from Chicago. They live in a six-room condo, brand new. One of those places with a laundry room on every floor and—well, it's like a hotel. If you call and the person's not in, the front desk picks up and takes a message. Someone comes in and changes the linens twice a week. They have their own medical staff. It's for so-called senior citizens."

"Like Grandpa's place in Florida," I said.

Rose shook her head and was a moment in answering. "Not really. I would imagine Carl's is different." She glanced in the rear-view mirror. "Though who knows? You never can tell. The only reason they got in is because Carl's wife is over sixty-five. Carl's just sixty himself. And pretty well tied to his wife's apron strings. She's a big Zionist. They were thinking of moving to Israel but they took the place in Cherry Hill instead."

"Well, what was it like talking to him after so many years?" I asked.

Again, Rose was a while in answering. "Fine," she said, with finality. But then she continued, "I think he was a little shocked to hear from me. And it was pretty late at night when I decided to call. I forgot the time difference, it being an hour later east. I woke him up. And you know how some people are when they get up, confused. Carl didn't catch right on who it was. Though maybe he was pretending if he and his wife sleep in the same room and she was right next to him, maybe he was pretending so she wouldn't make a scene. 'Don't faint,' I said. 'I'm just calling to say hello.' "

"You must have been nervous," I said. "It took courage to call."

"Not really. I had you and your father as examples. The point is you do whatever you want to and it's all right if it's for . . . *love*. I had no idea that life was so simple." She let out a long sigh.

"Are you going to see him?"

"Carl? What would the point be? I *loved* him for his beauty and I'm sure that's gone." Rose laughed; the car drifted toward the lane to our right and a truck blew a long terrifying note of warning.

"You haven't mentioned your father and I being back in the same house again," Rose said, moments later. "I thought you'd have a *lot* to say about that."

"To be honest with you, I'm surprised."

"I knew it! I know what you think of your mother."

"No, you don't."

"You're surprised your father would come home?"

"No. I'm surprised you'd have him back."

"The woman died. Her kids went to her sister and he was all alone. He called me five weeks ago, pretending he wanted to talk about you, we had dinner, he asked to come back, and I said it was all right with me. I didn't have any reason to play hard to get or any other games. I don't give a damn what people say. I've always been that way. An independent. When the welfare man used to come to my mother's apartment, I used to spit right on his nice brown shoes. My mother was afraid I'd get us thrown off relief but I didn't care. No one takes my dignity away, or my self-respect. That's something no one can do. Not the welfare department, not the cops, or the FBI, or the Board of Education, not your father, and not you. No one!" She paused for a moment. "I like being with Arthur. He's my best friend. He's my *husband.* And I know you know how he used to love me. Worship me! Really, it *was* like worship. He used to follow me around the apartment with his hands out in front of him, like he was sleepwalking. But things got confused. They bogged down. I wasn't as nice as I could have been. Resentments build up. It's not so unusual. He used you against me and that made things worse. But that happens, too. Believe me, the Axelrods aren't the only little family who've had a few failings. I think we've done better than most. At least your father and I have upheld our ideals. I'm proud of that, at least."

"You should be," I said. "It's hard to be a socialist in this country."

"You're damned right it is!" said my mother, with a surge. "And no one says thank you. That woman's children? The boy is going into the Army but he wants to go to college for a couple of years so he'll be made an officer. He wants to go to Asia and burn yellow people to death. And the daughter wants to be a clothes model. This is what you get from the Negro people. I don't know *what* their mother believed in, but it certainly wasn't justice or progress."

We turned off the expressway and drove through ghetto streets. Some of the buildings were still boarded up or in ruins, as they had been since Martin Luther King's assassination. It made you think that most would never be rebuilt; trapped between past and future, we lived with our own archaeology.

"Look at this," Rose said. "In the richest country in the world. Is your door locked? Poverty . . ." her voice faded; she speeded up to make a green light. "People take their own feelings so seriously," she said. "I try not to. People exaggerate their feelings, and I try not to do that either. Arthur is a man I've known for more than thirty years and when he came to me with tears in his eyes and asked to come home, well, I could have said yes and I could have said no, but I said yes. And it was fine. And getting better. *I* think we may have even been falling in love. Again, I mean. But then you called . . . I'm not trying to blame you, David. I'm glad you got in touch with us. I only wish it had been sooner. But then you called, finally, and Arthur had a heart attack. I don't blame you. I hope you don't blame yourself, either. Maybe he was just waiting for a time when you'd be able to know before he let himself collapse. Maybe he was holding out until then. Maybe he would have held out forever if you hadn't called. How could you know that? And I'm glad you called. It should have been earlier, but at least you called. And he's doing all right, as I told you. There's been no brain damage. He still has his functions. Only a very minor bit of tissue damage in his heart. He looks fine. Better than he did before the attack. Just one night's sleep and staying in bed. It's amazing. I was so frightened last night. It was a relief seeing him this morning—I stopped to visit before coming to get you. But now I'm scared again. That's why I've been driving so slow and going a little out of my way. I know a shortcut that could have knocked fifteen minutes off this trip but I'm a little afraid to bring you to see your father. I have this terrible feeling that seeing you is going to make him worse, maybe even give him another attack. Will you at least promise me one thing? If he seems to be getting weak, or if I give you a signal, because I could see something that you'd miss, then will you just pick yourself up and get the hell out of his room no questions asked? Will you promise me that?"

"Look for yourself, I'm fit and healthy as a horse," said Arthur, as we took our seats next to his bed. He was propped up, with the *Sun Times* resting on his lunch tray. His thin gray hair was mussed and his eyes were disconcertingly bright—he looked merry, impish, even slightly drunk. His loose-fitting hospital gown was open to the top of his belly and the hair on his chest glistened: someone hadn't wiped all the petroleum jelly off after his last EKG. He held my hand, clumsily but with strength. The letters on his plastic identification bracelet were dark violet and smeary. "Dr. Pokorny threatens to kick me the hell out of here unless I agree to look a little sicker. He says it's bad for the image of the hospital." Arthur smiled, broadly this time, revealing the soft blackness at the back of his mouth where his dentures had been removed.

"Are you in any pain?" I asked.

"Nah," he said.

"You don't have to be brave," Rose said. "He asked: tell him."

"It's nothing. At first it was like getting kicked by a mule, but when I think of what some people have to suffer . . . this is *nothing*." He took a deep breath, closed his eyes, and gestured across the room, where a white curtain had been drawn around the room's second bed. Then, slowly and sadly, he shook his head.

No mention was made of my absence, no joy was expressed at my return. Reflexively, we spoke as if the room was bugged by enemies, as if the police had learned of Arthur's attack and now waited for me to be drawn into their net. Once in a while, Arthur would squeeze my hand and say my name under his breath, but he never used my name in a conversational tone and this, too, was deliberate. We didn't discuss what I'd been doing the past months, nor did he or Rose express any curiosity over what my future might hold. We spoke of Arthur's health—how good it had always been; we spoke of the weather—the remorseless sunless heat.

We talked as best we could, and we said nothing. We were tense, formal, and bewildered. The floor was not clean. My mother kept clearing her throat. My father asked me to crank up his bed so he could sit up but the crank was broken and I lowered him a few inches instead.

I said I wanted to go to the bathroom and went out to find Dr. Pokorny, an ex-comrade who was looking after Arthur. I found the head nurse and she told me Pokorny was at Michael Reese Hospital—that morning his wife had accidentally slammed their car door on Pokorny's fingers and they were being set at Michael Reese. "Who's going to take care of my father?" I asked. It seemed utterly calamitous; I couldn't understand how something so unlucky had happened.

"Dr. Lonnigan is covering for Dr. Pokorny," the nurse told me. "And there's nothing to worry about. Your father is doing fine; he's mostly resting anyhow, you know, just resting."

When I returned to Arthur's room, Rose was gone. She'd left her purse tucked under the sheet of Arthur's bed so it wouldn't be stolen in her absence. My father patted it, as if it were a sick doll.

"Where's Mom?" I asked. I'd already decided not to mention Pokorny's accident; soon enough he'd be at my father's bedside with his hand in a splinted bandage and they could both have a nice comradely laugh on it.

"Calling home," Arthur said. "We got ourselves a cleaning woman now and Rose wants to see if there's any messages. She can't get used to having someone in the house."

"She was always against it," I said.

Arthur shrugged. "Since I moved back. It's a big help. But I don't like having someone pick up after us. And Rose watches the poor woman like a hawk. You know how particular your mother is. It's no picnic cleaning Rose's house. But we pay her twice what other people pay, so there's that."

"Dad," I said, "you know—" I stopped; Arthur had grabbed ahold of my hand and the sudden pressure startled me.

"Are you all right?" he whispered. "Are you happy?"

I nodded.

"I want you to go back to her. Today. Tomorrow. Soon. It's a little risky here, until we work everything out with the court. I'm not saying some arrangement can't be made but until then I want you to be careful. You're taking a big risk coming here, I hope you know."

"I had to." I put my hand on the side of his face. "It scared me to hear you were sick. I really love you, you know. I love you a lot."

Arthur suddenly let go of me and his eyes focused on the white ceiling. Taking his cue, I sat straight in my chair and a nurse came in holding a tray with a glass of water and a little pleated cup on it. She had dyed yellow hair and wore dark glasses; she looked more like a waitress at a truck stop than a nurse.

"Medicine woman," announced Arthur. With great eagerness he grabbed the paper cup and poured three pills into his open palm. His face fell like a child's at a disappointing birthday.

"Three?" he asked. "Where's the little orange one? The . . . the . . . whatever it's called?"

"Doctor's orders," said the nurse.

"What do you mean?" Arthur showed me the pills and furrowed his eyebrows, as if asking my opinion.

"The orange was a sedative," the nurse said.

"Well, I need it," Arthur said, with a moan. "I'm not so relaxed." He stared miserably at the pills in his hand, like someone who's been underpaid.

The nurse held the water out to him. "Down you go," she said.

The disappointment left my father's face, to be replaced by a look of fear. He turned the pills over in his hand and shook his head. Across the room, from behind the curtains drawn around the second bed, came a low, distressing sound, a grating, bubbling noise such as one would make sucking up the last of a milkshake through a paper straw.

"Nurse," a voice said. The curtains parted and a tall black man emerged. "Nurse? It's making that noise again. You want to take a look?"

"Your mother is being drained," the nurse answered, exasperated. The man nodded uncertainly and disappeared behind the curtains. "Poor soul," the nurse murmured. "He's been sitting with that woman for eleven days and she doesn't even know he's . . ." the nurse's eyes happened to rest on the pocketbook Arthur cradled beneath the sheet, but with a shake of the head she decided not to notice.

Moments after the nurse was gone, Rose returned.

"Everything OK?" asked Arthur.

"Yes. Fine. Everything's fine." She pulled her purse away from Arthur and tucked it under her arm. She looked warily at both of us; she was sure we'd been talking about her. Then she looked over her shoulder to make certain we were alone and said, "That parole office Eddie Watanabe called the house about an hour ago."

"Oh boy," said Arthur, softly.

"Dinah took the call," said Rose. "She said that we were here."

I was standing. I walked to the window, expecting, perhaps, to see a squad car pulling in, but Arthur's window looked on nothing but other hospital windows, grimy and opaque, like the view from a cheap, desperate hotel.

"Did she say anything else?" I asked.

"Who knows?" said Rose.

"Did you say anything to her?" Arthur asked. "Does she know he's here?"

"I don't know. I may have," said Rose.

"You don't know?" said Arthur.

"I think I'd better be going," I said.

"Where are you going?" whispered Arthur.

"Back?" asked Rose.

"I don't know. I'm scared." But even as I said it, I knew I was leaving. I would leave without talking to Arthur's doctor, leave without discovering anything more about my parents' new and difficult truce, leave immediately to save myself.

I heard footsteps coming down the hall. They sounded deliberate, official. My life seemed to be balanced like an egg at the edge of a table but the footsteps passed—a doctor in surgical green.

"I better go right now," I said to Rose.

"I'll take you," she said.

"Thanks."

"But don't get excited. Don't react to things before they happen. Do you understand me? You'll wear yourself out just by worrying?"

I nodded. I was thinking: she's stalling; she wants me to be caught.

"You're a little fish in a big pond," said Rose. "I know how these people work. He was sitting on his fanny in his office, making calls."

Arthur patted the bed. "Come here for a minute," he said. "Sit."

I lost control. "No," I shouted, nearly at the top of my lungs. The world flapped like a flag before my eyes. "I want to get out of here right now!" My voiced echoed in the room. The enduring son peeked through the curtains around his mother's bed. Footsteps were hurrying toward us. "I really think I should be going," I said, bringing my voice as much under control as I could. My parents were looking at me, a huge beam of disapproval coming from their eyes: I was behaving like a fool, humiliating them.

I bolted from my father's room just as the nurse in sunglasses was entering. I jostled her but didn't look back. I hoped I was heading toward an exit. I heard running behind me and looked over my shoulder, against my better judgment. It was Rose, holding her purse like a football, moving with astonishing grace. I stopped and waited for her. In silence, we walked out of the hospital and we maintained the silence until we were in the car and she'd started the engine.

"Have you gone out of your mind again?" she asked, glancing into the rear-view mirror.

"Yes. Completely. Now please, take me to the airport. And you're going to have to loan me the money for a ticket, too. I'm broke."

"You think I carry that kind of money around?"

"Then charge it on a credit card."

"I don't know who you're talking to. I don't have a credit card, except from Weibolt's."

"Then pay by check. I don't care."

"I don't know how much money is in my account."

With a lunge, I grabbed her behind the neck and squeezed her with my fingertips. She let out a scream and slammed her foot on the brake. We both swung forward but I kept my grip on her, only incidentally aware of what I was doing. "Then take me to the bus station," I said.

"You're hurting me," she said, with a small cry. She reached behind and dug her fingernails into my hand.

I let go of her. I was shaking uncontrollably. I pulled my suitcase from the back of the car. Our car was stopped in the middle of Stony Island Boulevard and the cars behind us were sounding their horns. *This is how I get caught*, I thought to myself, but even fear seemed remote and distorted. Rose was rubbing her neck and staring at me—with fear, or hatred, I don't know, it could even have been pity.

"I'm sorry I hurt you," I said. "Please, if you could just take me—"

A couple of cars managed to swing around us. The rest— I don't know how many—were still sounding their horns.

"I'm not moving," said Rose. She rotated her head, testing the soreness of her neck muscles.

I closed my eyes, covered my face, and saw myself grabbing her shoulders, shaking her back and forth, back and forth, smashing her . . . I threw the door open and set off down the street, my suitcase banging against me like a separate self.

. . .

The bus route from Chicago to Stoughton was a complex one, and the bus that would bring me there left the Randolph Street terminal at four that afternoon, a three-and-a-half-hour wait. It seemed unsafe. Rose would know I was there; it would not be beyond her to convince herself that I was in the pain of psychosis and to take me out of my misery by turning me in. I could not stand to look at the people who filed around the station. Even the derelicts looked menacing—if they did not look like disguised cops, they seemed like omens. The devastating green watery light of the place; the shrieking odors of cheap food, disinfectant, old newspaper. I had enough money for a ticket to New York City. I wasn't sure what I would do from there but a bus was leaving in fifteen minutes.

I called Jade. She answered the phone herself and accepted the charges.

"I'm coming home right now," I said.

"What's wrong with you? Tell me what's happened!"

"I'm all right. I'm just in a rush. The bus for New York leaves in a couple of minutes, and I want to make sure I'm on it."

"Are you—" she stopped herself. She knew I was in trouble. "Well, get on it, then. I'm glad you're coming back. One night without you is all I can take. I miss you."

"I'll get there as soon as I can."

"I called your job and said you wouldn't be back for a week. All the puppies leave tonight. We'll have nothing to do except lock ourselves in our room and force ourselves to eat from time to time."

"I'm coming right away. I better hurry."

"Then hurry."

"Are you doing OK?"

"I miss you."

"How was Bellows Falls?"

"Intense. Horrible. I'll tell you all about it."

"God."

"I know. Also, Hugh's old girl, Ingrid Ochester, called. She says she has to talk to me. She's driving through in that van of hers. I'm having breakfast with her tomorrow."

"What does she want?" I asked.

"I'm not sure. She sounded very determined, though. She's been very messed up since Hugh. Therapy three times a week and all that. I think she's worked something out and now she wants to share it with me. If she only knew how much I didn't want to get into it. I really don't."

I held the phone, unable to speak.

"David?"

"I better go," I said. "I don't want to . . ." My voice evaporated.

"OK. Don't miss your bus. I'm waiting for you. We'll cry on each other's shoulder. It'll be wonderful."

I said nothing.

"David?"

"I better go."

"I'll see if I can borrow Colleen's car and maybe I can drive down to New York and pick you up. What time do you get in?"

"I don't know. Don't do that. I'll just take another bus. I have to go." I almost hung up but I held the phone very tightly and close to my mouth. "I love you," I said. "I'll always love you."

"Don't miss your bus, David."

"I won't." I waited a moment and then, finally, I hung up.

Time after time, during the long rumbling ride east, I went rigid in my seat, certain that *this* was the moment when Ingrid was telling Jade that it was me Hugh chased after just before his death. I had a dollar seventy-five to my name and I somehow turned all my anxiety and grief into a hunger I was too poor to satisfy. I had nothing to read, I could not sleep, and it wasn't until we were past Cleveland and it was long dark that I finally got a place next to a window.

I could have changed it all. I could have asked Jade to meet me in New York and then she would not have been able to meet Ingrid Ochester for breakfast. It would have only been a delay, but it would have been better. It would have engendered hope. Nothing is inevitable. Sometimes by stalling an event you contribute to its nonoccurrence. Ingrid could have left, gone somewhere far away, drifted back into the forgetfulness that had protected me for the past months, or perhaps dropped dead of a bee sting. It's crazy *not* to throw yourself into the path of a coming event, crazy to convince yourself that if it doesn't happen now it will happen quite soon, so what's the use. We *can* sabotage the future, with a glance, a phonecall, a misplaced message.

I arrived in New York around ten in the morning. I felt foul, exhausted, and what thoughts I had seemed bunched up in one small corner of my mind, like a throw rug that a dog's been pawing. I used the bathroom at Port Authority to change clothes and once I was naked in the middle of that vast tiled room I learned from the way people looked at me that changing your clothes like that isn't acceptable behavior.

I realized I didn't know where to begin hitchhiking to Stoughton. New York encircles you in a dense druidical mass and I couldn't imagine how to get out of it. I asked a few people at random in the bus station, but the only person who seemed to know anything about it was in a hurry and he only called to me over his shoulder, something about "getting on Henry Hudson." There were plenty of policemen around but I couldn't ask them for anything. It was against the law to hitchhike and for all I knew they'd been informed by the Chicago cops to keep an eye out for me—I knew my self-important fears were absurd, but knowing was no cure. I went to a ticket window and asked how much a ride to Stoughton cost—it was five or six dollars more than I had but . . . I don't know: perhaps I was expecting a clearance sale.

I had nothing worth selling and lacked the courage to beg,

and so I did the only thing I could to get the money for a bus ticket: I called Ann.

"I'm broke," I said, as soon as she said hello. "I need to borrow six dollars to get on a bus."

"Where's six dollars going to take you?" she said.

"To Stoughton."

"Did she kick you out?"

"No. Why? Why do you ask that?"

"I'm wondering, that's all. You sound like you're close by."

"I'm at Port Authority."

"I'm wondering what you're doing here without any money. But I recognize there are many things beneath heaven that are none of my damn business. Come by. I'll give you some money. But you can't stay. I've got a date for lunch and I'm nervous as a cat."

Taking two wrong subways and a long walk, I made my way to Ann's. She met me at the door and put a ten-dollar bill in my hand.

"You're late," she said, "and making me late, too. I wish you were staying around because you're just the person I'd like to tell whatever happens today." She touched her forehead. "I feel pregnant with anecdote."

I looked at the money in my hand. I felt my eyes filling with tears.

"That's a loan, remember," Ann said. "My finances are in shambles."

"I'll pay you back. I've got money in . . . Stoughton."

"Don't be shy about saying it," Ann said. "I'm *glad*. I know it's not my place to be . . . to be anything about it. But I'm glad. You two belong together."

I nodded.

"And besides, I don't want to lose you."

"Then don't," I blurted out. "Stay loyal to me. Try to understand. No matter what happens."

Ann nodded but she didn't know what I was talking about; she felt a soft wave of embarrassment over how ardent my plea had been, but she was letting it pass right by. It was just as well.

"OK," said Ann. "Off you go. I'm going to be late and for all I know my Mystery Man is as punctual as death." She smiled, but a little uncertainly, as if she suspected she'd said exactly the wrong thing.

I put the money in my pants and shifted my suitcase from my right hand to my left.

"How come you're in New York?" Ann asked.

"I had to go to Chicago and I only had enough money to get this far. Didn't Jade . . . ?"

"No. Of course not. That's the condition of our truce. Jade wants an old-fashioned relationship, based on kinship and ignorance—what she calls respect. And I think she's absolutely right; it's the only way it can ever work between us. Did you ever tell her about the night you and I spent here?"

"No. There was never a reason to. It wouldn't matter. It would only—"

"I agree. It'll go away on its own."

Coming in through the open windows at the front of Ann's apartment was the sound of church bells, ringing in the quarter hour.

"OK," she said. "Out. Away."

"Let me in," I said. "I have to tell you something. I wasn't going to but I have to. I want to now. You'll know soon enough anyhow but I want you to hear it from me."

"No. I'm late. And I'm not sure I really want to know. I hate confessions. They always make me think I'm supposed to match them with a bit of breast-beating of my own. I don't want to get into it."

"No. You have to. You want to know."

"You are *so* wrong. I don't. At least not today." She put her hand on my face and rubbed her palm against the grain of my whiskers. "You look strange unshaved. I don't think it suits you. You're not growing a beard, are you?"

"No. I just haven't shaved."

"Good. I think you should get on the bus, get up to Stoughton, and hope to God that Jade's not home when you arrive and you'll have time to shave—and bathe."

"Ann, I want to—"

"No," she said, stepping back and preparing to close the door. "Not now. If you want to tell me something, write a letter. I hope that the mere fact that you've found my daughter won't forever discontinue our correspondence. I like you in letters and I love writing to you. Confess to me in a letter. Now go."

She closed the door and I heard her footsteps going back into her apartment. "I killed Hugh," I whispered to the door. I thought of shouting it out, but it would be stupid, it would be cruel. And—this thought presented itself in a tone distinct from the others—what did I really know? Maybe Ingrid wanted to talk to Jade about something else. Wouldn't it have been a waste to try to expose myself before Ingrid exposed me, only to find that I'd really been in no danger at all?

It was eight in the evening when I reached Stoughton. The sky was a low inkwash and behind the swollen clouds lightning flashed, throwing a skittery bleak light that looked as false as a stage effect. It was a simple hitchhike from the bus to our house in North Stoughton, but I walked—past the Main Street Clothiers, past the church on whose lawn Jade and I took our lunch, past the art supplies store where I'd recently put ten dollars down toward a set of drawing pens for Jade, and finally into a Dunkin' Donut where I tortured my growling stomach with five donuts and three cups of coffee. Powdered sugar was on my lap and my hands shook. I looked down and my suitcase was gone—no, it was on the other side of the stool. I took it in hand and went to a phonebooth. I didn't think I should appear home without first speaking to Jade.

The phone rang at least a dozen times before I hung up. I felt a peculiar relief but it was blown aside by a rush of panic. A thought had been murmuring all day behind my will not to think it: Ingrid telling Jade the truth of Hugh's death might ignite a terror and grief in Jade that would make it so she wouldn't want to live. I put my last two dollars on the counter and left, already starting to run. It was at least three miles to home and within a minute I was breathing with effort and in pain. Carrying my suitcase was impossible and I tossed it aside, with the idea I'd come back some other time to retrieve it. The world before my eyes bounced up and down and I held onto my senses as if they would otherwise take flight and leave me forever. I was running as fast as I could. I had to rescue Jade, but I must have known that was not the case because already I was lying, telling myself that there was a way I could somehow explain myself to her: the real danger I wanted to rescue her from was the danger of holding Ingrid's information without me there to counter it.

The house was dark when I finally arrived and the door and windows were locked. I pounded on the front door and punched my finger against the bell a hundred times. Then I went to the back and started again. I went to the back of the yard where I could see the small darkened attic window and I called Jade's name. I threw pebbles against the window, ran out of pebbles, looked for a stone and couldn't find one, and finally tossed my shoes. The first shoe sailed past and landed somewhere at the side of the house; the second hit direct with a thud, but didn't break the glass. I waited and then the light went on. I don't know how much time passed but finally a shadow moved across the window and then I saw her standing, naked, looking down at me. I called out to her, lifting my hands—they felt so heavy.

She struggled to open the window and then realized she'd locked it. She turned the latch and the window slid open.

"Go away. You have to go away." She stared down at me. The light was behind her but I could see her eyes in the darkness. Her chest was heaving. "I know *everything*," she said. The window slammed down.

I raced to the back door and beat against it with open hands. My world, the only world I knew, the only one I wanted, was broken into pieces. I had no world. I could do *anything*. I beat against the door, I called her name, I threw my shoulder into the door hoping to break it down. It did not budge, and as I bounced off of it I brought my arm around, reaching over the railing of the soft wooden porch, and without a moment's hesitation pushed my fist through the kitchen window, through the old glass and the saggy wire screen as well. I withdrew, picked a piece of glass out of my knuckle, and tried to see through the darkness if I was bloody. I couldn't see but I felt the wetness, oily through the cracks of my fingers.

I climbed onto the porch railing and somehow got myself onto the window sill, an inch ledge of tender wood and peeling paint. My fingers gripped the frame and my stockinged feet did their best to hold on to the ledge; to keep myself from falling back, I leaned my weight against the glass and tried to knee a hole large enough for me to crawl in. I neglected to simply reach in to the hole I'd already made and unlock the window. On the third try the window fell away in two huge jagged sheets. I kicked through the screen and as I did, the light in the kitchen shuddered on. I lowered myself in and was hit in the shins—a terrible crack that knocked the wind out of me. The pain spread in every direction and then I was hit again and again. I held on to the window frame with its miniature Alps of splintered glass, three-quarters of my body in the house and my head sending cries into the night air. I was hit again—this time in the knees—and I let go, falling into the kitchen.

Jade was facing me, holding a broom, her hands baseball style near the straw, wagging the red handle at me. I took a stumbling step toward her and she swung again, missing me completely but causing me to stop.

"Don't," I said. I closed my hand and my fingertips ground a shard of glass into my palm.

She was naked except for her underwear. She was panting and shaking at the same time, as if running through a freezing rain. There were lines on one side of her face and her hair was flat—she'd been trying to sleep. She continued to wag the broom handle at me but her eyes didn't seem to be looking at me. She moved her head from side to side, swallowing hard. She stepped forward and threw the broom onto the floor, moved closer until she was near enough to touch, and there she stood, still and immobile. I reached for her, put my arms around her, pressed her unyielding body close to mine.

"We have to talk," I said. "I know what Ingrid told you and it's true. But it's not all. Jade. Jade?"

Slowly, her hands came up and pressed against my chest, pushing me back. "If you stay here, if you stay in this house, no, you have to go, I don't want to be near you, because if you stay in this house I'll kill myself, David. OK?" She breathed deeply and burst into tears. She covered her eyes and her fingers were ice white against her scarlet face. "Go away," she shouted through her tears. "Go away."

I turned, unlocked the back door, and left. And in my loss, which was absolute, I think I truly did believe Jade would reach out and stop me, or call out, but as soon as I closed the door behind me she rushed to it and turned the lock. I stood on the porch and looked at the wide open window but I had no heart left to climb through. I waited until the light went out and I listened for her footsteps as they went away, but she glided without a sound. A ghost.

A little time is missing. I was wondering where I would stay. I went to our neighbors, the Goldmans, but their lights were on and I shied away. I didn't know what I looked like that night: a shoeless man with a bloody fist, unshaved, unslept, panicked. I wandered, trying to collect my thoughts. My shirt was wet; it was raining. I wanted to think of somewhere to stay. When I'm particularly exhausted it feels like a low-voltage electrical charge snakes slowly across the top of my skull. In Rockville I tried to have it diagnosed but it apparently is nothing, what we call nothing. And then I was back home, in the yard, staring at the lightless house. There was no line of demarcation between the black roof and the rainy sky. It was all a mass looming before me. There was no longer any question of breaking back into the house but I needed a place to sleep.

I ended up in the kennels Jade had built for the dogs and their pups. I suppose she'd been waiting for me to help her tear them down. There was hay on the ground and two-by-fours and tar-paper to keep the rain off of me. The pen smelled reassuringly of the dogs, fur and shit and breath and milk and reality. I crawled in feeling very fortunate to have found a place so perfect and so near. I placed my head where I could see the house and tried to prepare myself for the morning when Jade would see me and we could begin the long process of making sense of what we knew. I thought about making love with her in the Hotel McAlpin and decided it would help if I remembered that night in every detail, but as soon as Jade asked me into bed I fell asleep.

I slept through the dawn. The light was on me and Jade woke up, looked through the window, and saw me asleep in the kennel. It must have terrified her, made her feel there was no dealing with me any longer. I don't know what the sequence of events was. She got dressed—but before or after she made the call? She put on a pair of khaki pants and a blue broadcloth shirt, rolling the cuffs midway to the elbow. Blue espadrilles. Then the call. I don't think, somehow, she'd call the police naked. She was probably hoping that in the time it took her to dress I would have miraculously awakened, that she would look out and the pen would be empty, the straw mashed down in my form. But

I was still there, asleep—no, beginning to stir. I remember opening my eyes before the police came, remember seeing the fresh pale sky, the smell of the straw, touching the cuts on my hand and falling asleep, deeper this time, submerging myself as if I knew I would not sleep in my miserable freedom again for a long, long while. "There's someone here who—" Jade said to the police. But who is what? Threatening me? Who has killed my father? Who has broken into my house? Who has gone mad?

I don't know how she described me to the Stoughton police. She didn't tell them I was wanted in Chicago because I'd been at the station for hours before they learned that. She probably just told them to come and remove me and didn't bother with explanations. And when they arrived, she came with them to the back of the house so I could see her as well as them. One of the cops kicked me in the shoulder and when I woke I knew exactly what had happened. "Get up," one of them said, in a fierce voice, as if expecting the worst from me. I hesitated for a moment, trying to think if there was anything else I could do, if I could alter the rush of events. The cop kicked at me again and Jade cried out. "You don't have to do that," she said, and one of the cops said something to her and I stood up. They grabbed me by both arms as if I were a truly dangerous man and they dug their fingers into me and yanked me this way and that, committing those small meannesses that break your heart. It was just a routine morning arrest and it should have been simple and calm; I don't know what secret revulsion I touched in them by letting myself be discovered in a dog pen. Oh, I'm sure I looked like a creep, but I was hardly awake and I doubt if I looked dangerous. I think it was because I looked so unprotected and so obviously uninterested in defending myself. They walked me away and I moved my feet to keep from being dragged. I tried to look behind me, to see Jade, but they grabbed me harder and I had that morning's first surge of terror: These guys really *hate* me, I thought. They pushed me into the back of their squad car. I could look back at the house then but Jade wasn't in sight. She was still in the back, looking down at the kennels, remembering the dogs and how we had raised them and how they'd almost gotten us to start a family of our own. And she was probably shaking quite a bit and feeling the beginnings of doubt over whether she'd done the right thing. The car sped along. I was in handcuffs but there was no wire fence separating me from the cops in the front seat, like police cars have in cities. I always had heard how much handcuffs hurt so it was no surprise, but I wasn't prepared for how violently the pain would turn my insides. I was sweating; I thought I might vomit into my lap and I had a huge icy fear of disgracing myself.

18

Whenever I had thought of the consequences of my leaving Chicago, I rooted my dread to the image of a return to Rockville, of pacing the grassy stretches, of the powder blue Wyon, Illinois, sky, and the blond children with their fingers wrapped around the black Victorian fence peering in at us. It was an image of exile, of fury, and, of course, of unacceptable loss because it meant that once again I would be forcibly separated from Jade. There were times during my life as a fugitive when the fear of capture was so great that it was nearly impossible not to torture myself further by imagining in detail what it would be like to be in Rockville again. But I was generally successful in keeping my mind off it, successful in keeping all the little ghoulish actors gagged and tied in their mental chairs, and it was just as well because what actually happened after I was returned to the authority of the Illinois State Police was far worse than anything I would have imagined—all of that dread would have prepared me for nothing, nothing at all. I was treated worse for violating the conditions of parole than I was for setting fire to a house and nearly burning a family to death. The first time I had broken the law of the world; but now I had broken the *police's* law, and they treated that sort of transgression with more severity.

After a series of delays, continuances, appeals, and what I suppose is normal bureaucratic foot-dragging, after questionings, tests, after transfers from one lock-up to another prison, and then to yet another prison, the court decided to send me to a medium-sized penal facility in Volkshill, Illinois, a small town about midway between Chicago and Wyon. I was placed in a cell with a man named Tommy Rita, a guy in his forties who was somewhere near the end of an eight- to ten-year sentence for black marketing cigarettes. Tommy looked vibrant, practically suntanned, and did two hours' calisthenics in our cell each afternoon to keep his small, stocky body in reasonable shape. At night, in whispers, he liked to tell me how getting popped for avoiding the state cigarette tax only proved how stupid the law was. He had, he said, beaten people to a pulp, firebombed a restaurant, committed innumerable burglaries, married a woman in Hegwisch and another in Michigan City, and all they could get him on was a "little shitass cigarette rap." I never believed Tommy's list of felonies.

There's nothing I really need to say about life in Volkshill. The fear was constant: even the depths of boredom and the mock heights of cynicism were laced with fear. The anonymity was crushing: you could be beaten to death, you could choke on a piece of pork, your brain could explode and no one would care —and perhaps no one would know.

It was my understanding that in less than six months I'd be out of prison, at which time I would not, of course, be free, but would be subject to some alternate, more lenient punishment. This should have made my situation infinitely more tolerable. Nevertheless, I wasn't equal to it. Though I believed that each day was bringing me nearer to the time when my case would be handled with more mercy, the days themselves, even as they passed, were intolerable: I felt like someone who has been swept out to sea by an undertow; each wave that rolls toward the shore only draws you further away.

I began to see everything through a haze, as real and disorienting as a thick morning fog. There was an accompanying loss of body awareness so that as the world outside of me became less real my own reality decreased as well. My dreams were so vivid and lifelike that I hardly thought of them, and in the midst of my slow, careful prison day there wouldn't have registered the slightest surprise in me if someone had grabbed my shoulder and shaken me awake. My appetite disappeared; sometimes the aroma of food—not to mention the *sight* of it—would cause a violent revulsion in me. I developed a limp; my hearing deteriorated. I talked to myself—at first, just to keep things organized, to remind myself of this or that, but then it became a habit and when someone would lean into my blurry line of vision and say, "Why don't you shut your fucking face?" I'd be surprised that I'd been at it again, or else I'd have no idea what they were complaining about. This led to an enormous sense of persecution —really, everything started to go. The world an inch out of orbit can end all life. I could not adapt; I couldn't recoup any losses; I only got worse. Every now and then in a moment of woozy lucidity I'd tell myself that all the madness, all the physical symptoms, all the unreality were somehow a product of my will, that I could still, if I truly wanted to, take the reins of my life in hand again. But it was empty comfort. I told myself I *wanted* to spiral down into madness, but even at the fullest pitch of self-accusation (which was somehow linked to self-congratulation) I couldn't see or even imagine an alternate mode of behavior.

Rose and Arthur came to visit me in the humanely informal visitors' room—shiny geometric wallpaper, orange plastic bucket seats, Formica-covered tables around which families could huddle, a portable Panasonic tuned to the local pop music station supplying the background noise. I don't know what I said or how I carried myself but I made it clear that I was eroding and soon they increased their efforts to have me transferred out of jail and into a hospital. They spent money they couldn't afford to keep the pressure on the state, and three months into my stay at Volkshill I was suddenly placed in the infirmary for psychiatric observation. I took the familiar tests and was interviewed by a pair of prison psychiatrists—first a Dr. Hillman, who looked like a big pink friendly animal in a children's book, and then by Dr. Morris, a young black doctor with an Afro and some kind of enormous fang hanging near his throat. I said whatever popped into my mind, with the objectivity of someone calling numbers at a bingo game. I felt under no obligation to answer their questions or follow instructions and in the end they both agreed that my psychological state was in critical disarray. They recommended I be placed in a state institution, and that's exactly where I would have been sent if I hadn't had parents who were willing to struggle for a better alternative and were willing to pay for it.

And so on January 15, 1974, I was transferred back to Wyon, Illinois, and readmitted to Rockville Hospital. I was delivered in a police car, sitting in back with a middle-aged prison official who didn't say one word to me for the entire journey. We ran into a snow squall and had to stop for new windshield-wiper blades. I was freezing cold, shivering; I kept my fingers tucked under my arms. The stubble in the cornfields looked like a world in ruins.

After Volkshill, it was a relief to be back at the hospital. The symptoms I'd been accumulating in prison gradually receded, but I was always in anticipation of their return. Sometimes in the middle of the night I would wake for no apparent reason and not know exactly where I was, and this momentary confusion would frighten me into believing that everything was falling apart again. And then talking to Dr. Clark—trying to be open now, believing I needed help—I'd sometimes burst into sobs that had no obvious relationship to what we were discussing and these sobs seemed to fill the sails of my turmoil and send me as far from shore as I was during the worst days at Volkshill. At first, Dr. Clark encouraged my crying, but I would be so affectless and withdrawn afterward that before long he did his best to intervene. He disapproved of drug therapy but he put me on Lithium. I always had a bad taste in my mouth and I began taking two-hour naps in the middle of the afternoon, but my moods leveled out and I was glad for that.

Whereas my first stay had passed with my anonymity virtually intact, the second time around virtually everyone knew my name. I wasn't one of those natural leaders and no one looked to me as the vanguard in the eternal struggle between patients and staff—which of course existed even in a genteel asylum. I was liked because I was older, knew the ropes, and because I was given more responsibility than others were. When new patients checked in, it was I who gave them the second-day tour around Rockville. I was like a failed career officer, soft and toothless, with a yarn or two and a shoulder to cry on. I couldn't fail to notice that whenever someone really was at odds with the Rockville staff, they turned on me as well.

I learned how to use a Super-8 movie camera and a simple editing machine, and before long I was the all but official film-making instructor. We did the ordinary, expected things: movies of people jumping up and down, zoom shots, slow motion, Keystone Kop parodies. I co-scripted a twenty-minute movie we called *The Attack of the Gigantic Mommy*, in which we photographed a patient named Sally Walsh from below a glass table, where she stood surrounded by tiny trees and cows, such as decorate the domain of a Lionel. I'm sure it was terribly therapeutic for all involved. Also to my credit: when Mitzi Pappas freaked out on some LSD her eyebrowy brother smuggled in to her, it was against me she huddled for comfort; when Myron Friedman stood perched on the verge of suicide (or, more likely, compound fracture), it was me who got him off the fourth-floor ledge with the slogan: "Myron, on my hands and knees I beg you to get your skinny white ass inside!"; and when dreamy Michael Massey failed to return from a group outing into Wyon, Dr. Clark appointed me a member of the five-man search party even though I was still strictly forbidden to leave the Rockville grounds, and it was I who found Michael, staring into his hands in the back yard of a boarded-up house.

On June 3, 1974, a letter arrived for me, and it was from Jade. It was given to me by Dr. Clark after a session in his office. "I'm not going to lie to you," he said. "It came yesterday and I read it. I gave myself a night to decide whether or not to give it to you and—well, here it is."

Dear David,

I'm still in Stoughton, but not in school and not living at Gertrude anymore. Except to move my things out, I haven't been back to the old house since the day. I live on the second floor of that little green and white house near the North Stoughton post office. It's a little too large for one person but it gives me all the privacy I need. I suspect you may raise your eyebrows, but I've learned some meditation techniques. Keith learned them from a guy he works with and we all share the same mantra, which is the words you say to yourself when you are beginning your meditation. It's marvelous how fifteen or twenty minutes of sitting and breathing can make you feel so renewed. Now that I'm a College Graduate, I am using my expensive education by working as a salesgirl at Stoughton Stoneware. It's a wonderful job in some ways because I think their stuff is so great—I've got enough "seconds" to make a service for forty-eight—but it's exhausting being on my feet all day and putting up with customers, many of whom treat me as if I were their personal servant.

I've been going to Boston a lot in my spare time. It started when I signed up for this course in psycho-drama, which was pretty strange to begin with! Twenty strangers from twenty separate private lives in this old former ware-house near some North End wharf, acting out our deepest feelings. Or trying to, anyhow. For me it combined a long-time interest in theater and in the newer modes of psycho-therapy, two fields of study I've never had a chance to explore as much as I would have liked to. I must say, at the end of the course I was left with more of an interest in theater than in therapy, but then Ira Woods (the teacher in the psycho-drama course) would say that's because I shy from the implications of psycho-drama and what it re-vealed about my "deepest feelings." Maybe I am running away from myself, but I've signed up for two theater courses—one here at Stoughton in theatrical design, which the college is letting me take (without credit) free of charge, and the other in beginning acting, in Boston, taught by this absolute marvelous madman named Rud-yard Lewis.

It's been very good for me to shift my center a little toward Boston. It's not New York, but at least it's more of the "real world" than Stoughton and the best thing about Boston is I've met a lot of good people and have made my-self a few actual, bona fide, dyed-in-the-wool *friends*. Mostly theater people, which I guess is limited because they're all pretty crazy, but I've met a lot of people from outside the theater too. Everything from an absolutely great and beautiful woman from Senegal who works in a health food store to a fifty-three-year-old corporation lawyer who lives all alone in a fantasy penthouse, reads people's astrological charts, and knows all there is to know about the Comédie Française.

I got a terrific reaction on my thesis, by the way, and I've always wanted to thank you for that because you did a lot of the work. Some people who've read it have been trying to encourage me to have it published, but I think I'll leave that particular limelight to Ann. I don't see who'd publish it anyhow, but it certainly is a boost to the old ego to have someone say that it could be.

Ann's publishing ventures are starting to pick up. *The New Yorker* bought three stories from her, all in one day. I don't know when they'll appear, but whenever it is I probably will decide not to read them. As I said to her recently, I'd like to see her face before I study her masks. At least one publisher has written her and asked if she was working on a novel and he hadn't even *read* her stories yet. He'd just heard about them from someone who works at *The New Yorker*. I'm sure Ann is on her way to success. I wonder how it will affect her. I think when Ann was a proper young New York girl she fully expected the world to beat a path to her doorstep, but college and finding out how her father used the United States Foundling Homes as a source of his own personal enrichment and then marrying such a strange fellow as Hugh and getting saddled with a family, all of it combined to make her forget her girlish dreams. But I have a feeling that success will make Ann young again. She also seems to have a serious relationship in the offing with this guy who sells paper to printers. I was my usual outraged self when she first told me about him, largely because they met through one of those "personal" ads you see in the back of some magazines. It seemed very degrading and dangerous, but strange things have a way of working for Ann. I have to admire her gutsiness— I'd be afraid to even meet someone like that, just a box number and three sentences describing how lonely and eligible he is. But Ann's used to it. She seems pretty happy with this new guy. They're planning a trip to Europe— by boat, since the guy is terrified of airplanes. I haven't met him yet; I figure if he lasts six months, I'll look him over.

Keith is eternally himself. He's been as steady as a rock for me this year, always *there* when I need him. He and I got totally involved in redoing his old farmhouse—with the money from Pap's insurance, Keith bought the place he's been renting up till now. I spent ten days on my hands and knees doing nothing but scrubbing the old wooden floorboards. Talk about occupational therapy! By the time I discovered those dark walnut floors were really bright pumpkin pine, my mind was as empty as a cup. Keith's been such a good brother and a good friend, it's been great rediscovering him. He's smart, funny, and wise as an owl, and the most loyal man on earth.

Sammy continues on his march toward the presidency. He's a freshman at Harvard now and the scourge of the Yard, I'm sure. He is so devastatingly handsome. A Greek Orthodox priest has fallen in love with him! It's getting a little difficult figuring out just what Sammy believes in at this point. I think he's getting too educated to believe in Universal Justice; now he talks about a Decent Chance for a Decent Life and it sounds all right but rather politician-y, too. He's doing super well in school and modeling at Jordan Marsh in his spare time, to the tune of thirty-five dollars an hour! Last week I saw a picture of him in the Boston *Globe*. He was in a dark corduroy suit and had the preppiest grin this side of Groton. Sammy is the only Butterfield who has to cope with temptation. The rest of us can only be what we are and our choices are not only narrow but tend to be singular. There are no forks in our road, no momentous decisions. But Sammy can do anything. He can be a revolutionary, a liberal Democrat, a preppy, a student, a monk, a heel, and no matter what he does he'll get applause. I suppose I *do* envy him, but his life has been such a constant series of choices. I don't know if I could really stand it. He's over-optioned, as Ann says.

I've had this letter on my desk and in my purse and on the kitchen table and just about everywhere I go for the past week. I don't know how personal to make it. Knowing you and keeping myself open to experience whatever it is that happens when we're together has meant, among other things, that everything we say turns out to be intimate. I know that I'll never stop thinking of you. I've tried to but now I don't even try. You are my past and I've come to realize that it's better to have a frightening, upsetting, largely unhappy past than to have no past at all. But that's silly, too, isn't it? Who cannot have a past? Even amnesiacs stare at paintings. If it was only grief I think it would be easier. I wish I could mourn for us simply and cleanly. But knowing that you are locked away, even though you're not in jail and are back in that good hospital, and knowing it was me calling the Stoughton police that put you there. It's so complicated and my feelings are so divided against themselves. It's like finding the black and white markers for your Go set mixed into the same messy pile: by the time you have them sorted, you don't feel like playing the game.

Do you remember the night we went out to dinner after I spent the day with Susan Henry? I told you about what she said, how I used you to act out all the aggressions I had toward my family. Now with Hugh gone and knowing you lured him into the traffic as he walked around Fifth Avenue with his new girl, I can't help thinking: in a way I would have wanted to do that, too. It's very hard sometimes for me not to think of myself as the worst kind of monster. It makes it difficult for me to get close to anyone. Only Keith, because he accepts anything and everything about me. Sometimes I can be in the middle of doing something and I'll have an image of you being dragged off that morning by the police and I'll think it should have been *me*. Just as I was a part of you when we made love, I was a part of you when you caused my family so much harm. When we made love we seduced each other, but when it came time to strike out at my family, I'm afraid it was I who seduced you. I don't want to hurt you or confuse you by saying this. But maybe knowing my feelings will help you locate your own and maybe that will help you go back into the world again, where I sincerely believe you belong.

I know we will probably never see each other again. I look at loving you as living outside the law and I never want to do that again. I've lost a part of my nerve and it's just as well because that kind of recklessness only leaves room for itself. Everything else is blown away. We could never have a life. It seems so strange to tell you, but I still believe in our love and still love you. Yet I've put it aside, truly and forever, and will never see you again.

I had no more mail from Jade for the next year. I didn't write back to her, save for a pictureless postcard thanking her for writing to me. I didn't write to Ann and I did my best not to think of any of them, which meant I tried not to think of them all day long. The only visitors I received were Arthur and Rose, but they no longer came as regularly as before. As I felt their visits becoming more infrequent, I asked them only to come once a month, and that made everything a lot easier for all of us.

I remained on Lithium, there was no talk of making me an outpatient, but my progress was good. Sometimes I thought I had merely adjusted to my situation, become so familiar with the longing and disorientation that I didn't notice it in the same way. Other times I was absolutely sure I was getting better. But, if someone were to have asked me what that meant—my getting better—I don't know what I could have answered. My goals were very modest: I wanted to get through the days without the crunch of emotion. In a strange and gradual way, I was adjusting to the life of a madman.

And then one day what was left of the bottom dropped out. It was February 1, 1976, and my parents had braved a blizzard to come out for their visit. Arthur wore a black Russian fur hat and when he took it off and shook out the snow, I saw he had lost nearly all of the hair in the center of his skull and the long hair on the sides had turned dull silver: he looked nicely distinguished, like a delegate at an international conference of trade unionists. He had lost bulk; his cheekbones showed now and though he wore his plaid wool shirt buttoned at the top, it hung loosely around his throat. Rose looked positively ravishing. The cold had painted her cheeks a dark raspy pink and the nervousness of the day enlarged her eyes. She wore fashionable leather boots, a gray skirt, and a turtleneck sweater; she smoked a cigarette in an Aqua-filter and exhaled the smoke in a long smooth upward stream that pierced the sunlight like a spear.

"I bet you thought we wouldn't make it," said Arthur, embracing me.

Rose stood at the window, looking out at the weather, probably wondering if the storm would perversely institutionalize her for the night. Now, when one of my parents spoke, the other looked away and gave no evidence of listening, the way people do when a foreign language is being spoken.

"You know what I was thinking about today?" I began, when we'd settled in. "My first day at Hyde Park High. You guys took me shopping at Polk Brothers a week before and I insisted on buying a pair of red pants. They were sort of like jeans, but not really. Like khaki, but red. No one wore red trousers; I'd never even seen a pair. I thought you were both being very easygoing, letting me buy them. And when I chose them to wear for my first day at school neither of you said a word—I remember I was a little worried, thinking you might stop me. But God, did I suffer for wearing them." I laughed; Rose and Arthur looked uneasy, like two claustrophobes in an elevator. They'd come to speak of other things and I'm sure they thought it wasn't a Good

Sign that I was talking about my first day in high school. "I was stuck with a reputation. I was the boy with the red pants for the entire year, though I never wore those fucking pants again. And I was thinking today how a little thing like that can temper your whole life, how it can tilt the way people see you and how that influences the way you see yourself, how it circumscribes the arc of your behavior. It's amazing you let me go to school with those pants on. Maybe you thought it was something boys my age commonly wore? Was that it?" I looked at Rose.

"I have no idea," she said. "I don't remember what you *wore* on your first day of high school."

"Well, I do," I said, with a small, defeated grin. "Red pants. Redder than any apple. Much, much redder than blood."

"We have some news about Jade Butterfield," Rose said.

"What is it?" I said. My anxiety was instant and total. I sat with my legs a few inches apart, my hands on my knees, leaning forward. I heard the wind and, from somewhere, a radio: it was the Kinks singing "Lola."

"You have to realize it's for the best, though I'm sure you do," said Arthur. Had he thought my mother had already told me, or did he want to skip over the announcement and go straight to the consolation?

"What's happened to her?" I said. I'd never felt so insubstantial; only words separated me from immeasurable sorrow. She's been in an accident. She's dying. She's dead. It would end my life.

"Nothing's happened to her," said Rose. "Except that she's found herself a husband."

"We got an announcement in the mail," Arthur said. "I don't know who sent it. It wasn't signed."

"Do you have it? Give it to me."

"I forgot it," said Rose. "It doesn't say anything. She's marrying a Frenchman. We couldn't decide if he was French or American."

"Where is it?"

"I told you. We didn't bring it. It was just a very simple card. I don't think I've ever seen a cheaper-looking wedding announcement in my whole life. Not that nice old-fashioned fancy print most people use."

I felt the beginnings of relief that nothing had happened to Jade but the comfort was devastated as soon as it appeared.

Rose was continuing: "All it said was Mr. and Mrs. Denis Edelman blah blah blah the marriage of their son François to Jade Butterfield. Then the name of some synagogue in Paris, France."

"When?"

"A month ago," said Arthur. "On January fourth."

"And you've known?"

"We just got the card a few days ago," Arthur said.

"I don't even know who sent it," Rose said. "But I thought you should know anyhow."

I stood up. Even the slight motion made the room race. I faced my parents; my father sat very still, absolutely erect; my mother was tapping her foot and glancing at it. I wanted to throw myself before them, to create a miraculous moment of family and comfort. I felt very weak and very ugly.

"Help me," I said, bowing my head. I felt my knees going weak and I wanted to fall, but I wouldn't.

"Help you?" said Rose. "I don't understand, David. I just don't get it. What can I do?" She looked at Arthur, her eyes at once frightened and annoyed.

"What's past is past," Arthur said, in a murmur. "There's no turning back. Forgive me for this, David, but I only hope she's happy."

"What can I do to help you?" Rose said. "I ask you. I've never known. Just tell me. You ask me for help and I don't know what to do. You're talking about red pants from twelve years ago, you're white as a sheet, and I don't know what to do for you anymore, if I ever did, to be perfectly honest."

I was sorry I'd said it. I drew myself up and tried to look masterly. It cleared my mind to take a long, deep breath. I walked to the window. I saw a boy named Howard Kerr, dressed in his unvarying black, walking with his parents toward their car in the visitors' parking lot. The Kerrs walked with their arms around each other while Howard walked in front, his head down, jacketless and hugging himself, his long hair dancing.

"It is for the best," I said. I watched the Kerrs getting into their LTD. Howard brushed the snow off their windshield with his forearm. "I mean it's a relief. Otherwise, there'd probably always be a question. I feel a weight being lifted off of me, I already feel it." I listened to my parents breathing behind me; my legs were aching from the tightness of my muscles. Mr. Kerr rolled his window down and Howard stepped back, bent at the knee to speak. The exhaust from the car darkened the snow to pale ash. Mrs. Kerr's long red fingernails appeared at the open window, waving goodbye. The car pulled away and Howard stood and watched as the taillights disappeared into the haze of the storm.

"You'd better be going," I said to my parents. It was dark enough outside to see their reflections in the window, propped up in their chairs like two oddly angled playing cards. "People are already leaving and you've got a long drive. In this snow. It's not letting up, you know." I saw Arthur beginning to stir; his hands went onto the arms of his chair and he took a deep breath; soon, he'd be at my side, his arms around me. I turned quickly, stopping him. "The best thing, the best possible thing, for right now I mean, it's kind of strange right now, a little hard to adjust to, so I think you should both leave."

"We could talk, David," said Arthur.

I nodded. "I know. But I've been talking for about five years and it hasn't . . . I'm a little talked out, is what I mean. Maybe we can talk some other time."

Rose and Arthur left with very little additional protest. I stood at the window and watched them walk to the parking lot;

they didn't touch but they seemed to be talking. As he opened the car door, Arthur turned around and waved in the general direction of my window, but I stepped back, plastered myself to the wall, as if avoiding gunfire. I sat in one of the armchairs, wondering with an empty, obsessive repetitiveness if there was any significance in the fact that I'd chosen to sit in Rose's chair and not Arthur's. The volume of the radio someone was playing seemed to have increased and the sound of it climbed up my spine like a monkey.

I stood up, my fists clenched, and I strode out into the corridors. The doors to some of the rooms were open. Families visiting. It was important to remember the whole world wasn't in a hospital, didn't meet in tiny rooms with single beds, on Sunday. Finally, I found the radio, on the floor above my own. It was in Bruno Tesi's room. He held it on his lap, a huge portable with the antennae completely extended and quivering. Bruno was with his older brother, who sat in a trenchcoat with his long legs crossed, smoking a brown cigarette. Bruno, soft and unformed, with skin like flan, smiled when I came into the room. A Steve Miller record was on, monotonous and snide. Bruno turned the volume down because even he knew I'd have to shout to be heard over it. I said in a voice only loud enough to be heard: "If you don't turn that thing down and keep it soft I'm going to cause you excruciating pain and then I'm going to kill you."

It was a grave error threatening Bruno. Both he and his brother reported it and my actions came under closer scrutiny. My favored position at Rockville withdrew just as effortlessly as it had appeared, backing out of circumstance's door, hat in hand.

It was just as well, I felt. My will was largely gone and I felt myself sinking into the marsh of my worst self. I had one last rational thought before letting it all slip out of my hands:

perhaps Jade had moved to Paris to increase my chances of release.

The loosely guarded secret of Rockville was that the staff tolerated sexual contact between the patients. It was usually discreet, so much so that in all my years inside I knew only of two or three instances when two people were known as a couple. During my first stay, Dr. Clark told me that if I ever had a romantic encounter with a patient the important thing was that I should not be ashamed of it, that I would speak to him of it, "share it." This was the Rockville strategy on sex: rather than control it, they wanted to make it a part of the general rehabilitative atmosphere. We were all of us there, after all, to help one another, and this meant genuine human contact—and how could there be genuine human contact with sexuality strictly off-limits?

In April, a couple months after learning of Jade's marriage, I made friends with a sixteen-year-old patient named Rochelle Davis. Rochelle was quite beautiful in a sultry, unwholesome way. She wore prune-colored lipstick and nail polish, black clothes, smoked Camels incessantly, and presented herself as an authority on suicide. She had categories of suicide: revenge suicide, accidental suicide, instructional suicide, and others that made even less immediate sense, such as lavender suicide, cheesy suicide, and astral suicide. She had no friends, neither inside the hospital nor out. In the world she was too aggressively strange, and in Rockville most felt too vulnerable to risk friendship with someone so fascinated by self-termination. Rochelle—gaunt, green-eyed, her chestnut hair combed Elvis style—gave no evidence of caring what people thought of her, but she did seem very keen on knowing me. It was obvious that my increasingly unstable social position in the hospital was a large part of Rochelle's interest in me, but it wasn't that simple, as it never is.

The first time we made love was in the bathroom on the first floor reserved for nurses. It was a strange, fussy little room, with pink walls, dull tile floor, an armchair, and a dressing table holding Johnson's Baby Powder, dental floss, Arrid deodorant spray, and a spray cologne called "Sunday." We made love in the armchair, three or four times over—not out of an ever-increasing passion but because each time it was clumsy and the satisfaction we gained only irritated our huge store of static lust. At first, we didn't have the boldness to take our clothes off—as if it might somehow be better to be discovered with pants down to the knees rather than naked altogether. We made love with Rochelle on my lap, her bony, bluish feet pressed on the back of the chair, her head dangling between my open legs, her navy blue underwear quivering like a trampoline between her thighs as she shook her constricted legs with nervous, discomforted passion. Then we helped each other come with our mouths and then we made love on the cold floor—naked now, but it was too late: we were already growing incurious and it was clear that the yearning we attempted to serve would remain immune to our efforts.

Nevertheless, I became obsessive about her. That night, I lay in bed and when my cock lifted at the thought of her I followed its ascent and was in her room moments later: Nurse Seroppian was asleep at her post, her enormous purple eyelids shuddering, and she was known for the dependability of her nightly doze. I spent the night in Rochelle's bed and entered her once after she'd fallen asleep. She woke for a moment, didn't seem to mind, and slipped back into sleep. It went on that way for weeks; we made love like people beating their heads against a wall. It sometimes amazed me she was only sixteen and so bereft of romantic illusion, but mostly I didn't care. I didn't discuss this liaison with Dr. Clark—I knew it would give him trouble—but I did slowly gain a secret sexual reputation: for endurance, if nothing else, or just plain availability.

Before long I took a second lover, a girl from Chicago named

Pat Eliot, who had curly yellow hair, cupid's-bow lips, prodigious breasts, and who pronounced her first name in two syllables. Pat was in her early twenties, an actress. She was actually a success in the world: she'd appeared at the Goodman Theater in many plays and had had a good role in a Hollywood movie, though it hadn't been released. She was a wonderful lover, tender and powerful, without a trace of athleticism. Her breasts fascinated me but they were so huge they also made me shy, which pleased her because I would guess people had made too much of an issue about them. And so I had two lovers, and then a woman named Stephanie was admitted to Rockville.

Stephanie was just twenty and already a graduate student at the University of Chicago. She had brutal nightmares and wandered about in her sleep. I didn't know her last name. But I was fixated on the idea of making love to her, and as soon as I had an opportunity to approach her, I did. She had no interest in making love with me and not much interest in knowing me. But I pursued the matter with increasing single-mindedness. Like any losing gambler, I could think of nothing else. I stared at her, followed her, dreamed of her, thought of her when I was with Rochelle and Pat, wrote notes to her, and finally lured her to my room, where I threw myself at her with odious abandon. She ran from my room, not exactly screaming, but saying "Christ sakes" in a loud, excited voice, and within the hour I was taken down to Dr. Clark's sunny little office, where he waited for me behind his desk, drumming his fingers on its polished surface, empty except for a folder that turned out to be my records.

We talked for a long while; I told him I was "sexually active," and he said that he knew I was. He told me that nothing unfortunate was likely to come of my friendship with Pat, but with Rochelle I was involving myself with a "girl of mysterious pathos," and that with Stephanie I was simply behaving like a jerk and a bully. The peculiar thing was that the reprimand didn't end in a warning; my actions were not directly proscribed.

I continued to pursue Stephanie despite my failure to interest her and despite Clark's words with me. I cannot even remember what attracted me to her or what I wanted: I analyzed the attraction as sheerly magnetic and I gladly surrendered all memory and forethought to an urge that really wasn't quite so blind as I would have liked. I felt myself capable of any low behavior. I imagined forcing myself on Stephanie, grabbing her from behind, sneaking into her bed at night. I took these empty, frustrated thoughts as signs of vitality, and so I welcomed them even as they destroyed me from within. The real point, of course, was not to think of Jade, and in this all illness served its purpose: if it had not been erotomania it could just as well have been hysterical paralysis. Finally, one day I convinced Stephanie to come to my room; I think my persistence was beginning to work on her, added to the emptiness and loss of self that was growing inside her as her stay at Rockville became longer and more routine. I had gotten her into a conversation about Nobel Prize winners and we were going to check in my almanac how many Americans had won the prize for literature. Rochelle saw us leave and a few minutes later she went to her room and uncovered the cache of Librium she'd been hoarding over the past couple months and attempted to commit what she might categorize as a revenge suicide.

Rochelle was saved without much difficulty, but the day after—with the entire hospital in a nervous hush—Dr. Clark told me that he was recommending that I be "released" from Rockville. I knew that it was only bad news, but I asked if this meant he was recommending me for outpatient treatment, if I was going to be allowed to return to Chicago.

"You know very well what it means and what it doesn't. I'm a little surprised, even as your doctor, that you'd use this as an occasion . . . Well, never mind. The answer is no. The decision is limited to one consideration: we don't feel that we can treat you with any great hope for success. At this point, your presence is disturbing the overall therapeutic community. I'm afraid your treatment is going to have to continue in a setting in which community is not as important. And who knows? It might be the change you need."

Right . . .

My grandfather Jack wasn't paying part of my hospital charges any longer; my breaking parole and Arthur's affair with a black woman launched Grandfather away from us and our interminable problems. My parents had been able to negotiate a slightly lower rate with Rockville, but it was still a lot more than they could afford. When it was decided that I could no longer stay in that permissive Wyon hospital, a cursory search was begun to find another comparable institution in the state of Illinois, but nothing suitable seemed to present itself—and the truth was that my parents couldn't afford to pay for private treatment any longer. At the recommendation of the court, my psychiatric files, my body, and my fate, were transferred to a state-run hospital called Fox Run, in Highland Park, a Chicago suburb. Breaking it to me—the details, that is—Arthur tried to be encouraging. "I think this is just the kind of place the court wants you to stay in before you get your release. The trouble with a place like Rockville is it's got a reputation, and the thinking is if you're spending your time here you're not getting helped and you're not getting punished."

"Then why'd you put me here?" I asked.

"It's what you wanted," said Arthur. "You said it was."

"And now you're putting me in Fox Run? I've heard about Fox Run, you know. There's been people here who've spent time there. It's a goddamned hole is what it is. Oh God, can't you feel what's happening? I'm getting lost in the shuffle. Fox Run is the kind of place you disappear in. You get beaten to death, or drugged to death, or forgotten. Fine. OK. I'm not going to care, not another word. I just want to suggest that you both take a good look at me. If you think I'm bad now, next time you see me you're not going to recognize me at all. I swear, it's the end of me."

On July 1, 1976, Eddie Watanabe and a rabbinical-looking

staff worker from Fox Run took me by Ford to my new quarters in Highland Park. As a parting favor, Dr. Clark had given me a whopping dose of Stelazine and the bright neon anxiety I'd been feeling was now encapsulated in a soft, faintly transparent gel. I was bleary, silent; I sat in the back seat with my valise and a paper bag, watching the cornfields turn to suburbs, the sky turn from the blue of robins' eggs to the blue of faded denim, to the barely decipherable blue of smoke. Eddie and the fellow from Fox Run talked about the mayor and the governor and the federal budget and then about things they'd believed when they were younger. Finally, Watanabe said, with weary pride, that they were both "survivors of the sixties," and the fellow from Fox Run nodded in agreement.

The joke at Fox Run was that we, the patients, were the foxes and the staff was the hounds. They tried to get us to identify with them by continually informing us of the neighborhood's attempts to have the hospital shut down; every third day, it seemed, part of the staff would be off somewhere fighting for the life of the institution, testifying before a citizens' group or a state committee, defending Fox Run from the charges, the thousands of charges made against it. We inmates ranged in age from eighteen to ninety-three; many of us were without family; a large number were without rememberable pasts. We were Oriental, Appalachian, East European, Mexican, black, and most of us would be spending the rest of our lives in this hospital, or in another.

One of the principal complaints of the people who lived around Fox Run was that security was so patchy that patients, supposedly at will, would leave the hospital and wander through the community, peering into windows, shitting in bushes, staring mournfully at the children in shorts and halters. As soon as I learned this, I resolved to escape and soon I had an opportunity. I was mopping the floors in a ward when I heard a supervisor tell an orderly that a fire exit door was jammed and had to be repaired because it could neither open properly nor close. I slyly patrolled the corridors, looking for the defective door. I found it in short order and stood before it, breathing heavily and adjusting to the idea of freedom—of the bright, vast world that stretched out beyond that door.

I waited until the corridor was quiet; I could actually see the light coming through the door, an iridescent strand. EMERGENCY EXIT ONLY was stenciled in red across the door. This is an emergency, I thought to myself, as I pressed on the long lever and pushed. The door wedged open, swinging uncertainly on its broken hinge; the world leapt into view. Then just as suddenly I was grabbed from behind and dragged to a small room that was rumored to exist solely for the corporal punishment of patients and in which I was slapped, shaken, bounced around, and pummeled until I lost consciousness. The supervisor and two orderlies who caught and beat me never reported my attempted escape and I, in turn, never reported them. No one asked me about the cuts, lumps, and bruises that covered my body. It was a month before the pain disappeared and even longer before the limp and the headaches receded. Being beaten like that is so extraordinary, there's no point in describing it. Those who haven't been punished like that will never know how it feels, even if a genius describes it, and those who have, know it all too well.

In October, on a Sunday, Ann came to Fox Run. An orderly found me in the men's fifth-floor television room watching the Bears play the Oakland Raiders. "Visitor," he said, tapping me viciously on the shoulder with his index finger. I'd been feeling woozy that week. I asked if it was my parents—surprised, because I remembered our huge fight the week before and my asking them not to come to see me for a while. "No, it's an aunt." He showed me the white slip in his hand. Date, time, patient's name. Visitor's name: Ann Axelrod. Relation: Aunt.

She was waiting for me in the visitors' room, sitting in a low green chair and studying the posters on the wall: gauzy photographs of couples walking hand in hand, swans silhouetted on the water, a waterfall, and a huge red and white striped balloon with the words "Up up and away" written on it. There were about twenty other visitors and as many patients, with five orderlies sitting around, looking the scene over.

I saw Ann before she knew I'd come into the room. I waited, giving myself a chance to feel whatever it was that seeing her again would awaken in me. I felt slightly nervous, embarrassed because I knew I didn't look good and because it's always embarrassing to be locked up. But other than that, my feelings couldn't come forward; they remained pressed beneath the overwhelming weight of my circumstances. She'd gained a little weight, but it looked good on her. Her hair was almost solid gray—I don't think time alone could have changed the color of her hair so radically. She wore a brown skirt and a soft, expensive-looking white blouse. She looked so elegant; I glanced around to see if everyone was noticing her, but no one seemed to.

"Surprise," I said, dropping down into the chair next to her.

"David," she said. Her voice suddenly disappeared, like a coin in a magic trick. Was she going to pull it out of my ear? She cleared her throat; color was rising in her face. "I told them I was your aunt."

"I know."

"I'm so bad at getting away with things," she said. "I felt sure I'd get caught in my . . ."—she glanced around—". . . lie. But now that I see you, I think I've actually pulled it off." She smiled. Conspiracy. Triumph.

A surge of emotion ripped through me. All at once, I took Ann's hand and held it, and then I lifted it slowly to my lips and kissed the back of her cool, faintly tanned hand. My nose was pressing against her; there was a faint cucumbery taste on her skin, and when I finally stopped kissing her and she let her hand drop into her lap, I saw that her hand was wet. I stared at it, hoping she would wipe it dry and horrified that she might.

"I'm in town at the behest of my publisher," she said, quietly. "Promoting my book."

"So you finally wrote a book," I said.

Ann hesitated, nodded. She'd expected me to know. A slight overestimation of her own celebrity. I felt ashamed for her. How dare she think I would know *anything*.

"I miss a lot of what's going on in here," I said.

"Of course. And even if you weren't here. Maybe ten thousand people in all the world know my name. It's a small world, the book world."

"It's about time you wrote a book. Think of it: a real book."

"You look OK, David," she said. "You really do." She glanced around the room, as if to say: Better than the others, at least. Someone was having a coughing fit, a patient. His family was pounding him on the back to make him stop.

"I saw myself in the mirror yesterday," I said. "And I thought, 'Hey boy, you look like someone in a public fucking nuthouse.'"

"You look good. Your voice is deeper."

"It's the drugs. It relaxes my face and makes me look old. They give you a lot of drugs here. Remember how we used to love drugs? Well, it's different here. It's serious. They have to give them to us or else we'd tear the place down. Burn it. That's why my voice is so low, too. The drugs. I'm glad you noticed. I wasn't sure it was true, and I didn't know who to ask."

We were silent for a few moments. The cougher was still coughing. An orderly stood with his massive arms folded, watching the family pound the cougher's back.

"What do you do while you're here?" Ann asked.

"But I'm always here!"

She looked around, shrugged. "What do you do?"

"Look. I want to ask a favor. Now you're a famous writer. Why don't you write a story about me? But not a story. The truth. What happened to me. I'm sorry. I'm forgetting what I'm not supposed to say. But the point is I'm here and it's been a very long while, don't you think? My case is sitting on someone's desk, on the bottom of the pile. Don't you think a little publicity would help? If you wrote a story to tell the world what's happened to me, and maybe others like me too. I just need to get out of here. Even if I seem old and different, I'm still alive. I'm still the exact same person. It's me, Ann. It's me. It really is. I'm holding on. I'm making it day by day. But I don't know, I really couldn't say how much longer I'll be able to hold out. They want you to change. That's what it's all about. I might even do it if I thought they'd let me out after. But knowing how it is I could turn myself into shit and they'd still keep me here." I grabbed for her hand again but let it go when I saw her eyes were blurred with tears.

"I don't think you belong here, David," she whispered. "I never thought you did. It's a damn outrage and you're absolutely right to be angry."

"I'm not angry, I'm dying. And I want to get out."

"I never thought you deserved it. That's why I came, to tell you. My plane leaves at three but I had to chance missing it to tell you and to see you. If there's anything . . ." She swallowed a sob, covered her eyes for a moment. "That sounds so false. I'm sorry. But it's so. If there's anything I can do, any way I can stand up in your behalf, I will. It's not a matter of family anymore. It's a question of right and wrong and it's plainly wrong for you to be punished any longer." She started to get up but I held on to her arm.

"How did you know I was here?"

"Your father told me. Weeks ago. I called."

"That must have been weird. Was it all right?"

"Your mother got on the line. She started to scream at me. Your father hung up and then I did. It *was* weird. I have to go. I want you to take care of yourself. You—"

"Does Jade have a baby yet? Is she all right?"

"She's OK. Her husband was transferred to Brussels. She doesn't much care for it. And no, they don't have children."

"Yet."

"I don't think she's anxious to. I think I've queered her on motherhood."

"What's your book about?"

"Hugh. I'll send you a copy."

"Hugh?"

"You're in it, too. But not as you. It's not what you think. It's about before. Falling in love with him. The beginning." She stood up.

"It was very nice of you . . ." My head was dropping. I covered my eyes and then I was afraid to uncover them and find her already gone. I felt her hand on my shoulder. I stood.

"Don't lose faith in yourself, David," she said. We were standing very close; I could smell her perfume. I breathed deeply, drawing the scent into my blood.

"I don't have any faith in myself."

"Yes you do. You've just got to find it. It's no wonder you can't here. You've got to get out. You don't belong here." She reached up, put her hand against my face. She held me in her eyes for a moment; I wanted to hug her but something told me not to. I felt tears streaming down my cheeks. Ann stepped back, looked at me in the way you do when you want to commit someone to memory, and then she turned.

I watched her walk across the visitors' room, toward the glass doors. Her shoulders were back and she was trying not to walk fast. In a moment she'd be gone.

"Thank you," I called out to her, cupping my hands over my mouth like a man at sea.

She raised her hand without looking round. She waved good-bye with her fingers, lowering them one at a time, as if counting down. Five, four, three, two, one.

The next September my father died, at home, in his sleep. A massive heart attack, though I don't know if it would have taken a huge shove to loosen his grip on life. As soon as he was gone, it was clear to me that he'd been preparing his own death since Barbara Sherwood's. Rose came to Fox Run to break the news. We were alone in the visitors' room, on a Wednesday. Her face looked utterly white, as if she were hovering in a state of semi-shock: there are windows in the wall separating life from death and when you peer through one of them it changes you. I knew something was wrong as soon as I sat next to Rose, and when she laid her cold, small hand on my wrist I was ready for the worst. It was already three days after the fact: Arthur died at eleven thirty Sunday night; his body, as per his promise, was already in the University of Chicago Medical School, "donated to science." I felt too neglected, too behind the roll of events to cry. I felt only a deep soreness within, as might be caused by a disease.

A month later I was given a round of psychological tests. Nothing new. Adding columns of numbers. Who was the first President of the United States? What is the sun? Questions to see if my brains were addled, if my hold on reality was at all sequential and ordinary. Inkblot tests, complete-the-story tests, spatial perception tests, memory exercises, and finally a kind of Ph.D. oral in front of a panel of three psychiatrists, in which I spoke of myself and answered their questions. If you could have any job in the whole wide world, what would it be? If you loved a gal and she didn't love you, what would you do? I was weak from the effort to appear normal, and I had even forced myself up toward a level of acuity in which I recognized that if my efforts were too apparent—or too successful—then I would be defeating myself. It was important to remain at all times vulnerable to their judgments of me; confidence and determination would be interpreted as symptoms of disassociation.

Two weeks after my round of tests, I was informed by Dr. Donner, who was supposed to be my psychiatrist, though I only saw him an hour and a half weekly, that I was fit to "take a crack" at being in the world again. He gave me several words of friendly advice, said I should "think seriously" about seeing a psychiatrist once I was released, that I should "feel free" to call on him if I had a problem I wanted to discuss, and that he hoped I'd learned about myself and how to deal with my problems while I was at Fox Run. "Especially with the hospital under constant attack by intolerant community people and opportunistic budget-cutters, it feels fine to be sending someone home with the feeling that we've done him a measure of good."

And so I was released. I left Fox Run, walking across a bridge made of your marriage and Arthur's death. I returned to the old apartment on Ellis, to recover from my long hospitalization and adjust to my freedom. I'd been through it all before, but what made it different was now I hadn't the slightest illusion that everything might be transformed suddenly by the huge unreasonable magic of Reunion. I never once expected to see you from my window, even as I got out of the bed I'd slept in when I first joined my heart to you, the bed I had lain in in agony, waiting to rejoin you. When the phone rang I never thought it was you and the sight of the mailman shouldering his big leather pouch of letters and cards never tempted me to even *wish*. Arthur's small estate had gone to Rose, but she divided it in half and so I was, for the first time in my life, solvent. Now, I could move out whenever I was ready, but I wasn't ready. I needed to be home and Rose needed me there, too.

Jade. I don't want to say it, I truly don't . . .

It was difficult to find a job. I had a criminal record and it was worse for me to have been punished in a hospital than in a prison, in terms of how other people looked at me. I had very little education and not much of a work history. I was close to twenty-eight years old. I wanted a job in a large company, something to put me in contact with many people. Friends of the family tried to help but no one had anything for me; everyone was retired or simply too old to have much influence. I lived on my small legacy and took courses at Roosevelt University. It doesn't matter what I took, though it wasn't astronomy. I needed something that I was sure would help me find work and everyone told me that astronomers were having a very hard time of it.

On the good days, I felt like a shipwrecked man spotting the signs of some nearing but still invisible shore: a taste in the wind, a softness in the light, a sudden passage of gulls.

I hope this day finds you well. You don't have to read a word of this, you know. I don't want to make your husband nervous, or to embarrass you, or to make you remember things you've decided are best forgotten. I've come to the end, finally. Not of love. But of my power to say another word. I've no more need. My life is taking shape. I'm living with a woman and maybe someday we will marry, though I doubt it. She paints, too, by the way. Even better than you used to. She teaches at a university and is a full inch taller than I am. I won't bother to tell you where I'm living now; it makes a more perfect sense for you not to know.

I don't want to say it, I truly don't, but if you've gone this far I suppose it's obvious that what was ignited when I loved you continues to burn. But that's of small importance to you now, and that's how it should be.

Everything is in its place. The past rests, breathing faintly in the darkness. It no longer holds me as it used to; now I must reach back to touch it. It is night and I am alone and there is still time, a moment more. I am standing on a long black stage, with a circle of light on me, which is my love for you, enduring. I have escaped—or have been expelled—from eternity and am back in time. But I step out once more to sing this aria, this confession, this testament without end. My arms open wide, not to embrace you but to embrace the world, the mystery we are caught in. There is no orchestra, no audience; it is an empty theater in the middle of the night and all the clocks in the world are ticking. And now for this last time, Jade, I don't mind, or even ask if it is madness: I see your face, I see you, you; I see you in every seat.

A NOTE ON THE TYPE

The text of this book was set on the Linotype in Janson, a recutting made direct from type cast from matrices long thought to have been made by the Dutchman Anton Janson, who was a practicing type founder in Leipzig during the years 1668–87. However, it has been conclusively demonstrated that these types are actually the work of Nicholas Kis (1650–1702), a Hungarian, who most probably learned his trade from the master Dutch type founder Dick Voskens. The type is an excellent example of the influential and sturdy Dutch types that prevailed in England up to the time William Caslon developed his own incomparable designs from them.

Composed by The Maryland Linotype Composition Company, Inc., Baltimore, Maryland
Printed and bound by The Haddon Craftsmen, Inc., Scranton, Pennsylvania
Typography and binding design by
Virginia Tan